GLOBAL★STAR.

by R.A. JONES, MICHAEL VANCE AND MEL ODOM

PRO SE PRESS

GLOBAL STAR
Copyright © 2012, R.A. Jones, Michael Vance & Mel Odom

"Funerals Are Fun In Singapore", Copyright © 2012, R.A. Jones
"Sewer Savage Scours City", Copyright © 2012, Mel Odom
"God Bop", Copyright © 2012, Michael Vance

A Pro Se Press Publication

The stories in this publication are fictional. All of the characters in this publication are fictitious
and any resemblance to actual persons, living or dead is purely coincidental. No part of this
publication may be reproduced or transmitted in any form or by any means, graphic, electronic, or
mechanical, including photocopying, recording, taping or by any information storage or retrieval
system, without the permission in writing of the publisher.

Edited by- Nancy Hansen
Editor in Chief, Pro Se Productions-Tommy Hancock
Submissions Editor-Barry Reese
Publisher & Pro Se Productions, LLC-Chief Executive Officer-Fuller Bumpers

Pro Se Productions, LLC
133 1/2 Broad Street
Batesville, AR, 72501
870-834-4022

proseproductions@earthlink.net
www.prosepulp.com

Cover Art, Book Design, Layout, and additional graphics created by Sean E. Ali

GLOBALSTAR®

IN THIS ISSUE:

FUNERALS ARE FUN IN SINGAPORE

by R.A. Jones

"**A**pril 13. At approximately 2:37 P.M. Eastern Standard Time, the American Airlines 747 in which I was flying was sucked up into the belly of a huge alien spacecraft.

"God ... I hate when that happens."

Ace Montana shut off his micro-cassette tape recorder and returned it to the pocket of his leather jacket. He then twisted his muscular six foot tall frame, rising from his first class seat.

He seemed oblivious to the panicked outcries of his fellow passengers as he ambled to the front of the compartment. Turning to face them, he paused to run both hands through the thick mass of his slicked back black hair. He calmly pulled out a pack of unfiltered Camels and lit up.

"I'm sorry, sir." A harried looking stewardess came racing toward him. "But you can't smoke on this flight!"

"Yeah, right." His voice was a low rumble. "What're you gonna do, babe... kick me off the plane? Now get the *u*k outta my face. I got an important announcement to make."

Stunned by his bluntness and the metallic sound of *u*k, the stewardess meekly backed away from him. He took another slow drag on his cigarette, and then raised one hand.

"People, people, people!" he said loudly. "You wanna shut the *Uc* up?"

Instantly, the cabin fell silent.

"That's better." Ace grinned a cocky grin. "Now then; as you probably know—unless you're so f*c*i*' stupid you need a road map to find your own ass we've been captured by aliens."

He paused to let this sink in, and then continued. "I'm just here to tell you that we have nothing to worry about."

"Excuse me, young man?" Ace looked down to see a petite, elderly woman tugging gently at the leg of his blue jeans.

"Raise that hand a little higher, lady, and you'll make my day."

"Oh, my!" The woman released her grip and fell back in her seat, blushing a bright crimson. Ace leaned over closer to her.

"What is it you want, sweetheart?"

"Are you a police officer?" she asked softly.

Ace straightened abruptly, as if he had been slapped in the face.

"Give me a *****e break. I'm better than a cop... I'm a reporter,"

He looked over the crowd of anxiously staring faces, assuring himself that they were suitably impressed.

"As I was telling you, we've got nothing to worry about. I've been through this routine a dozen times. The aliens will let us go as soon as they get what they came for."

"And what's that?" a nervous passenger called out.

"Here's the scoop: they'll take us into their rec room, strip us naked, and take photographs. Simple."

"Photographs?" The elderly woman placed a hand to her heart as though she was about to have a seizure.

"Sure. You don't think they travel billions of miles just to hang out in shopping malls, do you?"

"Whew," sighed the nudist on aisle three. "For a minute there..."

"Trust me, Grandma." Ace smiled leeringly and blew out a stream of smoke. "I'll probably be the most fun you've had since Calvin Coolidge was in office."

"Barely," she answered.

———— ✦✦✦ ————

"**P**ersonal reminder: write a letter of complaint to the head of the airline. If stewardesses get any uglier I'm traveling by boat."

Ace made his way through the dingy corridors of La Guardia Airport, heading for the baggage claim area. Just as he had predicted, the episode with the aliens had been time consuming but uneventful.

Well, almost so. There was the scuffle that ensued when the little old lady didn't want to leave the alien spaceship.

Ace shook his head in amusement thinking about the incident, and then stopped at one of the airport newsstands. A stocky salesclerk asked if he could be of assistance.

"Yeah. Give me a pack of Camels."

"Right. Filtered or unfiltered?"

The clerk yelped helplessly as Ace grabbed him by the front of the shirt, dragging him halfway across the counter separating the two men. The reporter's face was livid with anger.

"Do I look like a f*****' Commie to you?"

"Wha what?" The clerk was clearly befuddled.

"I said, do I look like a *****n' Commie to you?"

"I d don't know about your s sex life," the clerk stammered. Ace jerked hard. "No! N not at all!!"

"That's better." Ace released the clerk. "Don't you ever try to sell me a pack of filtered cigarettes again. You understand?"

"No, sir. I mean, yes, sir. I mean I won't, sir?" The clerk slid the cigarettes to Ace, refusing to accept payment for them or to ask how Ace was able to say f*c*i*g.

Ace paid no mind to the puzzled stares he was getting from other travelers. He was still too incensed. The ignorance of the American public never failed to amaze him. Didn't they know that filtered cigarettes were part of a Communist plot to sap the vital juices of American men?

"God knows what they do to women!" he muttered to himself. At the thought, he pulled out his micro-cassette. "Note to self: Find out what brand of cigarette Roseanne Barr smokes."

A row of the current edition of his newspaper, the Global Star, strung across the newsstand's racks caught Ace's eye. The headline read: Child Pornography Exposed. The byline was Ace Montana. He felt the tingle of secret pride run up his spine that was almost better than money.

It'd been a tough assignment. The twelve year old director had shown a clever turn; kids filming adults. But a story is a story, and he'd proven the old adage: there are no small roles, only small actors.

The story probably wouldn't win him a Pulitzer... but his cameo role in the movie was sure to make him a contender for an Academy Award.

Ace breathed a sigh of relief as his cab pulled up to the curb in front of the Menaheim Building on Lexington Avenue. Close encounters with aliens didn't faze him, but a ride with a New York cabbie could still raise his hackles.

He eyed the cab's meter, and then shifted his gaze to look into the smiling face of the cabbie. The man was of Arabic extraction, and had kept up a steady stream of dialogue all the way from the airport. Ace counted out the exact amount of his fare, gave it to the cabbie, and then stepped out of the car.

"Please to be excusing me, sir." Ace turned back to look at the disappointed driver. "But will you not be having me a tip?"

"You want a tip? Okay, here's a tip ... learn to speak the *U***' language. Now, hit the road, Jack."

Ace smiled smugly as the cabbie gunned his taxi and sped away from the curb, and then called cheerfully after him, "Oh, and have a nice day!" Unconsciously, he touched a small, triangular scar on the rough skin of his neck.

When Ace stepped out of the elevator onto the 39th floor, a familiar feeling came over him. The feeling of coming home, except home wasn't this clean, and it usually had more women in it.

As always, the editorial offices of the Global Star were a whirlwind of activity. Land phones were ringing right and left. The city editor stuck his head out of his work cubicle, yelling for a reporter to run downstairs and check out an accident involving a crazy Arabic cab driver.

Ace loved it all. Global Star was the most widely read, weekly tabloid newspaper in the world—and he was its premier reporter. Had been for nearly ten years. He'd received many offers to leave, juicy offers from the New York Times and the New York Post, but he had always turned them down. No, he preferred real journalism.

He made his way through the chaos, exchanging greetings with various other reporters. But he didn't stop; he was on his way to the private office of Frank Gephard, managing editor of Global Star.

As he approached Gephard's office, Ace smiled approvingly. As always, Gephard's personal secretary, Uge Nochers, was on duty at her desk outside the office.

Nochers was a busty, big-boned blonde of Swedish decent. She was a few points shy of adequacy in the I.Q. department, but she was highly proficient in controlling traffic in and out of her boss' office. Ace strongly suspected she provided other services for the managing editor as well.

"How's it hanging, Uge?" Ace asked cordially as he sauntered up to her desk. She looked up from her model of a gallows, fingers sticky with glue, and smiled. A tiny figure of Gephard's wife swung silently on the model at the end of a tiny rope.

"Ace! Good to see you again. Go right in; Mr. Gephard's expecting you."

"Sure thing, babe." Ace headed for the door leading into Gephard's office, then paused and stepped back to the secretary's desk.

"You know, Uge, I heard a really interesting story on the radio today. It seems that the government is ordering the recall of all D-cup bras."

"Oh? Why's that?" Uge cast a surreptitious glance down at her chest.

"Get this; it seems some idiot at the manufacturing plant accidentally mixed nitroglycerine with the nylon while they were making the damn things." Ace stopped to light up a cigarette.

"So?" Uge said, urging him on.

"So this; if a lady happens to be wearing one of these things and her body temperature goes up-they tend to explode. Wild, huh?"

Ace pretended not to notice Uge clutching at her bosom. Instead, he simply turned away and stepped into his editor's office.

"Come in, Ace," Frank Gephard called from behind his desk. Ace pretended to ignore the small stepladder next to the editor's desk.

"Shhh." Ace placed a silencing finger to his lips as he crossed the threshold into the office and not quite closed the door completely shut behind him. He then reached into one of the pockets of his jacket and pulled out a small paper bag.

Gephard watched with puzzlement as Ace proceeded to blow into the bag, inflating it with his breath. When it was expanded to its full capacity, Ace pulled it away from his mouth, holding the top closed with his left hand.

Bringing it close to the opening in the doorway, Ace slapped the bag with his right hand, causing it to pop loudly. Instantly, a blood-curdling scream came from the area of Uge Nocher's desk.

"What the hell was that all about?" Gephard growled.

"Bursting someone's bubble, Frank. I tell ya, that Uge is a real jewel. You ought to marry her."

Gephard coughed. "I'm already married, remember?"

"Oh, yeah. Well, in that case, you should just sleep with her."

"You're a card, Ace," Gephard said, chuckling. He loved to listen to his star reporter's banter, and Ace knew it. "So... what have you got for me?"

"See for yourself, Frank." Ace tossed a file folder down on the desk.

"Please, Ace--call me 'Chief', okay?"

"Yeah. Right." Ace dropped down into an over-stuffed chair. "Look it over, Frank."

Ace studied Gephard as the editor scanned the contents of the file. His bulldog face screwed up in concentration. Occasionally, he would run one hand through the close-cropped gray hair of his square head. Gephard was fifty-three years old but, as Ace was fond of saying, he didn't look a day over sixty-five.

"This is terrific!" Gephard exclaimed when he finished his perusal. Ace had presented him with the story of a Swiss woman who had given birth to a baby that was half cocker spaniel--complete with color photos of the child.

Gephard then poured over Ace's expense voucher clipped to the reporter's manuscript. He obviously saw something he didn't like, for a frown twisted his lips.

"Ace," he said slowly, "you've got a dry cleaning bill here for $150. What's with that?"

"Hey, man--you ever had a f*c**n: dog-boy sit in your lap?"

"Oh. All right." Gephard was satisfied with the explanation. "Good work."

"That's the only kind I do. I got a new UFO story for you, too. Nothing spectacular, but a nice filler. I can have it for you first thing tomorrow."

"Never mind that." Gephard rose and walked around to the side of his desk, placing a foot on the first rung of the stepladder. Ace braced himself. He knew whenever Gephard took that position, he was about to ask for a favor.

"Actually, Ace, there's something else I'd rather have you do if you don't mind. Excuse this, " he blushed, pointing at the nearby stepladder. '"Wife's got me on the old exercise/diet regimen again."

As with the entire staff, Ace didn't mind the lie. He knew it was to hide Gephard's greatest, unjustified shame, his size.

Gephard was a pygmy. An albino pygmy, at that. Not that Ace cared much; one of his most torrid love affairs had been with a pygmy. Good things do come in small packages.

"What are you grinning about?" Gephard asked.

"Nuthin'," Ace grunted, flicking ash off of the end of his cigarette and steeling himself for small talk.

"Right. Thanks anyway. You remember that no-good brother-in-law of mine, don't you? Fred Hertz?"

"Ethel's husband? The one who left your sister to marry a circus fat lady?"

"That's the one." Gephard stepped up the ladder.

"What about him?"

"Well, his daughter's in town for a day or two, and..."

"Don't say what I think you're gonna say, Frank."

"What? I was just hoping you could show her around the city, that's all." Gephard stepped down the ladder.

"That's what I was afraid you were gonna say. Sorry, Frank. No way. "

"Why not?"

Ace collected his thoughts before replying. "How can I put this delicately, Frank? Your sister's so *u*k*n* ugly even you won't kiss her. And as for Fred-- the fat lady's probably better looking than he is."

"So?" Gephard stopped on the ladder's middle rung.

"So, what kinda daughter's gonna appear when those two breed? You get what I'm saying, don't you?"

"Oh no, no, no, no, no, Ace," Gephard hurriedly assured him. "Trust me. Payne is real window dressing."

"Her name is Wyndow Payne?"

"Yes. No!" Gephard glared from the ladder's top rung, almost out of breath. "Her last name is Kyller."

"Payne Kyller? Forget it, Frank. I'm outta here."

As Ace rose and turned to leave, the door of the office suddenly opened inward. A young woman walked in who caused the reporter to freeze in his tracks. She was tall and willowy, with auburn hair falling down over her naked shoulders and a face that could only be called angelic.

Ace liked what he saw, and she definitely felt the same way about him. They openly appraised each other, until their eyes met and locked. A smile tugged at the corners of the woman's mouth, making her look painfully more beautiful.

"Ace... this is my niece, Ms. Payne Kyller."

The journalist tore his eyes away from the woman and looked at his editor with approval. "Well, I gotta admit, she's a real pill!"

"Ace!" Gephard hurriedly descended the stepladder. "He's a real card," explained the editor as he blushed.

"It's a pleasure to meet you, Ace." Payne stepped forward and took his right hand in hers. Electricity seemed to leap between their fingertips. "I've heard a lot about you."

"And you were still willing to meet me?"

"I've been looking forward to it."

Gephard stepped closer to the pair. "Payne, I've asked Ace here to show you around. I hope you don't mind?"

"Not at all, uncle."

"Ace?" Gephard looked up at him expectantly.

"Well, as yet, I'm feelin' no pain--"

"Ace!" chided Gephard.

"But that can change. I'd love to, Frank."

As the young couple turned to leave, Gephard stood on tip-toes and whispered in Ace's ear. "Thanks a lot, Ace. I owe you one."

"Forget about it, Frank. I'm in no mood for small change."

The initial broad smile on Gephard's face began to fade.

Ace escorted Payne out the door, closing it behind him. He smoothly slid one hand around her waist, and was delighted when she moved closer to him.

"Shall we start with a tour of the offices?" he asked. "I guarantee it'll be pain free."

Payne giggled. "That would be fine."

"All right. To our immediate left is the desk of your uncle's secretary, Uge Nochers. As you can see, Miss Nochers is presently occupied cleaning up some sort of nasty spill under her chair." Ace turned back to stare deeply into Payne's eyes.

"As for the rest ... well, you've already seen the most interesting thing this place has to offer. So, what say we skip right to breakfast. I mean dinner?"

"Sounds great."

"All you can eat?"

"Mmmm," Payne moaned breathlessly. "I love it. But I have to warn you... it always makes me incredibly horny!"

"No problem. In the orchestra of love, there's no such thing as too much... brass."

"You're a brave man."

Payne walked ahead of him, heading for the elevator. Behind her, Ace clenched his fists triumphantly and turned his smiling face upwards.

"Thank you, God."

He finally understood a 'musical score'.

On the wall behind their booth hung a framed photograph of Hannibal the Cannibal holding a fortune cookie and grinning. A piece of paper was pasted on the bottom of the photograph. It read: You Are What You Eat.

Ace and Payne had chosen that booth because Ace loved the photograph. He also loved the All You Can Keep Down buffet at Shanghai Sally's. He'd had the Octopus Plate and Payne had the Swordfish Snout.

"Prepare to attend a party where odd customs hold sway."

Ace reread the slip of paper that had come from inside his fortune cookie. He knew, of course, that these fortunes were seldom wrong. He just wasn't sure exactly how this one would come to prove true.

He slipped the fortune into his pocket and pushed back slightly from the table. The dinner had been excellent; the company even better. Payne had briefly excused herself to go to the restroom, but now she was returning.

Ace's eyes never left her as she crossed the room and again took a seat beside him. She leaned over and kissed him lightly on the chin, then rubbed away the lipstick stain she'd left behind.

"Dinner was delicious, Ace," she purred contentedly. "Now, what do we do?"

"I suppose we could go dancing."

"That would be nice."

"But I know you'd be happier if I just took you back to my place and jumped your bones, sweety."

"You sound awfully sure that's what I want."

"I am."

"Was I that obvious?"

"Nah. But when a beautiful chick holds onto my family jewels all through dinner, I get the hint, honey."

"No wonder Uncle Frank thinks you're his best reporter. Before we go, though, could I ask you one question?

"Sure."

"It's about your name. It seems awfully unusual. Tell me the truth; is it real?"

Ace shrugged. "You caught me, babe. No, it's not. I made it up when I first got into the news business."

"Well, then, what is your real name?"

Ace hesitated, and then spilled the beans. After a helpful waiter cleaned up the beans, Ace took a deep breath and began to speak.

"Wyoming."

"Huh? Your real name is Ace Wyoming?

"No, no. My real name is Wyoming Montana."

"Oh."

"Now it's my turn to ask you a question, pretty lady."

"All right. Turnabout's fair play."

As was his wont, Ace first pulled out a Camel and lit up. He then fixed Payne with a penetrating stare.

"I've been watching the way you walk" he began.

"The way I walk?" Payne pulled a few inches away from him, licking her lips nervously.

"Yeah. I'm a trained observer, you know? So, I couldn't help but notice that you walk a little funny." Ace glanced down at his smoldering cigarette, then back up at the woman. "You wouldn't happen to be a web-footed geek would you, babe?" It was more of a statement than a question.

Payne hung her head, no longer able to meet his eyes. "Yes," she said in a voice so soft he could barely hear it. "It's true. I wanted to tell you—really I did. But men tend to run away when they find out..."

Ace didn't bother to tell her that any real man has a tendency to run away from every woman he's been with. Bad enough she had to go through life looking like a duck; no need to shatter all of her illusions.

She raised her head. Opalescent tears were rolling down both cheeks as she reached out to clutch his hand. She squeezed tightly.

"My real name isn't Payne Kyller, either. Does this change your feelings for me?"

Ace chuckled softly and patted her hand reassuringly. "Don't worry about it, sweetheart," he said. "So, what is your real name?"

"Payne Hertz."

Ace ground his cigarette out in his plate. "Like I said no worry."My feelings don't run that deep anyway. Besides, I work for the Global Star, remember?

"Some of my best friends are geeks."

"**P**ersonal note, Saturday, April 14: Send a tape of last night's session to Beth Francher, ASAP. Let the bitch know how a real woman spends her evenings."

Payne Hertz giggled as Ace tossed his micro-cassette recorder to one side. "You're a monster, Ace."

"Yeah. And that's one of my better traits."

Payne pulled her silken bathrobe more tightly around her as Ace lit a Camel.

"You... you didn't really make a tape of what we did last night... did you?"

"Hey!" Ace snorted." Great performances need to be preserved, babe. I'm callin' this one 'Ace in the Hole'. Besides—I got a deal with Kirsten Lane. I swap her my tapes in exchange for the use of her apartment."

"But, why would you need to use her apartment when you have such a lovely place of your own?"

"Uh ... well, sometimes, I deal with people who I don't want to know my home address." Ace's cigarette bobbed as he spoke.

"Oh-h. Dangerous types?"

"You could say that." Ace didn't feel it necessary to mention that these 'dangerous types' were all female. He had a sudden thought and again reached for his recorder.

"Personal note to Kirsten Lane: Hey, babe—my tapes are the best thing that ever happened to your career as a novelist and to your love life—so is it too much to ask that you keep a couple of **ck*** beers in the refrigerator? Gimme a break. And start putting the CDs back in their cases, for Gods sake.

"Now, where were we, sweetheart?" Ace took a deep drag on his Camel, rubbed the small triangular scar at the base of his throat, and then pulled Payne close to him. "Hertz me, baby," he grinned. "Make me feel cheap."

She moaned into his mouth as they kissed, pressing her ripe young body against his. He eased her down on the sofa, his hands moving to the belt holding her robe closed. Then, the doorbell chimed the theme from the movie Close Encounters of the Third Kind.

"Son of a bi***," Ace yelled as he leaped to his feet. Payne sat up, closing her robe, smoothing her mussed hair and taking the lit end of Ace's cigarette out of her mouth. "Can't they ever leave me alone?" Ace growled as he padded toward the door.

Payne felt an additional swell of pride that she had spent the night with a man who was obviously so important.

Ace jerked the door open, causing his caller to yelp and jump back in surprise. Ace sighed as he saw that it was "Rollover" Rover, the Global Star's genetically engineered dog-boy, half-Shiatsu and half sheepdog. Ace had nicknamed him "Rollover", but Rover's official title was 'cub reporter'. In actuality, he was little more than a glorified lapdog and office boy, doing whatever struck the fancy of Frank Gephard, but, at night, he was just one more of the thousands of super-heroes that cluttered up the city.

At night he was Mighty Dog.

"What are you doing here, Shi**u?" Ace scowled. "It's June. At the first sign of summer, you usually flea." Behind him, Payne giggled.

"Don't bark at me like that, Ace." Rover panted. "I'm just doin' my job."

"Come in, you stupid Shi**u."

Rover cocked his left to the left, puzzled.

"Sorry, Rollover. This thing in my neck confused S**tzu with s**t, admittedly, an understandable mistake." Ace waited for Rover's reaction to his insult. It didn't come. He took a copy of The New York Times and began spreading its pages on the floor for Rover.

"No need. I brought my own scooper, Mr. Montana."I'm sorry to disturb you." Rover nervously licked his left paw and wiped his left cheek with it. The awe in which Rover held Ace was plain to see. "Especially on a Saturday. But Mr. Gephard told me to come over and drive you back to the office. Are you ... in pain?"

"I woulda been if you hadn't showed up. The Chief sent you to fetch me? Why didn't you say, so, boy?"

Ace's mood changed instantly. There was only one reason Gephard ever sent a driver for him, and that was when he had an important overseas assignment on tap. The mere though of a new story was enough to send Ace's adrenal gland into overdrive.

"Come on in, boy. I just want to have a bite of breakfast, and then we can go."

"Ace, you forgot to introduce me," interrupted Payne.

If Rover had thought it strange that the reporter would be eating breakfast at noon, such thoughts left him as he looked at Ace's pained expression. Payne took his paw and he tried to smile. After all, Rover was a bit naive and innocent—but he wasn't stupid.

"I'm Payne Hertz.," purred Gephard's niece.

"Pedro!" Ace yelled, "Where the h**l's our breakfast?"

There was no response.

"Get you're a** in gear, Pedro, chop-chop!! You want to be castrating bulls back in Mexico again, hombre?"

There was still no response.

Finally, the swinging door leading into the kitchen swished outward and a middle-aged Oriental man, dressed in a white apron with the bird emblem of the quasi-mercenary Blackhawks air squad on it, entered the room. He was carrying a steaming breakfast tray in one hand and a small hatchet in the other, riding a small, white donkey.

"That's more like it!" Ace declared, clapping his hands and preparing to dig in. The smile vanished from the reporter's face when Pedro set a platter of pancakes down on the coffee table in front of Ace and Payne.

"Pancakes? Why the ***k did you cook p*nc*k*s and p*rkch*ps? I told you I wanted scrambled eggs!"

Pedro said nothing. Rover asked, "Why did your V-chip bleep out pancakes, Mr. Montana?"

"Because, when Pedro makes 'em, they're obscene."

Pedro set a second platter of pancakes in front of Payne, and then rode back into the kitchen.

"*****n' Chinaman," Ace snapped in exasperation. "He's inscrutable, I tell you. He never listens to me and he refuses to speak."

"Uh, I don't think he can, Mr. Montana," Rover commented meekly, scratching vigorously behind his right ear with his right paw. "Remember?"

"Yeah? Why not, Rollover?"

"Because he's a deaf mute."

"Hah! That's what he wants you to think! But he doesn't fool me. You hear that, Pedro?" Ace yelled at the swinging doors.

No response.

"What did I tell you?"

Ace turned back to talk at the swinging doors.

"One more screw up, Pedro, and it won't matter what I promised after I slept with your mother, your sister and your Aunt Sophie—I'm runnin' the story about the cozy little love nest you kept with Bill Clinton!"

"You mean Hillary Clinton, don't you, Ace?" asked Rover.

"Heh! I'm not cruel!" Ace shook his head. "You're a good dog, Rover, but you don't have a lick of sense."

"**R**ollover" Rover likewise maintained silence as Ace sullenly ate his breakfast before excusing himself to shower, dress and pack a bag.

When Ace came bounding out of the bedroom and headed for the front door, Rover yapped discretely and jerked his head to remind Ace that Payne was still waiting expectantly on the sofa. Ace took a leftover pork chop from his plate and tossed it to the dog-boy.

"Just how is life treatin' you," asked Ace in a rare moment of what passed in the reporter as concern.

"Ruff," barked Rover.

"Why don't you get the engine warmed up, Rollover? I'll be down in a minute. That's a good Sh* t**."

"Sure thing, Mr. Montana."

Ace walked over to the sofa and sat on one over stuffed arm. Leaning over, he kissed Payne lightly on the forehead.

"So long, babe. Just let yourself out when you're ready to leave, okay?"

"Sure." Payne did nothing to hide the disappointment in her voice. "I'd planned on going visit my little nephews today, anyway, Ace."

Nephews?"

"Cute little kids; Mega and Giga."

"Mega and Giga Hertz?" asked the reporter.

"Ace, will you call me when you get back home?"

Ace smiled wistfully.

"Probably not, kid." He chucked her lightly under the chin. "But don't you ever forget you were the best geek I almost had."

Payne smiled bravely as Ace stood and headed to the door. He paused as he opened it, glancing toward the kitchen.

"I'm leaving now, Pedro!"

No sound.

Ace looked back at Payne, shrugged and headed out the door. As she fought back tears, the woman thought she could hear him grumbling about inscrutable Chinamen. She glanced down at her breakfast and saw that dog-hair covered the arm of the sofa.

Oh well, she thought, wrinkling her nose, slumping down on the sofa, and picking at her breakfast. Shiatsu happens

⸺⸺⸙⸺⸺

Rover deftly steered the classic Pinto provided by Global Star through the afternoon traffic that made Manhattan a snarling maze. He had driven in silence for several blocks, pulling unconsciously at the short hair covering most of his face and all of his body, silently cursing the dog days of summer. His pork chop sat on the seat next to him in a pool of congealed grease.

"Watch out, Rollover!" Ace yelled, as a homeless man stepped off the curb and into their path. "Heel!! Heel!!"

Rollover yanked hard on the steering wheel, swerving just enough to miss the staggering derelict by mere inches. The derelict glanced up, his face contorted with fear, as he clutched as his disheveled toupee.

"Get a f****ng job, ya low life b*****d!" Ace yelled, hanging his head out the car window. "That Donald Trump is a real nuisance, Rollover! This is all Hillary Clinton's fault, ya know," he declared in exasperation, pulling his head back into the Pinto.

"Everybody knows the b**** has a thing for bums, and now that she's living here, they've descended on this town like fat molecules on Rush Limbaugh's belly."

"Gosh, Mr. Montana... how do you know Mrs. Clinton has a thing for bums?"

"Are you kiddin'? Look who the h*** she's married to. That's clue # 1. "Ace leaned back in his seat.

"And #2... dressin' up like a bum's how I got in her pants."

"Wow! That must have been something else!"

"What can I say? She's no Monica Lewinsky... but I wouldn't kick her outta the Oval Office for eatin' crackers, if you get my drift."

"I never do," Rover replied. He pursed his lips quizzically, and then he spoke again. "Can I ask you another question?"

"Go right ahead, kid. I'm a f*****g fountain of information."

"How come you can't swear any more?"

"Huh?" Ace's voice took on a defensive edge.

"Well, no offense, Mr. Montana, but... you cuss all the time. Have for as long as I've known you."

"Have for as long as anyone's known me, kid," Ace replied, chuckling lightly. The tone of pride in his voice was unmistakable.

"My first words were, 'Hey, b****, bring me a f*****g beer!' My pa was so proud."

"So what went wrong?" Rover pushed. "Now, whenever you try to cuss... all that comes out is that garbled noise."

Ace's left hand reflexively came up to the base of his throat, his fingers tracing over the jagged edges of a three inch long scar.

"Don't ask, Rover," he muttered softly. "Long as you live... don't ever ask me again."

An uncomfortable silence fell over the vehicle, and Ace's mind raced back to that horrible moment just six months earlier.

He should have known better. Every reporter's instinct he possessed had cried out to him: Don't ever get involved with a televangelist's wife.

But Edna May Slicker was no ordinary TV trollop. Oh, sure—she wore more makeup than a rodeo clown and more jewelry than a 42nd Street pimp, just like most of her kind. But there was something different about her, something special.

Maybe it was the fact that she had previously been a contortionist at the Bungling Bros. Circus. Maybe.

Or maybe Ace had simply grown careless in his efforts to get the dirt on her husband, the Reverend Billy Bob Jimbo Slicker.

'Dirt' was the operative word. Slicker had gotten rich-—filthy rich—selling tiny bags of dirt he claimed had come from beneath the fingernails of Jesus and the Twelve Apostles.

In turn, he had used the money to buy political favors through the political action committee he had founded: The Christian Conspiracy (Their motto: Democrats aren't the only people who go to Hell. So do Jews, queers and Commies.)

Ace knew the man was a fake the first time he heard him speak. Slicker had quoted scripture from the gospels of Matthew, Mark, Luke and Zeppo.

It was only natural that Ace tried to get to Billy Bob through his wife. Totally unnecessary—but natural, if you were Ace. It hadn't been hard to seduce her. A diamond necklace and a box of bon-bons did the trick.

But the trick was on Ace. He awoke the next morning with the mother of all sore throats. There was no trace of Edna May, except for the imprint of her face which her make-up had left etched on Ace's chest where she had rested her head.

And there was also a note, explaining what had happened. Ace had blissfully passed out the night before, following a little trick Edna May had called the Third Coming. When he did, she opened the door to a team of Fundamentalist Physicians, a hard-nosed team of surgeons who believed every world published in the Journal of the American Medical Association came directly from God.

The physicians had surgically implanted a special V-chip inside Ace's vocal chords. From that moment on, any effort he made to swear resulted in garbled speech.

For several days after learning this, that meant he could say nothing.

But that wasn't the most insidious part of their plan. If it had been solely the V-chip they had implanted, it could have been easily removed. After all, Global Star employees belonged to the same HMO that served the local Meat Packers Union.

But the surgeons had implanted a second device, in a... more delicate part of Ace's anatomy. If any attempt was made to remove either device, a neuro-electrical charge would be triggered, rendering Ace permanently impotent

And while he dearly loved to cuss, an Ace Montana without sex would be like Elton John without his gay houseboy—unthinkable.

So, for now, Ace had to do without his ability to swear, much as he hated the very thought. The Slickers had gone underground, their exact location unknown. But Ace had sworn to find them, no matter how long it might take. And when he did...

"I'll f****n rip their f*****g heads off and s*** down their f*****, C*****, M*******t throats!" he growled aloud.

To Rover, it sounded like radio static coming from Ace's mouth.

"Can I ask you a question, Mr. Montana?"

"Sure." Ace picked Kirsten's latest paperback, Raging Hormones, out of the pocket on the back of the driver's seat and looked at it. "Bark."

"You...uh...you know Miss Lane pretty well, don't you?" Rollover licked the back of his hand and stroked his cheek with it.

"Rollover, I know Kirsten in every way a man can know a woman-including in a Biblical sense." Ace put the paperback back in the pocket with a look of disdain and symbolicly 'washed' his hands by rubbing them together.

"Gosh!"

"Keep your eye on the road. Good boy. That raghead cabbie in front of us could do something stupid at any minute. That's why they're here, you know— to disrupt America's transportation system."

"If you say so. About Miss Lane?"

"Right. What do you want to know?"

"Anything. Everything."

"How come?" Ace looked over at the ugly and earnest young reporter, the only son of a Greek shepherd. No wonder it's so hard to find virgin wool, he thought. "Holy ****f You've got the hots for her, don't you? Lookin' for a little heavy petting!"

Rover started to whine a denial but Ace cut him off

"If's nothing to be ashamed of, boy. Half the staff of the Global Star could say the same thing, including that d***ed dyke over in broadcasting, Beth Francher. They'd all like to get in Kirsten's pants. But let me tell you—and I'm speaking from experience here—she'd chew a pup like you and spit you out in a single night."

"But, I'm not just talking about sex, sir. I'm talking about the possibility of a real, meaningful relationship."

Ace laughed sharply. "Believe me, kid, there's less chance of that happening than there is of finding out that Pee Wee Herman is a Martian transsexual."

Rover started to share that Pee Wee was, indeed, a Martian transsexual, but Ace shushed him with an upraised hand. He finished his micro-cassette recorder out of the pocket of his leather jacket and switched it on.

"Personal reminder: check for possible links between Pee Wee Herman and Martian transsexual community. Start with Mars bars. "

Ace returned the recorder to his pocket and turned his attention back to "Rollover".

"Listen. Kirsten Lane has only two qualifies that I admire. The first is that she would kill her own grandmother if it meant getting a story. The second is that she will **q* anything that moves without feeling an ounce of human emotion. She's almost as good as a man in that respect. So, give up any notions of puppy love you may have about her."

Ace popped a Camel into his mouth and lit up. He exhaled the first noxious fumes out through his nostrils, looking out at the passing skyscrapers. Rover panted, his tongue between his canines. It was, after all, the Dog Days of Summer.

"Nah. You can trust me on this one, boy. Where that woman is concerned— many are balled, but few are chosen."

Rover pulled into the spacious underground parking garage beneath the Global Star building, and parked, letting his passenger out near the elevators. Ace could tell from Rover's hangdog expression that he was sinking into depression, so the veteran reporter sought to cheer him up.

"Hey, 'Rollover', you know Gephard's niece is still back in my apartment. If you want, you can go over there and, uh, throw her a bone, if you get my meaning."

"Nah--but she's your girlfriend," Rover growled.

"No problem. I'm through with that mutt, boy."

"But we live in t-two different w-worlds, Mr. Montana."

"Believe me. You're both from the Geek Islands. Let me tell you something, boy. When God created man, He told him he was gonna have to work his ass off and die old and broken. But, in return, he could have all the sex he wanted."

"Are you sure about that?" Rover asked, licking his chops.

"Love Hertz. It's in the Gospel of St. Ace. Now, doggoneit, get the *u** outta here."

Ace smiled as the dog-boy gunned the motor and roared out of the parking garage, his head hanging out of the window. He felt like he had done a good deed today. Twice.

Ace was still smiling as he entered the editorial offices of the Global Star. He loved the sights and sounds that surrounded him, drinking them in as he strolled through the bustling bull pen—the subtle smell of pulp and ink, of stale after-shave, of hidden bottles of booze in desk drawers, the musky scent of the Minatour being interviewed at a back desk. What a beef he had!

His eyes twinkled mischievously as they locked on Uge Nochers, seated at her desk outside of Gephard's private office. She was bent over the desk, applying copious quantities of correcting fluid to an office memo from the 'managing' editor which had probably taken her an hour to type. Ace shook his head sadly as he watched the white liquid slide down the face of her computer screen.

As usual, she was wearing a low-cut blouse from the Britney Speared collection that showed off her greatest attribute. Ace smacked his lips, then sauntered over and planted himself on one corner of the secretary's desk. He never tired of the view—a tiny cameo necklance with a picture of him that he'd given Uge on her twenty-seventh birthday.

Her tongue protruded from one side of her mouth, her face twisted in concentration, as she painstakingly whited out yet another misspelled word. Finally, she took note of Ace, looking up to smile at him as she absently brushed a strand of hair away from her blue eyes.

"Hi, Ace. Mr. Gephard's waiting for you. Go right on in."

"Sure thing, Uge." Ace hopped off the desk, then paused dramatically. "Uh, Uge?"

"Yes?"

"No. Never mind. " Ace hesitantly turned aside and started to walk away.

"What is it, Ace?" Uge's voice quivered ever so slightly with trepidation, and Ace knew he had her.

"It's nothing, really."

"Please tell me."

"Well... okay. " Ace returned to Uge's desk, planting his hands on one edge and leaning toward her. Her face was raised expectantly.

"Tell me, Uge... have you ever heard of tit mice?"

"Uh!" Uge gasped, and reflexively clapped her hands over the scooped neck of her blouse. "What...what are tit mice?" she asked, in that tremulous voice that turned weaker men's knees to jelly.

"You don't know? I thought you'd keep abreast of stuff like that." Ace actually managed to sound concerned as he leaned even closer to Uge. "T'hey're just about the most vicious little beasts God ever saw fit to put on this planet, that's all. They're all over the place. And, once they set their sights on their prey, well, nothing short of death will stop them from devouring it."

"Their chosen prey?" Uge's heart was beginning to pound frantically. "What's their chosen prey?"

Ace let his gaze drop down the front of Uge's dress, then back up to her face. "I'll give you two guesses," he whispered.

"Ooooh!" Uge's enormous eyes grew even bigger, and she began to scan the floor all around her. Seeing nothing, she looked back up at Ace, and a sceptical expression began to grow on her face. "I think you're just titillating me again, Mr. Ace Montana, star reporter! I don't think there is such an animal."

"No? I'll prove it." Ace glanced around the newsroom, and a wolfish grin stretched his lips as he looked past the paper's religion editor, Maharishi Mephistopheles, a hell of a writer, and saw Beth Francher walking in their direction.

Francher was anchorwoman of the Global Star Tonight television show, which made her the natural enemy of a print journalist. She was also a lesbian, which made her the natural enemy of a man like Ace.

"Yo. She-male! " Ace called out as she passed Uge's desk. She stopped dead in her tracks, turned slowly, and glared at him.

"What do you want, Neanderthal?"

"Relax, babe. I just want to test how smart you are. You ever heard of tit mice?"

"Don't be a moron, moron. Everybody's heard of tit mice."

The broadcaster then jumped with surprise as Uge Nochers let out a blood-curdling scream. Chalking it up to the fact that the secretary seemed to have an I.Q. somewhat below that of cauliflower, Beth shrugged and continued on her way.

"I rest my case," Ace stated matter-of-factly, pushing himself away from Uge's desk and heading toward Gephard's office.

As he opened the door to enter, he glanced back to see Uge now standing on top of her desk. He wondered if she knew how lucky she was not to be working at that rag of a newspaper, Washington Post.

She wouldn't last a week at that Mickey Mouse outfit.

—⊗⊗⊗—

Frank Gephard was talking animatedly on his cell phone, but he motioned for Ace to enter and take a seat. Hanging upside down from gravity boots ratcheted onto the cealing, Gephard's face was flushed with blood—or anger—and his hair looked like a stiff plug of long, unmowed yard grass.

"I'm sorry, but at this point it just doesn't sound like our kind of story. Yeah. Sure. Right. If you come up with anything more, let me know. Right."

Gephard returned the phone to his shirt pocket from which it promptly fell to the floor. He grinned and gestured broadly at Ace. "Retirees! Walter Cronkite heard that a blood bank was robbed here in town last night, but he didn't have the sense to find out who did it. Bloody fool. Bad enough he can't keep his clothes on, he's with the 'Let me entertain you, let me entertain you…all the time!' If he wasn't a channel for Gypsy Rose Lee, no one in this town would give him the time of day."

The editor looked down enquiringly at Ace. "So, what was all that commotion I heard outside, Ace?"

Ace shrugged, making a mental note that, hanging upside down, Frank looked a lot like Don King. "Uge is just up in the air about something. So, what's up, Frank, besides, well, you?"

"Please, call me 'Chief.'"

"Yeah. Right." Ace lit a Camel. "So, what's up, Frank?"

Gephard grunted. "Okay. Here's the deal; I'm sending you to Singapore."

"Great. I love dolls made in China. So, what's the scoop?"

"At this point, all we've got are unconfirmed rumors. But, they're juicy ones. Seems there's an 18-year-old girl there who's been displaying miraculous healing powers lately."

"Big deal. Faith healers are a dime a dozen. I go to one myself. F*c*ing HMOs."

"No, no. Listen. That's not the real angle on this story. The thing is, the little lady just gained these powers recently... after she was visited by the ghost of Marilyn Monroe!"

Ace made a sound of disgust as he exhaled a small cloud of smoke. "H***. Can't any of these ***kin' celebrities just die and stay that way for a change? If they're not zombies, they're ghosts. If they're not ghosts, they're reincarnations. If they're not reincarnations, they never fu***W died in the first place."

"But, for Gods sake, Ace--Marilyn Monroe! Is that hot, or what?"

"I don't know, short stack. Sounds to me like it could be a wild ghost chase."

"Don't call me that, Ace." Gephard struggled to lift himself at the waist to reach his boots. He failed. "C'mon, Ace; I'm a little short of time."

"No kidding. Listen, tiny dancer, I don't know if this one is worth my time or not. Maybe you should give it to Kirsten. She's been wanting an overseas assignment."

"No way. Only my top man goes on this one. Besides, I just got off the phone with Kirsten a little while ago, and she's up to her neck in caca. Seems she's in some jerkwater little town in Oregon, looking for monsters in sewers."

"Jeez. I feel sorry for the town. If the monsters don't destroy it, Kirsten probably will."

"Yeah- just the way she's destroying my expense account. But, back to this story, Ace; there's another twist I haven't told you about yet. It seems that after this little girl in Singapore had performed her first few miracles, she just up and vanished. No one's seen her in over a week, and no one knows what's become of her. Rumor has it she's been taken out of the mix by a bunch of televangelists; looking to reduce competition."

Gephard saw an involuntary shudder pass over Ace as his top reporter's hand kneaded the triangular scar at the base of his neck at the word televangelist. He could see that he had also finally piqued Ace's curiosity, and he moved in for the kill.

"We could be talking massive conspiracy and cover-up here, Ace." He struggled again to reach for his boots. "This could be the biggest story since you learned that Jim Bakker was really Howdy Doody!"

Ace expertly flipped his smouldering cigarette butt into the Munchkins wastebasket next to Gephard's desk, exhaling loudly as he did so.

"Aw, what the f***, short order. I didn't have anything planned for this weekend anyway. I'll do it."

"That's the spirit! I knew I could count on you." Gephard wore a wide smile as he twisted in his boots and pointed to a packet on his desk for Ace. "There's your airline tickets. You're booked on the next flight out of Kennedy,"

"I'm thrilled." Ace stuffed the packet into the inside pocket of his leather jacket and rose to leave. Just as be opened the door, Gephard called out to him.

"Ace? If you can get Miss Nochers down off her desk, would you ask her to come in, please? I have some ... er, dictation... to do. "

Ace smirked. "Dictation. I never heard it called that before, Frank. Are you sure it isn't shorthand you're needin'?"

Gephard coughed nervously.

"That's a stretch, even for you. But I think you got a more pressing problem at the moment," Ace added as his head disappeared around the comer of Gephard's door. It took every ounce of self-control for him to stifle an outburst of laughter.

Uge looked at Ace from behind her desk, her face a mask of confusion. She wore a mouse trap on her Dollie Parton brand blouse over each breast.

"What problem?" stammered Gephard.

Ace withdrew his head back into Gephard's office and leaned against the doorjamb.

"Your wastebasket." Ace was already closing the door behind him as he began to exit.

"It's on fire."

⊸∞∞∞⊶

"**M**onday, April 16. What a *****n'waste of an airplane ride. We didn't encounter a single alien spaceship, ozone storm or time warp the entire trip. On top of that, the only movie they had to offer was Rollover's favorite, All Dogs Go To Heaven. My stewardess, who was a genetically engineered human mutt, was so shaken, she accepted Lassie as her personal savior.

"The only thing that made it worthwhile was the knockout English stewardess in First Class. We'd have made it into the Mile High Club if she'd known how to convert from kilometers. I'd give her a call if I could remember her name for sure. I think it was Mary Poppins or something."

Ace switched off his micro-cassette recorder and dropped it into the pocket of his denim shirt. Rising from the bed in his hotel room, he walked out on the balcony of his Motel 5 ½, cursed Gephard for his cheapness, and waved away the pigeons with the odd, slanted eyes that had perched on the railing. He looked out over the city.

Singapore was just as he remembered it from his last visit. A bustling port that never seemed to sleep, its diverse citizenry crawled all over each other like worker ants.

And, as always, the sticky, humid air was thick enough to swim in. Within seconds, Ace could feel the sweat begin to bead on his forehead and pool under his armpits. He retreated back to the air-conditioned comfort of his room. Thus far, the reporter's stay in the city had proven unproductive. None of his contacts could even tell him the name of the girl he sought. He still had one hope: an old friend who had promised to call him.

Ace glanced at the sundial on his wrist. His friend was not expected to contact him for another hour yet. Until then, there was nothing Ace could do but wait.

Actually, it occurred to him, there was one bit of business he could take care of while he waited. He reentered his room, dropped down on the bed, snatched up and flipped open the cell phone there, and began dialing the offices of Global Star. While he waited for the overseas connection to be made, he lit a Camel, savoring its bite. On the third ring, Uge Nochers answered.

"Uge? This is Ace."

"Hello, Ace. How are--SNAP!" Her words were cut off by the unmistakable sound of a sprung mousetrap.

"Uge? What the hell's going on there?"

"Oh, it's all right. Frank ... er, Mr. Gephard... uh... he just caught a tit mouse."

"Atta girl. Don't let one of the little b**t***s sneak up on you. Listen, you think you can snap out of it long enough to tell me if I've had any messages?"

"My pleasure. You had a call from a Dr. Schlomo Reynolds. He claims to have proof that the tobacco companies are putting chemicals in cigarettes that cause people to exhibit aggressive behavior."

"Who the hell's gonna believe that kinda bulls**t claptrap? Remind me to tear his head off when I'm back," Ace snapped, taking a deep drag on his Camel.

"That's what I told him. He must think we're idi–" BLAM! Ace recognized the unmistakable sound of a gunshot.

"What was that?" he demanded of the cell phone.

"Oh. I borrowed a gun from a security guard, Ace. Did you know that Mr. Gephard's shoes look exactly like tit mice?"

"I've long suspected they were related. Any more messages?"

"Yes. Delta Burke's attorney called. He's threatening to sue if we don't retract our story about Delta being possessed by the spirit of Orson Welles."

"Gimme a break. Reynolds had to gain twenty pounds to move in! Who's the public gonna believe, me or a shyster who represents that giant Japanese lizard?"

"I think your confusing Delta with Della, Ace. She doesn't work for Perry Mason. "

"Oh. Never mind. Anything else?"

"One more thing. A woman who is a fan of your stories showed up here this morning. She says she wants to have your baby. "

"Who am I, Paul Anka?! "

"That's the name you gave the last one, Ace."

"Oh, yeah. What does she look like?"

"Kind of like Bo Derek, only prettier."

"In that case, have her sign the usual contract, give her a number—say, 10—take her phone number, and tell her I'll put her on my waiting list."

"Gotcha. Anything else?"

"Yeah. There is one other little thing, babe. Tell me, have you ever heard of that problem called Parton's Dropsie?"

"Parton's what?" Nochers tittered.

"Dropsie. I was reading about it in a medical journal on the flight over. It's the downward force gravity exerts on a woman's ta ta's."

"You're kidding."

"Swear to Playtex. It's what makes them sag as women get older. And naturally, the bigger the headlights, the worse it is. The magazine had a photo of a forty-year-old who has to tape them to her ankles."

"Oh, no! Is there a-any c-c-cure, Ace?"

"Yeah. Vigorous massage twice daily with limburger cheese. Gotta run now, Uge. Have an uplifting day."

"Wait! Don't hang up! What about tit mice? Don't they love limburger cheese?"

"Only the German ones genetically engineered by Walt Disney." He could almost see the tears rolling down the distraught secretary's cheeks. "Check for tiny little swastika's and round, flat ears." Then, just as he was setting the telephone receiver back in its cradle, he thought he heard the sound of yet another gunshot--followed by Frank Gephard's screaming. He knew that, from now on, Gephard wouldn't have to worry as much about toe fungus.

Ace lay back on the bed with his fingers laced together behind his head. As he stared up at the mirror on the ceiling, he began to chuckle softly. He finally knew the answer to one of life's great mysteries.

Was Gephard a man or a mouse?

***

Ace again checked the address he had written down on a sheet of hotel stationary against the address on the building, confirming that he was at the right location. From a hidden speaker, an instrumental version of an old disco song that Ace couldn't place filled the air. It was Kung Fu Fighting.

"Tuesday, April 17. This may prove to be the weirdest piece of ***t I've ever stepped into since Edna May Slicker and the Christian Conspiracy. My old buddy, Roger Castle, has arranged for us to meet at a f*****n' crematorium! Guess I better get my ash in gear!"

Ace shut off his recorder and stepped inside the unassuming building. There was a strange smell to the place, an odd mixture of incense and disinfectant. For once, Ace felt no urge to light up a Camel.

"Ace Montana! Ace, old chap! Over here!"

Roger Castle approached from one of the crematorium's side chambers. He was dressed as a "Biker" in leather pants, vest, and cap. Castle had started as the arts reporter for The New York Post covering Post Modernism before the scandal had reduced him to writing obituaries at one of Singapore's daily newspapers. He and Ace had painted the town red together in their younger days. They'd been kicked out of town by the Local Painter's Union.

"Glad you could make it, old boy," Castle said in his clipped British voice, and tipped his cap. "Today is a jolly 'oliday!"

"Right-o. But, why 'ere?" Ace was feeling more than a little uncomfortable in his present surroundings, and Castle's phony accent didn't help. Castle was from Hell's Kitchen, and it wasn't the one in New York state.

"Oh, we're burying my Mother Bun, my mother-in-law, today. "

"Are you s*****n me?"

"Not at all." Castle cocked his head to the left and looked puzzled at Ace. "I thought we could bag two kills with a single bash, so to speak, what?"

Now Ace had to light up a Camel. "Suits me, but you're not exactly dressed for a funeral, are you? Shouldn't you be wearing white, Castle?"

"I tried, but the buggin' 'ittle 'amburgers wouldn't stay on. You forget where you are, old chum. We do things with a little different slant here in Singapore. Come on in."

Castle directed Ace into the side chamber. Half a dozen people were already there, each dressed as either an Indian, a policeman, a carpenter....

Ace immediately recognized them for what they were, a chapter of the Village People cult. They all seemed very unconcerned, certainly not in deep mourning.

"This has got to be the biggest mother-in-law joke of all time," Ace whispered into his recorder. "All we need is some music, and we'll have a real disco inferno going." He suddenly recognized the song coming faintly over the public address speakers: Burn Baby, Burn.

At that, the words written in his fortune cookie came back to him. Odd customs did indeed hold sway here.

"Personal note: Try to find out who writes the fortunes in fortune cookies. The guy's a f*c*i*' genius." Ace touched the scar on his neck and winced.

Ace's attention was drawn by a sudden splash of color as a new participant entered the chamber. It was a young Buddhist monk, dressed in a saffron yellow robe. Walking to a small table at the front of the room, the monk lit several sticks of incense. Quickly, their sweet odor began to fill the room. In deep tones, the monk then began to recite a prayer for the dead.

Ace was, of course, extremely fluent in Chinese, but he quickly lost interest in listening to the prayers. At that point, his ears picked up another sound from nearby: a hushed, roaring noise.

Only then did he see the black metal door set in one wall of the chamber. He felt a heaviness in the pit of his stomach as he realized this was the oven in which the body of Roger Castle's mother-in-law was being incinerated. Ace leaned closer to Castle and tugged lightly at his sleeve.

"Tell me the truth," Ace whispered. "You hated the old battleaxe, and this is your way of getting even with Mother Bun, right?"

"Not at all!" Castle looked somewhat indignant. "I dearly loved Mrs. Bun. She had a wonderful sense of humor. But, in this part of the world, we've come to accept death as the inevitable conclusion to the cycle of life. It's commonplace to have a bun in the oven.

"Ah! I see we're ready for the final ceremony."

Ace opened his mouth to speak, then closed it. Two attendants had removed the cremated remains of the old woman from the oven, and now wheeled them over to where the family members were waiting. To his amazement, each of the 'mourners'—including Roger Castle—produced a pair of chopsticks and began to pick through the bones and ash. They would pluck out bits and pieces, depositing them in an ornate urn decorated with scenes from Travolta's movie, Saturday Night Fever, that would serve as their final resting place.

"What the hell," Ace muttered, finally accepting this practice as being no more bizarre than an Irish wake. "When in Rome..."

Roger Castle deposited a bit of bone in the burial urn. Looking up, he smiled with bemusement and shook his head. Ace was standing opposite him, holding a single chopstick. He had managed to find a marshmallow among the food offerings the family had brought to give to the presiding monk, spiked it on the end of the chopstick, and was now casually roasting it over the still smouldering remains of the dearly departed.

When the funeral was ended, Ace and Castle excused themselves and went for a walk through the streets of the city. The avenue they chose to stroll was lined with open air stands in which all manner of goods were being bought and sold. Castle bought a bootleg Cd by Michael Jackson: Killer. The Chinese still had trouble pronouncing t's.

There was no need to worry that their conversation could be overheard by unwanted parties, for their words were lost in the verbal rumblings that surrounded them. Besides Chinese, people were speaking in Malay, Tamil and English, creating a supermarket Babel.

"So, tell me," Ace said, dodging a young man on a bicycle," were you able to dig up anything on this chick with the magic hands?"

"Very little, I'm afraid," Castle replied. "She hadn't made her presence known for long before she vanished."

"A flash in the Sai Pan, eh. What do you know?"

"A name, old chap. She's called Sueng Lo."

"Sweet chariot, at least that's something to go on. Have you seen this babe yourself?"

"No. But I've spoken to a man who claimed to have seen her cure a woman in a wheelchair. The man's usually a reliable source of information, but, quite frankly, I have a hard time believing in all this miracle healing sort of tommy rot."

"Believe me," Ace replied, "I've seen stranger things; babies with two heads, a shaved Big Foot, politicians with brains..."

"Yes, I imagine you have, old chap, given your particular beat. Damn, but I envy you, Ace. The press is kept on a pretty tight string here. Nothing but hard news: UFOs, the Loch Ness monster, hauntings. Just the 'beyond a doubt' stuff. "

"Hey, pal, we each do what we can. One more question. The girl was just starting to make a name for herself, so why would she up and disappear?"

"According to my contact, she didn't do so voluntarily. She was kidnapped," he said with obvious contempt, "by those who worship the Hantu."

"Don't knock it," said Ace, pulling his pack of Camels from his shirt pocket. "In rare, and I do mean rare, instances where I couldn't find a woman, I've worshiped the hand, too,"

Castle stopped Ace in midstep with a hand on his shoulder. He looked for even a hint of humor in the journalist's eyes. There was none.

"The Hantu," he said slowly, "is a mysterious religious cult, old boy."

"Hey! I knew that! " Ace spat, jerking his shoulder from under Castle's hand.

"Exactly who or what they are and want, and where they've taken the girl, he couldn't tell me. Sorry, but that's all I know, old boy."

The two men had reached the end of the avenue, having left the market stalls behind them. It was relatively quiet now, except for the sounds of passing traffic. Ace lit up his Camel and stared out over the city.

"I'll just have to dig up the rest on my own," he said.

"So, what's your first move, old chum?"

"First, I find myself a good restaurant." Ace smiled jauntily. "That little snack I had with Grandma Bun just made me hungrier. And, listen, Castle. Don't ever invite me to another of your family *U*k*n* ghoulish 'celebrations'. One was enough for a lifetime."

"As you wish," said Castle, picking at his teeth with a sliver of Mother Bun bone. "As for me and mine, nothing says lovin' like something from the oven."

The little hotel sign hung motionless in the fetid air. It read: Hotel Tao Main. Ace glanced up from his egg fu yung buritto and through the fly-specked window by his table at the sign. He looked down again at the greenish mess on is plate. He decided to give Pedro a raise when he got back to New York City.

The afternoon sun was like a blowtorch, and Ace's lunch was not resting easy. Even the soothing balm of a Camel did little to relieve his discomfort.

He had combed the streets for hours, searching for leads to the whereabouts of Sueng Lo. All it had netted him was sore feet and clothes dripping with sweat. (Well, there was the hot little number he met in the Yoo Man Chu laundry, but, at the moment, even thoughts of the delicate cycle brought little comfort.)

Finally, he'd decided to retreat to the coolness of his room. Night would bring a little relief from the heat, and he would again hit the mean streets.

His feet were dragging as he walked from the elevator to his room, and his stomach was rumbling loudly. As he opened the door and stepped inside, he suddenly felt even more sick at the faint but familiar odor of Barbeque after-shave lotion.

"***t!" he snarled. "Ask for a room with a window, and I get a room with a phew! "

An intruder was in his room, waiting for him. The man made no hostile moves, but rather grinned at Ace. The smile revealed crooked, yellow teeth, set in a face even a mother couldn't love. Dirt brown hair hung loosely down over his forehead, though not so low as to obscure the beady little eyes that would have done any pig proud.

Ace winced as he looked at the ugly little man in the light pink, dirty, polyester suit. His name was Walter Sleize. He was the top reporter for the Global Star's main competitor, the Enquirer-Trib. Ace knew the man well enough to thoroughly despise him, especially after the incident in Stockholm a few months earlier.

Ace had been on the trail of a really hot story. A teenaged boy, suffering from the effects of too much monosodium glutamate, had begun to hallucinate to the point where he believed people were nothing more than giant Swedish meatballs with legs. While suffering under this delusion, the boy had eaten his entire family. And the household pets. And at least two top-ranked tennis pros.

It would have made for a great human interest piece. But Ace couldn't file the story because he was cooling his heels in a Stockhohm jail. Only later did he learn that the authorities believed him to be a spy for Chef Boar Adeize, thanks to a tip from Walter Sleize. So Sleize got the scoop while Ace was nearly getting engaged to a Swedish convict named Odin--who was a damned fine dancer for an axe murderer.

"What the hell are you doing here, sleaze?" Ace demanded bitterly. "Ya beat the rap for molesting the Little Mermaid?"

"The name is pronounced SLAYZE, Montana—but I'm not surprised you can't say it." Even the man's voice was codfish oily. A toothpick bobbed in his mouth as he spoke. "And she was of age."

"Yeah, like that story has legs. That don't change the question. What the hell are you doing in my motel room?"

"Waking for th' bedbugs to bite, old buddy. And, here you are!"

"And how'd the 'other white meat' get in?"

"Cute. Nah, I just told the manager I was your long lost, twin brother." He scraped something from under a fingernail with a toothpick and wiped it on his shirt sleeve.

"Jezz. He should've known that if I'd ever lost a hog like you, I'd want to keep it that way, buddy."

"You'd hurt my liddle feelings if I had any, my brother from another mother," he grinned, sticking the toothpick back in his mouth. "You gonna keep roasting me all night?"

"No way. I'll kill you long before sun-up."

"I detect a real note of hostility here, brother. " Sleize stood up. "Maybe I'd better just take my news tip, make like a tree, and leaf."

"Hey, what a great story idea. Enquirer-'Trib Go-Fer Finds Door With Both Hands.' And, here I thought you had chittlins for brains." Ace opened the door, prepared to usher out his uninvited visitor. "Hit the road, sleaze, and don't wear a helmet, Porky."

"Ba-depp, ba-beep, ba-deep, that's all, Ace!" Sleize headed for the doorway. "I'm sorry I bothered you. I just thought you'd be interested in hearing my rendition of Sueng Lo."

At mention of the girl's name, Ace roughly slammed the door shut, blocking Sleize's exit. His hands shot out, grabbing his rival by the lapels of his loud sport coat. He felt something slimy under his left thumb.

"This is my story, sleeze. What the *u*k are you up to?"

"Hey, hey, hey!" Sleize shrieked, puffing away from Ace's grip. "You know the rules of this game, tough guy. A story belongs to whoever can find it."

"It's whomever, and you couldn't find your f****e a*& with both of yer pig knuckles, sleeze. So, what do you want from me?"

"Sharp as ever." Sleize grinned again, and Ace had to fight the urge to punch that crooked mouth. "All right, Ace. I'll be straight with you."

"I'm not asking for a change in life-style, Miss Piggy."

"You want to hear what I got? If not, I'm out the door, Your call." Sleize reamed an ear with the untrimmed, dirty nail of a pinkie finger.

Ace was seething with anger and suspicion, but, as always, the desire to get the story overcame his emotions. He took a deep breath and reached for a Camel.

"Okay, sleeze. Flap your jowls."

"That's more like it," Sleize grinned, wiping his pinkie finger under the left armpit on his coat. Sleize turned and strutted back to his chair. He leaned back in it, propping his feet up on the bed. In three strides, Ace was across the room, swatting Sleize's feet away and nearly sending him tumbling out of the chair.

"Not on my playground, sleeze. You really are a f**k**' pig?"

"All right! You don't have to get physical!!" Sleize struggled to compose himself.

"Let's get things straight, sleeze-ball," Ace barked. "I'm this ***kin' close to having myself a pork pie, okay? Now, you tell me why you're here, or you're a Luau." Ace snapped his fingers sharply, "You got that, or do I need to repeat it in Pig Latin?"

"Yeah. I got it." Fear sparkled in Sleize's little pig eyes, and something else far deeper. He began to talk, digging nervously at one fingernail with the fingernail of his other hand.

"As you can tell, I am obviously on the trail of the same little miracle worker you are. Unlike you, however, I give a little thought to an assignment before I go stumbling in blindly." Unexpectedly, Sleize sneezed hard.

"So, I've scoped this scene out plenty good. And I've seen enough to let me know that there could be a hell of a lot of danger involved in this whole mess. Danger of the potentially fatal variety." He could find nothing to wipe his nose.

"And when I might be facing death, I don't like to do it alone. I go looking for help." Sleize wiped his nose on the sleeve of his coat.

Ace could hardly believe what he was hearing. "Hold on there, sleeze. "

"Slayze!!"

"Are you trying to say that you want to work as a team, you human snot-rag!?!"

"That's exactly what I'm saying. How about it?"

Ace responded by picking up the land-phone next to his bed. "Hello, doctor? I got a *****n 'crazy man in my room. Send up the butterfly net, and a bottle of bourbon for me."

Ace returned the phone to its cradle and stared balefully at Sleize. "Does that tell you what I think of your brilliant idea? You couldn't write an obit for Little Miss Muffet."

"I never touched her tuffet, and you know that! It's a lie!!" Sleize's head jerked nervously back and forth. "What's wrong with the idea of the two of us working together?"

"I'll tell you what's wrong with it. Did Einstein consult Elmer Fudd? Did Martin need Lewis? Did Woody Allen have to marry his mother?"

"Of course he did; she was preg–"

"That's where it's stupid. I can see what you get out of it. You're scared shi***ss, so you want somebody to protect your flank. But, I ain't scared. So, what's in it for me?"

"Information." Sleize picked his nose, smiled his disgustingly twisted smile again, and scooted forward in his chair.. "I got a nose for news."

"You got snot for brains!

"What have you come up with on the girl so far, Ace? Hub? Zilch, that's what."

"What makes you so sure?"

"'Cause if you had anything at all, you never would have agreed to talk to me in the first place. Am I right?" Sleize picked his nose and wiped his finger on his pants. Ace decided to borrow a page from Pedro's book and give no response.

"I know I'm right," Sleize continued. "'Well, I haven't done much better than you. I don't mind admitting that. But I do have something you don't." He put his finger in his mouth.

"You mean besides more venereal diseases than a Bangkok cathouse?" Ace hated to get information from such a despicable source, but realized he was in no position to be choosey.

"I've got a lead that just might tell us where the girl has been taken." Sleize picked his nose, wiped his finger on his pants, and put the finger in his mouth. "I've got a meeting set up for tonight. You can be there with me."

"Damn straight I'll be there." Ace had fallen victim to his greatest weakness. He'd make a deal with the Devil, and had, if it meant getting the story.

"Good. " Sleize was again on his feet and heading for the door. "I'll call you and set up a meeting place for this evening. Can I have your cell phone number?"

"No."

Sleize merely smiled, picked at his nose and started out the door.

"And, Sleaze?"

"That's Slayze!" He put his finger in his mouth.

"Whatever. Do me a favor."

'"What's that?" Sleize wiped his finger on his pants.

"Introduce your body to some soap and water before tonight. And remember. It's nose, pants, mouth. Nose, pants, mouth. Not nose, mouth. Nose–"

The angry slamming of the door gave Ace no satisfaction.

"Whoever tagged it 'yellow journalism' must have caught a glimpse of that man's jockey shorts," he said to the empty room.

—∞∞∞—

Ace cursed softly as the end of his cigarette sputtered and hissed, turning mushy as falling rain soaked it. The only good that could come from this would be if Sleize was getting drenched as well. He had forgotten just how wet and dreary Singapore could be. The thought of using an umbrella against the downpour never entered his mind. Only wimps, The Penguin, and women used umbrellas. He pulled up the collar of his leather jacket to keep the rain from running down his back.

Ace was seated on a bench within the city's famed Tiger Balm Garden, waiting for Walter Sleize to appear. He cast an impatient glance at his wristwatch and fought down the instinctive urge to reach for another Camel. On a corner opposite him, a shadowy figure squatting by a wall shouted "Shazam!" A flash of lightning tore through the curtain of the night sky, casting an eerie pall over his surroundings.

"D*%n Gomer Pyle," Ace muttered, "and his electrical outlets. Get a room!" he yelled and turned away.

"I always knew it," a cheery voice called out from behind him. "You don't have sense enough to come in out of the rain."

Ace turned to see the oily countenance of Walter Sleize, grinning at him from beneath the protection of a garish, plaid bumbershoot. "And you just confirmed my theory about umbrellas," he snapped at the rival reporter.

"I won't even pretend to be interested," Sleize replied icily. "Come on. We don't want to be late for our meeting."

"Lead the way, pork rind. "

Sleize set out from the park, with Ace beside him. Walter began to bounce from curb to street, twirling his umbrella and whining, Singing In The Rain, until Ace slapped him hard on the back of the head- Ace's hand came away greasy.

Ten minutes of brisk walking brought them to the Bruce Lee housing project, one of many such in the city. One of the ways the island nation had sought to create national unity among its many diverse races was to destroy the various ethnic slums and relocate the people in newer, high-rise flats. The plan had proven to be successful, at least to a limited degree.

Ace stopped in the lobby of the high rise, shaking the water from him like a great hound. He slicked his hair back into place with both hands, then reached for a Camel.

He sighed contentedly as he exhaled the first lungful of cigarette smoke. No question about it, he thought, next to sex, tobacco was the greatest pleasure a man could ever know. His lips curled back in a snarl as he caught Sleize staring at him. "You got a problem, hamhock breath?"

"Those things will kill you, you know," Sleize observed. He hocked up phlegm and spat it on his left shoe.

"Huh! Shows how much you know. If you ever read a real newspaper instead of that cheap rag you work for, you'd know the truth. Cigarettes don't cause cancer. Polyester causes cancer, moron."

"You're kidding." The stubble on Sleize's yellow face quivered.

"That's why I wear nothing that isn't natural... cotton shirts, wool pants, pig skin shoes." Ace looked down at his feet, then eyed his rival coldly. He raised his feet. "Oink Oink twice if that's you, mama Sleize.

"You, on the other hand, are wrapped in enough polyester to kill the entire Green Bay Packers team."

Sleize felt his skin crawl, and shivered. "Forget it. Let's go."

With his eyes averted, Ace followed Sleize as he headed up a nearby stairway. They didn't stop until they reached the third floor landing. The hallway was rather dark, save for a flickering light that came from the open doorway of one of the apartments.

"This is it," Sleize said, his voice falling to a melodramatic whisper. He wiped a finger under his nose.

The two reporters slowly walked toward the light. When they stepped through the doorway, Ace's eyes danced back and forth, soaking in the details as quickly as possible. The living room of the apartment was sparsely furnished. a sofa and chair pushed against a wall. The flickering light came from thousands of Sesame Street birthday candles scattered about the room, leading to a framed picture of Bruce Lee in his role as Kato from the old television series, "'The Green Hornet".

"You goddamn Yankees?"

Sleize jumped with fright as the shrill voice called out to them. A small Chinese woman stepped out from behind the door, looking them over wanly. Her tiny hands pressed down against her pale blue dress, smoothing out imaginary wrinkles. Sleize relaxed when he saw who she was.

Yes. It's us."

"You take you goddamn time." She laughed a weird, high cackle of a laugh.

"That's quite a vocabulary she's got there," Ace observed dryly.

"She learned English from a Marine chaplain," Sleize explained.

"Come on," the woman snapped, turning and walking toward a beaded curtain that separated the living room from the rest of the apartment. "You know karate, kid?" she asked.

The reporters pushed their way through the curtain. Ace paused, letting his eyes adjust to the dim light in this room, cast by a single Cookie Monster candle in one comer. The rest of the room was empty.

Or almost so. Ace squinted as he caught sight of a squat figure in the center of the room. As he peered closer, he could see it was a young boy, no older than five, seated shirtless and cross-legged on a pile of Big Bird plush pillows.

Outside of his obsession with Sesame Street, there seemed to be only one unusual feature about the boy. He was easily the fattest child Ace had ever seen. His bare middle bulged obscenely, hanging over the waistband of his Bert and Ernie shorts.

Ace then noticed yet another peculiar physical feature. The boy had three navels. They sat like the points of an inverted triangle in the center of his distended belly, moving up and down with his breathing.

"So, what's Porky Pig's story," Ace whispered. "Let me guess. He ate Elmo."

"His name is Opie," Sleize answered. "He's Jim Henson's love child, and he was born with a bowling ball in his stomach."

"You're *h*t*i*' me? Who was his mama, Miss Piggy?"

"Yes. And the bowling ball's a Dunlop. Ten-pounder.

"Wow! I ain't seen nothin' like that since I covered the Italian girl who carried her own twin inside her gallbladder."

"I remember that. How did it come out?"

"The twin or the gallbladder?"

"Never mind. This kid is the one we've come to talk to. He may be able to give us some information."

"About what? How to make a 2-10 split?"

"Just shut up and listen for a change, Montana."

Sleize looked at the boy, then turned his back so the child couldn't see his lips.

"Opie is special," Sleize explained. "I don't know if it's because of the bowling ball or what, but something has given him psychic abilities."

"He might be able to give us a lead on where Sueng Lo has been taken."

"What do goddamn whispering Amerlikans want?" the Chinese woman demanded.

"Just arguing over who's gonna get to take you to the prom, sweetheart," Ace replied. "'Why don't you just leave us alone for a few minutes?"

"Take it easy," Sleize hissed. "She's the boy's foster mother."

"Oh? That's different." Ace turned back to the woman and smiled. "Why don't you just go**mn leave us alone?"

At this, the woman chuckled and padded out of the room. "See, Sleize," Ace said, "you just gotta know how to speak the language. Now, close your mouth."

Only then did Sleize realize his jaw had dropped in surprise. He clamped his lips together tightly, then walked toward the boy. Ace followed suit.

"Do you speak English, Opie?" Sleize whispered.

You goddamn light I do!" the boy exclaimed, so loudly that Sleize jumped back several feet.

"Like mother, like son, eh, Sleize?"

"I suppose so." Sleize again approached the boy. "Listen to me, Opie. Do you know about the girl named Sueng Lo?"

"She right down my alley," Opie replied.

"Uh...yeah. That's the one." Sleize looked at Ace, shrugging his shoulders. "My friend and I are trying to find Sueng Lo. Do you think you could help us?"

"Why should I?"

"We're going to give your foster mother some money."

"Gutter ball. What for me?"

Sleize seemed stymied by this question, so Ace pushed him aside. "Let me handle this, Supersleize."

The reporter leaned forward and whispered something into Opie's ear. The boy made no response, sitting impassively with his eyes closed. Ace whispered again into his car. At this, Opie started and his eyes popped open wide.

"I can tell you," he assured them, flashing a conciliatory smile in Ace's direction. "Strike!"

"What did you say to him?" Sleize asked, spraying saliva.

"It was simple," Ace replied. "First, I promised him a new definition of gutter ball that he'd never forget. When that didn't work, I told him I'd rip out his intestines and sell them to McDonald's."

"You didn't!"

"Child psychology, Sleize. Learned it from watching Oprah. It works every time. Go ahead and ask him your question now."

Sleize hesitated briefly, unable to tear his eyes away from Ace's placid face. Finally, he looked back at Opie. The boy was still smiling warmly, trying unconsciously to stick his thumb and two fingers into his navels.

"Okay, Opie. Can you tell me where Sueng Lo is?"

"I goddamn tly."

Opie again closed his eyes, and began to concentrate. His breathing grew more shallow as he entered an almost hypnotic state. His belly seemed to expand to an even larger size, making him look like a great toad. Ace watched in surprise as the skin of the boy's three navels bulged outward, looking for all the world like buttons about to pop off. Then Opie slumped forward, coming out of his trance. He gasped for air, looking up at the two men leaning expectantly toward him.

"She not in Singapore no more," Opie stated in a small voice.

"Where is she?" Sleize asked.

"Light down lane. Malaysia."

"Malaysia? That's a hell of a big country, Opie. Can't you narrow it down any more than that?" Sleize was agitated. He popped a pimple on the right side of his jaw.

"Terrengganu plovince. I think."

"You think?"

"Therefore, I am. That' all I can spare."

"That's all right," Ace assured him, "You done good. Your candy bars'll be in the mail. Now, we gotta split."

"And pletty guts?"

"Stay right where they belong—wrapped around that beautiful bowling ball."

Ace and Sleize then turned to leave the room. As they did, Opie's foster mother came forward, her hand thrust forward, palm up. Sleize sighed, pulled out his wallet, extracted a ten dollar bill and gave it to the woman.

"Give me a **c**n' break, sleeze!" Ace barked. "You gotta be stupid and cheap? Give the lady more money."

Reluctantly, Sleize withdrew two twenties and gave them to the woman. She winked at Ace as she shoved the money down the front of her dress.

"You goddamn good!" she proclaimed, patting his arm. "For capitalist pig."

"You got that light, sister. I mean right. And if we weren't in such a hurry, I'd show you just how 'g**d^!n good' it can be."

The woman was snickering like a schoolgirl as the reporters left the apartment.

It was two hours later that she discovered that Sleize had given her $20,000 in Monopoly game money.

"**H**ere's more good news for you, Ace," Sleize commented as they passed a window in the high rise's stairwell. "It's stopped raining." An orange cat hung outside the window, gripping the pane by suction cups on the bottom of it's paws.

"No kiddin'. As a news flash, that ranks right up there with Pearl Harbor, Sleize." Ace slapped the window, dislodging the orange feline which fell backwards and down, cursing.

"What's wrong with you, Montana? We just got a terrific lead." Sleize flicked something from a finger. They both listened to the diminishing scream of "lasagna!!" outside of the stairwell window as they descended.

"Hope he had Aflac," quipped Ace. "Now all we gotta do is slog through a thousand miles of jungles and rice paddies till we reach a sign that reads: Sueng Lo this way.

"Hold it!!" Ace thrust an arm out, stopping Sleize cold. Sleize started to protest, but closed his mouth when he saw the grim expression on Ace's face. Ace was staring intently at something moving at the bottom of the stairway, and Sleize swiveled his head to see it.

At first, he could make out nothing but shadows. Then, one of the shadows seemed to separate itself from the others, and slide forward. As it did, Sleize could make out that it was a man dressed in a baseball uniform, his cap pulled down over his eyes. The only exposed skin was a narrow band revealing a pair of cold, dark eyes.

"Ninja! Outfielder, I'd guess," Ace hissed.

"Chicago Cubs!" Sleize gasped. "I wonder if he'd autograph my card...?"

"What the he*l is a Ninja doing in Singapore?" Ace interrupted out loud. "And it's a St. Louis Card, you rump roast."

"What difference does it make? There's only one of him, and two of us."

No sooner had Sleize spoken than more shadows emerged. Four more men in striped cotton shirts and caps joined their comrades at the foot of the stairs.

"Three strikes," snapped Sleize, "and we're outta here!"

"Now you're talking. When I move, you head for the roof like your **s was on fire.

"What are you--?!?" Sleize hissed and jumped back from the lit match held by Ace to his backside.

"Setting your **s on fire. Yaaah! " Ace screamed and leaped into the air. At the first sound, Sleize bolted up the stairs. Ace hurtled downward, feet first, slamming into one of the advancing Ninjas. The dark assassin flew backwards, colliding with his comrades. Ace saw two spiked mitts fly into the air.

All of them went down in a jumbled heap at the bottom of the stairwell. Ace was the first to regain his footing, and he began to jump up the stairs three steps at a time.

He could hear the Ninjas behind him, but he forced them from his mind, concentrating instead on making it up the stairs without a misstep. When he reached the final landing of the building, he was not surprised to find that he had caught up with Sleize.

"Come on, lard-*ss," he said, grabbing Sleize by the collar and dragging him up the last few steps leading to the roof. He ignored what he felt on Sleize's suit under his grip.

When they passed through the fire door that separated the stairs from the roof, Ace slammed it shut behind them and threw the bolt to lock it. He knew it would not delay the Ninjas for long, but it might buy precious seconds.

Ace used a few of those seconds to survey the rooftop. Humid steam rose off the asphalt like heavy fog all around them. Except for a few wooden planks left lying about, the roof was bare.

Still dragging the panting Sleize, Ace headed for the edge of the roof. He stopped and jumped upon the ledge, peering through the darkness to gauge the distance to the next rooftop.

"Da**! he tried to curse against the electronic impulses of the v-chip embedded in his neck. "It's too far for me to jump, Sleize. At least there's a silver lining. There's no way you'd ever make it across."

"Then what can we do?" Sleize was almost blubbering with fear. His nose was running, and Ace grimaced at the distinct smell.

"Don't mess your pants, man. They're minor leaguers. I'll think of something."

Putting action to his words, Ace raced over to examine the wooden planks lying on the roof. Doing a bit of quick mental calculation, he decided only one of them was of sufficient length to be of any help. He snatched it up and scurried back to the ledge where Sleize was standing as though paralyzed, drooling.

"Give me a hand, Sleize! " Ace bellowed, snapping his rival out of his stupor. Together, they pushed the plank out over the ledge, extending it until it bridged the alleyway below and came to rest on the ledge of the next building.

"Go on, Sleize. I'll hold the plank in place while you get across it." Ace pointed at the opposite roof.

"I can't." Tears were rolling down Sleize's dirty face.

"Do it, ****it! This's the bottom of the ninth!"

"But, what if I fall?"

"Then they'll miss your flyball and you'll break your neck. Which'll still be better than what I'll do to you if you don't. Now, slide, Sleize, slide!"

Sleize stood up on the narrow plank, took two tentative steps and fell to his knees. Sobbing softly, he began to crawl across the span. Only once did he dare to look down, and then the pavement seemed to rise up to meet him. He closed his eyes and gripped the plank so tightly his knuckles turned white.

"Hurry up, Sleize." Ace could hear the Ninjas pounding at the fire door behind him, and knew they would be swarming over the rooftop at any second.

Sleize continued his forward progress, moaning sickly as the plank bowed beneath his weight. It was all he could do to force his hands and knees to keep moving, but, at last, he reached the opposite end.

He slid over the edge, watery knees almost buckling beneath him. Ragged breaths wracked his lungs as the adrenaline continued to pump through his body. Looking back across the alleyway, he saw Ace beginning to climb on the ledge, prepared to follow him across.

Suddenly, the fear left Sleize as a new plan of action sprang to mind. He grabbed the plank he had just traversed and shoved it off the ledge.

Thrown off balance as the plank slid from beneath his feet, Ace tottered on the edge of the high rise. His body swayed forward and he could see the plank hurtling downward, his only passage to safety finally being lost in the darkness below. Seconds later, he heard it strike the pavement.

Pushing himself backwards with his legs, Ace fell back onto the rooftop. He scrambled quickly to his feet, his eyes seeking out Sleize across the gaping alleyway.

"What the h**l are you doing?" he demanded.

"Just slidin' into home plate, Ace," came the glib reply.

"What's that supposed to mean?"

"The Ninjas, Ace. I'm the reason they're here in Singapore. It's just a little something I neglected to tell you. You see, I was covering a story in Japan before I came here. You know how it is when you're after a story, Ace. You do whatever it tales. Only problem is, what it took this time involved a cocker spaniel, a Shetland pony and the Siamese twin sister of a Yakuza mob lord. I'm afraid he didn't appreciate my journalistic initiative. So he must have sent the Ninjas after me."

"And now you're gonna let 'em tag me out while you escape free and clear?"

"That pretty well sums it up, yeah."

Ace's face grew flush with anger. "I"ll get you, you sonuva*****. You hear me?"

Sleize was already backing away from the edge of the building, slinking back into the darkness of the night.

The sound of splintering wood interrupted Ace's tirade, causing him to spin around. As he watched, the fire door leading to the roof was shattered and torn from its frame. He inhaled deeply as five Ninjas crept onto the roof. Spying him, they spread out, each grabbing his crotch and spitting to his left.

"Alone with Ninjas," he murmured to himself "What could be worse?"

In reply, thunder boomed from the sky and the driving rain again began to fall. Ace turned his gaze from the black clad assassins and looked up with anger at the swollen clouds.

"It was a rhetorical question, God!" he screamed.

Walter Sleize parted the tall grass before him and was startled to see Robin Leach with a microphone. The announcer, in his famous, loud, clipped English accent, was interviewing Lord Greystoke, King of the Jungle.

"Me Robin," the announcer grinned, thrusting the microphone at the ape-man's head.

"I'm so sorry," said the bored Jungle King. "Does it hurt?"

It had been done to death and Greystoke was only half the man he'd been since Cheeta had run off with Jane, so Sleize let the grass close. Walter rose and moved to a wall of vegetation as he reflected that he envied the rich and famous life-style of the television host, but he liked his name even more.

Sleize hacked at the thick vine in front of him with a machete, clearing a path for himself. His left foot caught in the undergrowth and he toppled forward, hitting the ground with a woosh of escaping breath.

He simply lay there for a moment, sucking in fresh air—fresh, but hot and carrying the smell of decay. He slapped at the back of his neck as yet another insect sank its stinger into his fleshy hide. Sweat dripped from his scalp, scalding his eyes with its saltiness.

Sleize had been staggering through the steaming jungles of eastern Malaysia for the better part of two days, following a vague lead he had picked up in one of the small coastal towns. If his source was right, Sueng Lo was being held in a tiny hamlet nearby.

The reporter pushed himself back to his feet and continued to plunge ahead, flailing about awkwardly with the machete. The ground rose steeply ahead of him, and he had to go on all fours to keep from sliding backwards.

"Hot damn!" The words came out in a hoarse whisper as he topped the rise. From the peak of the hill he looked down at a shallow valley. At the far end of the valley, farmers were working in neatly tended rice paddies.

Directly below him were the dozen small grass huts that made up this isolated hamlet (or "kampong" as the natives would call it). Sleize dropped to his belly to insure that no one would see him. Ripping at his backpack, he withdrew a pair of binoculars and scanned the circle of huts. He stopped at the familiar arches rising above one.

McHut," he whispered, and licked his lips. "And I'm lovin' it."

He could detect little movement in the village. A small boy played on the dusty main trail with his dog. A woman with a basket of dirty laundry balanced atop her head was obviously making her way to the laundromat. And outside one hut stood two swarthy men dressed in tuxedos, arms crossed as they looked from side to side. Sleize felt certain they were there to guard something or someone inside the squalid hut. Whether or not it was Sueng Lo, he had no way of knowing.

He quietly slithered over into the shade cast by a nearby tree. There was nothing he could do now but to wait and watch for some sign that would tell him if his tip had been accurate or not.

Sleize lay beneath the tree for over an hour, the heat and the monotonous hum of insects nearly lulling him to sleep. Then a high pitched scream of pain snapped him alert.

Native women spilled out of their huts at the sound of the screaming, looking about for its source. Moments later, another woman came running into the village. She was carrying a small child in her arms, its cries of pain and fear growing louder and more persistent.

Sleize snatched up his binoculars for a closer look. His stomach rolled slightly as he focused in on the crying child, an infant girl, surely no older than three. She was obviously distressed. Her left arm dangled at an awkward angle, indicating it had been broken.

The women circled around the child, trying in vain to calm its fears. Finally, one of them broke away and trotted over to the hut where the two men were standing guard. Sleize watched intently, wishing he could hear her words. It was obvious that she was arguing with the men, who kept glancing at the hut behind them and trying to chase the women away.

She was not to be deterred, however. One of the men finally shrugged his shoulders in resignation and stepped into the hut. Within seconds, he emerged, dragging yet another young woman by one arm.

Sleize's breath caught in his throat as he saw the girl being dragged. She was the right age, no more than in her early twenties. Her figure was slender and willowy, her face pretty even though it was twisted in a grimace as she resisted the guard.

The man paid her no heed, roughly pulling her toward the cluster of women in the center of the hamlet. The girl continued to struggle against him until she became aware of the child crying in agony. At that, she ran forward even as the guard released his hold on her.

Brushing shiny black hair back away from her face with one hand, the young woman quietly approached the child. Saying something in a low, calm voice, she reached out to take the child from its mother.

At the first touch of the woman's hands, the infant grew silent, sniffing back a last few tears. Sueng Lo (for Sleize was now convinced this was indeed who she was) smiled and cooed meaningless words of comfort to the small child.

She then reached out and gently gripped the little girl's broken arm. She slowly raised the snapped limb, pulling it up until it was straight. Holding it in that position, Sueng Lo closed her eyes as though praying. When she opened her eyes, she released the child's arm.

The little girl giggled and began to bend the arm normally. She reached up and ran her chubby fingers over Sueng Lo's smiling lips. The miracle worker then handed the girl back to her furious mother.

Words were shared. Sueng Lo was obviously confused. Suddenly, to Sleize's horror, the mother broke the little girl's left arm again with a sickening snap. She bent down before the screaming girl and dangled a finger back and forth in front of the girl's genitals.

It struck Sleize like an axe. The woman had broken the little girl's arm because she was left-handed, a sure sign of devils. She'd brought the child to Sueng Lo for an entirely different cure.

She wanted the girl to be a boy.

At that moment, Sleize realized he wanted nothing more in the world to become the King of Sueng. He'd fallen deeply in love with the faith healer.

The old woman fell to her knees before Sueng Lo, clutching her child to her and begging the miracle worker. The other women began to chatter excitedly, reaching out to touch Sueng Lo's simple cotton dress.

But then the guard broke through the circle of women. His fingers encircled

Sueng Lo's right wrist in a grip of iron and pulled her away from her admirers. The women cried out in protest, but the man paid them no heed. He returned to the hut where his partner still stood, and shoved Sueng Lo back inside.

The other women pressed in around the guards, yelling invectives at them. In response, one of the men pulled a long, wicked looking knife from his belt and waved it. The women pulled away, finally breaking up and returning to their own huts.

Sleize grinned coldly as he lowered his binoculars. He had found what he was looking for. All that remained was to find some way of rescuing her from her captors. He had no doubt he could do just that.

The sun had been down for three hours when Sleize made his move. The last fire had been extinguished in the hamlet. The McHut sign was dark.

Crawling on hands and knees, Sleize descended from the hills where he had been hiding and watching. Unseen creatures could be heard moving about in the jungle but he felt no fear, so caught up was he in expectation of snatching Sueng Lo and getting his story.

He took his time, weaving his way through the thick vegetation until he reached the back of the hut where Sueng Lo was being held captive. He left the shelter of the jungle and made his way to the grass structure.

The little, swinging doggie door cut in the hut was too small for Sleize to use for entry, so he gingerly pushed his machete blade through the woven wall of the hut, then began cutting a larger opening. He didn't rush the work, stopping periodically to listen for any sign that he had been detected.

At last, he succeeded in hacking out an opening wide enough to enable him to slip inside the hut. When his eyes adjusted to its deeper darkness, he could make out the shape of the young woman sleeping in one corner.

Scurrying to her side, Sleize reached out and clamped one hand over her mouth. Sueng Lo instantly awoke, her instinctive cries stifled by the reporter. He leaned down close. She wore nothing but panties and an Oral Roberts teeshirt that read: Expect a Miracle.

"Shhh! I'm an American! I've come to rescue you. I'm, uh, William Shatner!"

So softly did he speak that he wasnt sure she could hear him until her body relaxed beneath him. It was a certain sign that she'd either accepted him or fainted from the smell of his hand. Tentatively, he removed his hand from her mouth. She made no sound, but merely smiled up at him.

"Would you look at this!" he gasped, looking at his hand. "You cured my hangnail!!"

Holding her hand, Sleize guided the young woman to the back of the hut. He pulled aside the cut section of the wall and motioned for her to exit. Sueng Lo didn't hesitate. Sleize smiled in self satisfaction and followed her out.

"Hey!" he shouted as two sets of muscular hands grabbed his arms and pulled him to his feet. Sleize looked back and. forth frantically at the pair of tuxedoed, native guards who had seized him. He saw no signs of humanity or mercy in their grim faces.

His head snapped forward as he heard Sueng Lo's voice calling out in protest. A third guard came stepping out of the jungle. His arms were wrapped around the struggling Sueng Lo's waist, half carrying and half dragging her back to the hut.

The three natives carried Sleize and Sueng Lo back into the village proper, where they were joined by the two men who had been guarding the girl earlier in the day. The men spoke among themselves in a dialect Sleize couldn't understand. Not that he needed to; he knew full well what his punishment would be for attempting to free the girl.

Suddenly, a glaring light cut through the night, splashing full in the eyes of Sleize, Sueng Lo and the natives. They were all momentarily blinded, helpless as they heard a guttural roar issued from the jungle.

Sleize squinted his eyes, and by doing so could just make out a vague form that came crashing out of the primeval forest. It was proceeded by the ray of light and accompanied by the ever more deafening roar.

"Sonuvabitch!" Sleize yelled as he was at last able to make out the details of the apparition. "It's…"

It was none other than Ace Montana, sitting astride a Harley Davidson motorcycle. Ace gunned the cycle, which lept forward like a raging beast. The machine plowed right into the midst of the stunned natives, sending them flying. Sleize also was thrown to the ground.

"Hop on, baby," Ace yelled above the growl of the cycle. "We're blowin' this joint!"

As Sleize watched, Sueng Lo obediently swung one leg over the seat of the Harley. Her arms circled Ace's waist, gripping tightly.

"Hi-Yo, Silver!" Montana whooped. Only then did Sleize notice that the back of Sueng Lo's teeshirt read: elcariM a tccpxE.

Ace cranked the throttle. Dirt and pebbles flew from beneath the spinning rear wheel of the cycle as it screeched forward. The Harley flashed down the center of the village and then disappeared into the jungle.

"Wait for me!" Sleize screeched, scrambling to his feet. He started to run after the fast departing cycle, only to pitch forward as a pair of arms wrapped around his ankles.

Sleize rolled onto his back to see a native guard sitting astride him, long knife raised in a threatening posture.

"Oh, God!" Sleize gasped, struggling to keep himself from dirtying his pants. He knew he faced certain death. Ace would indeed scoop him. But at least there was one silver lining to this angry cloud.

He realized that Sueng Lo had cured his BO as well.

Ace swerved, barely missing a leopard hidden by the dark. He laughed heartily as he revved up the engine of the Harley. It was a challenge, keeping the cycle on the narrow jungle path at night, but he welcomed it. When Sueng Lo tightened her grip around his waist, however, he was reminded that he had another life in his hands, so he began to slow to a more sensible speed for the terrain.

Ace swerved to the left, missing an orangutan by a hair.

It was well that he slowed, for the path grew fainter and more winding. It took all of Ace's skill to follow it. The thick foliage overhead blocked what little light the stars provided, and even the cycle's strong headlight could not cut far through the gloom.

He swerved, missing Robin Leach, the broadcaster's hands over his ears, Tarzan, his hands over his mouth, and Leach's cameraman, his hands over his camera lens, all squatting by the side of the trail.

Ace never saw the jagged rock that ripped through his front tire. He simply heard the sickening pop of escaping air a split second before losing control of the skidding cycle.

He fought to keep the motorcycle upright, to no avail. The Harley fell to one side, sliding off the trail and into the underbrush. Ace lay stunned for a moment, but quickly forgot about his own welfare.

"Sueng Lo!" he called.

"Sweet chariot!" Tarzan commented , examining the fallen motorcycle.

An answering groan came from Ace's right, and he crawled toward the sound. He found the young woman lying on her back in the middle of the jungle trail. She was barely moving when he reached her side.

"Are you all right, sweetheart?"

She opened her eyes slowly. "I think so," she said in a soft voice as she attempted to rise. The effort was too much, and she fell back.

"Just take it easy," Ace ordered. He proceeded to run his expert fingers over her t-shirt, checking for any sign of broken limbs or internal injuries. He breathed a sigh of relief. He ignored the silly smile suddenly on Oral Roberts' face.

"Okay, babe. Just lean on me and we'll get you up on your feet."

He took note of how light his slender companion was as he lifted her upright.

Hanging onto his arm for support, Sueng Lo took a few tentative steps, then let go as she regained her own equilibrium.

Knowing that she was all right, Ace moved to check out the damage done to his motorcycle. Even in the darkness, he immediately saw that it was a lost cause. The front end was wrapped around the trunk of a tree.

"Can you fix it?" Sueng Lo asked.

"No way. I guess you'd have to say it's gone to Hog Heaven."

"What do we do, now that your vehicle is in Pig Paradise?"

Ace studied the girl's face to see if she was now making a joke, but he could read nothing in her expression. For a second, he wondered if she might be related to Pedro.

"There's only one thing to do, babe," he said. "Unless you got a chariot, we walk."

Ace took Sueng Lo's hand and led the way down the jungle path. It would be rough going, he knew, but he wanted to put as much distance between them and the village of her captors as possible. They walked in silence for some time, until the woman finally spoke.

"Who are you?" she asked. "Are you Evil Knieval?"

"The name's Ace Montana."

"The American reporter?" There seemed to be just a touch of awe in her voice. "You write Global Star?"

"All the important stories. You've heard of me?"

"Of course! I learned all about America from reading your wonderful newspaper. Tell me--does Elvis Presley really work at a Burger Barn in Skokie?"

"Nah. Last I heard, he's an ice cream vendor in Brooklyn, New York. The poor slob; ever since he died, he hasn't been able to hold down a steady job. Keeps failing his blood test. Doesn't have any."

"And Liz Taylor is really going to marry a plumber and raise chickens? Or was it marry a chicken and raise plumbers?"

"That was last week's news, babe. Now she's decided to become a Buddhist monk and sell Amway."

"Oooh. It must be wonderful to know so many famous people."

"Don't be fooled. They take their pants off one leg at a time, just like you. Only if they're women and with me, more often. And some thave three pants legs."

So intent was Sueng Lo on listening to Ace that she didn't notice he had stopped moving. She walked into his back and staggered back a step from the impact.

"What's wrong, Ace Montana?"

"Nothing. I hope. Look."

Sueng Lo peered into the darkness. At first she saw nothing but jungle. Then she made out a lighter colored object to one side of the trail. She quickly realized that it was a solitary grass hut. It appeared to be in a state of great disrepair.

"Stay here, babe," Ace whispered. "I'm gonna go check out the joint. Unless it's made of gingerbread and gumdrops, we've got reservations for tonight at Hotel Montana."

Sueng Lo started to protest, but before the words could come, Ace had left her. Dressed in dark clothing as he was, he blended in with the night and eluded her sight. When the seconds grew into minutes, and he did not reappear, Sueng Lo grew anxious. Just as she was about to set out after him, she saw the reporter leaving the hut and returning to her side.

"It's empty, all right," Ace said. "Has been for quite a while. Looks like it'd be a good place for us to flop for the night. It should even be safe to light a fire."

True to his word, Ace soon had a small blaze going in the middle of the hut's dirt floor. Leaving Sueng Lo again, he returned with armloads of leaves to make bedding. Sueng Lo smiled at him as he then came to sit beside her.

"Thank you," she said, with obvious sincerity. "You've been wonderful. But why did you leave the dirty man?"

"Sleize? To introduce your kidnappers to his rod and his staph."

His answer was met with the furrowed brow of confusion. "May I ask you another question, Ace Montana?"

"You just did, honey, and the answer is sure."

"I don't mean to look the gifted zebra in the teeth, but... why did you rescue me?"

Ace tossed another stick on the fire. "Well, I could lie to you and say I just have a weakness for beautiful women...and Sueng dancing. " Ace paused as Sueng Lo's head dropped, her cheeks blushing hotly. "Hasn't anybody every told you that you're beautiful?"

"No. Never."

"Jeez. The boys in your neighborhood must be blind."

"No. Most village boys do stop just before they need an optometrist." Her voice trailed off. "They did not notice me."

"Not until you started healing people," Ace finished for her.

"You know about that?"

"Of course I do. Did you forget? I'm the guy who discovered Adolf Hitler as a chorus girl in the Follies Bergere."

"So that's why you save me." There was deep disappointment in Sueng Lo's voice.

"No." Ace reached out and cupped the delicate girl's chin in his hand, turning her face so she had to look him in the eyes.

"It's the reason I came looking for you, sure. But when I saw you being rousted by those goons back in the village, I'd have rescued you no matter what."

Sueng Lo stared at him intently. "Yes, I think that's true, Ace.

"Hey, babe, there's a lotta things I'd do to get this or any story, but lying to you ain't one of them."

She smiled and took his hand, gripping it tightly. "What happens now? Can we get away from them?"

"Come here." Ace pulled Sueng Lo close and wrapped comforting arms around her. "There aren't any guarantees in this world, little lady. But, Sueng Lo, I'm comin 'for to carry you home. Safe."

Sueng Lo nuzzled close against him, and rolled her eyes in unbelief at the joke she'd heard a thousand times. As she stared into the flickering flames of the fire, she realized that, even though she was in the middle of a hostile jungle, she had never felt more safe in her life.

Ace realized she'd just cured his hemorrhoids.

The rising sun cast its baleful light through the open doorway of the dilapidated hut, striking Ace full in the face. He blinked his eyes several times before coming fully awake.

He found himself looking at the dirtiest pair of feet he had ever seen. "Go' mornin', Sleize," he said, half awake.

Raising his eyes, he saw that the feet belonged to one of the Hantu who had held Sueng Lo captive, barefooted but still in a tuxedo. Nor was he alone; six other scowling natives stood around him.

Ace tried to leap to his feet, but the Hantu swarmed over him like locusts. Their combined weight dragged him down, pinned him to the floor.

"Run, Sueng Lo!" he yelled. "Run!"

The woman, awakened by the sounds of the struggle, ignored his command. Instead, she threw herself into the fray, kicking and clawing at the natives. With a vicious backhand slap, one of them laid her low.

"You filthy ba*&*d!" Ace growled, then grunted as a dirty foot slammed against the side of his head. His vision blurred.

The natives pulled Ace and Sueng Lo to their feet and dragged them out of the hut. More Hantu were waiting outside, along with Walter Sleize. He looked worn and disheveled, with his arms tied behind his back. Ace and the woman were likewise bound and placed on the path that would take them back to the village.

"I'm afraid we're done for, Ace," Sleize whined.

"Nah. I'll get us outta this, you filthy piece of slime." Ace smiled and winked reassuringly at Sueng Lo. Her look told him that she believed him.

He just hoped this turned out to be the first and last lie he ever told her.

"Yeah," sneered Sleize, wiping his nose on his sleeve, "Like you got us outta that Medusa thing 'untouched'."

"Hey! Your child support can't be all that much, pork chop. I mean, it's not like they need haircuts."

"God, I hate bugs!"

Ace shook his head in a vain attempt to dispel the cloud of gnats that were circling about him. They scattered momentarily, then swarmed around him again. At least they weren't genetically altered Disney gnats. He hated singing gnats more than singing plates.

To Ace's surprise, the natives had not returned their captives to the village from which they had escaped. Instead, they set them on a path that led deeper into the jungle. As the sun rose higher in the sky, the heat and humidity rose with it, growing increasingly oppressive.

"I got more sweat in my shorts than you or a Times Square hooker on Saturday night," Ace grumbled.

"I can't believe you," Sleize said from behind him. "These aborigines are probably going to kill us, and all you can worry about is insects and jock itch!"

"Yeah, well, you know what they say, sleeze; the coward dies a thousand deaths, the brave man only one. I figure you must be up to what—number 204 by now?"

"Not funny, Montana."

"What are you talking about, chum bucket? My bodyguard here thinks I'm a laugh riot. Don't you, chuckles?"

Ace turned to the native who was walking beside him and smiled. The Hantu scowled and slapped the reporter in the back of the head.

"Name not Chuckles," he spat. "Name Guffaw."

"Everybody's a critic," Ace growled, staring balefully at Guffaw. "Tell me, Tarzan, does your father know about your mother's inordinate fondness for your sister?"

Guffaw raised his hand to deliver another blow. "Yes, and name is Guffaw!" Before he could begin his swing Ace spat full in his face. Enraged, Guffaw lunged for his captive, grabbing him by the throat as he wrestled him to the ground.

Other Hantu rushed forward, prying their comrade's fingers away from Ace's neck and dragging him to his feet. The leader of the band, a tall man with a scar running across the bridge of his nose, spoke harshly to his underlings, ordering him to the rear of the column. The scarred man then bent to help Ace to his feet.

"Ah, a helping Hantu. I think Bwana love me," Ace sneered. "What's your name, Big Guy."

"Big Guy,"

"Good. Now I know what name to put on your tombstone."

Big Guy smiled coldly. "Idiot," he snarled.

"Putz," Ace rejoined, adding a one fingered gesture that couldn't be edited by the v-chip in his neck.

"Fool." The Hantu flipped his fingers from beneath his chin.

"Dip s***k" Ace stopped the upward thrust of his arm with a hand at its crook.

"Monkey turd!" Guffaw kicked a cloud of dirt over Ace's shoes.

"Limp stick!!" Ace stuck a thumb in each ear and wiggled his fingers,

"Pond scum!!!" Hands on his hips, Guffaw launched another dust cloud.

"Spitball!!!" Ace stuck his tongue out and thumbed his nose.

"That's it!!! Yer outta here! Yer outta here! That's it! Yer outta the game!!!!"

"Hey, you're pretty good. I'll be sure to tell your sister that the next time I **** her."

The native looked at Ace, puzzled.

"The next time I *c*** her," said Ace, frustrated.

The native cocked his left eyebrow.

"Aw, s*&*w it," grumbled Ace.

Guffaw inhaled sharply. "I should remove your excuse for manhood for Big Guy, Deuce Montana."

"All yours, dummy," he said, waving an invitation to take Sleize. "The name's Ace."

The native leader gritted his teeth as he mumbled expletives in his own tongue. He then turned and walked away, shouting instructions at his followers. With much pushing and shoving, the captives were set back to their marching.

"You crazy son of a bitch," Sleize gasped, thankful once again that the word bitch was more than just an expletive. "What is your problem?"

"I got no problem, sleeze, I just don't take bulls*** off anybody."

"How did you know he wouldn't kill you on the spot?" Ace watched a drop of sweat leave a dirty trail down Sleize's face.

"Because I'm immaculate. I don't have a spot on me."

Sleize snapped his mouth shut before he could get in any deeper. He wasn't able to maintain his silence for long, however. "I've gotta know, Ace. How the hell did you ever get away from those Ninja ball players?"

"You mean the ones you left me to face alone while you ran off like the scumbag you are, sleeze? Those Ninja ball players?"

"Look, Ace, I'm sorry about that. Really. But you know how it is."

"No, I don't. But, then, I've never had to live without a spine.

"Fine. I'm a coward. I admit it. You happy? I'd still like to know how you got away."

"Why should I tell you? You, the great investigative reporter? You, who thought the Pulitzer Prize was an award for roosters?"

"Don't egg me on, Ace. We're probably gonna be dead in a few hours anyway. What harm can it do?"

"I need a cigarette," was all Ace sighed in reply, but with his arms securely tied behind him, he knew such solace as a Camel would bring was denied him. He looked back over his shoulder at Sleize, saw the most pitiful, hang-dog expression on the man's face, and shivered.

"All right, all right. First, these Hantu are your 'ninja ball players'. Secondly, I just bribed the jerks."

"You bribed Ninjas?"

"You didn't expect me to fight them, did you? Man, there were five of them. I'd of killed them all. They were outnumbered."

"I know. I just can't believe that mere money would be enough to buy off a Ninja." The scepticism in Sleize's voice was so heavy it fairly dripped.

"Listen to me, Sleize. They weren't Japanese Ninjas! And I had something a lot more valuable than money."

"Like what? A nude photo of Judge Judy?" Sleize asked, drooling.

"Like a Babe Ruth and a Stan Musial baseball card."

"No! I'm starvin' and you're hoardin' a candy bar!?"

"Shut up. I always carry a pair in my coat pocket. Of course, that's all I carry, so we had two cards and five pajama boys to split 'em. While they were busy hacking each other to bloody pieces to see who got the baseball cards. I just took a leisurely stroll off the roof to safety. Of course, the cards are fakes. Ninjas are stupid that way. Willing to kill each other over a couple of baseball cards."

"And a candy bar," corrected Sleize.

———⊶⊷———

In the late afternoon, the band reached the banks of the narrow River Bic, named after the notorious Hantu jail on its banks north of them, the Bic Pen. They paused to rest on its shore.

It was the first opportunity Ace had to get close to Sueng Lo, and they sank down on the ground next to an historical marker.

It was red. Someone had left the cap off. It was dry.

"You all right, sweetheart?" Ace asked solicitously, tossing the marker aside.

Sueng Lo tried to smile, then had to bite her lips to hold back the tears that began to well up in her almond eyes. "I'm scared, Ace."

"I know, babe." Ace silently cursed the ropes that prevented him from putting his arms around the woman. "But I think everything's gonna be okay. These slugs are probably just looking to make some money by putting the snatch on you. I'll talk to the Big Kahuna again and let him know my paper will pay whatever he wants for your release. You'll be back home before you know it."

"His name is Big Guy," corrected Sueng. "Do you really think so?"

"You think I'm gonna let anything happen to you before I get my story? Huh?"

Sueng Lo returned Ace's smile, then leaned over to rest her head on his shoulder. He kissed her on the forehead even as his brain began to race, searching for a way out of their predicament. He lost the race.

Five minutes later, the natives roughly jerked them to their feet, and Ace again found himself separated from Sueng Lo. Their captors continued to march them at a relentless pace deeper into the jungle.

When the sun at last sank below the horizon, Ace expected the column would stop, but such was not the case. Crude torches were lit and the march continued. An occasional break in the foliage overhead revealed a beautiful full moon shining on a warning sign which read: DEER CROSSING.

As they approached, Bambi crossed the clearing

The strain of the long, forced march was beginning to show on all the captives. Ace could hear Sleize behind him, puffing and panting like an aged steam engine. The column was forced to stop at one point when Sueng Lo fell to the ground and was unable to rise. Two of the Hantu held her up by the arms and carried her as they continued to march toward their destination. Ace's instinct was to throw a knockout punch, but he knew he'd lose at Hantu Hand combat.

The first indication Ace had that they were about to reach their final goal was a muffled, indistinct sound that began to intrude on his consciousness. At first, he thought it was merely his own pulse, pounding in his temples, but then he recognized it as the persistent beating of drums. Another warning sign was posted in their path. It read: PANTHER CROSSING.

They paused as a panther slunk into view, then disappeared in the jungle.

The music grew louder as they marched, and their captors grew visibly more excited. They pushed their exhausted prisoners to move even faster. Minutes later, they broke out of the jungle and into a large clearing.

Ace was awestruck by the eerie tableau that spread out before his eyes. The light of the onlooking full moon cast a pale blue glow over the clearing, Even more natives were gathered here. All were dressed in white cotton baseball uniforms with stripes, and caps, clustered around three drummers who continued to pound out their haunting melody. Sputtering torches added their light to that moon, giving all an other worldly look.

On the opposite side of the clearing, a small, solitary mountain peak jutted up like a pustulant blemish on the face of the earth, strangely out of place against the jungle surroundings. In its side could be seen a cave. By the cave, a warning sign read: NUN CROSSING.

Three sisters smiled and genuflected.

Several of the natives who had just entered the clearing now rushed to join their compatriots, donning identical robes. Those who remained behind to guard the prisoners pulled out machetes and cut the ropes that bound their arms.

Sueng Lo threw herself into the comfort of Ace's encircling left arm. He squeezed her reassuringly, then shifted her slightly so he could reach into his jacket and retrieve a cigarette. He sighed with pleasure as he puffed on it and thought about how he'd make a great Hantu.

Ambidexterious.

"What is all this?" Sleize asked. "Some kind of cult ceremony?"

"They're a poor but proud people," Ace replied. "They live Hantu mouth."

"That's crazy. I thought all the people of Malaysia were Moslems. This looks more like something out of an old King Kong movie!"

"Some of the people of this country still follow the old ways," Sueng Lo explained. "They worship the Hantu."

"What?" Sleize looked puzzled. "There were times when I couldn't find a woman..."

"Like your entire life," interrupted Ace.

"...that I worshipped th..."

"Spirits?!" interrupted Montana. "Ghosts. Spooks. Casper the dead baby." He exhaled a small cloud of cigarette smoke. "Right now, the only spirits I'd like to see are ones named Johnny Walker and Jim Beam."

"This is serious, Montana," Sleize snapped. "What are they up to, and why do they want us? Are they going to… eat me?!?"

"They don't eat pork. It's Sueng Lo they want, Sleize. You and me are just along as a bonus. Why they want her, I haven't a clue."

"We've got to get out of here."

"Right. And how are we gonna do that?"

"You create a diversion and I'll run away."

"That's one hell of a good plan you got there, ass***e." Ace flicked his cigarette away, watching as its glowing butt disappeared into the darkness. He thought of the triangular scar that still functioned imperfectly since some English words act both as profanity and socially accepted descriptions.

"Well, what do you suggest we do?" Sleize's voice rose into a squeal.

"Don't *h** your pants. All we can do for now is wait and watch. Can you handle that, babe?" Ace looked down at Sueng Lo, pulling her even tighter against him.

"I think so," she said softly, "As long as you're here with me."

An ear-splitting scream erupted from the native dancers, and they raced toward the three captives. The dancers circled them several times in movements similar to Lo's own when she was in a healing trance. Then they reached out to grab them. With the prisoners in tow, they began to move across the jungle clearing, heading for the small mountain peak.

"They're dragging us into that cave!" Sleize shrieked.

"Prepare yourself for possible Hantu Hand combat," Ace said coldly.

Torch bearers pushed the entourage into the yawning cavern, lighting additional sconces set in the stone walls as they went. The sconces were carved in the Hantu's most sacred icon, a hand with the thumb and index finger forming a circle. They were followed by the Sueng dancers and three drummers who continued to pound out the maddening rhythm of their sacred music, I Wanna Hold Your Hantu. The three captives tried to hold back at the mouth of the cave, but were prodded forward by machete blades poking against their backs.

"They're going to kill us," Sleize moaned. "I just know it. They're going to kill us."

"That's the way," Ace replied calmly. "Just keep thinking those happy thoughts."

"What's wrong with you!" Sleize barked. "Are you just too stupid to be afraid?"

"Hey. I just happen to think there are some things worse than death."

"Yeah? Like what?"

"You. Or no sex," barked Ace. "But that's redundant. Or worse yet, sex with you."

"This is all my fault," Sueng Lo said solemnly "If not for me, you wouldn't be here."

"I don't want to hear that kind of crap, babe," Ace said. "You didn't bring us here—the story did. And any reporter worth his salt is more than happy to die for the story."

Sleize simply gurgled and belched.

"Right," Ace finished for him. "Besides, it ain't over till the fat lady Sueng's."

His rival reporter spun to one side and threw up, spewing vomit down the tuxedo leg of one of their captors. The native cried out in disgust and slapped Sleize.

"Nice move, slick," Ace commented. "Next time you feel like dropping your cookies, let me know. I might be able to use the distraction to get Sueng Lo outta here."

The stone floor of the cave began to slope at a mild angle into a tunnel that lead down deeper into the bowels of the earth. The drummers began to bang more incessantly as they descended, and now the other Hantu started to chant in unison, their sing-song voices echoing hollowly off the tunnel walls. They repeated the same words over and over, each time more loudly, hugging themselves or gesturing wildly.

"What are they chanting?" Sleize asked his fellow prisoners. "It sounds familiar somehow. And those gestures..."

"Maybe it does to you, Sleize," Ace replied, "but it sure ain't on my Hit Parade. Sounds like they're saying 'okay Cann Sea'.

"I've got it!" Sleize grew more animated. "Can't you hear it? They're rapping the Star Spangled Banner!"

"Give me a **c*i*' break. Even Americans don't sing the Star Spangled Banner."

"No, really. I'm sure that's what they're rapping. We've got to let them know that we're Americans. Maybe then they'll let us go. Do you have an American Express Card? What?!? You left home without it!?"

Raising his voice, Sleize began to say, Oh, Say Can You See repeatedly. Scowling at the reporter, one of the Hantu swung his machete sharply. The flat of the blade struck Sleize full in the mouth, causing him to double over in pain. Blood dripped from his split lips, and he groaned incoherently.

"Not bad," Ace said. "It's got a good beat and it's easy to dance to. I'd give you an 85."

"Fug oo, Ace," Sleize managed to gurgle from between clenched fingers.

"No, thanks. I think I've already been royally 'fugged', just by being here with you."

They marched on in silence then, continuing their gradual descent. A short time later, the ground began to level off noticeably. The torch bearers leading the group could be seen passing under a low arch in the tunnel. On the other side of the arch, the tunnel opened into a large, vaulted chamber, its granite walls rising up nearly four stories in height.

The torch bearers ran around the outer walls of the chamber, lighting fresh sconces. As these flared up, the entirety of the chamber was illuminated. In the center of the cavern, Ace could see what he at first took to be a thick, natural stone stalagmite.

He quickly realized it was far more than this, however, when his captives proceeded to bow down reverently before it. Looking closer at the object as the flickering lights allowed, Ace then recognized it as being a stature.

The roughly carved stone image was of an incredibly fat woman wearing a baseball uniform and cap. One hand clutched the crotch of the striped uniform. The features of the statue's face were not clearly defined, but its mouth was opened wide, as though in song.

With that, it all fell into place for Ace, and for the first time he felt genuine fear. The statue of the fat woman. The song the natives continued to now chant. Ace knew then that there could be only one explanation: they had fallen into the dirty hands of a cult of Roseanne Barr worshippers.

"It happened back in the late '80s, I was told," Ace explained to Sleize and Sueng Lo. "I thought it was a rumor. A troupe of celebrities came to entertain for the Peace Corp somewhere. A small band of natives were watching the show from the jungle.

"When good old Roseanne came on stage dressed in a baseball uniform and started to belt out the Star Spangled Banner, they were fascinated. When she clutched her crotch and spat, they nearly dirtied their loin cloths. They'd never seen or heard anything like it before, so, naturally, they assumed she was a divine spirit.

"They made her the center of a new religion. No one knows much about it, except that its followers are real fanatics."

"But, what does any of that have to do with me?" Sueng Lo asked. "I have nothing to do with Roseanne. I don't even know who Roseanne is."

"Beats me, babe. We'll just have to wait and see."

The captives then turned their attention back to the ritual that was continuing around the statue of the actress. The drums seemed to grow louder still as the natives danced to a Sueng band around the idol, alternately clutching their crotches and spitting.

A new Sueng dancer carrying two roses came out of the shadows and joined them. It was their leader, Guffaw. He was dressed in the finest uniform of all. He bit the flower off of one stem and, chewing it, presented the other rose to Sueng.

It was a second Hantu rose.

Guffaw clutched his crotch, turned his head to the left, and spat. "Play Ball!!" he yelled, maniacally.

At first, Ace thought the skull of a monkey was perched atop his head like a small crown, its empty eye sockets glowing with reflected torch light. But on closer scrutiny, Ace realized it was a man's shrunken skull. Tom Arnold's shrunken skull.

"I always heard she left poor Tom a shell of a man," Ace muttered.

Guffaw whirled like a dervish in front of the pitted stone statue, his voice rising above all others as he joined in the sacred chant.

As Ace watched the ceremony, his eyes came to rest on an object which had escaped his notice earlier. There was a second stone object in front of the statue of Roseanne. It was little more than a flat, oblong trough standing perhaps four feet high.

Roseanne memorabilia. Very impressive, Ace thought. At first, he also thought the trough to be made of iron, for its surface appeared to be blotched with rust stains. But on closer examination, the grim truth came home to him. The splatters were actually dried blood. Ace looked anxiously at Sueng Lo, but kept his awful suspicions to himself.

The native drummers pounded faster and faster on their instruments and the Sueng dancers quickened their pace to keep time. Hot Dog Hantu's hawked their ballpark franks. Sweat glistened on their dusky skin, often flying off in a fine spray as they whirled about.

One Hantu, caught up in the religious frenzy, began to literally froth at the mouth. He pitched to the ground, writhing like a worm, as he shouted words that made no sense.

"Batta batta batta!! Batta batta batta," he screamed. "Sueng!"

"Is that fu****' disgusting or what?" Ace snorted. "They're selling the franks for five bucks each!"

"Maybe they'll all freak out like that," Sleize offered, "and then we can slip out of here, Ace."

Suddenly, the dancers all yelled out in unison. Even as they did, the drumming stopped. The sudden silence that descended on the cavern was disquieting, and the three captives shifted about nervously.

When the music stopped, the dancers had all fallen to their knees (except, naturally, the poor fellow who was still flat on his back, jerking convulsively). Guffaw was the first to rise back to his feet, followed by the others. In his left hand was a baseball bat.

Turning his back on the sacred statue, Guffaw started walking slowly toward the captives. Ace instinctively moved to place himself between the natives and Sueng Lo. True to form, Sleize in turn took a step back so that he could cower behind the woman. Guffaw slapped the bat into the palm of his right hand.

As the Hantu drew within a few yards of them, Ace stepped forward, one hand held up. "That's far enough, Guppy. Now, how about telling us what's going on here, huh?"

"Name Guffaw!" Guffaw drew himself up to his full height, clearly affronted by being addressed so cavalierly (since he'd served in the Army, not the Cavalry).

He sneered and tossed two pasteboard cards at Ace's feet. Babe Ruth and Stan Musial.

"I think you know, Ace Nevada," he said in stentorian tones. "We are here to proffer blood sacrifice."

"In this day and age? That's un-****in'-believable, man. Does your mother know what you do? And, the name's Ace Montana."

Guffaw was taken aback by this. "Of course she does. Does your mother know what you do, Montana Bob?"

"Hey--leave my mother outta this. The only blood that goes into my work is my own. Now, let's cut the carp here. Bottom line... whose blood are we talking about?"

"Why, the woman's, of course."

Ace heard Sueng Lo gasp, felt her step up closer behind him. Likewise, he heard Sleize sighing with relief. "Yeah. I had a feeling you'd say that, But it won't work. Sueng Lo, here, just ain't that type of girl."

"What type is she, Colorado Cody?"

"Type A. And the name's Ace!"

Guffaw raised the bat and took a step towards the reporter.

"Very well, Jack Utah. If you will listen, I will tell you. Once,

we were children, playing children's games. Pin the tail on the gorilla. Spin the collarbone. Slit the throat of the white lackey Presbyterian missionary. We were ignorant savages.

"Now, we celebrate the most sacred ritual of our religion," Guffaw chortled. "Once each year, on this holiest of nights, we must sacrifice a virgin to our goddess, Roseanne.

"Even in our isolated village, we have heard of the miracle worker who lived on the island. We, just like everyone else, have our rumor mongers... or did until they went to work for CNN. She has obviously been touched by heaven also, and will therefore make the perfect sacrifice, Cleveland Jones. She will heal our spiritual wounds."

Guffaw would have continued, but he was interrupted by the sound of Ace chuckling. The native's face twisted into a scowl. He spat a stream of tobacco juice to his left side.

"Why you laughing, Peadmont Ohio?"

Ace felt so good, he chose not to answer immediately. Instead, he took the time to reach into the pocket of his jacket and pull out a Camel. With a snapping flourish of his right arm, he flipped open the lid of his Zippo and lit the cigarette. In unison, the Hantu drew

back and gasped.

It was obvious they were afraid of second Hantu smoke.

Inhaling deeply, he stepped closer to Guffaw and then exhaled. The Hantu coughed as the smoke entered his eyes and lungs. He wiped away the tears that rose in his eyes.

"Like they say," smiled Ace, "where there's smoke, there's a sire. I got a news bulletin for you, chief. There ain't gonna be no sacrifice. "

"Is this a sleight of Hantu?" Guffaw sneered. "You cannot stop us!"

"I already have."

"You talking crazy, Wes Virginia."

"Crazy like a fox, man. Or, in this case," Ace grinned rakishly, obviously proud of himself, "like a stud."

"This is foolish." Guffaw turned to his followers and, in their own tongue, ordered them to take the woman.

"Hold it right there!" The commanding sound of Ace's voice brought the natives to a startled halt. Wearing a cocky grin on his face, Ace put a friendly arm around Guffaw's shoulder and leaned close to him.

"You know, Chuckles, I fell like an idiot trying to carry on a conversation with a guy who wears a tuxedo and a monkey on his head."

Guffaw grew indignant and tried to pull away, but Ace held him close. "Come on, man. You've lived Hantu mouth so long that you've forgotten how it is. One Hantu washes the other. You help me, I help–"

"Let me go, Washington Smith," Guffaw hissed through clenched teeth.

"Let's talk, Man-to-Hantu. You gotta have a virgin to sacrifice, am I right? Well, I don't know how to tell you this but, uh," Ace pulled even closer to Guffaw, "as of last night, thanks to Your's Truly, the little lady here is no longer a member of the virgin species, if you get my meaning."

A collective gasp rose from the natives. Guffaw pulled away from Ace, his face contorted with surprise and fear.

"No. This can't be! Is this true, woman?" Guffaw directed his question straight to Sueng Lo. When a crimson blush rapidly spread over her face and she dropped her head to stare down at her feet, he knew it was indeed true.

"How could you do this thing?" he asked Ace.

"You don't know how? Guppy!"

"No. I mean--of course I know how! I mean… this is horrible, Selma Alabama."

"Shows how much you know, Laugh Riot. It was terrific."

"You don't understand. This is the only night on which the sacrifice may be made! Without it, our crops will fail, our women will remain fertile, and we'll have to abandon Sueng dancing and start doing The Monkey again.

"We have no hope," Guffaw continued. "We might as well kill ourselves now."

"Whoa. No need for Hantu hand combat. I might be able to help."

"You would do this for us, Little Rock Arkansas?"

"Why not? You need a virgin, right? Well, Sueng Lo is no longer a virgin—repeatedly, I might add. And, of course, I haven't been a virgin since my kindergarten teacher first laid eyes on me. So, who does that leave?"

Every head swiveled at the same time. While this discussion had been going on, Walter Sleize had been slowly edging his way back toward the exit of the cavern. He now froze in his tracks, a sickly grin chiseled on his face.

"How 'bout you, sleeze?" Ace asked. 'You wouldn't happen to be a virgin by any chance, would you?"

"No!" Sleize looked indignant. "He's lying!!"

Ace took a drag on his cigarette. "You don't lie any better than you write, slick. There's your sacrifice, chief"

Sleize shrieked and ran for his life. The Hantu swarmed up the tunnel after him, easily catching him before he had covered fifty yards. Half a dozen pairs of hands lifted him, kicking and screaming, above their heads and carried him back into the main cavern. They then lowered him to the ground, whereupon he fell to his knees sobbing. Ace walked forward and stood over him.

"A virgin. At your age. Sleize, you're a *u*k*n! disgrace to the whole male gender."

"I... I've got kids! With snakes on their heads!"

"Sleize, do these look like ignorant savages? You'll have to do better than that."

"Ace!" blubbered Sleize, greenish pus running beneath his left nostril to his mouth. "You gotta help me!! I'll do anything! I'll admit I stole the Swedish Meatball story!"

"Ancient history." Ace sucked at his Camel.

"I'll give you Madonna's phone number! That' s it! You always wanted Madonna, remember, Ace?"

"Got it. Had it." Ace began to exhale.

"I'll convince my newspaper, the Post to hire Beth Francher!"

Ace paused. Smoke seeped from his half-opened mouth. An anticipation of silence filled the cave.

"Well?!?"

"I'm thinking, I'm thinking," he said with some regret. "Naaah."

"Ace! Ace! You can't let me die before I've fulfilled my one great ambition!! Please! You're a man!! You understand! It's Kirsten Lane!"

"Oh no. No. You don't mean…"

"Yes! I've wanted her ever since she was just wet behind the ears and ghosting the Whoreoscope column in the Star!!"

Ace leaned down close to Sleize, grinning contemptuously. "I'll be sure to tell her that, next time I sleep with her."

Ace straightened and turned to face Guffaw. "He's all yours, laughing boy. One virgin sacrifice, comin' up."

Sleize began to scream hysterically as the natives dragged him toward the sacrificial stone. "Help me, Ace," he yelled. "For Godssake—I'm a reporter!"

"Ex-reporter, sleeze," Ace muttered softly, lighting up another cigarette. "And not even very good at that."

"You have done us a great service, outsider," Guffaw said solemnly. "In return, I give you your life."

"And the woman?"

"And the woman."

"All right! You're a righteous dude, Giggles."

Ignoring the puzzled expression on the native's face, Ace put his arm around Sueng Lo and steered her toward the tunnel that would lead them out of the cavern. Walter Sleize's screams for help continued to echo behind them, growing fainter, and Sueng Lo looked back again anxiously.

"What is your plan, Ace?"

"I plan to get us as far away from here as I can."

"You're really going to leave him there?"

"He'd have done the same thing to me—and has. Just be thankful you and I are getting out alive."

"I am, of course. Still, I can't help but feel sorry for him."

"Forget it, babe. Roseanne is the one I feel sorry for." Ace remembered Shanghai Sally's, Payne Hertz, and the photograph of Hannibal the Cannibal that hung where they'd sat.

"After all. You are what you eat."

Ace stood on the balcony of his hotel room, smoking a Camel and looking out over the city. The Asian edition of Global Star lay by his free hand. He and Sueng Lo had been back in Singapore for twelve hours, with most of that time being spent either sleeping or soaking in a tub of hot water. He now felt refreshed and renewed, more like his old self. Even the humid heat of the evening didn't bother him.

Sueng Lo came out to join him on the balcony. Her arms snaked around his waist, squeezing tightly as though in fear that he would turn to mist and drift away. She was smiling as she looked up into his eyes.

"Thank you, Ace Montana."

"What for?"

"Everything."

"Hey, I haven't done everything. Not yet, anyway."

"You know what I mean."

"Yeah. I know."

She pressed her cheek against his bare chest, drawing silent comfort from the feel of him. "I suppose you'll be leaving Singapore soon."

"Probably. But not until I get the rest of the story."

"What do you mean?"

Ace turned in the circle of her arms so that he was facing her. "There's one last thing I need to make the story complete... and I need your help to get it. I want to see Marilyn."

"Annapolis, Maryland?"

"No."

"Marilyn Manson?"

Ace smiled at her little joke but said nothing. Sueng Lo reached up to stroke his chin. "If that's what you want, Ace, that's what you'll get."

"It won't hurt you, will it?"

"Oh, no. I actually experience a great sense of tranquility when she appears. When do you want to do it?"

"Right now?"

"Of course. " Sueng Lo stepped back into the hotel room. She moved the sparse furniture around so that a space was cleared in the center of the room. She then sat down cross-legged on the floor.

"I rather envy you, Ace," she said. "I have to go into a deep trance to summon her, so I don't actually get to see her. I only feel her presence and know she's with me."

Ace reached into a dresser drawer and pulled out a video-camera. "Tell you what... I'll make sure you get a copy."

Sueng Lo took a deep breath and closed her eyes. She folded her arms over her breasts and lowered her head. Then she looked up.

"Ace?"

"Yeah?"

"I'll never see you again after today, will I?'

There was a pregnant pause.

"Only in your dreams, babe."

Sueng Lo smiled wistfully. "Some day a woman will break your heart, Ace."

"You want to know a secret, sweetheart? They always do."

She again closed her eyes, and began to breathe in and out deeply. A soft groaning sound bubbled up from somewhere inside her. Her eyes snapped open, only to roll up and out of sight. Her head tipped back, and her arms fell limply to her sides. Ace squirmed uncomfortably, fearing for her well-being.

Then a strange stillness fell over the room, as though a bubble of nothingness had descended to cut it off from the rest of the world. As Ace watched in amazement, a faint ball of light appeared above Sueng Lo's head.

Up came his video-camera as the ball of light was growing larger, and now tiny spheres of colored translucence shot out of it in all directions, trailing streamers of blue, red and gold. And then a body began to take form inside the hovering ball of light. At first, it was so faint that Ace could easily have chalked it up to imagination, but the ephemeral figure rapidly solidified. Ace grasped in hushed tones.

There could be no room for doubt now. There before him, floating four feet above the floor of his hotel room, the greatest sex symbol ever captured on film had again come to life. Or at least a semblance thereof.

He had no choice but to believe that this was indeed the ghost of Marilyn Monroe, returned from the pale. She looked exactly the way she had in The Seven Year Itch, in that classic scene wherein she had stood above the grating of a New York subway. She was even wearing the same white, scoop-necked dress,

In a spectral replay of the movie scene, the dress was being blown by unfelt breezes, billowing up to show the shapely legs that had been the object of a million male desires. She giggled without sound as she tried to keep the dress from rising above her panties

Then she looked down at Ace. Smiling beguilingly, she extended her right hand, silently asking his help in stepping down from her invisible pedestal. Setting his camera aside, he reverently approached her.

Can a man touch a ghost? he wondered, even as he reached for her hand. The next instant, he knew. His fingers closed over hers, and a gentle electric fire spread throughout his body. It was like touching a little piece of heaven.

Even after she had stepped down to the floor, he couldn't bring himself to release her hand. All he could do was stare into those huge, innocent eyes that seemed to be constantly changing color from brown to green, with flecks of gold always dancing within them. Her full, rich lips were parted in a smile.

"It's true," he said when at last he regained the use of his tongue. "You're real."

"As real as I ever was. Maybe even more."

The voice was the same one that had caressed him from motion picture speakers, a breathless sigh that carried with it the essence of every woman who had ever walked the earth.

Ace shivered slightly. He fought back the sense of awe and tried to become only the reporter. He was at least partially successful.

"You've been gone for more than forty years. Why did you wait so long to come back?"

"I had no choice," she explained. "It's not as easy as you might think. I had to have the proper channel that I could move through. That channel didn't exist until little Sueng Lo was born. And even then I had to wait for her 18th birthday before she was ready. I just had to be patient."

"What's it like ... where you are?"

"Mmmm. It's wonderful. More beautiful than you can imagine. And it's waiting for everyone."

"Then why did you ever want to come back?"

Marilyn's face grew sad, and for a moment Ace expected spectral tears to roll down her cheeks.

"There was always a big hole in my life," she said at last. "I always felt like everybody loved me, but nobody ever listened to me. I had a lot to say. Really I did. But do one ever looked past my smile."

"Can you blame them?"

"No, I suppose not. And I didn't mind most of the time. But I wanted to be more. I wanted to do more. That's why I gave the healing power to Sueng Lo. Through her, I can do the marvelous things I was never allowed to do before. No one ever really listened to my words, but maybe they'll listen to my deeds."

"You've got someone who'll listen to you now, sweetheart."

"Really?"

"Really. I'd like to hear what you have to say." Somewhat to his surprise, Ace realized he was telling the truth.

For the next hour, Marilyn talked, a lifetime's worth of words spilling out in a cascade. Occasionally, Ace would scribble the words down in his notebook, other times, he would simply listen.

"I've really gone on and on, haven't I?' she said at last. "You must be bored to tears."

"You gotta be kidding."

"You're a sweet man."

"Yeah, I know. But don't let that get around. I got a reputation to uphold."

Marilyn giggled, and Ace felt the laughter rippling up his spine. Then she grew more serious.

"It's really getting late. I have to go."

"No. Not yet."

"I'm afraid so. Even here, we have rules. But before I go Ace, I really want to thank you."

"Are you serious?"

"Yes. I mean it. If you hadn't saved Sueng Lo from those horrible natives, my only life to the real world would have been lost forever. I never could have come back."

"Then, I'm doubly glad I helped her."

"And I'm also grateful to you for taking the time to talk with me."

"It was my pleasure. Any time you feel like doing it again, just give me a buzz. I'm in the book."

Once more the sparkling giggle that set his spine to tingling. "I just may do that. But seriously-- I'll always be grateful to you. Is there anything at all I can do to show you just how much I appreciate all you've done?"

Those words were all it took. A switch kicked off in Ace's brain, and his hormones took over.

"Anything?" he asked.

"Anything."

Ace stepped closer to her, staring her straight in the face. "There is only one conceivable thing that any red-blooded American male could ask for at a moment like this, sweetheart.

"You. Me. Here. Now."

"What do you mean?"

"I want to make love to you."

"Oooooh!" Her eyes grew even wider in surprise. "But... I'm dead!"

"That's okay," he grinned. "We'll pretend we're married."

Ace smiled coolly, put his arm around her waist and pulled her against him. "Really, no problem, babe. After all, I've slept with half the starlets in Hollywood.

"I'm used to that."

A SUCKER IS BORNE
(Interlude: Part One)

His eighteen inch platform shoes fell with a thud on the top of Gephard's tiny desk. It had been a long day. Frank leaned back in his chair wearily, rubbing at his aching eyes, his legs crossed. He glanced down at his digital watch—he could not tolerate the short hand on analog watches. It was nearly midnight. And he still had an enormous stack of papers in front of him, crying out for attention.

This was the only part of his job that he really hated: going over the reporters' expense vouchers, especially when those vouchers belonged to Kirsten Lane. She was a hell of a good journalist, but Gephard was convinced she was out to milk the tabloid dry. Why else would she keep track of how many miles she walked while on the job, so she could try to get Global Star to pay for her shoes? Gephard reached out and punched the 'record' button on his transcription machine. He noticed a smudge on one of his elevator shoes.

"Miss Nochers, remind me to ask Kirsten if she's ever heard of the term 'anal retentive'." He thought of returning to the Midget race car circuit, but knew his racing days were over. He'd actually been slowly shrinking for years since his trip to Borneo, and could no longer reach the pedals.

Gephard returned to the stack of vouchers, but again his short attention span waned quickly. He stood up and walked over to the table set against one wall of his office. It, like all of his office furniture, had a portion of its legs sawed off to reinforce Gephard's self-delusion of normal height. A pitcher of ice water was always in place there, and he poured himself a glass, hoping it would revitalize him. If that didn't do the trick, there was always the pint bottle of bourbon he kept hidden in his desk drawer.

Gephard looked wistfully out through the open door of his office, exhaling deeply as his little eyes fell on the empty desk behind which his personal secretary sat during normal office hours. If he squinted his eyes just so, he could almost conjure up a vision of her, each softly rounded curve accentuated by the tight clothing he preferred her to wear. He imagined her reading Of Mice and Men.

He shivered slightly, forcing himself out of his reveries. If this continued, he'd have to pour the ice water over his head or down his pants. Again. He set the glass down and returned to his paperwork

He had only been back to work a few minutes when a soft tapping sound caused him to raise his head. A tall, skinny man was standing just outside his office, meekly knocking on the door frame.

Gephard had to strain in the dim light to make out who it was. He finally recognized the caller as being Lon Alucard, one of his staff photographers, a little backward, but a quick study.

"Evening, Lonnie. What' up?"

"Good evening," Alucard slurred. "Everything but you, sir. I brought those photos you wanted." Alucard spoke so softly that Gephard could barely hear him, in a voice tinged with an accent the editor could never place.

"I don't want to be a bloodless monster, but I'm sorta... tied up... with work right now, Lonnie."

"Thank Bella," said the photog.

Alucard made no move to enter the office. He merely stood and stared at the frame of the doorway, as though inspecting the wood. Gephard noted that Alucard deferred to his authority by looking at his neck instead of the editor's face, and he liked that. He sighed heavily. "Let me explain something to you, Lonnie. You see, I can't look at the pictures if I'm here and you're way over there, now can I?"

"Sorry sir. I guess I'm a little," he said as he made a circular motion with a bony finger by the side of his well-oiled hair, "Batty."

"So, what should we do about that?"

"What do you suggest, Mr. Gephard?" he answered lifelessly.

Gephard closed his little eyes as if in deep thought, then opened them and smiled wearily. "Here's a real radical idea, son. Why don't you come in here and show the pictures to me? The vouchers can wait."

"May I, sir?"

"Oh, please do. You've got a stake in this too, right son?"

Alucard seemed relieved by the cordial invitation and stepped into the office. Gephard stared at him quizzically. The man was without question the oddest photographer working for the tabloid. Sometimes, he seemed to be about two steps behind the rest of mankind.

"You wouldn't happen to be related to Uge Nochers by any chance, would you, Lonnie?"

"No, sir. Not that I know." Alucard coughed into his fist.

"Just kindred spirits, I suppose. Well, have you got something I can sink my teeth into here?"

Alucard produced a packet of glossy photos and reverently placed them on the desk in front of the editor. For several long moments, Gephard silently stared at the pictures spread out before him, saying nothing. Finally, he looked up at Alucard, giving the photographer a blank stare.

"I don't know how to tell you this, Lonnie... but I don't have the foggiest idea what these pictures are!"

"That's because you're looking at them upside down, sir." Alucard reached out and turned the photos around. As he did, Gephard noticed his fingernails were nearly as long as a woman's.

"That's funny. The dates of these pics are now upside down. Get a manicure, son."

"Yes, sir." His deadpan face expressed no emotion.

"We have an image to uphold, Lonnie."

"An image, sir?" Alucard coughed into his fist.

"You better watch that coughin'," observed Gephard.

"Always, sir."

The editor scooped up the photos and leaned back in his plush chair. As was his habit, he stuck a pencil behind one ear, occassionally tapping at its barrel with one finger. Then he put the pictures down, turning his attention to Alucard, who was standing as stiff as a corpse.

"Are these what they appear to be, Lonnie?"

"Yes, sir. Photographic proof that Oprah Winfrey is actually Barack Obama in drag."

"All right! I knew my hunch would pan out. We could be looking at front page material here. How on earth did you manage to get these shots?"

"Oh, I have my ways." Alucard hung his head shyly and lightly scuffed at the carpet with one foot.

"Why, you'd practically have to hang upside down from the rafters to get these kinds of photos. These are terrific, Lonnie."

"Thank you, Mr. Gephard."

"Drink, Lonnie? Stay awhile." The photographer reluctantly complied as Gephard opened a drawer and pulled out his secret bottle.

"Bloody Mary?" asked the droll photographer.

"Sorry." Gephard began to pour himself a shot. "I especially like this one, of Obama stuffing the Silly Putty into his bra."

"Yes, sir. That was my favorite as well," he added still looking to Gephard's neck.

Gephard set the photos aside. He was beaming as he looked across the desk.

"Good work, Lonnie. We won't bury these babies."

"Thank you, sir. The field's so crowded. It's nice to be appreciated... and to limit competition."

"You are good," Gephard assured him, ignoring his remark. "I'd tell you more often if only I saw you more often. You never seern to be around."

"No, sir. I guess I'm sort of a night person."

"I understand. I was that way myself, when I was younger. Hell, most nights, I wouldn't get to bed tell the sun was rising."

"Yes, sir. That's how it is with me."

"Ah, well... that'll change when you get married."

"I don't know about marriage, Mr. Gephard. I really don't date much."

"Why not?"

"I have a hard time finding a person who suits my taste."

"Really? Don't you even... neck?"

"Occassionally. You know, your secretary, Miss Nochers, seems like a charming young lady."

"Uge? Oh, yes, she's a wonderful girl. Like a daughter to me." Gephard eyes the photographer a little more closely. "Of course, you know I try to discourage inner-office romances. It sucks the life right out of an employee."

"Yes, sir. I understand." There was a discernible note of disappointment in Alucard's voice.

"But, don't you worry, boy. The right... person... will come along sooner or later. Maybe Beth Francher could find the right type for you." Gephard shrugged his shoulders.

"Any type is fine, sir."

Gephard leaned across the desk to make sure Alucard was fully conscious. When he did, he couldn't help but notice the photographer's pale, pasty complexion.

"You look like the walking dead. You need to cut out the nightlife and get a little more sun, boy," Gephard reached under his desk and retrieved a paper sack. From it he pulled an oblong object wrapped in cellophane.

"Tell you what, son; I was just about to take a break and eat a little something the wife sent with me from home. Why don't you join me?"

"No thank you, sit. I wouldn't want to impose."

"Don't be silly. Irma always packs enough to feed four men. Take a took at this."

Alucard glanced down at the desktop. Gephard had unwrapped a submarine sandwich that would indeed make a meal for an entire Third World country. Gephard tore off a section of the sandwich and graciously extended it toward the photographer.

"Give it a try, son. I guarantee it's the best meatball sandwich you'll ever taste. Irma uses her own special sauce, laced with just a touch of garlic. "

Alucard recoiled from the offering. "No, sir. Please. I'm highly allergic to garlic. "

"Are you kidding? No one's allergic to garlic. Well, then, how about this?" Gephard again reached into his sack and brought out a hot cross bun.

Alucard recoiled again. "I'm afraid I have a lot of allergies, Mr. Gephard. It's just something I have to endure."

"Yeah, well, you know what they say, Lonnie; life's a bitch, and then you marry one."

"Another joke, sir?"

"I wish."

Gephard took a bite of his sandwich, savoring its pungent flavor. He dabbed at the corners of his mouth with a paper napkin.

"Lonnie, have you ever worked with Ace Montana?"

"No, sir. I've never had the pleasure."

"Like to? Course, I wouldn't want you to bite off more than you can chew, but I bet you two could become blood brothers."

"Whatever you want, Mr. Gephard."

"You'd make a great team. He should be getting back from Singapore tomorrow night, I'll ask him about it."

"I understand he's a very good reporter. Efficient. Cold blooded."

"The best we've got. The boy's got ink in his veins. If you don't believe it, just ask him." Gephard chuckled softly. "It's in our blood. Ace kind of reminds me of myself when I was a hotshot reporter.... Did I ever tell you," continued Gephard, "the story about how I discovered President Kennedy's brain had been transplanted into the body of President Clinton?"

"Yes, sir. Several times."

"It was a shame it was still dead. Those were the days." Gephard stared off into space as he munched on his sandwich. He swiveled his head as Alucard suddenly rose from his seat.

"I really should be flying, sir."

Huh? Oh. Right, right." Gephard set his sandwich down. "Before you go, Lonnie, there's something I've been meaning to ask you. It's your voice. It sounds... funny. You're not from around here, are you?"

"Uhhh... no, sir.

"I didn't think so. Where, Vermont?"

"No, sir. Farther east than that."

"Ah. New Hampshire. That explains it. Good-night Lonnie."

Gephard returned to his sandwich as Alucard turned and walked out of the room. Only then did the editor remember another question he had wanted to ask the photographer.

He jumped up from his desk and walked out into the newsroom, only to find it completely deserted. Alucard was nowhere in sight. He did notice a few wisps of what appeared to be smoke hanging in the air, so he checked all the desktops to make sure no one—that 'no one' likely being Ace—had left a smouldering cigarette behind.

Looking around and sniffing the air, satisfying himself that all was well, Gephard then returned to his office. Taking his seat, he reached over and turned on his desk recorder.

"Miss Nochers... have somebody from maintenance check out the ventilation system in the newsroom. Smells like a bat is caught in there."

Picking up his sandwich and taking another bite, he resumed going over the stack of expense vouchers. Reading the top voucher, he scowled and turned again to the recorder.

"And ask Kirsten just why in Holy Hell she thinks we should pay for her damn birth control pills! Has she never heard of absten…abstan….ab….just say no?!?"

But reviewing the vouchers did nothing to relieve the suspicion in Gephard's mind. All of the signs were there; Alucard's nightlife, his long fingernails, his odd accent, his single life-style and his rejection of a man-sized sandwich.

He knew Alucard was gay.

SEWER SAVAGE SCOURS CITY

by Mel Odom

Inexplicably, she felt April fresh.

"Kirsten Lane, 2:31 P.M., April 13th, Friday, driving in from the Barbara Walters/Bigfoot Love Child story. What a hairy situation. Item, personal: remember to extend my thoughts to Gephard about this piece of garbage Pinto he rented for my trip home. It smells like road kill, and for a good reason. I found an empty six pack of Colt Malt Likker and the bones of Colonel's Country Fried 'Coon under the horsehair seat. People do still fly in this country despite the UFOs, Chief. And how much did the rental agency pay you to have Sarah Palin drive this potential firebomb from Alaska to New York City for them?

"God, I hate this backward burg. Someone tried to intentionally rear-end the Pinto. They were on a horse, Frank. And they didn't just say neigh, either.

"Additional expenses: gas purchase on the Global Star card (it's probably kerosene), and I don't want to hear a word about me taking the card when you weren't looking. You shouldn't leave it in that drawer. I warned you about that flimsy lock, and I refuse to be sent out on an assignment on short finances because you were short sighted.

"And, Chief? Twenty bucks waiting on me at the Western Union office (and feed store) is short finances, even for you, short stack.

"Expenses at CHARLIE'S PLUCK and CLUCK self-serve restaurant are also on the card. I don't know what the amount was, but you can bet your butt it was more than the fill-up at the convenience store, the BAG &MOUNT IT. I don't mind bagging my supper, Frank, but I'll be damned if I'll mount it.

"Also, add a pair of Leggs panty-hose to the list. The springs are sticking through the stinking horsehair seat. Phew! The horse they skinned must have been Whinny ther Pooh."

"Kirsten Lane, 4:47 P.M., April 13th, Friday, still enroute from Seattle. Item, personal: Chief, this Pinto should have been put out to pasture. I'd get out and shoot it right now if it wasn't raining, and I knew for sure the tow bill would go on the Global Star silver card. And I keep seeing these signs about fines for littering. You're fined if you don't.

"Between the constant shimmying, the misfiring, and the knowledge that driving this thing in traffic is considerably more dangerous that skateboarding with nitroglycerin strapped to my substantial chest, I'm not having fun here. It's been acting up for the last twenty minutes, so I'm going to pull off road see if I can scare up Mr. Goodwrench. If he can't fix the Pinto, he can at least fix my drive shaft.

"Wouldn't you know my Jitterbug cell-phone is dead, you cheap....

"I wish I'd kept my vow to never come back to this part of the country since you sent me to cover that story about the Neo-Nazi cult that was funding its purchases of nerve gas by doing an all-male roadshow of Mame.

"Item, personal: the next one of those sappy romance novels I do is going to be set in Oregon, and as far as life-threatening situations go, I couldn't think of anything more challenging than steering this frigging Pinto through the rain. Maybe I could have my heroine meet up with a lumberjack named Chip who's been in the woods for six months and is about to take his priestly vows as a druid. Of course, the guy doesn't have a chance when he meets this little red-headed spitfire, since the most seductive thing he's seen in months is a Maine Grizzly in heat...

"Unbearable heat, I might add."

"**K**irsten Lane, 6:23 P.M., April 13th, Friday, walking from Seattle now, Chief. Item, personal: it's still raining wildcats and bulldogs, Frank. I'm not sure the local sewers can hold them all, you miserable, low-life, pond-sucking, cheap bastard. I don't have an umbrella either, damnit! Who the hell is going to pick up even a hottie like me when all I've got to show is rain-drenched hair, torn panty-hose, and a cute little button nose-for-news?"

She attracted a lot of male attention when she walked across any room. Kirsten was slender and attractive, big brown eyes and red hair halfway down her back, the color so rich and dark it should have come from a bottle, but didn't. (Though it did come from a recipe left by ancient astronauts in Mexico. One thing you had to say about the Aztecs—they may have been blood thirsty-savages, but they had great hair.)

"Anyone outside of Ace, of course. He'd rear-end a Pinto, too. He's never understand that neigh means neigh."

—∞∞∞—

The antique jukebox was playing Vince Gill singing Beat It.

Kirsten Lane stood as close to the ancient pay phone inside the UCK NEKKED BAR and GRILLas she could, one finger in her ear to block the loud Country and Western music from the juke and the braying of the crowd. The B of Buck Nekked on the neon sign opposite her on the wall blinked on and off randomly, and the bull was not mechanical and very mad. She put her lips almost against the receiver. The thing that kept her from actually touching the receiver was the sight of the toothless men and women going into the bathrooms down the dimly lit hall. The stench of urine burned her cute button nose and left a foul taste on her tongue. It was hard to talk and breathe through her mouth at the same time, but she did it.

She gave the operator the Global Star phone card number from memory, then stood still, dripping in the yellow slicker with the happy faces of Patrick and Spongebob on it she'd 'borrowed' from the trucker who'd brought her into town. Guber hadn't followed her into Cadence, Oregon or the UCK NEKKED. The last she'd seen of him, the guy had been nursing a broken thumb and swearing he'd never pick up another hitchhiker. She didn't blame Guber for getting the wrong impression, but she'd had to stop him somehow.

Besides, she'd had sex with truckers before, and didn't care to repeat the experience. Their idea of foreplay was rednecking in the parking lot of the BATES and SWITCH MOTEL.

The phone at the other end rang and rang and rang. She read the messages scrawled on the wall next to the phone with lipstick. Good was misspelled on one. She wasn't interested in the job offer either, even if it was Bill Clinton.

"Hey, babe," a drunken cowboy called over the noise from a nearby booth. He wore Revi jeans (a Chinese knock-off), a western shirt with gold discs on the shoulders, and a cap reading FLOYD'S TAILPIPE CITY shadowed a badly listing smile. "C'mere a minute and talk to old Clem." He clapped his knee in invitation.

"What do the discs on the shoulders symbolize," she yelled back, half-heartedly.

"Cymbals," he grinned.

"Symbols of what?"

"Cymbals, like I jest said, baby."

Stupid Cadence rednecks Kirsten said inside her head. She turned away, thinking the whole hick city must be severely inbred. Wonder if he'll enjoy wearing mace for his aftershave? she thought as she fumbled for a cigarette from her purse.

On the fifteenth ring, the pre-recorded voice of a young woman answered the phone. "Menaheim Building. For Global Star, press one. For Global Star Tonight, press two. For a date with Ace, don't press your luck. For complaints, press 324-6800-2145-03877-9986436100333."

Kirsten pressed one as she continued to dig for her lighter. She couldn't find it. A yellow and blue flame flared to life in front of her, washing over Clem's befuddled features. The silver Zippo with a turquoise saddle insignia had a tiny motto that read: Happy Tails to You. Kirsten caught the flame with her cigarette and inhaled deeply, relishing the taste. She hadn't smoked in the eighteen wheeler because of all the Christian paraphernalia hanging from the sun visors. Of course, that was before Little Guber tried to finger her rosary.

"Thanks, Clem...?"

"Clem. Clem Clem," he said, smiling wide enough to show a healthy expanse of pink gum. "Don't mention it."

"Next time, I won't," Kirsten assured him, turning back the other way. On the dance floor, three mirrored globes started spinning and reflecting the colored lights that flickered on and off with the throbbing beat of Garth Brooks crooning Walk Like An Egyptian.

"Global Star offices," answered the male receptionist, Chip N. Dale. Music by Acorn played softly in the background. "All the news that we have a fit to print."

"Give me Uge Nochers," Kirsten asked. It was hard to keep her finger in her free ear while holding a lighted cigarette without singeing her hair, but she managed.

"I'm sorry. Could you speak up, please? This is Chip N. Dale speaking."

"Uge Nochers, Chip." She'd always thought the receptionist was a little squirley, but she fought to keep her composure.

The dancers whooped cowboy-whoops and danced in their Justin Roper boots as the bull brayed and Tody Keith rapped Eminem's Lose Yourself.

Taking a deep breath, Kirsten yelled, "I want Uge Nochers!" in a voice she usually reserved for Gephard when he wanted her to cover a story that had all the importance of a cat stuck in a tree. Many of the dancers turned to look at her. She realized the song had ended.

"I'm sorry, but you must have the wrong number. This is a newspaper, not a plastic surgeon's office."

"Cut the crap, Chip, and get me Nochers now!"

Clem walked in front of the reporter and leaned against the wall in a pose straight out of a Drysdale's Western Wear catalog. Kirsten guessed the man thought he was just oozing sex. She noticed he was oozing something. "Well, now, little darling, what you got may not be exactly prime cut, but I think if we fluff 'em up a little, they'll do right fine in a pinch." He grinned and winked at her.

Kirsten gave him a false smile, covering the mouthpiece and reminding herself to knock Chip's block off when she returned to GS, and to wash her hands as soon as she got some place suitable. "Just hold your horses for a few minutes, cowboy."

"Why, surely, ma'am. " He doffed his cap, showing the Grecian Gray stains along the inside brim. Then he grabbed the red and gold ponies stitched on his shoulders.

"Global Star, Miss Nochers speaking. "Who's there?"

"Kirsten, Uge."

"I'm sorry? I don't think I know a Kirsten Uge."

"Uge! It's Kirsten Lane!! Put Gephard on!"

"Ooohh, I'm sorry, Miss Lane, but Mr. Gephard is, uh, er, all tied up at the moment. Can I take a message? You can talk fast. I know shorthand."

"Uge, untie Gephard and put him on now!!" Kirsten thought furiously, searching for some excuse that would get past the secretary's feeble defenses, then remembered who she was talking to. "I've been bitten by a loan shark. I need to know if my medical coverage will take care of the reconstructive plastic surgery."

Concern filled the secretary's voice. "Ooohh my, that's just terrible. Does it hurt?"

"Only when I fill out my company expense vouchers, Uge."

"Well, then, I wouldn't fill one out if I was you. Mr. Gephard can be quite the little dickens, when he wants to be, you know."

"I know all about Gephart's little dickens..."

The phone crashing on the desktop echoed in Kirsten's ear despite the new assault of Clint Black belting out Sussudio.

"Kirsten?" Gephard's voice sounded strained, hollow from using the speaker-phone in his personal office. He grunted with effort. "What the hell's this about a shark?"

"Forget the shark, Chief. I'm stuck in Cadence, Oregon–"

"What the hell are you doing there? That car, I mean, you're supposed to be back here first thing tomorrow morning."

"The Pinto is at the glue factory. I had to leave it on the highway right next to the Izzit Inn. They've got a great 'all-the-road-kill-you-can-eat' buffet, Frank, and a great little short-order cook named Tom Izzit you'd just love."

"You did what? Do you know how much money the paper has tied up in that Pinto? How the hell could you just go and leave it there?"

"You bet on the wrong horse. It died on me on the highway. I didn't have a choice."

"Did you put gas in it?"

"Yes, Chief. In all four tires. Even had a priest bless it to ward off horse flies."

Leaning into the phone so she could be heard clearly, Kirsten said, "Listen, Chief, being left stranded in the midst of the Minnie Pearl Memorial Highway in the middle of a downpour is terrible. Having to walk for miles before I could catch a ride with a multi-cultural truck driver with Russian hands and Roman fingers is terrible. Losing the Pinto was a lot like having a hemorrhoid operation: a pain in the butt until it's gone. But none of that is like the hell of a woman named Kirsten scorned."

"You sound like you're in a bar," Gephard said, ignorning her. "Are you in a bar?"

"No, I'm in the Guggenheim Museum, Frank, discussing Picasso's little known Western paintings with John Wayne." She looked at Clem. "And if the local Gabby Hayes, here, decides to let his fingers do the walking, I'll let the Global Star lawyers do my talking."

There were more sounds of struggling, then an unintelligible whisper from Uge Nochers. A second later, Frank Gephard screamed with real feeling. Remembering the evening ritual of slap-and-tickle Gephard and his secretary went through thinking no one else at Global Star knew, Kirsten supposed it was really possible the editor was tied up. That would make him...

"Dope on a Rope," she muttered to herself.

"Kirsten," Gephard said an instant later, sounding short of breath, "I'm at the end of my rope. Call you back?"

"No way are you going to short change me again, Chief. I'm stranded here. No way are you squirming off the hook like the worm you are. Send over your old buddy buddy from Smallville, Superman."

"He's out on assignment," Gephard lied. "But, seriously, I'll get you home. Don't worry about it."

"I'm worried about it. Plane, Chief. P-L-A-N-E. Think flight, Wright Brothers, coffee, tea, or, for once, me. I'd even hitch a ride on Peter Pan's shirt-tails."

"Maybe I could send you some fairy dust, Kirstin. I just found out that Lonnie Alucard is a tinkerbell."

Kirsten shook her head in disbelief. "No he's not. He's just light-hearted like everyone living in The Big Apple, including me. Now quite stalling. I have a home there, at the Gilligan Apartments. I'm late for a three hour tour, and I've got a book due next week."

"Are you still cranking out those romance novels?"

"Tell her I just loved Love Bites, Frankie," Uge Nochers whispered. "But I think she can cut back on some of the sex she puts in them. Hold still. I've almost got it."

Gephard screamed again. It could barely be heard over Randy Travis singing Jumpin' Jack Flash on the jukebox." You're going to have to make a decision," Gephard gasped, "about whether you're a romance writer or a reporter."

"Frank," Kirsten said. "I'm the only reporter you've got who uses all ten fingers when they type."

"I don't want to hear it. Ace can type almost as fast as you with one hand."

"That's because he's had a lifetime of practice using one hand, Chief. The only thing bigger than Montana's ego is–"

"Kirsten!!" interrupted Gephard. "We all have our shortcomings."

"Speak for yourself, Gephard. And don't feed me that 'but he's still the best damn reporter the paper's got'. I know, that's why he gets flown all over the world while I get sent from Bugtussle to Kalamazoo to cover three-headed baby stories in a Pinto. No more infantile assignments, Frank."

"That was a good story," Gephard protested. "I gave it page five, above the fold."

"It was a lousy three-headed Chihuahua, Frank. You ever had a three-headed Chihuahua puppy throw up on you from every mouth at the same time?"

"Frankie," Uge Nochers whispered urgently, "how was I supposed to know the honey would stick to it? Now, be still while I peel it loose."

"Say, what are you and Uge doing in your office, Chief?"

"Uh, she was helping me prepare my speech for the International Beekeeper's Conference I'm going to. Then she spilled honey all over it."

"Let me guess. The title is To Bee Or Not To Bee."

There was silence. "How did you know that?" asked Gephard. He yelled again as Travis sang "it's a gas, gas, gas!"

"If you really thought of me as a good reporter," Kirsten said when the screaming subsided, "you'd give me some overseas assignments. Even Iran is sounding good right now. I could check out the rumor that Mahmud Ahmadinejad has become a Kiss groupie."

"That reminds me," Gephard said, "as soon as Ace gets back from Singapore, I need to get him out to Egypt. I heard a rumor from a contact in the State Department that archeologists have just uncovered an enema invented by Pharoh

Wazoo III that's supposed to raise the dead."

Abandoning her anger, Kirsten pleaded. "I want that story. Book me a flight and I'll go right now." In the background, Clint Black was singing Like a Virgin.

"I thought you wanted to interview Ahmadinejad?"

"I'll interview Saddam and Gomorrah if you'll just give me this assignment."

"Can't, junior. It's Ace. This one's... special to him. He was an orphan and never knew his mummy.

"Kid, look, I'll take care of you. I always do. You're one of my favorite people." There was a strange, surpressed giggle, then the editor whispering frantically. "Dammit, why did you have to bring the feathers?

"Remember all those expense vouchers for panty-hose I've signed for you?" Gephard went on. "Kirsten, you and I both know you don't go through that many pairs of panty-hose. Hell, even Marv Albert doesn't own that many pairs of panty-hose.

"I got to go," Gephard said. "Call me in the morning and we'll see what I can do. This must be costing you a bundle."

"It's going on my expense sheet," Kirsten said. "I want a plane, Chief, I–"

The phone clicked dead in her ear. Gephard's voice was replaced by the jukebox's tinny music. k.d. Lang was singing My Girl.

"Damn!" She slammed the receiver onto its hook.

"Did you know," Clem asked, "that I've been told women really love a man without teeth?" He grinned widely to display the pink gums again. "Want me to tell you why?"

"I know why. It makes it easier for women to pull their tongue out and cut them off at the root." Kirsten gave Clem the best smile she could fake while seething with anger, realizing she had just found a Frank Gephard surrogate. "Come here, lover boy, and you can tell me everything."

Clem stepped forward, wearing his wide-open and empty grin. Stepping out of the telephone booth, Kirsten stepped into his embrace and pulled his head to her shoulder. He started kissing her neck. Steeling herself, she pulled his head in tight, not releasing him, then swiped his lighter from his shirt pocket and brought her knee up into his groin forcefully three times. Clem made URKmg sounds as he gasped and tried to get free. His face looked greenish in the dim lighting when she pushed him away. Clem flailed wildly, running backwards off-balance, then spilled over a table where two cowgirls were arm wrestling.

Kirsten sighed and lit another cigarette with her new lighter. Thank God Clem had no teeth to lose.

And that she still felt April fresh.

The sleazy Bates and Switch Motel was one brick short of a Motel Eight. It was also the only motel in Cadence, which was almost a ghost town except for the annual Cadence Parade of Percussionists. The motel had no sign. A clown stood on a curb of Rat-A-Tat Street with a piece of cardboard that read: THE INN IS NEAR.

Once a year, percussionists gathered from across the country to attend seminars and to march in the 'big' parade down Rimshot Avenue. Each year, one major performer was brought in to draw the crowds. In the past, they had hired Buddy Rich, Gene Krupa, Ginger Baker, and Mike Huckabee. Kirsten could imagine nothing more boring each year than marching to a different drummer.

"Did you happen to see what started the fight, Miss Lane?"

Kirsten put on her most innocent face, the one that had made televangelist Anita Lott O'Toole confide a year ago that she'd kept a private stock of male prostitutes on her church's payroll.

"Beats me, marshal. All I know is one moment everybody seemed to be having a good time, then they were fighting."

They stood in the doorway of the motel room she'd rented. Light from the interior framed a yellow rectangle on the broken sidewalk outside the door. A mercury vapor security light drew the man in long, hard lines, emphasizing his over six feet in height. His badge glittered burnished gold. He also wore a tiny puce ribbon pinned above the badge.

"It's not marshal, " the young Deputy Sheriff said, doffing his hat and looking bashfully at the brim. "I'm a Deputy. Deputy Whey Layd."

Extending her hand, Kirsten said, "Well, it's been a pleasure meeting you, Deputy Dog. I'm Kirsten Lane."

"Layd. Layd. I'm Layd."

And quite often, I'll bet, thought Kirsten. He took her hand and pumped it vigorously. "Yes, ma'am it has been a pleasure." He put his hat back on. His cruiser was parked near a curbstone behind him, its lights playing out over the rain-slick street. It was the first pickup truck she'd ever seen used as a patrol vehicle. Two crossed drumsticks beneath the town's name had been crudely painted on both doors.

A manhole cover made a dark inkblot a few feet in front of the bumper. "It's really been a strange night," he said with a puzzled smile. "First off, we had this trucker in the emergency room swearing he'd picked up a naked woman on the highway who'd broke his finger. Then, we got this fight at the Uck Nekkid bar." He smiled again. "But, I'm glad you got out of there okay."

"Thanks to you," Kirsten said. She didn't feel bad about flimflamming the young Deputy at all. Except that seducing him now would have been totally out of the character she had portrayed for him. And he looked like the kind of guy who could really work the kinks out of a girl. "What is that little puce ribbon for, Deputy Dog," she asked, pointing at it.

"They wont let us notch our guns no more, so each ribbon is one queer wasted. I only got one 'cause I'm a rookie, but I'll get me more.

"Well," the Deputy continued, shifting his Sam Browne belt across his lean hips, "I guess I'd better get back to it. Don't want the Sheriff to think I'm slacking off. You know what they say—a queer a day keeps th' liberals away."

"You take care of yourself, Deputy," Kirsten said, thinking how Lucky Jr. it was that she'd been stranded here instead of Beth Francher. Fate had saved her Fanny again.

"Yes, ma'am and if you need anything else, you just give me a holler, like this: Suuuuueeeece!"

Trying not to smile too broadly so she could maintain her innocent look, she said, "If I should get into any more trouble, I'll just tell your desk sergeant I want Layd."

Deputy Layd's neck colored dark crimson. He wiped his lower face with a big hand. "Uh, no, ma'am You'll be talking to the dispatch officer, Mr. Kurds. And just tell him you want Whey."

"I'll try to remember, Deputy. Call Kurds, ask for Whey. Call Kurds for Whey. Kurds. Whey. Kurds and Whey."

Looking puzzled, Layd turned and walked through the light rain to his pickup cruiser.

Kirsten waved from the door, sighing and wishing he'd just said "go ahead and make my Whey". Going to bed horny even made old Clem sound interesting. She watched as the little yellow lights above the bumper diminished in the night, sighed again, and said to no one in particular, "Oh, well. I guess there was no Whey, ma'am."

Sudden movement and a feline yowl of fear drew her attention to the manhole cover in the street. She watched as a gray and white tabby streaked for the other side of Rat-A-Tat Street, still spitting in fright. Looking back at the manhole cover, she thought she saw it move slightly, then dismissed the idea as a product of a tired and overactive imagination. The cat stopped under the awning of the Al Bundy Hardware store on the other side of the street with its back arched.

"You're a stupid cat to be out on a night like this anyway," Kirsten said to herself. She wasn't terribly fond of felines... hadn't been since she'd discovered they were the main ingredient used by a wellknown hamburger chain that used its profits to support Satanic cults, Burger Thing. The story was a whopper and burger sales soared when it broke, confirming that Kirsten's distaste for cats was almost universal.

She closed the door and peeled off the yellow slicker, totally naked underneath except for a pair of torn panty-hose. She sneezed and hoped she wasn't coming down with a cold. She also worried about her own faltering political correctness.

Nowadays, entry-ways to sewers should be called personholes.

Her working title was His N Whoremones.

Suddenly realizing the love scene in the romance novel she was writing had transgressed from passionately writhing sheets and butterfly kisses to raw sex, Kirsten took her laptop computer from her knees and put it on the carpet.

She was itching for a major new assignment.

Still sitting on the floor, she crushed out her latest cigarette amid the others overflowing the tinfoil ashtray that had come with the room. She leaned forward, stretching her back, putting her palms flat on the carpet, luxuriating in the pain. Then she got up and walked to the mirror

"You're the best damn info-babe on television," she told her reflection. It was a nice idea that had no basis in reality for the newspaper reporter. But, someday...

Her hair still hung wet, looking wine-dark against the plush white bathrobe she'd stolen from the Beverly Hillbilly Hotel in Beverly Hills during the coverage she'd done on the Hollywood buy-back of the missing Leave It To Beaver and The Honeymooners episodes from the Belligians. As a story, it had been passe, strictly a buy-back of taped shows from a bunch of aliens no one had ever heard of, who were only now receiving the original broadcasts. But the benefits had been great. She'd gotten her own byline on the story and two more robes just like this one.

And a copy of the almost forgotten episode of Ward Cleaver wearing June's pearl necklace and high heels. The Beaver certainly didn't know what to make of that.

It reminded her of her first big scoop; an exposé of Hollywood's efforts to disgrace television evangelists. They had planted subliminal messages inside the makeup used by preachers' wives. Messages like: "Doesn't your secretary look good enough to eat?" and "Wouldn't you like to be a bimbo's personal savior?"

It was an insidious plot that Kirsten had uncovered just in the nick of time. The subliminal message in the last batch of makeup had read: "I want to commit a felony so I can have Bubba for a girlfriend. No doubt it would have sparked a massive crime wave, and, anyway, she'd been dating Bubba at the time. Best of all, Ace's attempt to horn in on her exposé ad. led to the implantation of the v-chip in his neck that distorted his cursing.

"You know what your problem is," she told her reflection. "You need Layd in a bad way. Or in any way."

No Whey was the answer Kirsten knew she must accept.

⸺⟳⸺

Kirsten took her cigarette pack from the pocket of the bathrobe and discovered it was empty. Sometimes, she wished smoking and drinking weren't mandatory for all good reporters (at least, that's what Ace had told her.) Cursing, she crossed the room to her purse and took out a fistful of change. Still in her bathrobe, she pulled on her hiking boots from her suitcase because her other shoes were still soaking wet, and walked outside to the small laundry/snack room of the Bates and Switch Motel.

A very young couple watching a dryer were chanting, "I see London, I see France, I see Doody's underpants"; "I see London, I see France, I see Clara's underpants..."

"Howdy Doody," Kirsten said, and waved. She noticed the couple was naked below the waist. Doody did not answer, his attention riveted to the dryer window. It made no difference to Kirsten. His delivery of his lines had been wooden, and disrupting such a traditional ritual of young, broke newlyweds seemed a waste of time.

Kirsten plunked her quarters into the cigarette machine. Overtaken by the chant despite her best efforts, she muttered, under her breath, "I see New York, I see Spain, I see Gephard in a lot of pain." She punched the button, relaxing when her brand dropped into the delivery slot in one piece. Ripping the cellophane top off, she shook one out as she glanced at a television screen mounted on a wall.

Fanny Francher, Global Star's own TV personality, was in the middle of an Elvis interview. Kirsten thought the woman had done one with the King only last month, but couldn't be sure. It seemed like the ageless rock star was around, more now that he was dead, especially since he and L. Ron Hubbard had become singing partners. She fumbled in the pocket of her bathrobe, then realized she'd left her lighter in her room. She snarled an oath on her way to the door, startling Doody and his belle, Clara.

"Fanny's had her face lifted three time, you know," Kirsten lied to the couple as she paused in the doorway. "Her bombs would sag to her knees if she hadn't had two Ompa Lompa's implanted in 'em. They use two cameras for each show: one for her body and the other for her head so it won't look so much larger. Hell, she even intimidates Arnold Swartzenager and Sylvester Stallone when she takes her shirt off. This is a big woman I'm talking about. And once you get to know her, she makes even Joan Rivers on a bad day sound like Mother Teresa."

Amazed, Doody turned to Clara and shrugged his shoulders.

"How can you stand to sit there and watch that drivel?" Kirsten demanded. "Well, it's none of my business if you don't mind that TV causes impotence."

Realizing they had been watching the dryer instead, Kirsten stomped out of the laundry in her hiking boots, ignoring the twin screams of horror behind her.

It was raining again, but she ignored it. She decided to write another anonymous letter once she was in her room to Global Star Tonight, demanding that Francher be replaced with someone younger and prettier, like Eleanor Roosevelt or Ed Sullivan. She smiled. She'd be generous this time and mention the possibility that once the station canned Fanny, the woman always had a career waiting for her in professional wrestling, splatterpunk movies, or as Jerry Springer's stand-in. Hell, the directors and producers would save thousands on makeup alone.

Kirsten put her cigarette in her mouth, then realized again she didn't have her lighter with her. Depression settled in on her with the rain. All she wanted out of life was a chance to fill Ace Montana's shoes or Fanny Francher's D-cup Maidenform bra just once. She knew she'd have to settle for filling both with cream of wheat again. She dropped the wet cigarette to the ground and muttered invectives as she jammed her hands in her pockets. With old GetHard running the show, though, she'd always have dibs on the runner-up position. She couldn't exactly sleep her way to the top. "GetHard" was too short to have a top. Unless she found that one story that would break her free from minor assignments and into the big time. She could have made survival wages writing those simpy romance novels for Good HouseKeeper, but being a reporter was in her blood.

"Sister?" a deep voice behind her asked.

She stopped, then turned around slowly, her hands still in her pockets. She was still too angry to be scared. The voice belonged to a bearded young man wearing a long, black trenchcoat and a black, slouch hat. She glared at him through the light rain. "What the hell is it with this town? Do I have nympho written on my forehead?"

"Actually, no," the man said, suddenly acting like he didn't know where to put his hands. "I just thought you looked lonely."

"Yeah, well, I think you look like you want to spend the rest of the night in the Cadence Hospital and Crematorium emergency room. Want to find out how right we are?"

The young man looked at the hiking boots she wore. He crossed himself and pulled nervously at his priest's collar. "Hail Mary," he stammered. He turned and vanished down the narrow walkway between the buildings, his running feet making spatters on the wet sidewalk.

"And my name's not Mary!" Kirsten yelled at his disappearing back. "And you're not my father!"

Kirsten scowled as she turned back to the door of her room. The poor schmuck really hadn't deserved that. It seemed that the angrier she got, the more miserable she was, the more she behaved like Ace. She shivered at the thought. Then, just as she put her hand on the doorknob and fumbled with the key, she heard a dog growl in fright and pain.

Turning around quickly, fisting the keys between her knuckles to protect herself, she saw the dog. The brown and white St. Bernard struggled to pull its leg from the open manhole in the street. It yelped in pain as its other three legs flailed away helplessly, toenails skittering like stones across the street pavement.

Unable to avoid the helpless look in its eyes, Kirsten sighed and started over. Before she could get there, the dog gave a final yowl and disappeared into the hole. Then something in the manhole stripped the bark away.

Not believing what she'd seen, she ran to the edge of the manhole, dropped to her knees, and cautiously peered inside. The raw, dank odor of the sewer pushed into her face. She felt for a moment like she was back in the Uck Nekked on the phone next to the men's bathroom marked The Genghis Can. Tiny rectangles of light glittered across the top of the dark water, outlining her shadowed reflection. Nothing moved. There was no sign of the dog. Feeling her hair prickle at the base of her neck, Kirstened back away.

She hated being wrong, and now she'd been wrong twice. It wasn't a manhole or a person-hole.

It was a Hell hole.

Then a slight smile came to Kirsten. It wasn't just sewage she'd smelled... it was news. She could see the headline already.

"Manhole bites dog."

<hr />

It was summer's eve.

Kirsten set the bottle on the dressing table and sighed. Something smelled in Cadence, but it wasn't her. She picked up the microcassette recorder that all

Global Star reporters carried on assignments. She put it back down and looked out her fly-specked window at the manhole cover in Rat-A-Tat Street. Something made her skin crawl... where the sun didn't shine. She turned the recorder on.

"Kirsten Lane, 10: 12 P.M.., April 13th, Friday, in Cadence, Oregon, Satan's cesspool of Rhythm and Booze. They've probably got a bungalow here with your name on it, Frank. Just for short stays

"I'm on a story here, believe it or not. I just saw something—maybe one of those Moppet horrors Henson created and passed off as puppets—drag a full-grown St. Bernard into a manhole. I just put in a call to Layd—Deputy Whey Layd—but he hasn't had time to get here yet. He's probably at a donut shop eating a drum roll. I'm not going to wait on him.

"Damn, if I'm lucky, this could be as big as the Loch Ness monster... or when John Candy ate John Goodman because Candy wanted to be the bigger star. I wish getting Layd wasn't so hard—getting Deputy Whey Layd, that is. Ah, forget it. It doesn't sound right no matter how you say it. The desk sergeant said Whey was, uh, on his way.

"Anyway, I'm going in after it, Chief, so if this mini-recorder somehow survives, or they find it later in a pile of monster droppings, I want you to know I was there first. My worst nightmare right now is that I'll get eaten alive and Ace will scoop me—literally—out of the monster's gut. Or worse yet, the monster will turn out to be Hanna Montana on a dog meat diet and Francher will get to interview her on television. She'll be remembered for my discovery because nobody ever reads anymore. Maybe I'll find Ren and Stimpy's love nest, on the other hand.

"Expenses are out of my cash, and I do have receipts even though the Bag & Mount It guy at the Convenience and Taxidermy Store didn't understand what I was saying at first: flashlight, four D batteries, Tim Taylor work gloves, a Picasso painter's mask, a bottle of Liz Taylor's perfume—cheap since she went on that onion garlic and limburger cheese diet—William Shatner super-glue and hairspray, E.R. surgical tape, a tin of Moppet bandaids and two lighters that undress Leonard Nimoy when they're turned upside down. Dinner expenses are a bag of chips and a large Pepsi. I ate the chips on the way back from the Bag & Mount It. Also, a new pair of panty-hose. You can't expect me to go monster-hunting in torn nylons. Round it off to say, seventy-five Buck Nekkeds and we'll call it even."

Dressed in Levi jeans with the legs tucked and laced into her hiking boots, a black turtleneck sweater, a dark blue cap, and the new leather work gloves, Kirsten took a deep breath and looked down at the manhole. Person-hole. Hell Hole. A chill thrilled down her spine when she realized it was equally possible that something had replaced the cover. A great, bloated, undead Kermit the Frog?

She gazed down the empty street in both directions and bit her lower lip in frustration. "To hell with it, Kirsten, climb down and get this story before someone beats you to it."

Sitting down beside the manhole gingerly, ready to jump if genetically engineered giant geckos appeared, she pawed through the sackful of supplies she'd purchased at the Bag and Mount It. Thinking the spicy aroma of the few crumbs remaining in the Doritos bag might attract whatever it was that lived in the sewer, she balled it up with the empty Hostess Ding Dongs wrapper and threw it down the street. The wind caught the cellophane ball and rolled it out of sight. For a moment, the only sound on the whole street had been the whispered stuttering of the bags.

She squirted a shot of breath freshener on her tongue. No need to offend whatever writhing mass of festering pestilence lived below. She's learned that from Bob Davis, a reporter on the Star. He'd been assigned to cover suspected cannibalism in the ranks of N.O.W., the National Organization for Women. What he'd found was a Greek Harpy who'd, thankfully, loved his cologne. They'd been married seven years, and had four little songbirds together. Well, songbirds that could only chirp half-notes.

And, it had been a big St. Bernard.

Containing a shudder and cursing her own fear vehemently, she returned to the cars parked in front of the Motel Seven long enough to rip a wiper arm free of a Toyota sedan. It tore loose with a loud squeak of tortured metal, but nobody seemed to notice. She made a hook of the broken arm and dragged the manhole cover back.

Only a lot of darkness seemed to be inside, And the smell. She choked with it, fanning a hand in front of her face as images of the Hanna-Barbera horror movie starring a zombie Flintstone with slavering fangs shot through her mind. The Night of the Living Freds.

She knew the image was ludicrous ... most zombie cavemen practiced very good dental hygiene... gaping facial cavities not withstanding.

"God, Kirsten," she told herself just to hear the sound of a human voice, "You haven't covered zombies since you helped bust that Nursing Home scam in October of last year. And they were only interested in eating Spam the nursing home directors ordered." It had been her coverage of the unusual quantities of

Spam consumed by the residents that had eventually led to the Social Security scam bilking the federal government out of hundreds of thousands of dollars yearly. Luckily, there hadn't been a fight. Once the zombies had been informed of their deaths, they'd gone quietly to the grave, packing Alvin and the Chipmunks lunch boxes of Spam as a final bribe.

She took the painter's mask out, sprayed it liberally with the perfume, then put it on, bending the wire so it fit snugly over her mouth and nose. It reminded her of the time Gephard had assigned her to look for Martian hookers. She'd found them, but it hadn't been a big deal because they'd only been attending a National Quilting Bee. It hadn't been the first second rate story Gephard had sent her on.

Using the surgical tape, she secured the flashlight on top of her left forearm. She put the extra batteries for the flashlight in her over-the-shoulder purse, along with the perfume, tape and extra lighter. Leaving the purse open, she switched on the microcassette recorder so she could talk freely. She took the cap off of the hairspray and held it in her left hand. Shoving the super-glue in her right hip pocket, she carried the other lighter in her free hand.

She took a deep breath, then choked for a moment on the perfume fumes and wiped away the tears. "Now, Kirsten, if you're going to do it, you've got to do it now!" Her voice was muffled by the mask. Approaching the hole, she peered inside. Only darkness was there to be seen. Street lights glinted dully off the rungs of the ladder.

Clamping down on her courage, letting her nose for news lead her even though it was seriously handicapped from the perfume fumes, she stepped down inside the manhole. She shivered in sick anticipation. "Bite me, you son of a bitch, and it'll be the worst mistake you ever made. I'll go down harder than left-over microwave eggplant and peanut butter casserole." When nothing happened, she took another step down. Eight steps later, she was on the narrow ledge beside sluggish water.

The flashlight made a yellow oval as it splashed against the cinder block and mortar walls. Green slime oozed wetly down or up them; Kirsten couldn't decide. Black water marks showed where the water level had risen with flooding in times past. As it was now, the surface was about six inches below the edge of the narrow ledge. The water looked greenish in the flashlight's beam.

So did the heart with an arrow through it scrawled on the wall. Clem Clem and Candy were written in the heart. Kirsten made a mental note never to use that "cymbal" again.

"Damn," she said. She quickly trained the flashlight on the dark tunnel in front of her. The only thing that quelled her stomach was the fact that barfing in the painter's mask sounded even less desirable.

Sticking her arm out, she swept the beam side to side. It fell on a message scrawled on the opposite wall of the sewer. It read: for a good time, call.... but she knew it was a lie. For a teenager or a ninja turtle, Leonardo wasn't all that good.

She squirted the mask with another hit of the perfume. As she coughed and her eyes teared again, the flashlight beam wobbled across the tunnel. The tunnel was at least ten feet wide. Her stomach revolted when she even thought of guessing how deep it might be, or what the dark water might contain. There was no sign of the dog.

Making an arbitrary decision to go upstream, she walked carefully, dodging the white and. gray spiderwebs clinging to the ceiling. It looked like Peter Parker had had diarrhea. The water lapped at the sides like a slow-moving ocean. Pausing for a moment, she turned back around and shined the flashlight at the manhole. It was every bit of seven feet from the ledge to the opening. She shivered inside the turtleneck when she realized even if the thing hadn't been that tall, it had at least a seven-foot reach. Anything with arms that long had to be gigantic, like the huge octopus in 20,000 Leagues Under the Sea.

Or like Ace Montana on a date.

She stumbled over a loose rock and almost fell in, screaming as she flailed her arms wildly. Then she found her balance and leaned back into the cinderblock wall with both arms flattened out beside her, breathing heavily. The softness of the spiderwebs settled. over her face. She used an arm to brush them away, cursing loud enough to wake the dead, then hoped she hadn't.

She went on, moving slower now, realizing the shadows left by the flashlight could trick her into believing footing was more sure than it really was.

The tunnel split into a 'T' less than a moment later. She took the left branch because taking the right would have meant crossing over and she hadn't figured out how to do that. The sign pointing right for the Uck Nekked didn't hamper her decision either.

Peering around the comer cautiously, she found only more green-slimed walls waiting for her. Graffiti had diminished dramatically, so she knew that few had ever traveled this far before her... and Clem Clem. She deduced this from his message: Clem Clem was here here.

The tunnel dimensions were so close to the same that she couldn't tell if there were any difference. A rhythmic sound came from in front of her. For a moment, she had wild visions of Miss Piggy creeping unseen toward her with slavering snout and four inch high spiked heels. She could envision the headline Gephard would write: Reporter killed by PMS Porker. Just as she was getting ready to flee back down the way she had come, Kirsten spotted the dripping portion of the ceiling to the right.

Breathing a sigh of relief, she lowered the can of hair spray and the lighter. She tip-toed through the sewer, surprised and almost overcome by the lively breeze that came from behind her now. She applied more perfume and controlled her stomach. Trying to picture the Oregon state map she'd left in the defunct Pinto, she guessed that Cadence was close enough to the coast for the sewers to eventually connect there. Maybe the wind was coming in off the sea through one of the filtering plants.

Tearing spider webs away with her gloved hand, she went on, trying to psyche herself up for whatever lay ahead by thinking of the look that would be on Ace's face when she scooped him, assuming he could grasp the concept. The office joke unexpectedly flashed into her mind. What do you call a mole on Ace's butt?

A brain tumor.

Without warning, the tunnel ended.

Kirsten came to a stop ten feet away, shining the flashlight beam on the dulled gray cinderblock wall that loomed in front of her. The collection of spider webs was even more severe along the wall, looking like fog gathered at the juncture of the wall and ceiling. There was no graffiti. The water continued unabated under the wall, rolling out with little bits of... little pieces surfacing three or four feet in front of it.

"Damnit," Kirsten said with feeling. She glanced at the dark water swirling around the wall. "No way am I getting in there. You wouldn't find Sam Donaldson in that.... that stuff, and you damn sure won't find me..."

A soiled, sodden toupee floated sluggishly past her feet. Inside its lining, she could make out the words: Property of ABC.

Her words were lost in awe. She removed her cap and bowed her head in respect for a fellow, albeit lesser, fallen 'journalist'.

Her flashlight beam had found a four inch in diameter pink disk stuck to the wall. It was a giant Airwick stick-up. Now she knew the things must be female, which meant there was hope they were intelligent.

Noticing a slight discoloration, she played her beam across the tunnel walls, then over the blocking wall again. Cautiously, she moved forward. "Must be female," she repeated to herself, "because Elton John uses potpourri." She eyed the huge air freshener. Angry, fat-bodied spiders wadded up the webs as some of them hit the dark green water. "This wall is new." She examined the mortar closer. "This mortar's even a different color than the old stuff The only reason anyone would wall up a sewer is to hide something! Barney Frank? The Teenage Mutant Ninja Republicans? Geraldo Rivera?"

She scoured her hand across the cinder blocks, creating dust clouds that got in her eyes. A strange, trembling vibration ran the length of the wall. It hummed like machinery in one way, but different in another.

"Like a cat purring," Kirsten said, realizing of what the humming reminded her. "Is that what's down here? Some giant Sylvester that eats Chihuahuas? If that's how this stacks up, I've got a dynamite headline for my Pulitzer-winning, front page story, Chief.

Cat On a Hot Zen Woof.

Something big splashed in the sewer.

She stepped back and fell as she tripped over something that gave way beneath her weight with a loud crack. The flashlight tore loose from her arm but she hung onto the hair spray and lighter. The smell from the water seemed stronger at ground level. Her stomach heaved convulsively, bringing up the taste of Ranchflavored Ding Dongs and Hostess chocolate-covered Doritos. Gritting her teeth, she kept it down and struggled to her knees.

The flashlight was easy to find in the darkness. But she didn't expect the grinning skull.

"Oh, damn." She reached for the flashlight, unable to tear her attention away from the small skull. It was tiny, like a child's, colored a mottled ivory in the yellow glow of the flashlight. The small, pointed teeth were her second clue. The little, silver disc gave it away. She picked up the flashlight and played it around the immediate area. Bones littered the dirt-covered floor. Big bones and little bones, cracked bones, splintered bones, and whole bones, formed a mosaic of skeletons. Some looked old while others gleamed wetly, as if they had just been deposited there. She whistled softly, holding the skull in the palm of her hand.

"Alas, poor Lassie, they've done you foul," Kirsten whispered softly.

Metal bits flashed in her beam. Trembling, but unable to walk away, realizing Lassie would never come home, Kirsten picked some of them up. She held them, reading the raised letters on the different colored discs. They held a litany of names: Fido, Sparks, Morris, Garfield, Mouser, Joan Rivers, There was also information regarding vaccination. Two collars listed home addresses. Joan's listed her phone number. Metal caught fire under Kirsten's beam as she played the flashlight around.

"Damn, Chief, whatever lives down here has eaten at least a hundred cats and dogs. Wait, here's something else." She reached through a large rib cage that was surprisingly intact and pulled the object up. "Oh, my God, Frank, it's a kids shoe, a Nike tennis shoe, size five." She searched frantically for any sign of a child's skeleton, but found nothing except cat and dog bones, and skeletons of a few large mice. One of these skulls wore a blue, floppy cap. There was an odd, three-fingered glove.

"And apparently has gone south," whispered the infobabe.

Kirsten sat in the middle of the heap of bones and fished out a saggy pack of

Lucky Jr. Strikes. Thank God they weren't those unfiltered Camels Ace smoked all the time. The last thing she needed was to be beaten even to the sewers of Cadence by her rival and sometimes lover. But it meant someone else knew about whatever it was that was eating cats and dogs, little boys, mice (live and animated), and maybe even birds. She hoped she wouldn't stumble on mutilated pieces of little birds.

She hated shredded tweet.

When the dark green water suddenly sluiced up over the edge of the ledge, she realized the last thing she needed was to be eaten by the Spawn of Godzilla. She wondered if atheists even believe in Godzilla. Zilla sounded silly.

The stress was getting enormous. The second wave of stinking water spilled across her hiking boots. She grabbed for the flashlight, losing the can of hair spray somewhere in the darkness, and got to her feet.

Some kind of activity was taking place on the other side of the wall. The purring filled the static air, becoming audible now as it rose and fell in ululating waves. White water churned up in front of the wall.

Kirsten trained her beam on the seething action just in time to catch the St. Bernards head as it came bobbing to the surface. "Beethoven! " she yelled as she got her feet into motion. The flashlight jerked and whipped across the walls as she ran, making it hard to keep sight of the ledge.

Behind her, she was sure she heard the plop-plop-plop of wet, webbed feet, but she was afraid it would catch her if she turned to look. She had no desire to be sucked dry by a vampiric Donald Duck. She tripped and fell, getting green slime all over the front of the turtleneck before she could get to her feet. She ran harder, cursing her smoking habit as her lungs rebelled.

The plop-plop-plop sounded closer. She thought she heard a hungry hiss, wondering if the Pillsbury Dough Thing could eat a whole St. Bernard and still want a skinny reporter for dessert. She had seen it eat a hot cross nun once. When she caught sight of the ladder leading up to the manhole, she threw the flashlight over her shoulder, hoping it would slow the thing down. Then she had her hands on the railings and pulled herself up, screaming, "Car 54! Where Are You! "

Before she reached the street, darkness blotted out the street light and strong arms snared her wrists. She fought, kicking and snarling and screaming, as she was snatched out of the manhole.

"Hey, pilgrim," a male voice said. "Hold on. You're okay. Just simmer down."

A second later, Kirsten realized her nose was resting against the Deputy Sheriffs badge—a tiny, silver cymbal. Still dangling from her wrists, her feet well above the ground, she looked up into Deputy Whey Layd's handsome face.

"It's a good thing your name isn't Deputy Garfield. You'd be kibble by now!"

Layd looked puzzled. "Was that statement cymbolic?"

"No! I was almost killed and eaten by a damn cat eating monster!" But she knew her concern fell on deaf ears, for in a clash of minds, Deputy Layd was one cymbol short.

He looked like Curley Joe of the Three Stooges in his most famous role, The Postman Always Knucks Twice.

"I'm here to report a monster," Kirsten Lane said to the Deputy manning the desk at the Percussion County Sheriff's Office. It was 7:43 a.m. the following Saturday morning. She felt washed out from the lack of sleep, the long walk in the rain the previous evening, and the incident in the sewer tunnels. She was also unhappy she was going to miss the kid's block of programming on the Global channel. She loved the rock 'n roller, Prince, and tried never to miss his animated show, The New Adventures of The Artist Formerly Called Talented.

"I'm Kirsten Lane."

The Deputy glanced up from the rows of empty blocks on his crossword puzzle. He placed a thick, beefy hand under his lantern jaw as he regarded her. His name tag read: Moe Sheckles.

"Kinda early to be reportin' a monster, don't you think, little lady?" He talked slowly, but went on before she could answer. "Th' Sheriff, now, he don't usually allow no reportin' of monsters or crawdad's or scary stuff 'till at least after nine. And what do you want us to do, ma'am? Step on the big ole' hairy spider?"

A Deputy eating chop suey with tiny drumsticks from a soggy, paper container guffawed loudly at the other end of the desk, but didn't turn around. The advertisement on the sack for the Rean Cuisine Restaurant featured a gap-toothed Chineses man in a cowboy hat.

Keeping her anger in check, Kirsten shifted the heavy bundle of papers under her arm. "I called, Mr. Shingles. I made an appointment with the desk sergeant."

Sheckles smiled tolerantly and raked a big thumb through a stack of multi-colored message memos. "We don't have no desk sergeant, ma'am, but we do have a couple of old safes mounted in th' back. Hard to separate 'em, in fact. But at least they're doing safe sex!!!"

The Deputy eating chop suey fell to the floor, doubled over in laughter.

"Very funny," scowled Kirsten. "You're a regular Barney Fife."

"N-now, we d-do have," stuttered the cop between his own bouts of laughter, "a dispatch officer. H-he wears dis, hehehe patch on his shirt front!! Get it?!? Dispatch!".

"That's who I talked to." The front door opened and two men with swarthy skins walked in, talking in a language that sounded familiar. Without turning around, Kirsten watched their reflection in the window of the Sheriff's private office. The two men stood in the entrance talking and gesticulating. Recognizing one of them as Barabajagal from the Bag and Mount It, she raised the lapel of her Chicago Cubs windbreaker and turned away from them. "Look I'm kind of in a hurry, Mr. Chuckles."

Sheckles nodded. "Yes, ma'am, I expect a lady reportin' a big ole' monster would be right hurried like." He flipped through the message memos. "Do you know who you talked to, Miss Lame? And was it before your third quart and after your second of Johnnie Walker?"

"Boink, I think. I talked to him the first time when I was trying to get Layd."

"Ma~am?" Sheckles looked up suddenly, reaching into his pocket for a match stick and putting it in his mouth. When he realized he was sucking his car keys instead, he snatched them away.

"Deputy Whey Layd," Kirsten said with a belligerent glare, daring the man to say anything else, her stress building. "You know, two can play your game. Do you know what you call two identical door bells that no longer bing bong?"

"Huh?"

"Dead ringers. Like you and Chop Suey Barney over there. Two losers like you who no longer ring any woman's chimes."

"Yes, ma'am. He turned back to his stack of messages, obviously perturbed at her joining in their joke fest. "We don't have no Boink working here, but we do have a Peabody."

"That's him." Kirsten shifted the stack of newspapers on her hip, feeling at any moment they were going to slip and fall and call attention to her. Once Barabajagal recognized the reporter, things could get really dicey with the cops. The monster in the sewer would become the least of her immediate concerns.

"Yes, ma'ma I've got your messages right her, Miss Vain."

"My name is Kirsten Lane. I am not Vain."

"If you excuse my saying it, you do wear a bit too much makeup fer my taste, ma'am."

The Mount It store clerk and his companion drew nearer to the desk. The need to tell bad jokes rose with her stress. Barabajagal's voice was indignant. His reflection in the window showed bandages on two of his fingers. The other Deputy talked to them briefly, then turned to Sheckles. "Got a man here wanting to report a robbery with battery complaint."

Sheckles sighed, reached under the counter, and pulled up a clipboard containing official forms. "If you'll excuse me, I got some business to tend to, Miss Pain."

"Sure thing, Deputy Shingles," Kirsten replied, "I'll just stand here and pray you get a clue." She stared at the reflection of the two men in the window. She had the Cubs windbreaker pulled up to her temple and her neck scrunched down, wondering how the hell she was going to hide her hair color.

Sheckles looked at her suspiciously. "Got something wrong with you, Miss Tang?"

"Not me, but do you know what you call a door bell with its cover off?"

"Uh .... "

"A ring bare-er." The jokes were getting worse. "Is there a bathroom in here? I've got some medication I can take."

"Over there." The Deputy hooked a thumb over his shoulder indicating a door with the image of Britney Spears on it.

Kirsten went in that direction, letting the windbreaker drop only after she'd passed Sheckles. Starting to step around a Deputy leaning down to the water cooler in the hallway, Kirsten said, "Damned idiot."

The Deputy at the fountain rose up suddenly, gazing at her as he brushed water out of his mustache with blunted fingertips. He looked like someone had cobbled him together from knotty pine four-by-fours and not bothered to knock away the rough edges. He was the typical redneck who couldn't count that high so never bothered about fourplay. The mirror sunglasses gave her no idea at all what was going through his mind.

"Ma'am?" he asked, and tossed three coins in the fountain.

"What?" Kirsten stopped, physically and mentally, not knowing how to deal with the unexpected situation. "Did you address me?"

"Not unless you're a letter, ma'am," the Deputy grinned and touched the front lip of his cowboy hat in defference. "I just wondered what you wanted."

Taking a quick glance at the man's nameplate and seeing Dan Ashwhole there, Kirsten shifted her stack of newspapers again, trying in vain to find a more comfortable position for them. She used her voice of authority, mustering the business tone Gephard used at his conferences with his reporters. She jerked a thumb over her shoulder. "Moe Sheckles said you could tell me where the Sheriff is, Ashwhole."

The Deputy took his sunglasses off, breathed on them, then wiped them clean. "Don't have a desk sergeant. That there's Sheckles."

"Moe power to 'em, Ashwhole. But he was busy. Somebody just arrived with a robbery and battery complaint."

"Oh, you must be the new job applicant. Nobody else would know the difference between assault and battery."

Her experience had taught her to go with the flow rather than tamper with any perception that worked in her favor.

"Yep, that's me, Ashwhole." The stress was about to burst a blood vessel.

"I've seen women deputies before," Dan admitted, "but none of them as little as you."

"Hey, good things come in small packages. The only difference between me and Arnold Schwartznegger is one hundred pounds of muscle and a dress."

"But you aren't wearin' a dress, ma'am."

"I know. I'm also an ex-Shaolin ninja, drive the Daytona 500, pro wrassel, and love to shoot people. You might say I'm a Jill of all trades."

Ashwhole pushed his cowboy hat back with a gnawed thumb. "You ain't from Percussion County, are you, Jill?"

"What gave it away," she answered without missing a beat. "The fact that I have all my own teeth?"

"That capped it. But, no, you just don't talk with the native rhythm. And down here, it's unusual for women to shoot people. Most of them prefer stabbin'."

"And I'd love to talk that talk some more, but I have to see the Sheriff. Where can I find him, Deputy Ashheap?"

Ashwhole pointed down the hall. "In the pokey. Take the door down to the left."

"Pokey? Isn't that a, er, little hokey?"

"That's right. We name all our cells. The Hokey Pokey. The Slow Pokey. Pokey and Bess... that's in the women's section."

Kirsten stopped at the door and gave him a more friendly smile. "By the way. I'm Danielle Wesson."

Recognition spread across the Deputy's broad features. "Hey, you any kin to...?"

"He's my uncle."

"Tell him I said he makes a hell of a corn oil," Ashwhole said, patting the thirty-two ounce bottle in his holster with affection.

"I will, Deputy Ashwhole."

"I use it to grease the palms of my squeelers all the time."

"That's wonderful, and let's be careful out there." Kirsten pushed on through the door as Ashwhole gave her a quick salute. Kirsten regretted her close encounter of the right kind. They'd have been great together if he hadn't been so oily or so Charmin.

———— ❦ ————

Ammonia and stale sweat kicked her in the face as the door closed behind her. Holding cells lined the back wall of the building. At least a dozen male prisoners slept or lounged behind the bars. A lean man in overalls with a cigarette dangling from his lips and another behind his ear pushed a mop across the brick floor with no enthusiasm.

The little chalk board on the wall next to the cell read: Pokey and Beans.

Sheriff Cole Slaugh stood in front of a duty roster written in crayon hanging on the wall behind the desk to Kirsten's left. The lawman was pushing sixty hard, with a pot belly that stretched his tan uniform shirt. Short cotton-white hair stood up in short peaks like whipped meringue. A long-barreled pistol in a worn and scarred holster that looked uncomfortable to sit on hung from his belt. Yet, the way it was positioned—like the Duke had worn his—the man couldn't have had any other choice. As she approached, the man in the holding cells whistled appreciatively and Slaugh took a pair of reading glasses from his shirt pocket. She sat the copies of the back issue of the Cadence Beat newspaper on the desk.

"Sheriff Cole?" Kirsten asked, extending a hand. "You're quite the side order, ain't ya, honey? Sorta makes me hungry for pulled pork!"

"Actually, I'm a tad hot, ma'am " Slaugh said without turning from his surveillance of the duty roster. "Deputy Pork is on vacation rat now."

Kirsten held out her hand. "I'm Kirsten Lane, with the Global Star newspaper." She saw no recognition of the newspaper's name in his eyes. "And there's a terror in your toilets."

"Damn. We just can't seem to keep them dogs out of there! Last week, it was a poodle, the week before, a shitzu." Slaugh turned to face her, pulling his glasses down far enough for him to peer over. He had watery blue eyes that seemed to have faded with the decades.

"Not a terrier. A Terror. Like Opray Winfrey doing a spred for Playboy." Kirsten extended her hand again. "Or for anybody, for that matter." Kirsten's grin faded and she withdrew her ignored hand."You never heard of Opray, have you? Sheckles sent me over."

"Sheckles, eh. Did you know he was raised in one of our local cat houses?"

"Well... no, but..."

"Yep. Sheckles is a brothel sprout."

Laughter erupted from the cells. Kirsten realized that Slaugh enjoyed his captive audience, but only to a point. Slaugh yelled out "SHUT UP!!" with a voice like thunder. The prisoners did so instantly. Apparently, an order of Cole Slaugh was serious business.

"I'd like to know what the Cadence police plan to do about Rodan in your sewers."

"Myself, I'd use a shotgun," shouted an unseen prisoner, "on a Turd of Prey."

Kirsten didn't laugh. Slaugh sat a haunch, the one without the gun strapped to it, on the desk, and punched an out-dated intercom. "Shecky?" His eyes never left Kirsten. "Did you direct a young lady back here to bother me?"

"A redheaded, skinny little bone of a thing, Slaugh? Called herself Kandy Cane"

Inwardly, Kirsten seethed, but she didn't let any of it show. "I'm a woman, full growed," she said. "My name is Kirsten Lane."

"This is her," Cole said. "She's the one that got Layd in Cadence last night."

The prisoners broke up laughing, whistling loudly and cheering. After his point of appreciation, Cole yelled: "Shut Up!!"

The Sheriff didn't crack a smile. "That'll be all, Shecky. Cole released the intercom button. "Hope you'll ignore his remark, ma'am. New recruit. Shecky's green." Cole folded his reading glasses and put them away. "Speaking bluntly, I don't have time to have my men stepping on spiders for cute little lassies."

"That's a pretty weak excuse," Kirsten said. "Couldn't be you won't help me because of what Cadence police and the Keds people have in common."

"Huh?" drawled Cole.

"Dozens and dozens of loafers."

Cole glared at her. "Well, I reckon we could canvas th' area. Just to show you our sole's in the right place." He smiled at his own puns.

"Bigfoot is living in the sewers of this town," Kirsten said, "and it's eating every dog and cat in Cadence." She unfolded the top newspaper. "Look at this. Pages and pages, issue after issue of people who have lost pets here. Iguanas. Ferrets, boa constrictors, and even trophy wives have all turned up as missing in the want ads."

"Boa constrictors?" the Sheriff repeated. "Who the hell would keep a boa constrictor?"

"That Indiana Kid, Sheriff," one of the prisoners said. "He's that fourteen-year old punk with the fake name."

"I know, I know who Joe Indiana is," Cole said, wiping the back of his neck with a handkerchief. "That boy blew up the outhouse the Historical Society was preserving in Cadence last year."

"What are you going to do about it?" Kirsten asked.

"There wasn't anything I could do about it," the Sheriff insisted. "The boy is a minor, and there wasn't nothing left of that outhouse but toothpicks. Wasn't the biggest thing that ever hit Cadence," said Cole. "That'd be the day th' whole town turned out to see Pope Bruce."

"I remember Pope Bruce," said Kirsten. "He never could decide whether he was divine or just gorgeous."

"That there'd be a bad habit, alright," added an unseen prisoner.

"I gotta admit, I like him a whole lot better when he was just cock sure," Slaugh drawled. "But that's a Southern Fried Baptist for ya."

"What are you going to do about the thing in your sewers?" Kirsten tried to redirect the conversation back to her problem. "You can't just ignore it and hope it goes away."

"Nope, and I don't expect that's gonna work on you today, either, Ms. Cane." Cole shifted uncomfortably on the desk.

The door opened and a Deputy escorting an attractive middle-aged woman in cotton pajamas with sewed in feet and Curb Service printed on her chest stepped through.

"And what is that?" asked Kirsten.

"Just the hotest thing to hit Cadence since that cursive A on Sesame Street undressed and created Script Tease." The Sheriff looked up, crossing his arms over his barrel-chest. "You been hawkin' again, Sadie?"

The woman gave him a radiant smile. "Sadie hawkin' days? Not me, Mr. Cole, sir. Sadie is a class act." She turned around. On the pajama flap over her butt was printed: No Shoes, No Shirt, No Slut.

More catcalls issued from the prisoners, followed by gales of laughter and assorted bird calls.

"Shut Up!"

"Might give a girl a warning next time you hire a Deputy. And such a cute one at that." She reached down to pinch the Deputy's left cheek, starting a crimson flush that covered the upper ones. "Makes a girl almost not care about getting Layd to arrest her."

"Leave that boy alone, Sadie," Cole ordered in a fatherly tone. "Vance, get her in a cell away from those animals."

"Yes, sir, Sheriff. " The Deputy took the woman by the arm. She leaned on him like they were at a prom dance, sighing theatrically. The other prisoners cheered her on as the Deputy colored.

"It's eaten hundreds of animals. Even a Chia pet," Kirsten went on. "I found a child's shoe in there." She dug in her purse and produced the Nike in a plastic sandwich bag. When the Sheriff didn't take it, she dropped it with a thump to the desktop.

Looking at the tennis shoe, Cole thumbed the intercom. "Shecky."

"Yes, sir, Sheriff."

"Get me Layd in here."

"Yes, sir, Sheriff. You want th' whip or whipped cream this time?"

Sadie turned around, halfway into her cell. "Why, Sheriff, you naughty boy," she said in a bad Mae West impression. She dipped to reveal considerable cleavage and a tiny tattoo of Visa, MasterCard and American Express cards. "You know I give discounts to Piece officers?"

Kirsten stepped in front of the Sheriff. "Listen to me. Layd didn't see it last night."

Cole looked at her. "Did you?"

"No, not exactly."

"What the hell does 'not exactly' mean?"

"It means I dont have to see God to know that She's real," Kirsten replied. "It means I'm intelligent enough to see the bone pile Its been making in the sewer, and I'm wondering what It's going to eat next." She picked up the tennis shoe and dropped it meaningfully.

Angrily, Cole stabbed a finger at the intercom. "Sheckles, who's working missing kids right now?"

"Taco Bueno, mostly, but I think a few have been hired over at McDonald's, Sheriff."

"No, you idiot. Who's looking for missing kids!"

"Uh, er, Woody Allen??"

"I think it's Childs, Sheckles. Deputy Julius Childs. Send him in?"

"I think he's out getting Layd in the motor pool."

Sadie's high-pitched cackle punctuated the roar of laughter from the prisoners.

Releasing a tense breath, the Sheriff said, "Get him in here. And, Shecky? Let's use Deputy Layd's first name from now on, shall we?"

"You want to see this Barabajagal guy," asked the Deputy, "about that Cadence convenience store robbery and battery? His description matches the one that trucker gave us about the naked woman he picked up hitchhiking, the one what broke his finger."

"Give me ten seconds, then send him on in."

"Can't do, Sheriff. Th' trucker can only count up to nine..."

Kirsten reached into her purse for a cigarette and was about to light it when the Sheriff harumphed for her attention. He pointed to the No Smokey Pokey sign on the wall. Wondering if anything could make matters worse than no smoking and the store clerk about to enter the room, she put her cigarette and lighter away. Then she saw Clem Clem tossing restlessly on one of the cell bunks. She turned her back on the cells.

A lanky, bald Deputy wearing a black Stetson cowboy hat that had slid slightly askew walked into the room. "I'd have been here sooner, Sheriff, but I was out getting Layd."

"Why don't you arrest him, too?" sneered Sadie. "Or is it just women getting Layd that offends you, Sheriff Cole?"

Loud whistles, gay slurs, and raucous shouts shook the room.

Kirsten saw Cole was ignoring the reaction of the prisoners with increased difficulty. "Have we got any missing kids reports cooking, Julius?"

"No, sir, Sheriff. Not since Joe Indiana come home from his little three-day jaunt."

"Thank you, Childs," the Sheriff answered. "That'll be all." He picked the slime-encrusted tennis shoe up from the desk and tossed it back to Kirsten.

Kirsten put the shoe in her purse, "Is it worth jeopardizing the people of Cadence just because you doubt my word? I'm telling you, Sheriff, there's something carnivorous living in the sewers."

"There's a carnival in town? Look, lady, I don't care if Ralph Cramden is back living in the sewers, long as he don't stop up the plumbing. I'm familiar with that rag paper you write for. I canceled my subscription when it broke the story about Dolly Parton's sex-change operation. There's somethings a man would rather not know. But, if there was a monster living in one of my towns, I think I would know about it. So, just go find some other way to peddle yer papers."

"How do you explain all those bones? Layd saw those."

"Probably the refuse from our wiener factory. Biggest employer in Cadence, and famous too. You've probably heard their motto: You Can't Beat Our Wienies."

There was an audible sob from the cells.

The Sheriff shrugged. "Or maybe it's where the dogs and cats all go to die. Like one of them elephant graveyards."

"Sheriff, that's the weakest reasoning I've ever heard. You can believe in a sacred doggie graveyard, but not in a bone cracking, slime sucking, twelve-eyed…"

Deputy Layd walked through the door, escorting the truck driver who had his hand in a cast, and Barabajagal, who carried his bandaged fingers cradled across his chest.

Kirsten halted in mid-objection, staring at the two men. "…imaginary beast, created by the hysteria of a redheaded, skinny little bone of a thing?"

"I'll have Layd escort you out," the Sheriff said.

"I know the Whey. I'll see myself out," Kirsten answered, lifting her windbreaker to cover her face. "And thanks for all the typical male 'help'. It was about as useful as the nipples on your chest."

She stormed out of the room, giving Layd and the two injured men a wide berth, seeing only their feet beneath the edge of the windbreaker.

"I did not understand that she only wanted the receipts, Sheriff," Barabajagal said in heavily accented English. "Then, when I did, she insisted on more receipts than she had coming. Naturally, I had to resist her. That is when she bit my hand. And she never paid for the things she got."

Thinking the clerk had learned to talk better English awfully damn fast since last night, Kirsten scurried through the door and down the hall. It was undeniable the incident in the sewers had shaken her, even disturbing her dreams, the image from those nightmares still haunting her. The little man in the sewer in the little boat. The swirling, blue waters. Gurgling water sounds.

The little man's screams as he was sucked down a tidy bowl.

"Hey, Miss Lane, slow down."

Fearing the worst, Kirsten paused at the door, ready to bolt the instant anyone pointed an accusing (unbroken) finger at her. But she couldn't bolt. She had no nuts. It was an old Montana joke that intruded on her fear.

Deputy Whey Layd trotted over to her side. "Hey, I figured out what must have gone on back there. I tried to warn you last night that Sheriff Cole wouldn't have no truck with it."

She made her voice softer than it wanted to be. "I know, and I appreciate that, but I had to try." She couldn't help noticing how handsome was Whey. She wondered if he was a Kurd. It would be a very attractive combination. But that joke had been done.

"I still want you to call me if you need me," Layd said. "Don't be put off by what the Sheriff says. Under that gruff exterior..."

Kirsten felt like grabbing him by the shirt front and dragging him out to the back seat of the cab parked at the curb. Then Clem Clem came staggering through the door from the cell block, hitching his jeans up around his skinny hips. Desire melted.

"I'll call you if anything comes up," she said as she pushed through the door. "You do the same," she added hopefully.

——— ⊶⊷ ———

Kirsten pictured Gephard sitting behind his desk on a telephone book playing solitaire. That seemed appropriate since Gephard thought foreplay was a bridge hand. He must have answered her call while in the middle of a conversation with someone. She liked what she heard him say.

"... can you separate the women from the girls in a gay bar... With a crowbar! Hahaha Fanny keeps one in her trunk!"

Kirsten had only received one message at the hotel in her absence. The desk clerk had written it on a bar napkin from the Uck Nekked; Uck Nekked was misspelled. The message was from Frank Gephard. She returned the call from her room, changing clothes as she did so. "Frank, it's Kirsten," she interrupted sharply.

"Where the hell have you been?" the Global Star editor demanded, "We'll talk later, Alucard."

"With the local police," she said, pulling on a Kansas Jayhawks sweatshirt. Gephard signed. "What kind of trouble are you in this time?"

"None." Yet, Kirsten reminded herself silently, remembering the close calls she'd had at the Sheriffs office. "In fact, the Sheriff asked me to help him with an investigation he's been conducting." She pulled on a pair of ragged jeans.

"Kirsten, if you're in trouble, you've got to level with me. I've already got the bail bondsman standing by."

"I'm not."

"You expect me to believe the Sheriff asked you to help him with an investigation? He think you're Angela Lansbury?"

Kirsten sat down on the bed to pull on her hiking boots, cinching them up tight. She gagged with the smell that clung to them along with the green slime.

"What's wrong? Are you sick? And did you call collect? Answer the last question first."

"No, Im fine. Just a little nausea. And I did dial 10-10 CHEAP."

"Damn. You're pregnant. That's all I need, a Goodtime Blimp for a reporter. I can tell you right now, there's no way in hell you're going to get a desk job out of me."

"It's GoodYEAR, Chief, and I'm not pregnant. The world doesn't need another munchkin." Literally she added in her head. In his younger days, he'd already populated half of the Land of Oz. She looked in the mirror as she tied her hair back in a pony tail, then folded it under her Texas Rangers baseball cap. She reached for the leather gloves. "And that desk job thing. Isn't that similar to the position a guy holds who makes glass jars? A blow..."

"Kirsten! A nun of my professional stature isn't used to this kind of treatment."

"There is nun-such. Say, Chief, do you know what they call a guy who makes shot glasses?" When he did not bite, Kirsten unwrapped the flashlight she'd just purchased from a local department store.

"So, who was the bail bondsman you were going to aim in my direction?" Kirsten put the flashlight in her purse. She shoved the tube of super-glue into her pants pocket, "Like there's a jail that'd hold me since I interviewed Houdini's ghost?"

"Hog the Bounty Hunter."

"Damn, Chief, I thought Global Star had dropped him when they blew the Doctor Kavorkian thing. Didn't he swear they'd bring the Doc in over his dead body, and they did?"

"They had the low bid."

"The only kind you can reach; check. Never mind those Nazis tried to shoot me the last time they got anywhere near me. Only reason they missed was because I bent over to...er ... tie Ace's shoe."

"That's because you'd jumped bail. One of the clauses in their contract stipulates that they have the right to use any force they deem necessary to make sure you're there for your court date. And they didn't try to shoot you. They specialize in hog-tying."

"My 'court date' was with Judge Waffler, remember? The only TV judge who uses canned laughter."

"He is a highly respected judge."

"Everyone is highly respected when you're three feet tall, Chief." She paused to let it sink in. "So, why did you call?"

"I've got a plane ticket waiting for you at the Green Acres Memorial Airfield. You're booked on Knight Airlines."

"Kirsten lit a cigarette and rocked back and forth on her bed. "So, I'll fly by Knight from Cadence to L.A.?"

"Not exactly. Billings, Montana. I've lined you up for an interview with a rancher who claims Hillary Clinton's teeth pick up Rush Limbaugh's radio show."

"Forget it, Frank—there's no story there. And this could be the biggest story since they cloned Red Skelton because a mime is a terrible thing to waste. There's some kind of monster loose in the sewers of this town. It's already eaten hundreds of dogs and cats, " Kirsten saw the remains of the green-slimed tennis shoe in the baggie on the bed. "And one child that we know of."

"So what, Kirsten? We found teenage talking turtles in our sewers."

"A child, Frank." She fell silent, knowing from experience that not saying anything would be more convincing to Gephard than anything she could say.

"Was it a... big child?"

She remained silent, grinning at her reflection in the mirror because she could hear the tone of his voice change, signalling his slide over to belief

"Kirsten, you once told me that John Candy was a bathroom confection. "

"This is a Creature Feature. Front page, above the fold monster. Pulitzer Prize."

"An honest-to-God for real monster?" Gephard chuckled with the enthusiasm of a child given free run of a toy store. "The public eats that kind of crap up. Thank you, Lord, thank you, thank you, thank you. What kind of monster? Frankenstein? Cthulhu? Big Foot? Rosie O'Donnell?"

"It's a big one. Green scales and fangs are about all I can tell you now."

"Hot damn! Now we're cooking! When do you expect...?"

"Hey, sorry, Chief, but the Sheriff just pulled up outside and I've got to go." Kirsten hung up the receiver and ignored the sudden urge to call up Fanny

Francher to gloat. Clad in her sewer gear for the day, she shouldered her purse and wrapped the strap of the new digital camera around her wrist. There was one more stop she had to make before she staked out the manhole.

She'd have to meet her foe on neutered ground.

———⊕⊕⊕———

Kirsten Lane, 10:22 a.m., April 14th, Saturday, waiting by the monster's den in Cadence, Oregon. I know you're excited, Chief, so am I. I want a cover out of this one when I get the pictures. But, I'm here to tell you, this story isn't coming cheap.

"Expenses: the cab fare to the Sheriffs office in Cadence is on the company card. I tipped big because I wanted Singh to come anytime I sang no matter what time that was. Additional expenses consist of a new flashlight; I deep-sixed the last one fighting off the thing last night, remember?. And a new can of Don King hair spray, etc. etc.

"Oh, yeah, I had to buy a fat Siamese kitten from Heavy Petting, a store in Cadence. And a fishing pole. You know there's no love lost between myself and any smelly feline, Chief. But, my life depends on this sewer-sucking creature swallowing my bait.

"Hook, line and stinker."

———⊕⊕⊕———

As her flashlight played over the surface of the sewage below, Kirsten thought of her retrospective expose on the Navy of Saddam Hussein, and why the Iraqi had used glass-bottomed boats. They had had to make sure their bombs missed hitting the old Iraqi Navy.

Kirsten sat on a sidewalk atop a pillow she had taken from her motel room. She had removed the manhole cover leading down into the sewer, and a bright noon-day sun poured into it. She held the fishing pole tightly in both hands, staring intently at its line where it disappeared down the manhole. Cars, pedestrians, a bicycle, a boy on a skateboard and a one-legged woman on an inline skate using ski poles passed by, paying no attention to what she was doing. Apparently, no one thought it odd or out of the ordinary to see someone fishing in the sewer in Cadence.

"Item, personal: Do not eat at the Brown Lobster restaurant."

Growing bored, Kirsten lightly yanked on her fishing pole, causing the line to jerk. She was rewarded with a mournful meowing sound rising up pitifully from the blackness of the sewer.

Good. Her bait was still on the line. She felt no remorse for that bait because they were Siamese if you please, and they were Siamese if you don't please. Kirsten knew that it was odd that the independence she hated in cats was also what made Ace, Francher, and herself the best journalists around. But, then, you had to be odd to be a reporter.

Her thoughts were interrupted by the squeal of tires and a car horn. A '72 pickup truck full of rowdy teenagers screeched to a stop at the nearby traffic light. Their whistling and obscene comments were barely audible under the car-shaking music blaring from their radio.

Kirsten had never heard Sinatra belt out Smells Like Teen Spirit. If anything, death had made it easier for him to hit the low notes. Very low.

"How 'bout a Bud light, babe," one pimpled-faced teenaged boy yelled, "I'm Bud, and I'm on a diet!" At least one of those claims was a lie.

"Alight on this, Bud," Kirsten signed his I.Q. with one finger.

The passenger door opened and a rider with spiked hair appeared ready to get out. Then a second boy in the back seat with a huge nose ring pulled him back in and whispered to him, fear obvious on his face. The truck roared to life and drove on.

Suddenly, without warning, her fishing pole bent nearly in half. A mewling scream from below was cut off, and the pole was almost yanked from her hands.

"Holy Jonah," she muttered, staggering to her fed. "It's the Loch Ness monster!"

She pulled back on the pole with all her might, the fishing line squealing with protest. Then it snapped with a loud twang. Kirsten, thrown off balance by the sudden stack, staggered backward and fell on her rump.

Her eyes grew wide as a slimy, yellow-gray tentacle shot up out of the open manhole. It flopped wetly against the pavement, leaving a wet impression. The tentacle arched upward and dropped back into the dark green depths as Kirsten jumped back to her feet.

Another tentacle shot up out of the water with the suddenness of a frog snapping its tongue. As Kirsten stared at the mottled appendage, she experienced a strange, itching sensation. Something about this thing seemed uncomfortably familiar, like a half forgotten bad memory.

She hadn't felt this uneasy since she'd uncovered Ronald Reagan's lingerie collection.

Although the teddy had been nice.

It made no sense, but neither did her climbing down into the sewer. Next to the rungs imbedded in the manhole, someone had hung a book on a string.

Jokes For The John.

Kirsten screamed as the tentacle smacked into the wall by the book. Water splashed over her, reminding her of the painter's mask and perfume in her purse. She triggered the hair spray by instinct as the tentacle wavered up towards the infobabe. The lighter flicked twice before it caught, then she moved the flame up into the path of the hair spray.

The combustible fumes caught at once, creating a barely controllable blowtorch. She took a step, leaned forward, and held the flames to the tentacle.

The yellow-gray skin blackened and flaked away. An almost cat purr escalated into high-pitched dolphin squeals laced with fear. The tentacle drew back into the water with a tremendous splash that deluged Kirsten and put out the makeshift blowtorch.

Tucking the lighter and the hair spray into her purse again, she reached for the camera and switched on the micro-cassette recorder.

"I've got the damn thing on the run. It almost got me, but I've got it on the run," she hissed to herself. She raised the camera and took two shots in quick succession of the wavering mass under the unsettled water. Shoving them in the hip pockets of her jeans, she dodged back as the tentacle flailed again, managing three shots before it dipped back down.

Then it was moving under the surface, running upstream with no more apparent effort than a cloud scuttling across the sky. The shadow flattened and wavered, changing shape dozens of times. She homed in on the blackened spot near its center. There was no longer a tentacle, just the pancake-shaped mass undulating below the surface.

The mass had contained a kind of luminescence, like the greenish glow of a firefly. She was sure that, like the firefly, it gave off no heat even though it gave off enough light for her to find her footing on the ledge.

She dodged around the corner, stumbling for a moment, then finding her balance and going on. The high-pitched squealing hurt her ears. It was a struggle to think. Her finger kept working the button of her camera.

As the mass made its way to the blocking wall, it split into dozens of smaller luminescent pancakes no larger than a yard across. They filed under the new wall in quick order, like silver dollars, taking the keening dolphin-wails with them. And the light.

Kirsten stood in the darkness, suddenly shivering, afraid, and itchy.

"You hurt them," a voice said. "Nice."

Bones snapped and splintered under her hiking boots as she whirled. Kirsten grabbed for the flashlight in her purse. There was a scratching sound, then the flare of a match in the darkness. At first, there was only the image of light around the slouch hat the figure wore, and a glare that revealed the pack of Lucky Strikes Jr.s in his hand. As the hat tilted back, the features came into focus.

"Very nice," said the face. "I've never seen Sourpuss so... well, retractable. "

"Who the hell are you?" Kirsten demanded. "And what's 'Sourpuss'?"

Kirsten realized it was only a boy. Surely, he was no older than sixteen. She turned the flashlight full on his face.

"Name's Cleveland Smith. Do you mind getting that light out of my eyes, honey?"

He blew out the match, dropped it into the stream of sewage, and took a long hit on his cigarette. He blew out a slow circle of smoke for affect. Besides the slouch hat, he wore a khaki shirt with a half-dozen pockets, a brown leather bomber jacket, a thong barely visible above the waistline of his khaki pants, and black boots. A heavy, scarred, Telletubbies backpack dangled by its straps from the crook of his arm.

"Say, you're that Joe Indiana kid that blew up the old toilet," said Kirsten, lowering the flashlight. "And that get-up you're wearing..."

"Like I said, Cleveland Smith's the name, toots. Adventure is my game."

"That's a Cub Scab's uniform. Oh, great. You're in Montana's national fan club, The Boy Scab's of America. And Old Maid is more likely your 'game'"

"Slabs, baby. The club is Boy Slabs. Get yer facts straight, sister."

"Whatever. What did you think you were doing sneaking up on me like that? Working on your sexual harassment badge?"

"Got that already," he said, pointing at a small patch with a beaver on it. "Even got my President Clinton badge, too." The patch featured a cigar.

"Look toots, I didn't sneak up on you. I was already down here when you pulled your fireman-down-the-ladder number." As he talked, cigarette smoke drifted out of his nose and lips. His eyes and the Charlie Brown band-aide on his left cheek remained partially shadowed by the brim of the hat. "You were damn lucky. Sourpuss eats babes like you for lunch."

"At least it's got good taste," Kirsten insisted. "And luck has nothing to do with it. I came prepared."

"Prepared, baby?" Cleveland Smith reached into the backpack and pulled out a small propane hand torch. It caught fire at once, burning bright blue as he adjusted the flow. "Now, this's prepared." He turned it off and put it away. "Who are you, sweetheart."

"Look, junior G-string man, don't get cheeky with me, or I'll give you an Underroo wedgie you'll never forget. Just don't be forgetting who's the adult around here."

"I ain't forgettin' nothin', sugerbeets. Bye the way, that was one of my Sourpusses. I found them first."

Checking for the low-key hum of the micro-cassette recorder in her purse, Kirsten asked, "Those are your things? It figures, with your fixation on outhouses and sewers you'd like being in deep do-do, but..."

"They will be mine as soon as I catch one of them."

Disappointment edged into Kirsten's voice. "Then you didn't whip them up with your Montana Jr. Chemistry Set? What are they?"

"Not me, mommy, er, uh, sweet thang," Cleveland Smith replied, tugging unconsciously at his thong. "And I don't know what they are." He squatted on the ledge and stared into the green depths. "So, what's a loose babe like you doing in a sewer like this?"

"Ms. Kirsten Lane, to you, little boy peep. I'm a reporter with the Global Star, but then I'm sure you've never heard of the world's leading newspaper. Too busy reading Jack and Jill magazine." She didn't join him on the edge of the ledge, thinking Sourpuss might not always glow in the dark. "I even did an article on you Cub Scabs. Testosterone Totts Titillate Topless Trollops."

"How many times I got to tell you it's 'Slabs', lady. We would have been Cub Studs but the juvenile division of the carpenter's union had already copyrighted it. And I never heard of your article. I was busy in Toledo doing vaudeville and supporting my family. I'm the best Thong and Dance man around."

"Well, you do look a little light in the loafers. And, by the way, what's with the empty chest? Where's your merit badge for virginity?"

"I lost it."

His head swiveled on his shoulders, his eyes still masked by the shadow from the brim of the slouch hat. "Toots, I've had three articles published in Tile and Toilet Magazine, and there's a potty fragment I found two years ago that's on display at the Smithsonian. Katie Couric did a 60 Minutes segment on me: Cleveland Jones and the Temple of the Heated Throne. I may be young, but that don't mean I'm unlearned, savvy?" He dropped the butt of the Lucky Jr. into the water and the ember died with a short hiss that filled the tunnel. "I was potty trained at two."

Ignoring his comments, Kirsten inspected the dark stains on his face. It couldn't be beard growth. The kid was just too young. "What's on your face, Cleveland?" She felt an unexpected urge to spit on her fingers and wipe his cheeks. The ones on his face.

Cleveland Smith felt at it with a hand, then examined his fingers. "Five o'clock shadow. I was trying to shave when you started screaming."

"Uh-huh. With a Schick electric pudding-pop. You're about as macho as G.

Gordon Liddy in drag at the Fairy Tale Ball."

Whirling suddenly, dropping to one knee as he scooped a slingshot from his thong, Cleveland Smith clipped two fingers into a pouch there, pulled back the slingshot, and let it fly. Ten feet farther back down the ledge, a rat the size of a terrier jumped convulsively and died. Its feet kicked up toward the ceiling.

"Think whatever you want to, honeypot. It's a free world." He walked along the ledge, grabbed the rat by its hairless tail, and came back.

"What are you going to do with that, Teddie boy?" Kirsten asked.

"Try to find out how bad you hurt Sourpuss." He took a roll of kite string from his Teletubbies backpack and tied it around the rat's neck. He stepped past her, leaning against the wall as he lowered the rat's body into the water.

A moment later, the string jerked taut in his hand. He fought with it, then the tugging stopped. When he pulled it free of the water, only a rat's shiny white skeleton remained.

Slinging the rat onto a pile of bones, he said, "At least they're still hungry. That's a good sign. You probably only scared them."

"What about the one I burned?"

"Sourpuss eat their wounded. Tastes like chicken."

Kirsten swallowed hard, feeling her ham sandwich trying to force its way back up.

"They eat everything," Cleveland Smith said as he dipped his head to light another cigarette. "Except people. And broccoli. So far. And they won't touch hot dogs."

"They don't eat hot dogs?"

"I don't blame them. Do you know what goes into hot dogs?"

Recalling the story she did in Juarez, Mexico six months ago about a family-owned meat packing plant, Kirsten Lane leaned over the sewage and gave up the fight to retain her ham sandwich.

"I guess you do know," Cleveland Smith commented.

Kirsten shook the retching off. Holding up her hands, she said, "Don't tell me. Besides being an accomplished archeologist, you're a biologist as well, right?"

"I've done some studying in that field. Mostly on my own at Kirkegard's funeral home in town after dark, and at the Uck Nekked at Happy Hour, but I've learned a lot." He turned, pulled his pants down slightly, and displayed a long scar on his left butt cheek. "See this? I got this while doing an autopsy on Shirley Maclaine. She came back during the thing and almost tore me a new–"

"I crack myself up sometime, too," interrupted Kirsten. When I stand on my head, she thought. "Just how old are you, jailbait?"

"Fourteen. But I've never thought that age should make a difference in a relationship."

"Aren't you and your hand the same age?"

"Don't beg, toots."

"Is this clever banter your idea of foreplay?"

"No. My idea of foreplay is 'Wake up, baby!' Anyway, don't get any ideas. I work alone."

"So do I!" Kirsten tried to figure out where exactly she'd lost control of the conversation. "How long have you known about these... Sourpuss...es?"

Cleveland Smith shrugged. "A couple weeks, I guess. I first noticed them when I was at the Lail Refiltering Plant checking out the system. I was alone in the building at the time, but I saw a school of them get sucked into one of the refiltering vats. Took them almost half an hour to get away. I figured they had to be from somewhere further up the line."

"On the other side of this wall?"

He nodded and Kirsten noticed his Cub Slab badges bob as he did so. A bronze one featured a paper bag on fire on a porch. It looked like Gephard's porch. "Somewhere beyond there and the other side of Cadence. There's another wall at the end of the main line too."

"Like someone tried to pen them in? Who?"

Cleveland Smith shrugged. "That I don't know. But they may be the mutated waste products of the local factory, the Cadence Wiener Works and Recording Studio."

"The label that produced Cadence Clearwater Revival?" asked Kirsten.

"You heard that through the grapevine, didn'tja, doll." Cleveland eyed Kirsten suspiciously. "John Fogarty was my uncle, until his operation. Now he's my aunt. You're a real quick study... for a dame." Cleveland Smith flipped his cigarette butt into the water.

"Don't try my patience, Little Mr. Mini Ace, or I'll give you a good spanking and send you home."

"Gee," he said, looking totally unimpressed. "I hate it when that happens."

"I'm beginning to think this whole town is anal retentive. What we need is help. I could get Layd back."

Shrugging, he said, "Hey, so could I. But I believe in business before pleasure."

Kirsten wondered how a thong wedgie might feel as she leaned against the wall, digging at the mortar with her fingernails. "You know, I bet if we had the right tools, we could remove some of those cinder blocks. If we could find some gigantic hot dog buns..."

"Not me. I've got my eye on Mrs. Wilson's Blowhole Scuba Gear. She's getting ready to put on her Summer Blowout sale, and I've been sweeping up at the Uck Nekked to save enough to buy it. I make an uck a day."

Feeling her stomach revolt again, Kirsten swallowed bile. "You'd swim through that …"

"Hey, its possible there's a whole nest of Sourball creatures on the other side."

"Sourball?!? I thought they were called Sourpuss?"

"Only the girl ones," Cleveland continued. "If they operate off of hive mentality, you could be releasing a horde of monsters you couldn't stop. If you slip in under the water, they may not think they're being attacked." He eyed the reporter from under his slouch hat. "You got to have a clear head if you're going to tangle with the unknown, toots."

"Swimming through a sewer in scuba gear doesn't impress me as being exactly clear-headed. Especially since these things are carnivorous."

"What do you suggest, sweetheart? We send them an embossed invitation to the next Cadence Wiener Roast at Snare Drum Park and grill them there?"

"For starters, I suggest you drop the bad Humphrey Bogart impressions.

"Humphrey who?" asked the Cub Slab.

Kirsten looked at him and shook her head in resignation. "We could tell the Sheriff. He wont believe me, but with you backing my story up, he might. Or we could contact the National Endowment For The Arts. They love artsy-fartsy crap. "

"Leave the funny cracks to me, babe." Cleveland Smith shook out another Lucky Jr. and lit up. "My mom would kill me if she found out I was mucking around down here."

"Well it does give new meaning to diphthong."

"And the Sheriff," he continued, ignoring her remark," hasn't liked me much since I blew up the Historical Society's outhouse while I was experimenting with explosives found in nature. It wasn't my fault, but they wouldn't listen. There was more methane in there than in a herd of contented cows."

Taking the micro-cassette recorder from her purse, Kirsten said, "Then I'll just take this in to prove it."

"Hey, whatever we do is a crap shoot, toots." Cleveland Smith blew a series of smoke rings as she grinned in the silence that followed. "You wouldn't do that. It would ruin your exclusive and you know it. There's no way in hell old Sheriff Cole would let you back down here even if he did decide to send someone to check it out." He stood up and started back the way he'd come, the backpack dangling from his arm. As he walked away, Kirsten reflected he should have been nicknamed Long Thong Silver.

Kirsten dropped the recorder back into her purse and followed. "We could drop Rush Limbaugh into the sewer. He'd eat the Things... if they aren't

Republican."

A chill sped down Kirsten's back as she remembered the St. Bernard's head popping up out of the water. "Damn. " She kicked a small dog skull into the dark green depths, then dropped her flashlight in line with the ledge and hurried after the boy. By the time she'd made the comer, Cleveland Smith had vanished into the darkness.

Cursing with passion, she made the climb back up the manhole. She felt miserable inside and out as she trekked back to her motel. Before she reached her room, she stopped at the vending machine at the foot of the stairs for a soft drink. Kirsten opened the vertical door only to see Coors, Budweiser, Stax, Miller, and several brands of bottled beer she'd never heard of before. She closed the door and sighed. Trapped in Hillbilly Heaven. She turned only to spot a dark blue sedan with military plates, sitting in the motel parking lot.

She cursed yet again. The military had a hate-on for her and the paper, ever since the Star broke the news that the entire first Gulf War had been staged on a Hollywood backlot by Speilberg's Dreamwerks studio.

"I may have to kiss brass big time," Kirsten muttered, slipping into her hotel room. She tried out one of Montana's mindless axiom's to see if it fit.

"This time, the s*i* has hit his fan."

━━━∞━━━

Kirsten was still flushed with excitement.

"Hello? Front desk? This is Kirsten Lane in 116. Look, I just came in from the parking lot, and there's a car out there with its lights on. I thought you might want to notify the owner before the battery runs down." She read off the tag number from her notepad then sat the empty Popeye Spinach can that was the hotel land phone down on the table next to the bed. The cotton string ran from the bottom of the can to a wall plug. Kirsten shook her head.

The reporter crossed her room to the patio window. It was a piece of thick plastic held in place to a window jamb with duct tape. She lifted the curtain patterned with tiny drummer boys to peer outside.

A few minutes later, a man in his early thirties approached the car. He had short black hair in a military cut, skin darkened by the sun, a trim physique with wide shoulders, and a manner of walking that cried out for calls of cadence.

He reminder her of the Electrocutioner, a mercenary she'd done more than interview. It had been the first real time in her life or her career that she'd been shocked. The interview had been startling, too.

The officer gave his vehicle a one-fingered salute when he discovered its lights weren't on. It spoke volumes to Kirsten that he used the wrong finger. "At least this grunt can count to one," she muttered. Stepping out of her room, Kirsten fumbled in her change purse as she walked toward the miniature laundry room. No cigarettes should be a good excuse if he caught her following him.

The man studied the car's lights, then shook his head and went back to the motel.

Still fumbling in the change purse, Kirsten followed, maintaining a discreet distance. She noted the couple were still inside watching the dryer spin in the laundry.

The grunt's path took him through the laundry, to the other side of the motel. He used the key on room 132 and passed inside.

Pleased with herself, Kirsten paused at the vending machine and bought a Pabst Blue Ribbon beer. She opened it on the machine's bottle opener. It immediately spewed like a volcano all over the machine. She sat the half empty bottle on the cement in front of the machine in disgust. It had left quite a Pabst smear.

When she got back to her room, she discovered she'd locked the keys inside. "Yeah," she chided herself as she went through her change purse again, "you're a real sleuth, aren't you, newshound? I bet Miss Marple never smelled like cheap beer or locked herself out."

Where was a boy Scab when you needed one.

"Thank you for using AT&T. This is Anita Mound, your operator."

"Yes," Kirsten told the operator as she stood in a motel phone booth and looked at her bent and ragged-edged phone card. Talk about your monopoly. They'd even cornered the Popeye Spinach can market. "Person-to-person, please, for Billy Byrne." The night air outside the motel was brisk. The can was cold against her ear.

"Billy Barty?" the operator repeated. "There will be a small charge..."

"No. Not Barty. Barty's an actor; played on Fantasy Island or something. I'm using my credit card." Kirsten read off the number.

"We have no area code for Fantasy Island. Please hang up and call again."

"I can't hang up and try again. I only have fifty cents, and I'm on a public can."

"There's no need for sexual harassment, Miss. And what you do on a toilet..."

"Sexual har –?"

"Are you calling from a Coke machine?"

"A Coke..." A public can; Public! Not pubic phone, you ding dong!"

"Please wait." There was a long pause. "I'm sorry, but I can't bill that card number. It was filed as a lost card this morning."

Amazed that Gephard would even notice the absence of the phone card on a

Saturday when it had been missing for the past two weeks, Kirsten said, "There must be some kind of misunderstanding. Maybe my husband lost his. Oh, well, you can just bill it to my home number." She gave the operator Gephard's home phone number from memory.

"Okay, Mrs. Gephard," I'm putting you through now. Thank you for letting your fingers do the walking."

A brief image of Gephard in Fruit-Of-The-Loons flashed through her mind. She shuddered. "Thank you, operator. Bitemenow."

It had been this annoying ever since A. T. & T. T. had broken their union by hiring East Indian zombies. Her call was answered on the twenty-seventh ring.

"Yo?" a deep voice answered.

"Billy, its Kirsten. I'm calling from Cadence."

"Sorry, babe. What's shaking? Working on that wiener envy thing? Just wantya to know I've never envied yours,"

"Ha Ha. Got a little excursion into cyberspace for you if you're interested."

Byrne sounded cautious. "Hey, babe, don't mean to sound ungrateful or anything, but that last little excursion you got me mixed up in landed little Billy Byrne in the slammer for a couple of weeks. If I hadn't hacked into the police computers and released myself... I been looking for IRS death squads ever since."

"Ain't life taxing. Did you forget it got you that choice little spot on '20/20', Billie? And business is booming, right? And Byte Me, Incorporated is in the black for the first time since you hacked your way into the market? And who cleared your name in that 1-800-CALL-GIRL fiasco that almost cleaned your whistle?"

A heavy sigh hissed through the phone lines. "That was a blow. But, I don't need no trip to the slammer no more. It ain't my favorite Port 'o Call, if you get my drift."

"Yes. I've been there before, remember? It's where we met. You were in for messing with the Sesame Street numbers skits that almost cost Bert and Ernie their bookie business, and I was in for burglarizing Galt Whitney Studios for those unreleased pornographic cartoons made of Rikki Rat and his friend, Doofus."

"Yeah, yeah, I remember. They were animated little flicks. Old Galt almost quacked at the end, but he died before he could get them released to the public. Good thing, too. Galt as 'Ronald Duck' was a bit goosey. Ace's cameo in that one was really good, though."

"Aah, he used a body double and special effects. It was for the best. The public would have been shocked to learn, " said Kirsten, "Why she was called Many Mouse."

"Sure was a shame," Byrne commented. "I was always a Rikki Rat fan. Even belonged to the fan club. Sang 'R-I-K-K-K-I, RA...'"

"Get a grip, Billy. Except for Galt, they weren't real people, for Godssake."

"Hey, neither is Sean Hannity, but I love him, too. Now, what do you need this time? Background check on another armless politician thrown against a wall?"

"Hey, Art was a good guy! I've got a military tag number I need checked out," Kirsten said. "I need to know everything you can find out about the plate and the driver."

"You got a name for this car's owner?"

"Sure. Major Bunns. Major Wheet Bunns."

"Yeah, uh huh. I'll take a quick dip in the motor pool files and trace the assigned driver back from there. The motor pool maintains clean records so curious taxpayers will know every piece of machinery the government buys."

"While you're at it, check out the Cadence Wiener Works for any environmental waste violations. See if their bologna has a first name and if its m-o-u-s-e."

"Hey, Kirsten, how're you going to pay me?"

"The same way I usually do; you'll break into Global Star's bank account and take what's fair. And, Billy, honey, baby? Don't pull any punches."

"Kirsten, just remember my company moto: 'when its the right fee, you BYTE ME!'"

"**K**irsten Lane, 12:47 p.m., April 14th, Saturday, same hayseed motel in Cadence, Oregon. Things are starting to heat up concerning the monsters in the sewers, Chief. Yeah, creatures, meaning more than one. We're talking the cover of Global Star and a full-color photo insert, chum, if you want this one."

Kirsten didn't feel one hundred percent, but she had a job to do. With the micro-cassette in one hand, she opened the door to her room with the other, and stepped out into the parking lot of the motel.

"I just got another break in the story. It seems Military Intelligence is interested in our monsters as well. That's right, Military Intelligence. That's a stupid contradiction of terms if I ever heard one. Anyway, our boy on the scene in Cadence is Major Ashley B. Ho. A few years back, it seems Major Ho was assigned to the security section on something called Project Scratch 'N Sniff in 'The Triangle'. He worked his way up to head it.

"Project Scratch 'N Sniff is a closed file, even though my source was able to confirm that it was shut down shortly after Glasnost went into effect. That coincidental bit of information set my taste buds salivating, let me tell you. I believe the monsters in the sewers have nothing at all to do with a Military Intelligence officer who's been in town the last three days like I believe that Ace is really Mother Theresa. The missing cat and dog classifieds have only been around for the last four months that I know of. I'm itching to expose Ash Ho."

Kirsten closed the door to her room, suddenly overcome by an urge to scratch an itch unique to her gender.

"So, what's happened in the last four months to draw a Military Intelligence officer to this God forsaken backwater berg?

"Oh, and by the way, in case you think I'm really out on a limb after all this supposing...my source also tole me Ashley Ho fielded a platoon somewhere around the Wiener Works. They're not just here for vacation or the sights. They're equipped with military jeeps and tanks."

Kirsten looked around, saw no one, and scratched.

"I want the next couple days for my own investigation. If I turn up missing, you'll know where to start looking. I'll write out the names so you'll have them spelled r-r-right...

"Boy, howdy, would you look at that!" said a voice, and Kirsten turned, still scratching, to see Doody and Clara from the laundramat, finding new entertainment. Kirsten's hand stopped moving, and her face flushed a deep crimson.

"And, Frank, make sure 'Conn, Frad, Fibber and Loupe deWhole' are all versed in military law. Death by firing squad is NOT an acceptable way to go, and it's probably not even covered by the company's medical and health plan."

As Doody and Clara gawked, Kirsten did what her subconscious demanded. She began to moon walk.

Kirsten was still flustered by her encounter with Clara and Doody, his face covered by lipstick. It was obvious what they had been doing in the laundramat. She shuddered, even though she completely understood that Clara had to do her Doody.

"Can I help you?" Major Ash Ho asked.

Kirsten did a double-take on the door number because Ace Montana told her the double-take was the best thing she did. She hadn't let him know about her other faking maneuvers to hold the male ego in thrall. She could teach Alyssa

Milano a thing or two about those. "You're not Keith," she said in feigned perplexion.

"No," Ho said, "I'm not." He started to close his door. Kirsten noted he was Asian, probably Chinese. In Military Intelligence, that would make him a Chinese checker.

Thinking the Army major was a rude son of a dog, Kirsten burst into tears. She wore a white dress that showed off what cleavage she had to its best effect, and very little makeup. She'd used it several times successfully. Gephard, who'd seen her dressed like this only when he'd initially hired her, called it her demure, sensual look and compared it to the kind of look Black Widow spiders wore just before they cannibalized their mates. She had been working at the Global Star gift shop, handing out sample suppositories.

"Why you cry?" Ash Ho asked, peering out around her.

"You're not Baby Love," sobbed Kirsten.

"No. I Ho. Ho. Ho."

"What?!?," Kirsten wept. "You don't look like Santa Claus!"

"I Major Ashley Ho, Military Intelligence, formerly one of Ho Chi's men."

Through the crack in the door, Kirsten could see a full-dress uniform hanging from the wall, a .45 automatic sitting on top of a laptop computer similar to her own, and an episode of 'Gomer Pyle, USMC' on the television. She knew this would be a hard Ho to row.

"Baby Love was supposed to be here," she said in a squeaky voice. She used a flowered handkerchief smelling of lilac to brush away her tears. "He told me he'd meet me here, in room 132. H-he l-lied."

Major Ho opened the door wider, obviously confused about what he was supposed to do. "Who 'baby love'?"

Kirsten figured crying women weren't handled in the Officer's Handbook. She leaned against the wall and let her shoulders heave, staying at an angle that kept her cleavage on display while still hiding the toilet paper there.

"You been rooking for rove in all wrong places?"

"I-I know," Kirsten sobbed. "We had a fight. Oh, Baby Love... oh, Baby Love. I need you; how I need you." It was a supreme act of shameless manipulation.

"He hit you?" Ho asked, bristling immediately with macho enthusiasm.

"No, no, no," Kirsten replied, seizing the man by the shoulders. The last thing she needed him to do was concentrate on preening his masculinity. "His mother doesn't like me. Mother Love never has. I should never have agreed to try to spend the weekend there. He was always her baby more than he was my fiancee. I suppose I should have been suspicious of the fact that she still breast feeds him,

"We were supposed to be married next month. Now, I guess this means...

he... he..." She broke into a fresh onslaught of tears, burrowing into his reluctant embrace and laying her head on his shoulders. He wrapped him arms around her automatically, patting her back awkwardly and not looking directly into her face.

"It going to be all light," Ho said. "Hey, if this guy take his mother's jealousy over a nice dame rike you, he deserve what he get."

Kirsten had to steel herself to keep from kneeing the Army major in the groin for calling her a dame. She preferred skirt or broad. She cried again, flinging her arms around his neck. "Thank you. It's so nice of you to say that, but you don't have to, Major No."

"Ho. I mean, no. I am Ho, and no, I mean it. You as fine a hunk of womanhood as I ever seen. What your name?"

"Angelina," said Kirsten. "Angelina Jolie." Surmising that Ash Ho's security work had been low on tact as well as manners, Kirsten quickly disengaged the embrace. Wide-eyed, she covered her mouth, "Quick. Where's your bathroom?" she asked in a hoarse voice.

"What wrong, Angelrina? Nose need powder?"

I'm going to be sick." She let him help her to the door, closed it, waited a few seconds while she dry-retched some more, then flushed the toilet. She started to open the door, said, "Oh. God," closed the door and dry-retched again. This time after she flushed, she stumbled back into the room. When she saw the concern on Major Ho's face, she knew she'd given him enough time to step into his role of Rhett Butler to her Scarlett O'Hara.

"When was rast time you had something to eat?" the Army major asked as he slid into a sportjacket and hung the .45 in a clipon holster from his waistband, "Refs get something in tummy, Ms. Angelrina Jorie, and see if things rook rittle brighter. You rike IHOPS, International House of Potato Soup?" He leered. "Or maybe Burger Queen?"

Kirsten waved the lilac-scented handkerchief at him. "Oh, no, I've imposed on you enough, Major So 'n So."

"Well, if that the way you feel..."

She looped her arm through his. "But, if you insist, Major Snow, I'm not strong enough to say no to a strong-willed man. I need a strong man in my life." She fluttered her eyelashes at him and knew that, like most men, Major Ho was a rake.

Ash Ho guided her out the door. "Where you from, darrin'?"

"Raleigh," Kirsten replied. It was where the heroine in her current romance novel was having the same problems she was about to outline for the Major.

"As in North Carorina? That where I from!"

"I knew you weren't from around here!"

"It my Swedish accent. That what always give me away."

"Oh, well, I haven't lived there very long. David wanted me to move to Portland with him and his mother."

"I thought you said his name Keith?"

"It is. David's his first name. That's what his mother calls him. David Keith Steve."

"I understand. Some mispronounce my name, too."

Only when they pronounce it Ash Ho, thought Kirsten, smiling.

Kirsten eased up from under the bedspread that obviously belonged to the fastidious Major Ho. It was covered with action pictures of G. J. Joe. Major Ashley B. Ho slept on, kept completely under by the excessive number of Harvey Wallbangers he'd drunk during their meal as well as the three tranquilizers she'd put in them. Despite his best attempts, he had banged on her wall, not Harvey's, last night, just as planned.

Walking naked to Ho's laptop computer, she brushed the holstered .45 to the floor, grimacing with distaste. She took the computer, the telephone, and the meal receipt from Ho's pants pocket, and walked into the bathroom.

She called Billy Byrne's number on the bathroom Popeye can and charged it to Gephard's home. While she waited for the connection to be made, she sat on the closed toilet and turned on water in the sink. Ho was asleep, but that didn't mean he didn't bug his room for unannounced visitors. She did that herself at home. It was how she'd discovered Ace Montana was bringing girlfriends over to her apartment when she was on out-of-town assignments. She'd griped at Ace until he paid the rent she demanded, but kept some of the better tapes she'd made for mood enhancers. Her favorite tape was After The Ball Was Over. It was a short feature. Ace's expression was priceless when he discovered his dance partner had been a Ginger Rogers impersonator. Male.

"Byte Me."

"Billy, it's Kirsten Lane. Hey, I got some more computer stuff I need you to take a look at. We can pipe it in over a modem if you can tell me how to operate it. I see a setting here that says it's equipped. Which, by the way, is more than I can say for its owner."

"'What are we dealing with here?"

"Military software and a Popeye Spinach can. I'm a little short on time, here. Can the banter and get working, Sweetpea." Kirsten followed Byrne's instructions and set the computer into motion. While it operated, she returned to the bedroom and got dressed. As she zipped up the back of her dress, Ho turned on his side and belched with enough force to rattle the walls. Remembering last night, she whispered, "You know, Ho, after your first, last and only attempted deployment, I realize I should have called in a Marine to get the job done."

Ash Ho twitched, kicking the covers off. Kirsten sighed and shook her head sadly as she looked down at his nude form.

"Now I know why we need a 'new Army', Ho," she said, throwing the cover back over him. "In a major thrust today, small arms are useless."

At least she finally understood what Military Offensive meant.

Kirsten had an uncomfortable feeling that Sourpuss might leave the sewers like herpes leaves a hospital.

On crotches.

She had an unbelievable urge to scratch.

"Monsters created and financed by the American government?" Frank Gephard repeated over the phone. "In the Bermuda Triangle?"

Kirsten stood inside the greenhouse-hot phone booth at the comer of the street in front of the 6-Eleven. She was pleased that she wasn't talking into another spinach can. This one featured Sylvester the Cat on the label and had held succotash. She watched the clerk inside, breathing a sigh of relief when she saw neither hand was bandaged. "So, you're interested?"

"Hell, yes, I'm interested. This has gotta be the biggest thing since Ace discovered..."

"Then call me back. This is costing me." She read off the pay phone number, adding the area code, and hung up the phone. Opening the door to get a breath of fresh air, she rummaged in her purse till she found her cigarettes and the turqouise-studded Zippo she'd confiscated from Clem Clem in the Uck Nekked Bar and Grill. When you held it upside down, Janet Reno undressed. She'd barely touched the flame to the end of the cigarette when the phone rang, but held off answering it untill the fifth ring.

"It's me," Gephard said irritably. "Don't hang up again. I'm short of time."

"You're short of everything," she responded. "This is on your nickel now."

"So give. I'll have Klark Cent do a rewrite on your phone-in."

"Uh-uh, not till we establish some ground rules."

"Ground rules? Kirsten, this is Frank. You still owe me for assigning you that Bigfoot story when he murdered Doctor Scholl in Times Square for false advertising."

"Damn, you're right. I do KNOW you. You'll agree to anything at this point, then do whatever the hell you want to later on. So maybe I'll just call that rag, the Washington Post. They haven't had a decent story since Nixon's ghost gave his 'I am not a Spook' speech."

"Kirsten, oh ye of little faith. Remember the good things I've done in your life? Remember when I made Ace stop leaving those notes around the office calling you Princess Roundhells? Remember how I got him to stop leaving your home number on the bathroom wall of every sleazy dive he entered?"

"Yeah, I have misty, water-colored memories, Frank. It was you who were leaving my number. Luckily, you can't spell numbers correctly either. Barbara Streisand got the calls, which worked out since people who love people are the luckiest people in the world."

"Well, I still stopped it."

"So, tell me about the government-funded. monsters scam again," Gephard hastily added, pretending not to have heard her.

Flipping her notebook open, Kirsten cradled the can against her shoulder and moved her cigarette to the corner of her mouth. As she relayed the notes she'd gotten from Byrne less than a half hour earlier, she absently brushed ashes from her denim jacket. "Project Scratch 'N Sniff was put together back in the early 1970s as a biological retribution weapon to be used in the event of a successful Russian first strike with nuclear weapons."

Gephard interrupted. "How do you spell 'Retchtribution'?"

"G-E-T E-V-E-N. Military Intelligence had this guy, Dr. Hermann Pusey, who had a theory for the creation of living organism that could live through even a nuclear holocaust."

"How do you spell hollowcaust?"

M-R-S G-E-P-H-A-R-D. Damn, Chief." Kirsten stamped her foot impatiently. "Do you spell relief U-G-ET?"

"That's a lot better. Word selection, Kirsten, is very important in this business. You should know that. I mean, creatures summons up visual pictures of orgasms."

"Organism. The word is organism."

"Yeah, well, I like creatures better. Creatures is a journalistic term. It'll sell more copies. Especially if they turn out to be drooling creatures. Can you get them to drool? Can you get one to swallow a box of baking soda? Wow! Drool and Foam! That's a winner. Remember, this is a newspaper, and our purpose is enlightenment and entertainment."

"And lining bird cages." Kirsten let out a long breath. She'd always hated the way Gephard glossed over the facts in her stories and played up the sensationalism. He'd even downplayed Princess Fergie's divorce to play up her eleven toes.

"So, what were these creatures supposed to do?" Gephard asked. "Suck up all the vodka in Russia and trigger mass suicide?'

"They were supposed to eat Russians in the event of a nuclear attack," Kirsten replied.

"God, this is great. Not now, go away!"

Straining her hearing, Kirsten overheard Uge Nocher's petulant tones mumbling something about fluffy handcuffs. But she could have been mistaken. However, knowing Uge, she didn't think so.

"Pusey's creatures were supposed to be put into a geosynchronous orbit around the earth. Apparently, they're constructed from some kind of mutated bacteria and look like some kind of cousin to a jellyfish from the description. They grow best in warm, moist environments, but can go into metabolic hibernation when food isn't available. If America lost the nuclear war, this 'Sourpuss' creature was supposed to be dropped from their orbit and crash into Russian territory, devouring everything that stood in their path, except borsch. They also have the ability to reproduce by fission."

"I don't know what fishing has to do with it," Gephard said, "but the rest of this is reel exciting! I'm waiting for this story with baited breath, junior!"

"Did I mention that bad puns are like strawberry shortcake to these things? And that they just love strawberry shortcake, Frank?" Feeling exhaustion creep over her, Kirsten leaned back in the phone booth with the door open. "Listen, minnow breath, I'm tired of the clever banter. You don't do this with his holiness, Pope Montana, and I expect to be treated as his better."

"Hey, that's not true, Kirsten. Just the other day, I told Ace a joke about this cloistered nun and hooker..."

"You shouldn't make fun of a bad habit, Chief. What have we got in the morgue on Hermann Pusey? He's probably from Kliche, Germany. There was probably no brat worse...

"Give me a minute; I'll have Klark Google it."

Kirsten held the can away from her ear as Gephard bellowed orders. When the editor was back, she said, "According to my source, this Pusey disappeared from the military less than a year ago."

"I'm sure the military was shaken to the corps. But don't worry about this inventor guy, Kirsten, just get a couple dozen pictures of these creatures. We don't publish Scientific American here, honey. Now, here's how I see it. Headline (above the fold): Sourkraut Socks Sourpuss in Sewer System."

Kirsten shut the editor out easily through months of rigorous training. She sat down in the bottom of the booth just as Major Ashley Ho stumbled out into the parking lot in her underwear and his. 45 buckled around his waist. The Military Intelligence officer held both hands to his head as he screamed in pain and fell to the ground.

"What was that?" the editor demanded.

"The sound of a military career going down the toilet."

A rental car approached the motel at a slow twenty miles an hour, finally coming to a stop in the parking lot. When the driver noticed Ho slamming his fists against the concrete, he pulled the car to the far end of the lot.

"Klark's back," Gephard said. "The only thing we have on a Pusey relates back to James Bond of the British Secret Service in the sixties. And something on Chia Pets."

"That's probably about the time Military Intelligence got him," Kirsten said. She watched the driver get out of the rental car. "Ali, damnit! Mulligan Stu is here." She recognized the man's features as well as the porkpie hat. "First I've seen of him since I scooped him on that hippo that gave birth to a Volkswagen Beetle."

"Mulligen?!" Gephard's voice came to quick attention. "Mulligan of the Enguirer-Trib? That means the E-T may be about to break your story too."

"Like hell," Kirsten snarled. "This is mine, and it's going to be an exclusive. Got to go, Chief." She hung up and slunk out of the phone booth. The can started ringing again before she made it across the street. She took a quick glance at the lobby and saw Mulligan standing expectantly before the desk, then went on to her room, avoiding the fire truck that suddenly pulled into the parking lot with the lights flashing and the siren fully engaged. Yellow slickered firemen dropped from the truck and surrounded Ash Ho with thick hoses. When the officer got to his feet, one of the firemen shouted, "He's got a pistol!" A stream of water slammed into Ho.

"Not really," said Kirsten, pausing at a window. "He's just happy to see you." It was obvious that Bernie the fireman didn't know his Ash from the Ho on the ground.

⚬⚬⚬⚬

"**K**irsten Lane, 8:47 p.m., April 14th, Saturday, in Cadence, Oregon, Expense report supplemental: out of pocket cash includes a quick trip to a Safe Sacks Food Store for breakfast supplies and Monistat 7. This afternoon, there was the lunch with the Military Intelligence officer, name withheld at his request, for a total of $70.13. I have the receipt.

"Item: Chief, it would really help out if the newspaper morgue at Global Star wasn't such a dead end. It's been a disaster ever since you hired Kivorkian to run it. I need a picture of Pusey, damnit. I've got a hunch, but I have to see this guy's face to follow it up."

She turned off her micro-cassette recorder and shoved it in her purse in disgust. She looked over her shoulder at the entrance to the Oscar Meyer Memorial Library and snorted. The best she found there had been a ten volume set on the history of wienerwurst in America.

Frankly, she didn't give a damn.

Besides the Ginger Baker Memorial Public Library, which didn't carry twenty year old periodicals and thought microfisch were small crappie, Kirsten knew of only two places in Cadence that might have copies of the magazines she needed. She got the addresses from the Yellowed Pages. Neither was open, so she bought a flat-head screwdriver from the hardware store and used the back doors.

Howard 'Painless' Quagmire, D.D.S., kept an office that was a virtual treasure trove of Newsweek, Time, S & M Weekly,and Look magazine in braille on top of the 13" television magazines. The latter had Monica Lewinsky's and Bill Clinton's wedding picture on the cover. The best man had been a cigar store wooden Indian. The older stuff had been stored at the bottom of the coat closet in Brach's boxes under an autographed picture of Jack Nicholson from the movie, The Little Shop of Horrors. She left Mulligan's distributor cap at the back of a file cabinet drawer labeled: Doe: a deer, a female deer.

Kirsten sat in the middle of the reception room's floor and spread the magazines out across the threadbare carpet. She used her penflash to leaf through copies of Tooth or Consequences magazine. She flicked ashes off her cigarettes to the floor, but kept the butts because someone investigating the break-in might be able to get her blood type from the saliva. She'd done a story once involving the field of serology that had led back to a Zombie doing serial resurrections, so she knew how accurate the tests could be, and that one should never french kiss a Zombie. They were dead from the waist down and up, for that matter.

By 11:45, she'd found the first picture of Dr. Hermann Pusey accepting an international award as co-inventor of the Chia Pet. She ripped it out, folded it, put it in her pocket, then stuffed the rest of the magazine inside her jacket so no one would know what had interested her. Twenty minutes and two more pictures later, she stood up to go, leaving the discarded magazines scattered across the carpet.

A match flared in the darkness, outlining a slouch hat and a pack of Lucky Jr. Strikes.

"Jumping Jose, kid," Kirsten said when she got her breath back. "What the hell are you doing there?"

Cleveland Smith sat on the receptionist's desk, clad approximately the same way he'd been the first time they met. "Watching you," he answered and did a

Bogart lip spasm like he had something caught between two teeth that he was trying to remove without touching.

Regaining her aplomb, Kirsten demanded, "How long have you been sitting there?"

"Throughout most of the mid-nineties," said Cleveland Smith. "Off and on. It's understandable why you didn't hear me; I'm light on my feet. Used to be a Thong and Dance man on the stage, remember?"

"Didn't anybody tell you it was impolite to spy an other people, you junior jerk?"

"Yah, you. And I heard someone announce a 'Major Ho Down' on my police band radio. And I'm always warned about the forced entry charges. Lots and lots of warnings. Yet, here I am, candy hips."

"You've got a smart mouth, kid." Kirsten lit up a fresh cigarette, inhaled, and exhaled smoke. "Too bad the smarts couldn't move north a bit."

"Thank you. My mouth was educated at the School of Hard Mocks. Did you find what you were looking for, Ms. Cub Reporter?"

"Cub Reporter! Look, kid, I've got tooth picks older than you." Thinking furiously, Kirsten tried to figure out a way to use the boy's knowledge without letting him know what she'd discovered. After a couple of moments, she gave up. "Look, if I tell you what I know, you've got to promise to keep your educated mouth shut. Understood?"

Eyes narrowing against their combined smoke fumes, Cleveland Smith stared back at her. "Hey, nobody gives me orders, not even Mama Jones."

"I thought your last name is Smith."

"Adopted."

"Figures." Smiling with as much humor as a hungry shark closing in on a paraplegic in the water (she'd known one once named Bob) Kirsten sat on a desk. She batted her eyes at the boy. "Cleveland—I can call you Cleveland, can't I?"

The boy shrugged. "You just did, sweetheart. Or you can just pucker and blow, and I'll come running for you, baby cakes."

"Cleveland, let me put it to you this way. If what I tell you is passed on to anyone else, I'm going to rip off your 'stud' and sell it to the Cadence Wiener Works."

Cleveland Smith gave her a flat-line grimace. "Thank's cold, toots, real cold. Sooooo, okay, we got a deal." He looked despondent. "But I have to tell you, I don't work well under restrictions. I fight alone, and for truth, justice, and, when I'm low on funds, Deputy Whey."

"I'm not here to play Lois Lane to your Superman, kid. I'm a reporter scrambling for an exclusive. There is not a more dangerous animal in the jungle." Kirsten unfolded the ragged picture she'd ripped from the magazine and laid it on the desk. She used her penflash to illuminate Pusey's face. "Do you know this man?"

Cleveland Smith studied the photograph. "Sure, that's Mr. Aquino. He lives here in Cadence. His real name is Pusey?"

Kirsten ignored the question. "Give me his address."

He did. "Mr. Aquino is really Hermann Pusey?" he repeated. "Why would anyone change a perfectly good name?"

Kirsten did not mention she'd changed her name from Lois. Kirsten Lois. In clipped words, she explained Pusey and Project Scratch 'N Sniff.

"Euuuuuuuuuh!" said Cleveland. "I thought yeast made bread get big!?!"

⊷⊶

Fired with the reality that the story was almost in the bag, Kirsten retreated to the open back door and the waiting alley. Cleveland Smith followed, reluctantly. She paused at the mouth of the alley, watching the late night traffic carefully. A poster on the wall next to her featured Hulk Hogan in Fat On A Hot Tin Roof at the Dukes of Hazard Little Theater in Cadence. She thought the little blue dress looked tacky on the wrestler.

Most of the neighborhood excitement had died away when Ash Ho had been taken to the hospital by the firemen for removal of a hose from a certain sunless orifice.

"You can see Mr. Aquino's house from here," Cleveland Smith said, pointing to a blinking neon sign reading: Aquino's Taxidermy—We Hang On by the Skin of Their Teeth.

She followed the line of his pointing arm to the three-story mansion in the center of town. It was built narrow and tall, constructed entirely of wood, and surrounded by a ten-foot high, ivy-encumbered stone wall. No lights were on in the house. Even the starry sky hanging over it seemed dimmed by comparison to the other houses nearby.

"I wonder if he stuffs squirrels?" asked Cleveland. "Mr. Aquino moved in just a few months back," he added. "He bought the house outright and had an indoor swimming pool put in. According to the Yellowed Pages, he is the only Pusey in Cadence."

"Not by a long shot. That info explains a lot about this hick, jerkwater town." Kirsten looked at Smith. "How do you know all of that, Cleveland?"

"Mama Jones was the real estate agent that sold him the house. He doesn't like kids, especially teengaged boys fixated on the Maltese Falcon movie."

"And you've actually seen Pusey?"

"Once. My cousin, Sarah, was visiting from..."

"Cleveland!!"

"No, Tulsa. She brought her Siamese cat with her from Tulsa."

"Oh. And he doesn't like all kids?" Kirsten asked. "Or just you."

Cleveland Smith made a face of indignation beneath the slouch hat. "I didn't ask. Maybe I can ask him tonight. I'm told he's a regular chatterbox if you get him started. One thing you ought to remember, though. That house sits directly on top of the sewer line we were in. I know because I checked out the schematic in City Hall last week. And Pusey does have an indoor pool. Kind of makes you wonder what he keeps in it, doesn't it?"

As Cleveland Smith faded into the darkness, he called back to her. "See ya later, babe. I got a plan of my own to work on."

Recalling the episode with the St. Bernard and the tentacled thing the organism could bond themselves into, Kirsten shuddered. The only thing that made her take her first step was the knowledge that an exclusive story was her's for the taking if she was nervy enough to reach out for it. The only thing that kept her stepping was sure knowledge that Gephard would get Ace or Fanny to cover it immediately if she muffed it. Then she sternly reminded herself that she had never muffed an assignment before.

Unless you counted that tragic misunderstanding involving Mother Teresa and the New Delhi Vice Squad.

She unconsciously reached down to scratch herself when she heard a titter from the darkened alley behind the doctor's office. A bum leaned against a wall under the Hulk Hogan poster and snickered.

Blushing again, Kirsten grabbed herself and began to moonwalk her way out of the alley. She was beginning to doubt she would ever measure up to Gephard's standards, even though the "Enter If You Are This High" freestanding cardboard cutout at his office door was a Keebler elf.

⎯⎯◦∞◦⎯⎯

Dr. Pusey's neon sign blinked forlornly in the dark before sunrise. His house reminded her of Norman Bate's home in the movie Psycho. She remembered that Bates had been into taxidermy, too. After seeing the movie, she hadn't stuffed a squirrel for a week.

"Here to get your squirrel stuffed, Kirsten? I must be getting old; I don't see Ace anywhere. Is he holding your hand through the Psychic Hotline... this time?"

She looked up, still holding the aluminum ladder against the side of the stone wall. Mulligan Stu stood in the shadows clustered between the wall and the neighboring houses on this side of the mansion. The Enquirer-Tribune reporter wore a dark suit, the familiar porkpie hat, and a mistletoe stuck in the hat brim. She suspected he wore Depends adult diapers beneath the suit.

"Well, if it isn't Mulligan Stu," she said. "If it isn't, it must be the Lucky Stars leprechaun. Is the federal pen overpopulated again?"

Mulligan Stu was the stuff of legend in the journalistic profession. His claim to fame sprang from an encounter with a stewardess on a haunted flight from Ireland, country of the Druids and countless other supernatural troublemakers. Mulligan's stewardess had turned out to be one of the more palpable ones. As the story went, the E-T man had talked his way into the restroom with this particularly fetching stewardess. There, at thirty thousand feet, while essaying an energetic attempt to join the Mile High Club enroute to New York from Ireland, Mulligan had the misfortune to discover the stewardess was a banshee who'd been quietly allowed by the airline company officials to travel on board. In mid- flagrante delicto, she had exploded with a burst of maniacal laughter that knocked the jet from the sky into the ocean. No one had been injured, and the occupants had been picked up only minutes later by a passing freighter. However, Mulligan had been left unconscious and naked. There was no mystery about what he'd been doing or with whom. And then there was the matter of the mysterious ring of tattoos that had been burned on his body.

There is an old saying that God created whiskey to keep the Irish from conquering the world. And He created Mulligan, Kirsten thought, to add insult to injury.

Mulligan claimed Venusian flying saucers had mistaken him for a cornfield in England, and that the rings were the remnants of firey butterfly kisses from their butterfly lips. He had thanked his lucky stars he'd escaped with his life.

Mulligan stepped forward, a wide grin on his round face. "Just as soon as I overheard from Osama ben Laundry at the Bates and Swith Motel that you'd checked out without telling anyone, or paying, and with half the towels, I knew I could expect you here."

Stepping in front of the aluminum ladder she'd liberated from the Streak and Peek window cleaning business down the street, Kirsten said, "Forget it, elf-breath. This is a real news story and, therefore, it's mine."

"I beg to differ, my dear," Mulligen said, taking another step forward. "I've been trailing this particular story for many moons. I gave up coverage on a human sacrifice to be here tonight after I found out Ash Ho had vacated the government labs."

"You should have stayed with the human sacrifice story since you'd have been under no personal danger. Now, if they were sacrificing jerks..."

Mulligan spread his hands. "Kirsten, Kirsten... we both know that you'd die to be the sacrifice on the altar of my love. Anyway, this one's big enough for the both of us. Government corruption and cover-ups. God, I smell another Watergate in the wind if this thing is handled right. Remember, babe, how my story on how Nixon resurrected J. Edgar Hoover's ghost to bug Democratic headquarters got a hell of a lot of ink and a great picture of J. Edgar in a party dress.

"Let's cut the cute, Kirsten. You have as much chance of getting rid of me as you do of teaching Montana ballroom dancing. You will cover this story with me."

"And if I don't?"

"Then I call the cops, report a cat burglar, and you get drummed out of Cadence." Mulligen shrugged. "As you can see, you're left with little choice. It's me or a night in the slammer with Robodyke."

"And the difference would be...? This is the deal—we go in together, then it's every pseudo-man and devastatingly beautiful infobabe for him or herself."

"Well, since you're the pseudo-man, is Fanny Francher here?" Mulligan grinned and faked looking for the TV reporter.

Kirsten placed her hands on the ladder carefully, sure Mulligan hadn't seen what she'd done. "Climb up first and I'll hold the ladder, bladder head."

Mulligan shook his head. "And have you pull it down just as I'm almost at the top? No, thank you. No blarney for me, lassie. I still remember that cream pie episode you pulled in Newark. Brokaw quit the news business after that, and Couric was ticked. I've got a lot of years left. And it's hard to file, much less follow up, on a story with your leg in a cast. So, this is your chance to make like Ace and rise to the occasion."

Kirsten thought that would have only been an unfortunate turn of events. Now a broken neck, that would have been something a girl could hope for. "You want me to go up first, Stu meat?"

"Want me to whistle Moon Over Miami while you climb?"

Kirsten placed her hands on the ladder, her back to Mulligan, then stopped. She turned back to the reporter. "You'll stick by me like flop sweat on Fanny Francher?"

"Like camel hair on Sam Donaldson's head."

Kirsten believed him, but she didn't think he realized how tight that was truly going to be. She threw her bag over her shoulder and swarmed up the rungs like a monkey, almost catching Mulligan by surprise. Just as she felt the ladder shift beneath her, she leaped for the wall, grabbing a double hand hold as she slammed into it.

Mulligan screamed in pain behind her, then began cursing. "Kirsten!! You insatiable slut!! You'll pay for this!!"

Her rib cage still aching from the impact, Kirsten pulled herself to the top of the wall. Her hands were covered with broken ivy strands and her nose was filled with the pungent aroma of crushed flowers. When she looked down at the Enquirer-Trib reporter, she saw Mulligan flat on the ground under the ladder, unable to release it. She dug in her pocket and showed him the half-empty tube of Stuck on You super-glue. She laughed at him as he flailed away with the ladder and made clanking noises against the cold pavement.

"Sucker," Kirsten hissed. "And I'm not insatiable. I've certainly had more than enough of you, buddy boy.

"You know what your problem is, Stu meat? A lack of imagination, that's what. Nothing you can't hope to cure in your next life as a cross between a crocodile and a Shetland pony. That's a crockoshet, which is just another name for you and that rag you call a newspaper. I'll leave you now to stew in your own juices."

"Bitch!" Mulligan screamed. "You cheap, conniving, heartless bitch!"

"Never cheap, just affordable," Kirsten answered as she started lowering herself on the inside of the wall. "You know flattery will get you nothing where I'm concerned. And you'd better quiet down before someone comes out and shoots you for a burglar. You know how these little hick towns can be with their 'Make My Day' laws."

Mulligan stopped screaming at once. "You can't leave me here like this, Kirsten! I've got money! How about a real job at the Trib? What if I found ya a horny housepainter?"

"Pray he doesnt spackle. Of course, you do have the option of gnawing your hands off."

Kirsten dropped to the spongy ground. "You're used to bad taste, but I wouldn't do it. I know where those hands have been." She released her grip on the wall.

———⊷⊶———

All the doors and windows were locked. No sounds came from inside the residence. Cleveland Smith's words about the indoor swimming pool trickled down Kirsten's spine like tumbling ice cubes, summoning up images of the pile of bones in the sewer. Rather than risk the shrill squeak the old screwdriver could sometimes make when it ripped through a lock, she opted for a quieter method.

After checking for electronic surveillance equipment on the window and finding none, she applied long strips of Flintstones surgical tape from her purse to the glass. The tape was the choice of professional cat burglar's because it was cheap, durable and ouchless, and because Betty Rubble was one hot babe. She took care to leave a handle linking all the strips together. One blow of her elbow shattered the window, then she pulled it clean of the frame and went inside.

Tension filled her as her imagination refused to leave her alone and let her do her job. Puns welled up inside her like bile. It didn't help that the inside of the mansion looked like a mausoleum. Dust and cobwebs hung thick and heavy. Her penlight flashed over a dark, eight-legged body with beady little eyes. She thought she heard a skittering noise until she realized her flashlight had actually found a picture of Fidel Castro. She sighed with relief. She remembered that Castro and his communist cohorts had been the original target of the Scratch 'N Sniff Project. His picture here made sense. It probably shared wall space with Lenin, Stalin and Hillary Clinton.

She couldnt help thinking maybe it would have been worth it to bring Mulligan except that, unlike the sewer spiders, she couldn't grow eyes in the back of her head. She knew the Enquirer-Trib reporter would have fed her to the mutant bacteria in little bitty pieces if it meant getting an exclusive because she'd have done the same herself if necessary.

Taking a firmer grip on her penflash, the digital camera in her other hand, she moved through the rooms in the lower floor. Nothing was in any of the rooms except Cheese Whiz and Ritz crackers. But her fear was not of finding Ace Montana's favorite meal, but of what had eaten it.

The smell of stale water and the lapping of tiny waves echoing hollowly drew her on. It was the only sign of life in a house that had as much animation as a South Park cartoon... or Ash Ho. She shuddered at the simile—though it was one she would remember for her story for Gephard, knowing the editor would relish it—and thought the last thing she needed to do right now was think of George Romero zombie films and how George hadn't needed make-up or paychecks for his 'actors'.

Frankly she hadn't been this afraid since her father had been murdered. He'd been killed by street thugs full of beans, cabbage and garlic.

It had been a drive-by pooting.

———&———

The pool area was immense, cut in the center of the floor with an atrium area leading up through the other two floors. In the center bobbed either two buoys or Pamela Anderson floating on her back. After a moment's study, she knew they were buoys; Lee wasn't that convincing an actress. Dead plants clung to the walls and railings all the way up, looking black in the pale moonlight leaking through a dusky skylight at the top. A shaft of moonlight caught a pool sign. It read: You Don't Swim In Your Toilet, So Don't Pee In My Pool.

Keeping her penflash off now, she crept forward and touched one of the black patches. It felt gooshy, slick, and disgusting. She retreated back to the doorway to scream silently, wiping her trembling fingers on the wall. "Oh, God," she whispered to the shadows.

Everything about this place was vile and disgusting. Yet, again, she felt a strange sense of familiarity, of deja vu. Maybe it just reminded her of Ace's kitchen table where in April, among February's dishes, she'd learned the Joy of Sex wasn't a detergent.

Camera at the ready, she steeled herself and went after her story. She had never balked before (except once in the Balkans), and she refused to balk now. Spam-eating zombies. three-headed babies, self-impotent Ash Hos and others had all stood in her way at one time or another. She'd ultimately used them all as stepping stones in her career. She'd be damned if she let a half-dozen giant bacteria keep her from a shot at the title.

She just hoped the title wasn't World's Choicest Morsel.

She crept quietly to the pool's edge, trying to peer down into the water. Something shifted and the sound of a million cats purring filled the air.

The pool lights came on, bathing the water and its occupants in a lambent fluorescent glow. Dozens, maybe hundreds, of the bacteria creatures—and she thought of them as creatures, not organism, because the scientific term for them didn't do justice to what she was seeing—filled the pool under an inch of water. An island of them floated near the center of the pool by the buoys. On top of them, a man dressed in a loud, flowered shirt and Bermuda shorts sat up and pointed at her.

"Velcome to der Triangle," he said calmly. "I am Hermann Pusey, the yeast of your troubles, Kirsten Lane."

Before Kirsten could move, three yellow-gray tentacles seethed free of the mass of organic jelly and wrapped around her. She tried to scream, and did cross her legs, but one of the tentacles covered her mouth. Immediately discarding the idea of trying to bite it, she concentrated on not throwing up. As tight as the creature's grip was, there was no place for her stomach to purge itself except through her ears.

The man stood up on the island of collected, giant bacteria. He pulled a pair of thick-lensed glasses from his pocket protector and put them on, brushing at his cheek absently. Gray-cottony hair stuck out from his head. He wore no shoes. His toes poked through the holes in his socks. "Bring her here, Zourpusses," demanded Pusey in a squeaky voice amid the meanacing low rumble of cat purring.

A tentacle unwrapped from Kirsten's mouth, leaving a gagging odor behind. She kept from licking her lips to moisten them by remembering that you are what you eat. The interior of the mansion vibrated with purring as the creatures stacked on top of each other, extending slender stalks from their gelatinous bodies.

"Dis ist explosive stuff, here, si? Vy der camera? Do you know dat you are playing vit Gynamite, mademoiselle!?"

Kirsten knew there was no denying the camera in her hand. "W-what is Gynamite?"

The little scientist smiled, adjusted his glasses, and smoothed his hair back. "You know uf me? Sacre Bleu, I am flautuated."

Kirsten nodded quickly. "I know of your work with Chia Pets, Dr. Pusey. But ... these putrid... things..."

"Vell, vell, notoriety certainly comes to der most unexpected moments." Dr. Pusey placed his hands behind his back. "Still, I ban been expecting to be recognized for my gude vork. Dis ist America, after all. Yah?" He walked across the surface of the pool on a path the creatures obediently made for him, never allowing his holey socks to touch the water. "Und these 'dings' are der Gynamite, der children uff M'sieu Pusey."

As he neared, Kirsten could see most of the stains on the lab smock were days-old smears of Cheese Whiz topped by cracker crumbs. And he smelled as bad as the creatures.

"Who zent you, mon ami?" Dr. Pusey asked. "Time? Newsweek? The National Enquirer? Jack & Jill?"

"Scientific American," Kirsten lied without hesitation, playing to Pusey's vanity.

Pusey snorted. "Ach du lieber. Nobody reads dat. Efen I only buy it for der pictures... und der centerfold. "

"Uh ... and Reader's Digest, too," Kirsten added, grasping for straws. "I'm a stringer."

"Yumpin' Yumney Reader's Digest?" This had obviously piqued Dr. Pusey's interest. "Vould dey let me do one of dem Condensed Milk ads -- GOT MK?"

Yeah. That's right. It's for a new feature they've started: The Most Interesting Mad Scientist I Ever Knew."

"I rather like dat," Pusey replied, stroking the dried Cheese Whiz on his chin as though it was a beard. "Although," he added, " it is more correct to say "I'm 'miffed', not 'mad!." He fixed Kirsten with a maniacal glare. "No one ban efer called me 'interesting' before."

"Trust me," Kirsten continued, "When I get through with you, Pusey will be on the lips of every man in America." Just like Frankenstein, Dracula and Joe

Biden, she thought.

"As vell it should be, mademoiselle!" the scientist boomed. "I can see it now: me and my beloved children on der Letterman Show vit Dave, yah!" His eyes grew wider.

"Sure. Sure. You guys would be a natural for his 'Stupid Pet Tricks' segment. Maybe they could debone an elephant? Or purr 'Eat It!'"

"Vhat!?" There was indignation and true confusion in his thin voice.

"I mean Dave would love you. I could introduce you to him, I introduced him to Idi Amin He ate it up."

"What a devious vitch you ban be, si" Pusey hissed. "I like dat in a voman,"

He made a vaving gesture with one arm and the tentacles that encircled Kirsten loosened and fell away, dropping to the floor. Still, they were close enough that she knew attempted flight would be useless. Trying to buy more time, she slowly reached into her purse and withdrew her micro-cassette recorder.

"Do you mind?" she asked. "I like my quotes to be accurate."

"Not at all," said Pusey magnanimously. "The vorld needs to hear my story. To hear how der U. S. Military hounds me, tries to track me down so day can kill my bueno children."

"You think of these Gynamites as your…children?"

"I sacrificed my 'th' gene to create them, si?" He smiled slyly. "Donnervetter! Do you know vhat dey really are, young lady?"

"No, not exactly, no. Some experiment in Bermuda...?"

"Take der closer look, mon ami. Don't dey seem somehow... familiar to you?"

Kirsten shivered because it was true, though she wasn't about to admit it. "Look, Doc, don't try to tell me this thing is my long lost brother who was stolen by Republicans."

"Himmel! Your brother vas stolen by der Republicans?"

"Worse. Young Republicans."

"Der poor child. Vas he tortured by degrees?"

"Yeah. They were Masonic Young Republicans. Made for one hell of a story, though." She shook her head to clear her mind. "But, let's get back to business. You say I should recognize this stinking glob of—uh, I mean these blinking mobs as your children?"

"Si. You und efery voman on der planet, mademoiselle Lane."

"You don't mean you cloned them from the cells of blind dates?"

"Nein, nein, nein. Dink, my dear. Dink!"

Kirsten stared intently at the disgusting mass spread out before her, again feeling a strange itching sensation, almost a burning within her. She shook her head.

"Ace's dandruff? Sorry, Dr. Pusey. I'm whipped."

"I'll gif you der hint," he cackled, leaning forward. "Vagisil!"

Kirsten's jaw dropped in horror. "Oh-my-God! You don't mean...?

"YES!!" Pusey threw back his head and laughed like a drooling idiot. "My beloved Gynamite are nothing more dan a mutated form of der common yeast infection!"

"Noooo!" Kirsten gasped, rising to the occasion and reflexively crossing her legs again and shuddering at the mere thought. She hadn't felt so repulsed since the night she double dated with Michael Jackson, his chimpanzee Bubbles, and Fanny Francher. Fanny had gone ape.

"You... you..." she choked, "You must be–

Miffed?!" Pusey finished for her, then laughed again. "Uff course I am! Otherwise, I vouldn'd be der miffed. scientist, now vould I? I'd be der mad scientist, or a mild scientist, or a sensitive scientist or a soothing scientist, or a–"

"I get the point. Where did you come up with such a twisted idea?"

"Tvisted? Tvisted? You mean inspired, don't you, mon ami? I started when I vas a boy vorking on tourist fishing boats, baiting der hooks per squeamish vomens, by gar. I vas fascinated vit tiny, viggling things. I vorked hard as an apprentice until I rose through der ranks and fulfilled my first dream.

"I became a Master Baiter.

"Uncle Sam paid me to create dese dear Gynamites as instruments uff destruction, to breed dem vith a taste for godless Communists. Dey come in der small package, yah. Day are dynamite for der 'mysterious triangle'. Ergo, Gynamite.

"But den der whole vorld changed. Donnervetter! Vere der devil can you find a godless Commie nowadays outside uff a Unitarian church und Congress?" He began to pace back and forth.

"Dey considered using it on der N.O.W. gang, but decided Patricia Ireland was so uptight she'd resist infection. Zo, dey cut uff my funding for Project Scratch 'N Sniff. I could lif vith dat. But dey vanted to remove all evidence dat such und operation had efer existed. Himmel! Dey vanted to kill my babies!?" Pusey's eyes grew moist with motion.

"Sacre bleu! I couldn't let dem do dat. Zo, I've been forced to lead der life uff a fugitive; dwelling in isolation, subsisting on Cheese Whiz... despite its side effects."

"How on earth did you steal these things from the government lab?"

"I did not steal dem on der earth, mon ami. On der Dallas Cheerleaders. Dey visited der lab on a field trip on day."

"And I've been wanting to ask you about the Cheese Whiz."

"Yumpin' Yimney! Don't you know? It's der perfect dietary supplement, containing elements uff efery known food group... und a few unknown ones as vell, mademoiselle. But der side effects," he said, shaking his head. "It's der aphrodisiac. Und you pronounce Ws live Vs and THs like Ds, even if you're bylingual, like me. "

"Ah. How did you smuggle such a huge gob of creatures out of the labs with the help of Dallas Cheerleaders."

"Von piece at der time, by gar."

"Ah. Then I assume from the aphrodisiac side effect that there must be a Mrs. Doctor Pusey on the grounds?"

"Nein. "

"Girlfriend?"

"No."

"Kissing cousin?"

"Nyet. "

"Inflatable Kathie Lee doll?"

"No."

"Inflatable Regis doll? Then excuse me, Doc, and no offense meant, but... what the hell do you need an aphrodisiac for?"

Pusey scratched his head, dislodging several flakes of dandruff or dried cheese. "Bah," he said rather sheepishly, "I'm afraid I've been too busy to really dink about it."

"Maybe one of those 'dink' signs over your desk would help."

"I knew you'd understand, Miss Lane. You're obviously quite intelligent." He stared a hole through her. "Und warm. Und loving. Und round. Und soft. Und—"

Kirsten knew she had gotten his mind on the wrong track, and needed to get it back, quickly.

"This is all multi-fascinating, Dr. Pusey, but I have another question for you. I know this thing of yours has been snacking on dogs and cats around town—but what about people? I mean, it was designed to eat people, right?"

"Yah, quite right. Military objectives und all dat, don't you know. But now dat ve're on our own, I've gifen dern strict instructions not to ingest humans... yet. Do you know der kinds uff germs dey could pick up from eating Howard Stern? Donnervetter! I hate to dink uff it."

"You instructed them?" Kirsten's face twisted in puzzlement. "You talk as if these giant... giant yeast infections have intelligence."

"Oh, but dey do, mademoiselle." Pusey's features lit up with pride. "My liddle Sourballs are all quite bright! Just der other day, dey brought dere teacher und apple! Und Adams apple! HAHAHAHAHAHA!

"Und dey're actually very gentle," Dr. Pusey continued. "But, der military shouldn't misconstrue dat as veakness, by gar. If dey continue der hostilities, I may be forced out uff self-defense to loose der full fury uff my babies on humanity." His voice grew a pitch higher.

"If I zo desired, I could lead dem on a rampage der likes of vhjch mankind has nefer known. Himmel! Nothing could stop me, nothing. If I zo desired..." he paused for effect.

"I could rule der vorld!! "

Both Pusey and Kirsten glanced skyward and then doubled over, laughing so hard that they could barely breathe.

"Oh, oh, oh," he gasped at last. "Tell me, Miss Lane... did dat sound as incredibly corny as I dink it did?"

"Well, that and the corny accents prove you certainly earned your degree from the College of Cliches."

"I guess you could say I'm der first multi-cultural miffed scientist."

Still clutching his stomach, Pusey motioned Kirsten to follow him to a tiled wall. When there, he pointed to a framed certificate. It was a B.A. for Overused Accents from the Newark College of Cliches.

Pusey pointed to a second framed certificate. It was an MD in Gynecology from the Baywatch College of Hard Knockers. Next to it was a framed certificate proclaiming Pusey a Chicken Hawk Scout in the Boy Scabs. Kirsten was struck that each certificate proved what she had suspected. He had changed his name to Pusey to stop the snide jokes and teasing that had tormented him all of his life because of his birth name.

Norman Beaver was on each certificate.

⸎

"I can understand vhy Adolf Hitler finally faked his own death und retired to der lif uff a svord svallover in a Peruvian circus. Still, I always vanted to say it." He patted the pockets of his stained shirt.

"Could I interest you in a Vhiz, Miss Lane?"

"No thanks. I went at the Bates and Switch Motel."

"Probably good advice. Can't be too careful nowadays vhen using strange bathrooms, by gar. Und alvays practice zafe zex. You nefer know vhat you might contact nowadays, eh, mon ami?"

"Gynamite comes in small packages, eh, Doc?"

"Nein. Nein. Actually, in der small boxes, mademoiselle."

Kirsten opened her mouth to reply, then closed it. An ominous rumbling had begun to vibrate through the foundations of the building. The clumped mass of mutated Gynamites that had congregated in the swimming pool quivered as if in fear. "Sacre bleu!? Vhat is that?" Pusey snapped.

Dr. Pusey trotted across the room, his cheese-stained shirt billowing after him. A recessed panel in the wall creaked back as a large monitor screen flared to life. It was connected to video cameras which covered the grounds around the mansion. Dr. Pusey punched buttons, moving the view on the monitor in different directions.

"Can't be too careful. My enemas are everywhere."

Kirsten dropped her recorder back into her purse and began to ease toward a nearby doorway. The tentacles on either side of her twitched spasmodically.

"You!" Dr. Pusey bellowed, freezing her in her tracks. He pointed an unbroken finger at her. "You betrayed me! You led my enemas to me!"

"Oh, hell!" Kirsten exclaimed as she glanced at the monitor screen behind the scientist. Tanks and military humvees could be seen rolling down the streets of Cadence led by Mulligan Stu, who still carried the aluminum ladder glued to his hands. They were headed straight toward the mansion.

"Sacre Bleu!! You vant dem to hurt by babies!" Pusey roared in anguish. "I'll kill you for dat, mon ami!"

Kirsten swallowed heavily. "You know, Doc... some of that Cheese Vhiz would taste pretty good right about now."

"ARRRRRRGGGGGG!! " screamed the miffed scientist.

"Then again, maybe not. Well, infobabe, what do you do now? Dink, stupid, dink!!"

On the monitor, Kirsten watched Ash Ho raise and shake a fist at the Pusey Mansion. It was some small consolation, in the face of certain death, that the Cadence doctors had been able to remove the fireman's hose... but not the nozzle.

As Kirsten watched the monitor, two of the yellow-gray tentacles flailed out and grabbed her. One wrapped tightly around her upper body, crushing her arms to her sides as the other locked around her knees. She maintained her grip on her purse and camera as she was lifted high into the air.

"Donnervetter!! You told Ash Ho vhere to find me," Pusey raged. "You haf endangered my children!"

"NO!" Kirsten gasped. I vouldn't do that, Doc. Uh ... wouldn't. Child endangerment is against the law!"

"I'm der only law here," Pusey sneered.

"You think you could fix a parking ticket for me?"

"I dink dat could be..." Dr. Pusey slapped his forehead, sending bits of Cheese Whiz flying. "Himmel! Don't try to divert me. Your life ist hanging by a dread, mademoiselle."

"Actually, it's hanging by a piece of goo that's starting to ooze down inside by bra," Kirsten vamped. "Surely you wouldn't hurt a poor... helpless... soft... round woman?"

"Zure. If you find one, zend her over." Dr. Pusey plucked a piece of dried cheese from his hair, nibbling at it as he stared intently at Kirsten. A small stream of drool slid down his chin. The only thing that Kirsten found more disgusting than the sight of this dirty, slobbering, horny maniac was the knowledge that in times past she had seduced worse in pursuit of stories.

"Why don't you let me slip into something more comfortable than these tentacles, Doc, and we can talk about it," she cooed alluringly.

"Der ist nothing more comfortable." The doctor's mouth dropped open slightly and he took a step forward. Then the flashing images on his monitor screen again drew his attention. Mulligan's ladder had become hopelessly tangled with Ho's nozzle. Mulligan stewed.

"Business bevore pleasure, Lois," he declared. Kirsten wondered into which category he placed her.

"Go!" Pusey shouted down at the mass of mutated creatures clustered in the pool. "Go und destroy de soldiers und eferyone else in dis God-forsaken town, before dey can hurt us!"

At his command, many of the Gynamites melded together in a single mass, while others remained swirling about separately. All started to drop below the surface of the water, toward the drain that would lead them outside the mansion.

"Vait!" Pusey shouted. Responding, the oozing mass heaved upward above the waterline. "Don't forget to say Grace first."

The amorphous mass bowed over slightly for a moment, then again began its descent beneath the water. At the same moment, the mansion was jolted slightly as the first wave of tanks drew nearer.

"Dey'll all die, liddle girl," Pusey cackled. "But you'll be the first to go, by gar!"

"No! Take Toto instead!"

"Vhat?" The doctor was taken aback. "My babies are going to kill you!" The scientist grinned like a young boy who'd just found his father's stash of Playboys. "Yumpin' Yimney!! Now you'll see what a really miffed scientist can do!!"

"So, this is how it ends. Not with a bang but with a whimp."

The tentacles holding Kirsten turned her upside down. She found herself staring down into a huge, frothing "mouth" that had formed in the yellow-gray island of mutated flesh. Unbidden, the image of a giant breath mint came to her mind, the same image always triggered by Gephard. She now understood the giant air freshener that had been stuck in the sewer.

"Do it!" Pusey commanded. "Kill her!"

His final words were drowned out by a thunderous explosion that came from below. The floor of the swimming pool thrust upward then collapsed down. The main body of the mutated organism was caught in the undertow of the pool water cascading through the newly formed hole in the floor, and was carried out of sight.

Frightened by this sudden and unexpected turn of events, the piece of the collective organism holding Kirsten released its grip. As she plummeted down into the remains of the pool, the organism split into three smaller sections and slithered into the protective embrace of their creator.

At the bottom of the pool, Kirsten tried to rise to her feet. Small, jellied bodies -- portions of the main organism that had not been sucked through the hole blown in the pool floor -- began to wriggle toward her. From the corner of one eye, she saw the figure of a man rising up through the crater in the floor. One hand pulled back the hood of the vinyl slicker he was wearing.

"Hiya, toots!" Cleveland Smith called out by way of greeting. "What's wrong? Something eating you?"

Kirsten threw herself forward, sliding along the scum-slickened bottom of the pool like a baseball player diving into second base. She slammed into the startled Smith and they both fell back through the hole. She held her breath, anticipating a plunge into the brackish waters of the sewer below. Instead, she flopped onto something smooth and rubbery.

"Oh, hell!" she yelped, trying to crawl off of it.

"Hey!" Smith protested. "Take it easy. You'll overturn the raft!"

"Oh!" Kirsten threw her arms around the youth's neck and kissed him on the lips.

"What was that for?" he asked gruffly. Even in the dim light of the sewage tunnel, she could see his checks grow red.

"For showing up in the nick of time, kiddo!" Kirsten declared. Then she drew back her right hand and slapped him sharply.

"Ow! What was that for?"

"For calling me 'toots' again."

Smith rubbed his throbbing cheek, then turned his gaze upward. "Hey, Doc! What'll you charge me to take this dame back?"

"Kill dem! Kill dem gude!!" Pusey screamed in response. The three monsters surrounding him quickly slithered over the edge of the swimming pool.

"Get us out of here!" Kirsten screamed.

"What if I say nein, I mean, no?" Smith replied, folding his arms and smiling smugly.

Kirsten lunged across the raft, grabbing the boy by the throat. "What if I string you up by your Indiana Joneses?" Kirsten released him and he quickly fired up the small outboard motor attached to the raft. A small light mounted on the raft illuminated the tunnel as they sped away from the gaping hole in the pool.

"Hang on, toots," he yelled above the echoing roar of the motor. "I mean, Ms. Lane! I'll have us out of here in no time."

"I'm not sure that'll do us any good, " Kirsten said, leaning close to him. "By now, that creature's reached the surface, and it has orders to kill anything that moves!"

"Then don't move, toots. Pretend you're on a date. Seriously, I think I've come up with a– ouch!" He yelped as Kirsten popped him on the back of the head. "Hey! This isn't a Three Stooges reunion."

"What did I tell you about that 'toots' stuff, Beaver Cleaver. I expect to be treated with the same respect you've given any beautiful babe. "

"Well, if we're pretending, what can I call you? Sis? Misses? Bitch.com?"

"Why not stick with Ms.Lane?"

"Because that'd be a Ms. Take."

"Maybe that is too formal for someone who just saved my life. Make it Kirsten."

"Yes!!" Smith pumped his right fist in a triumphant up and down motion.

"By the way. What did you use to blow up Pusey's pool back there?"

"I kept a jar from the Cadence outhouse just in case, and I guess this was the case. Gases from nature are just one of my specialities."

"He calls them Gynamites. You know how to blow them up?"

The raft struck something unseen in the sewer, lurched to the left, and then disengaged. Kirsten would have sworn it'd struck Danny DeVito floating face down in a tuxedo looking like a bloated penguin.

"I found the answer by going over Dr. Pusey's research papers. Did you know he modeled his Chia Pets after Ted Koppel's hairpiece?"

"How'd you get your hands on those?"

"It wasn't hard. After he released 'Dame J. Edger, The Movie', the F.B.I. is so busy keeping an eye on Oliver Stone that they don't pay much attention to anything else. It's worth breaking into for the Nancy Reagan files alone. I hope I'm still that nimble when I get to be her age."

"I thought you were her age."

"I went over Dr. Pusey's notes from top to bottom. If my guess is correct, we're up against the mother of all yeast infections."

"Sad thing, isn't it, doll? After the age of 16, you women fall apart pretty rapidly. Prone to all sorts of horrible afflictions. Sags, bags, wrinkles. Gray hair. False teeth. Irregularity. And that less than feminine feeling. Nature's been pretty cruel to you ladies."

"What makes you such an expert on female physiology?"

"I watch the commercials during 'As The World Turns'."

"Were we talking about Dr. Pusey's Gynamites? If you know how to destroy it, why didn't you do it back at his mansion?"

"That's not why I was there."

"Is this newspaper delivery day? Were you selling Cub Scab urinal cakes?"

"I thought you might need some help getting away from him. And Cub Scabs don't sell urinal cakes, doll. We sell oysters."

Their raft sped past a wall poster from the National Endowment for the Arts. Gilbert Gottfried was the poster child. Smith clamped his mouth shut, focusing on piloting the raft through the winding sewer system.

"Oh, my God," Kirsten gasped. "You've got a crush on me, don't you?"

"Don't flatter yourself, doll. I like my women younger, sexier and a hell of a lot quieter than you." Smith cut the motor as they neared a manhole.

Kirsten grabbed the ladder mounted on the wall and scrambled up it. The sound of tank cannon, machine guns, and screaming filled her hearing before she had the manhole cover off. She got up onto street level.

Dr. Pusey's creatures covered the streets of Cadence, swinging from lampposts, clinging to buildings, dropping onto passing pickup trucks, and oozing through grills. Pandemonium reigned. The Gynamite appeared to be unstoppable, slithering through streams of machine gun fire that chipped bricks from walls and carved hunks from the pavement.

An out-of-control tank lumbered up a pickup, then fell over on its side as the treads whiffed endlessly. A jeep rammed through the glass walls of the Bag and Mount It convenience store as the driver fought a glob of slime encompassing his head. Soldiers who had been rappelling down the side of a building were now trying desperately to reclimb their ropes as creatures slid up behind them, ignoring the pull of gravity.

Kirsten captured it all with her camera, whispering, "Oh God, oh God, oh God..."

The street cracked in the center as a behemoth mass of the Gynamite surged through it. It waddled out like an angry bear. Dr. Herman Pusey rode where its neck would be if it had one. It swiped out a "paw" and knocked a tank over effortlessly.

"It's a tankless job, but someone's gotta stop it," said Cleveland. "We can stop it. I've made all the preparations, but we've got to get out to the airport."

At that moment, five pickups from the Sheriff's department pulled up a short distance away. White-faced deputies, grimly gripping shotguns, stepped from the vehicles. Kirsten spotted a familiar face among them. She motioned toward them while looking at Smith.

"I'm going to snap a few more pictures of that behemoth, Cleve. Meanwhile, I want you to go get Layd."

"I'd love to, dammit—but this is neither the time nor the place, doll!"

"No, you little jerk, I mean Deputy Layd. He can drive us to the Memorial Airport."

Kirsten was still snapping pictures when two cops pulled up alongside her in a patrol car. One cop was instantly down behind the door of his vehicle, his bottle of cooking oil pointing straight out ahead of him. "Wesson!" he bellowed.

"State IUD," Kirsten called out as she neared the man. She flashed her library ID, then put it away before Deputy Ansell could get a good look at it. "I'm commandeering this pickup. And try pointing a gun, Ansell. We're not frying bacon."

Ansell looked puzzled. "I thought you were a recruit." He glanced down at the plastic bottle in his fist.

"I've got no time to go into that now, Deputy," Kirsten said officiously. She stepped in front of him, guiding herself in behind the steering wheel. A plastic figure of Joe Friday sat on the dash still bobbing its head. "You're going to be getting high marks in my report for your cooperation in this, Ansell. Now got out there and give those Gynamite cholesterol poisoning."

"Yes, ma'am." Ansell saluted, hitting himself in the forehead with his bottle of oil, and moved out, joining the other Deputy at his patrol pickup.

Kirsten keyed the ignition and backed the pickup into the street just as a fire hydrant nearby exploded, killing a cocker spaniel relieving itself. The explosion threw a half-dozen amoebas that splattered onto nearby cars and walls. She whirled the pickup around in a tight one-eighty.

"Where'd you learn to drive like that?" Cleveland Smith asked as he buckled in.

"In Manhattan," Kirsten replied as she drove straight toward a Gynamite fragment in front of them. "I was undercover as a cabbie, searching for the 'Fare Killer', Singh Ramalamadingdong, the psycho cab driver who was running down pedestrians for not riding with him." The nose of the Sheriff's pickup slammed into the Gynamite, shattering it into a thousand little globs of creature. The globs retained 'life', clinging to the hood and throbbing like a gathering of tree toads.

Kirsten cut the wheel hard as more explosions and machine gun fire sounded behind them. She floored the accelerator, racing through the flames belched out by a flame-thrower as it tried to toast four of the creatures joining to form an even larger single creature.

"Jeeze, Louise," she mumbled as she side-swiped the creatures and broke them apart. The fire from the flame-thrower scattered across her side of the car and blistered paint. "These things are worse than Transformers or Gobots."

"I'll admit I thought you were one crazy broad when I found you in the sewers, doll," Cleveland said, shaking his head. "But that's changed. You're the gutsiest skirt I've ever met. Have you even stopped to think what'll happen if one of these Gynamites infects you?"

"That," said Kirsten.. "is the yeast of my problems."

"**W**hat the hell is this?" Kirsten asked when she saw the airplane. "The reason Howard Hughes became a hermit?"

A WING 'N A SPRAYER was scrawled in red paint on the side of the plane.

"It's a single-prop crop duster," Cleveland Smith replied, pulling the chocks from under the wheels.

"One question. Can you get it up?" Kirsten touched the flimsy body molding. There were two cockpits behind the double wings. She didn't figure her name belonged on either one of them.

"Sure," he said, swinging the double hangar door open with a creak of rusty hinges, He looked at her and grinned as he knocked dust from his hands. "I'm a teenaged boy, remember? But I think dinner and a movie are traditional on a first date."

"How is that supposed to help against those sewer Gynamite?" Kirsten added, ignoring Cleveland's remark.

"I'll admit liquor is quicker... But, seriously, the tanks are loaded with a chemical mixture that is a guaranteed poison for Pusey's bacteria," he replied as he zipped up his 'bomber' jacket, a Cadence high school windbreaker with Chess Club printed on the back. "We can release clouds of it over the town." He threw his backpack into the rear cockpit.

"It's vinegar and water."

A pickup truck roared onto the runway. One light was out, shining vaguely against the backdrop of approaching dawn. She turned back to Cleveland Smith as he threw a leg up into the cockpit and slid behind the controls. "I'm not going," she said. "I've got a story to file before anyone else beats me to it."

He looked down at her. "I can't do this by myself. I need help. A minute ago, you were worried about those people in Cadence."

The pickup closed in, pulling up to a stop by the hangar doors. "Get one of them to help you," Kirsten said, pointing to the pickup. "I'm done with heroics."

"Toots, if you'll remember, I saved your backside back there. You can't back out on me now."

"If it means I have to go up in this," Kirsten said, "I sure as hell can."

Cleveland replaced his slouch hat with a pilot's leather helmet. It had a Snoopy emblem over the right ear with the dog dressed as the Red Baron. He pulled his Snoopy helmet low, then hit the ignition switch. The prop spun fitfully, coughed, then caught full if uneven life. Streamers of black smoke poured out behind the prop.

Making herself walk away, Kirsten gritted her teeth, telling herself again there was no way she was going up in something that looked as if it had all the stability of Charlie Brown's kite. Then she saw the driver of the pickup clearly for the first time. Five men squatted in the pickup's bed.

Toothless Clem Clem threw up an arm at once, then hauled a horse pistol from his overalls pocket. "There she is! There's the woman who kneed me! I'd recognize that color of red hair anywhere!

Kirsten froze even as she noticed that Clem Clem now wore a protective cup. On the outside of his overalls. The others had to be part of his family, his kith and kin. In fact, they looked like they were part of a family that bad grown up close, perhaps in the same house for the last six or seven generations. They looked as much alike as the Clinton's that had invaded Washington, DC.

"Hey, that's my plane! " one of the Clems bellowed.

After throwing her purse and camera into the forward cockpit, Kirsten grabbed hold of a wing strut—prayed that it would hold—and scrambled aboard.

"There used to be seven Clem's," said Cleveland. "But they drove that pickup into the Cadence Lake and one of 'em drowned. The one who couldn't get the tailgate open!!"

The crop duster hit a bump as she pulled herself into the cockpit, and she spilled into it unceremoniously. She surfaced screaming invective, only to find Cleveland smiling at her as the plane jumped into the air.

"I see you changed your mind, toots," he said above the roar of the passing wind. "Strap in!"

Kirsten held her breath, mumbling her reporter's prayer for survival. "Now I lay my story down to print. I pray the editor my story to take. If I should die before it hits the stands, I pray for a posthumous Pulitzer to make." The ground spun away dizzingly. Then her survival mechanism kicked in and she turned on her digital camera.

Cleveland nodded, the brim of his hat ruffling in the breeze, somehow miraculously staying on. The crop duster rolled over and lost altitude, screaming for street level.

Kirsten hung onto the edges of the cockpit, watching as the combatants in the streets rolled first one way, then the other. The general consensus was that the Army was getting its butt kicked. She let go of her hold to start taking pictures.

"You see that lever up there?" Cleveland asked.

"Yeah." She snapped a picture of a giant glob with Dr. Pusey on its back jerking a turret off a tank. Another as the giant Gynamite opened a mouth in the center of its body. Another as the turret was tossed inside. And a final as the turret was spat out.

"Pull the lever!" Cleveland yelled. The crop duster was less than ten feet above the broken street surface.

Kirsten ignored the command, still taking pictures. "Next time, though," she yelled back. "I need these shots."

"You're crazy. Those things will kill us."

The three-story, man-shaped mass of Gynamite with Dr. Pusey on its shoulders swatted out a three-fingered hand in their direction, narrowly missing. Kirsten closed her eyes as Cleveland guided them sideways between three legs as thick as California redwoods. She managed to control her stomach as she turned around to take more pictures, working the zoom lens by reflex.

"You pull that lever this time, doll," Cleveland warned, "or I'll ram that thing and rupture the tanks myself."

The plane spun in the air, feeling like it had folded into itself, then dropped through itself. Kirsten shouted curses as she forced her eyes to stay open despite the over-riding impulse to squeeze them shut. She locked her hand around the lever, yanking it back as soon as the plane levelled off.

Jets of noxious fumes sprayed out behind them, trailing a long, yellow cloud across the street. The Gynamite started turning cyanide blue and dropping immediately. Without warning, a man-shaped, giant mass of figures reared up in front of them on three trembling legs. It was turning blotchy blue in places as the vinegar and water saturated it. Pusey screamed and shook his fists at them, only to go tumbling off the deteriorating mass' back.

The plane turned sideways, losing altitude rapidly as the giant arm swept over it. Wobbling unsteadily, the Gynamite fell and struck the street with a loud douche, and shattered into their individual selves. They were all blue by the time they stopped rolling. One of the wheels on the landing gear bounced from the top of a '64 Thunderbird, leaving a huge tear in the canvas roof.

A collective cheer rose from the massed law enforcement and military people below them as they realized the creatures were either dead or dying. A contingent of Army personnel had Pusey in hand. Kirsten took a final picture of the captured scientist.

"Can I land you anywhere?" Cleveland asked as he aimed them at the open sky.

She looked back at him as they cleared a shop for obese animals called Heavy Petting, and continued gaining altitude. Kirsten got out her lighter, then discovered her cigarette pack was empty. Cleveland Smith passed up his Lucky

Strikes Jr's. She lit one for both of them, giving his back.

"Don't you want to set this crate down and play the local hero?"

"Not me. If my mom finds out what I've been doing, I'm dead meat. And that T-bird back there? That was my dads car. He loves that car. You think I want anyone to know I was flying the plane that creased it? Let Clem Clem and his brothers take the credit. By this time tomorrow, he'll be convinced he was flying this plane even though he wont be able to remember where he left it. Me, I want to live to see fifteen, lose my virginity, and go through zits like everybody else."

"Right. So how does a flight to L.A. sound?"

"At the moment, pretty good. It'll give everybody a chance to cool down before I make my reappearance. Do you have money for gas?"

Kirsten flashed him a smile and her Global Star silver card. "Does Cheese Vhiz in der woods?"

He nodded. "What about you? Don't you want to bask in the glory for awhile?"

Recalling Clem Clem, the Christian trucker, Barabajagal, Ramalamadingdong and all the other confusion she'd left behind her - not to mention one severely angry Major Ashley B. Ho, Kirsten shook her head.

"Not me. Global Star pays me for being a reporter, not a hero. I've got a story to write up. Being a hero just kind of falls into the job description somewhere. What I wish I had right now is a cellular telephone."

"All you had to do was ask," Cleveland said. He unzipped his backpack and handed a cellular telephone over. Kirsten smiled.

It was a Popeye cellular phone.

Kirsten dialed the Global Star number and waited, knowing the switchboard could reach Frank Gephard at home even this late. She looked at Cleveland Smith in idle speculation as she waited for the connection to be completed. A feeling of amazing calm swept over her. "Hey, Smith."

"Yeah, doll?"

"'When we get to L.A. maybe I can help you out with that virginity thing. NOT!!"

"I thought this was where the hero always gets the girl like in one of Galt Whitney's movies."

"Get real, Cleaver," she smiled. But the idea must have struck a hidden cord. She caught herself humming the tune from Whitney's biggest animation hit.

Beauty and the Yeast.

SUCKER PUNCHED
(Interlude: Part Two)

Frank Gephard whistled softly as he sauntered down the corridor leading to the Photography Department. The heels of his platform shoes struck like flint against the floor. He tapped one finger against the pencil stuck behind his right ear, keeping time with the melody he was whistling, Short People.

It was going to be another late night spent documenting the extensive mentions of brand name products by every Global Star reporter that almost doubled the profit of the paper. Besides, Uge Nochers had remained behind to work with him tonight, slowly pecking away at her old manual typewriter. She refused to touch the computer on her desk. Something about a mouse.

Gephard stopped whistling as he reached the office of the Photo Editor. He didn't bother to knock, but walked in. He smiled as he was greeted by the sight he had expected.

Sol Trotsky, the Photo Editor, was standing in front of an enormous mirror that hung on one wall of the office. His head was bent in such a manner that its top was reflected in the mirror. Trotsky was gingerly running his fingers through his thick hair, looking for all the world like a monkey inspecting itself for fleas. The adult diaper he wore instead of trousers added to the simian likeness. Sol's little eccentricity was distasteful, but he was the best in the business, so Gephard had to pamper him.

"What?" said Sol without moving. "They were out of the eight inch heels, so you settled for six's?"

"You're a silly idiot, you know that, Sol?" Gephard said by way of greeting. "I've known you for what—45 years? And you've been afraid you're going bald that whole time."

"It's gonna happen, Frankie," Trotsky replied, smoothing his hair back down. "It's a genetic thing, you know? My father was bald, my uncles were bald. Hell, even my mother was bald."

"Only after the sex change operation, Sol."

"Sure, that's what the doctors wanted me to believe."

"You're sixty-two years old, Sol. If you were going to lose your hair, you'd have lost it."

"Oh? And since when did you know so much about it, Mr. Clairol? You been goin' to follicle school nights?"

Gephard sighed. "All right, have it your own way, you big baby. You're going bald."

"You think so?" Trotsky again tried to inspect his hair in the mirror. "Think some hair plugs might help? Topical lotion? Trump's Hair Sump Pump?"

Gephard considered where the plugs might best fit, but said nothing.

Trotsky took one last look in the mirror, then turned back toward Gephard. "So, what can I do for you, Frankie? Wife got you on short rations again?"

"Please, call me 'Chief'."

"What kinda caca's that? I helped raise you, Frankie. Well, not very high, but you forget that? I kept an eye on you even when you was a kid. I looked out for you." Trotsky shivered at an unpleasant memory, and stuck a large pacifier in his mouth. Its ring had been replaced by a cigar stub, but it fooled no one, not even Uge.

"I even took that ugly sister of yours to the prom so she wouldn't have to sit at home alone," he said around the pacifier.

"Yeah, yeah," Gephard said. "I don't have a sister. That was my mother, Sol, and you begged me to set you up,"

"What a relief. I actually thought it was your brother, what with all those little pieces of toilet paper on her face from shaving. What can I do for you, Frankie?"

"Take a load off," Gephard said, gesturing at a chair. At least it smelled like a load. "Okay, Sol, here's the poop. I just got a call from one of my stringers over in Jersey. He claims Donald Trump has truck a deal with an ex-Nazi doctor. Seems he wants to surgically connect Ivanna and Marla together at the hip. Like Siamese twins."

"Cut the alimony in half, eh?"

"Literally. Anyway, our stringer thinks he can get someone sneaked in to watch the surgery, so I thought it might be a good idea to send a photographer over there."

"You got it. Let's just see who's available." Trotsky took a seat behind his desk cluttered with squeak toys and empty baby bottles and began thumbing through his assignment book.

"We want just the right guy for this," he muttered. "Someone who can deal with the kind of harsh lighting you're gonna have in an operating room."

"What's the big deal?" Gephard asked. "It's not like you have to have a brain for this, Sol. I mean, anybody earn take a stupid picture!'"

"Sure. This from the guy whose eye level is Mickey Rooney's belly button." Trotsky snorted with disgust. "Course, that could be the angle. Hey, what is it with all you guys in editorial. You think you're better'n the rest of us pee pee-ons. "

"We are, Sol," Gephard replied smoothly, rubbing it in. "I think it's like the baldness, you know? Genetic. So you got someone we can send to Jersey, or do I have to give the job to my pimply-faced nephew?"

"Keep your shirt on, Frankie."

"You should do the same, Sol."

"Hey, I get rashes." Trotsky earnestly scanned the assignment book for a moment, then looked back up at Gephard.

"By the way... are you still schtooping that zaftig secretary of yours? The 'knock-knock joke girl'."

Gephard looked appalled. "What the hell are you talking about, Sol? Miss Nochers is like a sister to me."

"Nah, she's more like your sister to me." Trotsky stuck his nose back into his assignment book.

"You're too old to be talking like that, Sol, even if you are in your second childhood. Don't I overlook that?"

"Only when you tiptoe. And God forbid I should ever be that old. Do me a favor, Frankie. The day I lose my sex drive... put a bullet through my brain."

"Can't do. I don't own a small caliber pistol. Anyway, Sol, what would your wife think if she heard you talk that way? Edith is a saint."

"So who wants to boink a saint? She lost interest years ago. I think she gave it up to celebrate the Bicentennial." Trotsky mumbled something else that was indecipherable as he flipped through the pages of his assignment book.

"I suppose we could send the Feldman kid. No. I forgot... he's in the Midwest somewhere, doing that piece about circus freaks from Mars."

"You'd think they could find better jobs," Gephard commented. "After all, good things come in small packages."

"That's why I've never opened your Christmas presents, Frankie. They're all so sticky."

"You've always been jealous of the heights I've reached careerwise, haven't you, Sol?"

Trotsky continued down the page. "Hmmm. Castle's finished that axe murderer shoot, but he won't be back until tomorrow. Can't understand how anyone could kill a good axe."

"No good. I need someone in Jersey within the next two hours."

"Depends."

"You're joking. I thought you wore LUVs."

"Ha ha. Here we go. Alucard. He's hanging around somewhere, and he's good. In fact I think he's in the morgue."

Gephard pondered for a moment. "No. Not if we have anyone else available."

"Why not? You got something against his lifestyle?"

"I've got other plans for Lonnie."

"Such as?"

"Look, he's the best man you've got, right?"

"I'd say so, yeah. "

"So it occurred to me last night; why not team our best photographer up with our best reporter?"

Trotsky grimaced. "Oh, no, Frankie. You don't mean Montana? The guy brought up on statutory rape... of a statue?"

"It was a life-size Barbie doll and an honest mistake considering the similarities to what Ace usually dates. He's due in from the Orient any minute now. I thought I'd try to get him and Lonnie together."

"The big schmuck'll never go for it, Frankie. You know how he hates photographers."

"He just likes to take his own shots, that's all. Besides, he doesn't hate all photographers. Just you."

"I've never received a greater compliment."

"You never deserved one. It's just that Ace thinks you're a Communist."

"Where the hell'd he get a cockamammie idea like that? I voted Republican when trickle down still meant incontinence."

"Obviously. I don't know. Your name, I guess."

"Cripes, Frankie... doesn't he know that Trotsky's been dead for 60 years? Communism's dead, for God's sake."

"Sure. But you know Ace. He doesn't think a true Commie'd let a little thing like death stop him. It doesn't stop most celebrities."

"Well, that explains why the jerk never comes into my office." Trotsky paused to scratch his nose."'Course, now that I think about it, Lonnie never comes in here either."

"Maybe he thinks baldness is contagious."

"Yeah. I don't know if the kid's terminally shy or what, but I always have to go out in the hall to talk to him. He's sorta sickly looking, too. Anemic, I think. And no wonder; I've never seen the kid eat a bite. It's no wonder he's batty."

"But you have no problem with his work?"

"You're kidding. With the guy who finally snapped Prince Albert in the can? Who got the first pics of the Hemmorrhoidians of Uranus?"

"Yeah. But I don't know... there's something about him that doesn't seem quite right. I just can't put my finger on it."

"Don't worry, Frankie. You'll figure it out." Trotsky again peered into his assignment book. Gephard took a seat on the edge of the Photo Editor's desk and began to absently thumb through a pile of envelopes.

"Here we go, Frankie, I got the man for you. I'll give him a page and have him hustle over to Jersey."

"Great." Gephard seemed distracted as he took a closer look at the envelopes he had been rifling through. "Are these the paychecks for your department, Sol?"

"Huh? Oh, yeah. Someone from payroll dropped 'em off just before you got here. "

Gephard extracted one specific envelope from the stack, "Mind if I take a look at Alucard's check?"

"Scroungin! for small change again, Goliath? Maybe the missus should increase your weekly allowance."

"I want to make sure we're paying him enough to keep him happy."

"But not enough to make him think we really need him, huh, Frankie?"

"Get outta here." Gephard stood and walked to stand next to the mirror on Trotsky's wall. Someone had pasted a Baby On Board sign on the mirror. Pulling the check from its envelope, he grunted with satisfaction at the dollar figure written on it.

He started to slide the check back into the envelope when its reflection in the mirror caught his eye. He smiled at the way the writing in the reflected image appeared backwards.

Then the smile vanished from his face. He turned away from the mirror.

"Sol, did you say Lonnie was here in the building?"

"Yeah. At least he was half an hour ago. "

"I have to go." Gephard tossed the pay envelope down on Trotsky's desk and headed out the door. "Remember to get that photographer over to Jersey."

"Yes, Chief," Trotsky said in a mocking voice, knowing Gephard was now out of earshot. "Whatever you say." He chuckled softly. "Kiss my baby smooth butt, Chief."

It wasn't really an insult. They both knew Gephard couldn't reach that high.

⎯⎯⎯ ⚬✖✖⚬ ⎯⎯⎯

Gephard was surprised to find that Uge Nochers was not at her desk. He approached the closed door of his office, only to stop when he heard voices from inside. He pressed his ear to the keyhole, and could hear Uge speaking in pleading tones.

"Don't, Lonnie."

"I can't help it, Miss Nochers," came Lon Alucard's voice in reply. "You have such wonderful breasts."

"Sonuvabitch!" Gephard cursed aloud. "The little bastards trying to put the make on her in my office!"

Gephard perked up when he heard the sound of something striking the floor. Noises that seemed to be those of a struggle followed. Then came the sound of fabric being torn.

"EEEEEE!!"

Gephard pulled back from the door in surprise as Uge's frantic scream tore through the air. Scowling with growing anger and concern, the editor stormed into the office.

What he saw froze him dead in his tracks. Uge Nochers was standing in front of Gephard's desk. A Buck Buck bucket of chicken sat on the desk. Uge, white with fear, held a chicken breast in each hand, Suddenly, Alucard was on her, pinning her arms down with his weight against the desk.

The photographer's head snapped up as Gephard burst into the room. Alucard snarled like an animal and his lips curled back to expose teeth that were long and jagged.

Acting instinctively, Gephard grabbed the pencil from behind his ear and sprinted across the room. Leaving his feet, he slammed full force into Alucard. The impact threw both men off the desk.

As they hit the floor, they locked in a clench. Alucard hissed, and Gephard flinched as his nostrils were assailed by an odor more vile than anything but an open sewer.

Shifting his weight, Gephard rolled over atop the crazed photographer. As he did so, he could see Uge cowering near the door. As the struggling editor looked at the hysterical woman, he could not help but think that Alucard had been right.

She did have wonderful breasts.

GOD BOP

by Michael Vance

"**B**eth Francher, 8:45 a.m., Friday, April 13th, en route from Rose Butte, Utah to the first available airport. Copies to Wood in Global Star Tonight FX video and Gephard at GS print. Duplicates of transcription to Ace and Kirsten with this addition: you're scooped again, butteheads!"

A light rain began to spatter the windshield of the rented Ford Escort. Behind it, Rose Butte and a dissipating black smear in the sky above it were diminishing. Francher smiled at the secret knowledge that the rain wasn't drops of water. It was Hawaiian Punch.

She looked to one side and watched as Dianne Menace recorded that fact in the Global Star Brand Name Log. That thoroughness was just one additional trait that separated her work from that of her fellow reporters, Ace Montana and Kirsten Lane, who generally faked entries after an event.

"Research," Beth said into a micro-cassette recorder in her left hand," need definition of 'bebop'. Need psychological profile of cult fanatics, brief history. David Koresh. Jim Jones. Moonies. Hari Krishnas The Al Goreites The Obamalamadingdongs."

On the dash, the head of a toy puppy bobbed to the vibrations of the rental car.

"Graphics: punch, radical mix of religious icons and low-brow pop music for opening title. Boy George dressed like the Pope? Aim for Friday, next week, deadline. I'm calling this one... God Bop."

Francher sat the recorder in the car seat next to her camera'man', Dianne Menace. "And Wood better not screw this one up. It's better than the Voodoo Village piece that Kirsten will be watching..." Francher checked the watch on her right hand on the steering wheel... "in about ten hours from now."

"Give it a rest, Fanny," said Dianne, half asleep. "She isn't interested in what you've got to offer. And I thought you weren't offering anymore anyway. How about some radio?"

"Don't..." snapped Francher as Dianne flipped the radio dial on the car dash. In mid-verse, Madonna sang,"...virgin, for the very first time." It had been a long time since anything had been for the first time for Madonna.

Beth Francher and Dianne Menace shared a look of controlled relief. "And don't call me Fanny!" said the newshound.

"Sure, buttehead."

The tension in the Escort was broken with laughter. Suddenly, Beth jerked slightly, involuntarily. The edges of her vision blurred and music seemed to rise around her. There was no mistaking the signs.

She was about to have a flashback.

Wednesday, April 11th. Melanie Shelf ran her fingers over the bronze plaque screwed into the granite wall next to the entrance of the skyscraper. Her fingers traced the name The Menaheim Building in relief on the plaque, and recognized the famous emblem for the Global Star conglomerate—a four pointed star peeking behind the word STAR and an earth replacing the O in Global. She let her hand drop, picked up a large, rectangular leather case at her feet, and moved inside.

She found the floor for the broadcast, cable and satellite television news-magazine, Global Star Tonight, from a lobby marquee next to a battery of elevators. She punched the up button on the polished marble wall next to the marquee. A sticker by the button read: Up Yours. U.S. Elevator Union.

When the elevator doors slid open, Melanie stifled her reaction to the unexpected sight of an alien elevator operator. True, aliens were a dime a dozen, but this one wore no pants. She was doubly sure. "Twenty-seventh f-floor, " she asked as she moved next to the four foot tall, leathery extra-terrestrial.

"Ooooh," said the alien, "you see Fanny?"

"Well, like d-duuuh!" stuttered Melanie, wondering if this one had 'his' green card or had snuck across the border...of the Twilight Zone.

"Beth... Francher. We call... Fanny. Fanny... my friend. Famous... goood. Newshound. We call... Fanny."

"And what are you called," asked Melanie, still shaken by the creature's offer. She much preferred zombie elevator operators. Sure, there was the smell of rotten Spam to contend with... but at least you didn't have to make lively conversation with them.

"Ooooh... I called.... Deep Neck. Deep Neck." The digital screen above the inset of floor buttons blinked past twenty-five. "Menace call me pencil-necked geek. Menace baaaad."

"The elevator slid to a stop and Melanie moved toward the opening elevator doors. "Ace Montana call... illegal alien... foreign bastard. Ace... baaaad," added the alien.

"Who is Ace–?" began Melanie, but the closing elevator door cut off the alien's response. The elevator pinged forlornly, and Melanie Shelf felt suddenly very alone and very frightened. She looked down at her feet at the thick, plush shag carpeting and wondered why she had ever thought that she, of all people, had been chosen to save or damn everyone on Earth. She turned from the elevator, and faced a long hallway ending in a tiny desk, a tiny secretary and a great, metallic-gold Global Star Tonight sign on the wall behind the secretary.

The receptionist sat behind her beige, American-Modem desk, chattering on a phone. Blending perfectly with the pale, green walls, white carpeting and beige desk, she looked like a carefully chosen accessory... except for her third eye.

"This is, like, real drooly digs," said Melanie as she sat her case in front of the receptionist's desk. Oblivious to her presence, the human accessory continued to giggle and coo into a phone cradled on her shoulder and against an ear.

"Hey, like, slick chick?! Lady? Could you...?" Melanie stood in bleak contrast to the plushness of the Global Star Tonight office in which she waited, rocking impatiently back and forth on the heels and balls of her sandaled feet. Wearing tight, Retro-Chic Capri pants cut at mid-calf, a black, pull-over sweater, and a matching beret, she would have blended perfectly with the shabbiness of the Global Star newspaper offices many floors beneath her feet. At the moment, even if Melanie had known of the sharp contrast between the two competing sister companies, she wouldn't have cared.

"Say, cat," she tried again, "could you, like, drop the cornball jive and listen a–"

"...Oh, Ace, isn't that sorta, like, perverted or something?" crooned the receptionist to her beige phone.

"Hey, eye candy, yer dress is on fire!" Melanie shouted.

"Oh, oh! " faltered the secretary, patting franticly at her dress. She glanced up with her third eye without raising her head and lost her hold on the phone. "Ace, honey, I gotta go," she chirped into the barely balanced mouthpiece on her shoulder. "No, I gotta go. Customer. I'll call you back. Yes, we'll do it tonight, you silly–"

"I'm like, Melanie Shelf, and I'm here on really important stuff."

"Well, if you're just like Melanie Shelf, then who are you?" The receptionist giggled nervously again, looking for tongues of flame on her dress, and blushed when she found none. Brushing a strand of red hair back from her face, she dropped the mouthpiece of the telephone into its cradle. "May I help you, Mrs...? I'm Miss Molly."

"Good golly, Miss Molly, I'm, like, sorry to cut the hep-jive with your pash-pie short..."

"Oh," said Molly, "the only thing short about Ace is his attention span. Besides, it was just his answering machine"

"But, like, I've gotta make like crazy and lay my sweet peepers on Beth Francher, newshound for Global Star Tonight."

"I'm afraid Miss Francher doesn't allow anyone to lay their sweet anything on her anymore. Do you have an appointment, Miss Shelf?" asked Molly as she checked the angle of a book perfectly placed on a corner of her desk blotter. "Tuesday, Shirley MacLaine. Wednesday, Elton John. Thursday, Shirley MacLaine. Funny how she keeps coming back..."

"But, like, you don't see–"

"Please. I have 20/20/20 vision. I'm afraid a meeting with Miss Francher is out of the question unless you are her mentor from RLA."

"RLA?"

"Recovering Lesbians Anonymous."

"Then I'm afraid a meeting with Miss Francher is out of the question. She's a very busy and important person, as I'm sure you understand. It just isn't possible. She's in a viewing room editing a new feature. Could I schedule you for..."

"Listen, chick," Melanie interrupted. "If she, like, doesn't jive with me now, she'll be broadcasting to a big, blue marble full of dead couch potatoes in eleven days."

"Oh, dear," said Molly, cleaning the dirt from a perfectly manicured, rose-pink fingernail. "I hate it when that happens. Would four o'clock, say, in two weeks be okay?"

It was a dark and stormy room.

The lightning came from Beth Francher, news anchor for Global Star Tonight. She reclined in an overstuffed easy chair that couldn't hide almost six feet of lean, perfectly symmetrical curves and a stuffingly beautiful face. The viewing room shadows accented her high cheekbones instead of obscuring her features. Jade green eyes and a slight upturn of her nose added a feline intelligence to her face. Her Ellen Degeneris makeup didn't hurt either.

Angry, Francher leaned forward and jabbed a remote control in her hand at a television mounted several feet away on a wall. The image on the screen froze, and its hazy glow highlighted auburn hair that cascaded to Beth's shoulders in soft curls.

Beth Francher was beautiful. Greek goddess beautiful. She'd heard that all of her life, and grudgingly suspected her body had won her her first job in television, not her mind. She hated that. She saved that slumbering irritation for deserving editors.

"I dont like it, Charlie," she groused to a shadow seated in an identical chair to her right. "Does this conjure up images of zombies and rock and roll to you, Dianne?

A third shadow on Francher's right snored.

"Ms. Menace agrees, Charlie; these titles suck. I want it changed. Charlie? Are you listening? Do I need subtitles here?"

"Consider it done, Beth," answered Chaplin, twitching his smudge moustache.

"I'm not a 'consider-it' woman, Charlie. The mark of a pro is pride in his or her work. It should have been right the first time. Charlie? Charlie? I won't tolerate the silent treatment."

"If you have a problem with the graphics, Ms. Francher, I suggest you tell it to graphics. Or you can put it in a letter to the grievance committee of local Union 1427.

"I edit."

"And I have final edit, Charlie. Put that in a sandwich and feed it to that thing that lives in your bathtub."

"Violating my personal life is a breach of union contract."

"Do it before I change my mind. Dub in the B-horror version of Heartbreak Hotel that I requested, lose the Old English lettering on the titles and have it done by ten tomorrow morning or you'll be editing the Resurrected Adventures of Soupy Sales before that thing in your bathtub has tune to burp."

The silence in the dark and stormy viewing room was broken by the click of the remote control in Beth's hand. The title on the television screen—The Thing is Dead! Long Live the Thing—began to fade and segue into the newshound's face.

"Consider it done, Ms. Francher," said Charlie from the shadows, tipping his bowler hat in mock respect.

"Charlie," said Francher, "you're like a little kid sometimes. Better seen than heard."

Francher couldn't blame Charlie's obnoxious challenge to her authority. He hadn't been himself since Ted Turner decided to "Oralize" his old silent movies made when he was alive. The straw that had broken the mime's back, however, was when Turner picked Madonna as the voice of The Little Tramp.

After all, Madonna wasn't little.

———◊◊◊———

"This is Beth Francher with Global Star Tonight bringing you another in a series of exclusive interviews with world figures.

"This week, we travel to an isolated medical clinic and village in the Swiss Alps where Papa Doc Duvall has been redefining the term 'life after death'. But only for those who are very rich, very famous, and very... dead. "

On the preview screen, Beth directed her viewer's attention with a sweep of her arm to the beautiful Swiss, snow-capped mountains behind her and a sprawling clinic seemingly built in a pseudo Art Nouveau style from the 1950s.

"This is Saint Jimmie Hoffa Hospital, named after its benefactor, Jimmie Hoffa, former union leader with suspected Mafia ties. His generous donations to this facility were more a tax dodge during his lifetime, and you'll learn why here, on Global Star Tonight.

"You'll also learn how the influence of this clinic does not end at the Swiss borders, and how you may be financing Papa Doc's bizarre enterprise without even knowing it. From Wake Watchers frozen entrees, whose profits are funneled into this very medical facility, to Papa Doc's bizarre 'Death Insurance' for those frightened by unscrupulous resurrectionists, this man has infiltrated our lives... and our deaths."

The image of the clinic on the screen melted into the broad, black face of Papa Doc Duvall. Naked except for a top hat, nose bone, bone necklace and grass skirt, he grinned into the camera with a smarmy sincerity.

"And this man," continued Francher in a voice over the image, "is the reason that people are dying to get into Saint Jimmie's. Papa Doc Duvall, whose notorious exploits into tyranny and the occult, need no recapitulation for Global Star viewers who remember our expose, Papa Doc—Ghastly Guru or Graveyard Gourmet."

"And a sorry piece of reporting dat was," sneered Duvall into the microphone held by Beth. "Dey miss de entire point. Voodoo is much more dan de cult based on African deities and de white man's Christianity. It de cash cow, mon!

"And if dey don't come here, dey can go to Saint Elsewhere, mon."

Before she could stop him, Papa Doc flashed a cardboard sign on which was written his toll-free number: 1-800-UNDEAD.

Through the magic of film editing, Papa Doc and Francher were already moving through a long, white hall interrupted sporadically with doorways on either side. The walls of the hallway were covered with framed photographs and news releases, all in some way featuring Duvall. Duvall and Ed Guien in the stage production of Ghouls and Dolls. Duvall on The Today Show plugging his book, Mon and Supermon. Duvall with Colonel Sanders. Duvall on The Frugal Gourmet.

"Some of these seem in poor taste, Papa."

"What, no. Somethin' eating you, Beth? I prefer de term cheap taste. My budget am skin and bones, mon."

"Obviously," responded Francher, "it's difficult not to notice the bone in your nose is not bone, Papa Doc."

"Oh, dis? Gucci. Silver and hypoallergenic. I allergic to de chicken bone, see. It's all just for atmosphere, you know. Dat's why I couldn't be colonel. De bone necklace? Peacock. Chicken is so necessary but so... plebian. De point is we be respectable. Member of de Swiss Chamber of Commerce. I be president of local Rotary, Mon.."

"Highly profitable may be an understatement. Isn't it true that your patients must give all of their earthly possessions to your 'foundation' before they can receive your treatment or live in your village of the dead?"

"No. Day keep chicken bone. Look at dis picture," said Papa Doc, stopping and pointing with a chubby finger to a framed photograph. "A nothing, a nobody funny man until we have gib him de famous deadpan expression."

"That's Buster Keanton, Papa. Now, answer the question."

"Our prices be high. Our profits... our profits be low, Beth. Overhead is steep. I won't be gibing out trade secrets tonight, " he winked at the camera, "but de cost of eye of newt alone is staggering! Doze little pupils... it takes thousands for one treatment! Ob course, we cut expenses somewhat by using as much of de creatures as possible. Dere's our 'Newt Rockne Soup', 'Fig Newtons', and our popular 'If I'd newt you were comin', I'd a baked a cake' chocolate pudding. We hab our own in-house kitchen, you see. That last ones a particular favorite of Wayne Newton; he always says danke schoen."

At the end of the long hall, a niche in the wall stood at the junction of a parallel hall. A large, grey oil drum sat in a wreath of crumbling cement, highlighted by trac lighting. Francher and the voodoo man approached the shrine as they spoke.

"And, ob course, we use lots of chicken, tons of it, and what does one do wid chicken feet, mon? Our expenses don't end dere, either. Dere are the particular needs of the dead—maintenance costs—dat require outside benefactors and donations to maintain Saint Jimmie."

Duvall stopped again, pointing at a large, framed photograph of a rock and roll group. "Eben de dead need de recreation. Some of our citizens amuse themselves, ob course, like dese residents. Morrison. Holly. Hendricks. Joplin. Cass. Marley. Cobane. Dey lob to sing. An dis group here, I even gab them their names..

"Which is...?"

"De Grateful Dead. Just more satisfied customers."

They had arrived at the rusted oil drum. Francher ran her fingers across the raised lettering of a bronze plaque screwed into the wall next to the niche.

"I'm told your activities aren't always limited to the recently dead in your search for 'benefactors'. There are rumors that your services aren't limited to creating mindless zombies. That, in fact, many of your clients 'live' full, productive 'lives' in society, completely undetected by their friends, spouses and neighbors. Could you give us some of the names, Papa Doc?"

"De upkeep on Cleveland is also very expensive," said the doctor-priest, ignoring Francher. "We also get some deadbeats..."

"Cleveland?"

"Ohio. De 'village of de dead' you mentioned."

"Cute," said Beth, her expression one of slight distaste. "But I'd like names, Papa, of some of the living dead."

"Dat information is protected by de confidentiality of de witch doctor-zombie relationship. Many of our patients are only partially dead when dey come to us, it's true. Dead from the neck up—the deadhead syndrome. Dead from the waist down—the deadhead syndrome. Dead all over we call de married man. Bwhahahhahaha!"

"I believe mindless is the key word here in 'mindless zombie', Papa Doc. Isn't it true your patients lose the ability to think for themselves? That they are completely at the mercy of the attending physician? That they are, for all purposes, simply meat puppets?"

"Dat is not true, Ms. Francher. Don't take my word on dis. Ask our greatest benefactor, Mr. Jimmie Hoffa."

"I couldn't help but notice the memorial. But where is the infamous Mr. Hoffa?"

"He be de memorial. I'll open... de... lid... so. Jimmie? Jimmie? Are you asleep? You hab de guest here wid de questions, Jimmie!"

"Mr. Duvall," Beth scowled, shaking her head. "You don't really expect me to fall for the old 'hidden microphone-speaker' scam, do you? That's about as phoney as that fake Jamacian accent you've been using during this entire interview. What is it, Papa: dis or this; dere or there, de or the? You use them both with equal ease."

"Ms. Francher, I can make a detached pinkie finger crawl across a table like de worm. Why should you be surprised by Jimmie-in-de-drum. As for the accent..." he grinned into the camera, shrugged his naked shoulders, and offered the audience his upturned palms. "I talk softly and carry de big schtick."

Francher leaned over the lip of the oil drum and choked back a scream. There in a thick, red soup of scraps of flesh and body parts floated the grinning face of Jimmie Hoffa.

"Sweet Mother of God," Beth gasped.

"No," said Papa Doc. "Dis be Jimmie. Mrs. Koresh be in de other Link."

"Hey, baby!" said the dismembered head," nice bazongas. Hope ya don't mind my bluntness, but I dont get out much anymore.

"Yessir," it continued, "those are hooters a Kennedy would kill for, and have. As a matter of fact..."

Dianne Menace froze the image on the viewing screen with a remote control. "Ya gotta admit, thatsa classic shot," she said with a yawn. "Notice how I caught the red, yellow and green in the intestines near his left ear?"

"It's a good shot, Dianne, but I think it's too graphic to broadcast. We need to cut this, Charlie; its something even Ace wouldn't use," interjected Beth.

"That's because I got way more guts than Ace Montana," spat Menace, looking at the screen. "Literally."

"It's no more graphic than that piece you did on Jock the Ripper, the serial killer for the Oakland Raiders team," said Charlie, squirming in his chair. "To this day, I refuse to touch liver."

"I'll think about it, guys, but I'm not comfortable with this. Could you kick it in again, Di? I'm on a tight schedule. "

As the image of Beth and Papa Doc flickered into life on the screen, Francher glanced over at the shadow that was Dianne Menace.

Beth's photographer was, in everything, a counterpoint to herself. She had been with Beth, at Beth's request, ever since the Speilberg Conspiracy was uncovered in Houston; it was the feature that had won Beth national recognition and the job on Global Star Tonight as its primary anchor.

Francher mentally stored Menace's features again, as she had done a hundred times and for reasons that she did not understand. Menace was a little over five feet tall with curly, brown hair, a heart shaped face and clean, broad smile. Her green-grey eyes sparkled with intelligence. Menace hid that razor-sharp intelligence underneath a rough, streetwise facade that didn't mirror the woman beneath. She was the smartest woman Beth knew.

The images on the screen shifted and caught Francher's attention again as she watched herself in miniature walking along the edge of a grassy knoll overlooking a cluster of small bungalows.

"It was at this point that camera woman, Dianne Menace, and I killed the camera and requested a private conference with Papa Doc Duvall. Pretending complete disgust and depression over our lives as wealthy and famous television personalities, we told Papa we were interested in signing his suicide-contract and joining his village of lost souls... the sister city to Cleveland."

"Where dere's a will, dere's a way,' said Duvall.

"Ignoring another of his stupid puns, I asked him if we could talk to several residents of Cleveland-Swiss to help us make up our minds. He agreed if we left our camera equipment in his office.

"He could not have known that Menace was wearing a false left hand that was actually a mini-camera. Sorry, Papa, I lied to you.

"Now, I ask you to prepare yourselves for a shock," Francher continued as she pushed the door open on a small bungalow. "This interview will surely not be pretty as we dispel the rumors and half-truths that have shrouded the life and death of one of rock and roll's icons.

"Elvis?! Elvis, are you here?" Francher now moved into a small, dark hallway cluttered with empty food wrappers, beer cans and a Buck Buck bucket of Colonel Parker's Nuggets. On either side of the hallway hung framed photographs and news clippings. Most were askance, and the wallpaper was yellow, torn and dirty.

"We were told to expect no answer. The Undead don't answer questions; they answer commands," continued the newshound.

"Elvis!! If you're here, tell me where you are sitting or standing."

"Yes'm, ahm heah... in th' deadroom."

"That flat, emotionless intonation in a voice so world famous is... eerie. I'm steeling myself for the..."

Francher's voice faded as she turned a corner. The image on the screen shook slightly as Menace responded to what both newshounds, and now their audience, saw. It looked more like a gob of dough thrown against a ratty, plaid couch than the King of Rock and Roll. Sitting behind a coffee-table strewn with discarded bones, crumpled soda cans and wadded paper, Elvis wore his trademark white jumpsuit. It was smeared with mustard and catsup. In the center of the mess on the coffee-table was a plate heaped with pork chops.

"I thank ya'll forgot yer camera, ma'am. Ahm cain't feel th' lights."

Elvis moved his head in the direction of Francher's voice and smiled. One eye was blank, empty of pupil, and one ear hung slightly away from the side of his head against the high, white collar of his jumpsuit. His skin was a ghastly pallor.

"I'm sorry, Elvis, that I forgot. You will answer my questions. The camera is hidden in this ladies hand."

"I was wonderin' why she was givin' me th' fanger, ma'am. Ahm jest thrilled to death to talk with someone, but please 'member to tell me to answer or ah git kinda lost."

"Of course. Mr. Presley, are you happy liv... uh, being here at Papa Doc's little village? Answer."

"No'me, ah cain't say that ahm happy. Not sad neither. Sorta like inbetween shows, mostly, is how ah feels. Mind if ah ask yew a question, ma'am?"

"Why, of course not! Ask me a question, Elvis."

"Papa Doc didn't tell me who was comin' tonight. Jest who are yew two ladies? Hope yew ain't groupies 'eause ahm dead tarred tonight."

"I'm Beth Francher and this is Dianne Menace, my camera'man'. We work for the television show, Global Star Tonight."

An expression of distaste crossed Elvis' face, and he turned away from Francher's voice. "Ma'am, are yew th' one that keeps writin' those stones 'bout my face on the moon, that ahm gay and had four hunerd kids, ma'am? If yew are, ah don't think ah can say much."

"Oh, dear, NO," said Francher, moving to a ratty chair that faced the famous zombie and beginning to sit. "That's another 'newspaper entirely, Elvis—The Washington Post. If we just made up stories like they do, why would I bother to even come to talk?"

Elvis' frown of discontent melted into a smile as he turned to where Francher's voice had been, and he said, "That's good, ma'am, 'cause ah shorely wanted to talk. It gits kinda lonely 'round Cleveland sometimes."

"Tell me, Elvis... why the sudden decision to die? Most people thought you had it all—money, fame, success."

"It wasn't sudden, Miss Francher. An ah didn't have it all. There was this sled named Rosebud." The singer leaned forward and felt along the surface of the coffee-table until he found a pork chop. "An ah'd been dyin' on stage for years."

"Let me rephrase. Why did you want to die? Answer."

"Ah didn't! That's why ah came heah, ma'am. Ah figger livin' dead is better'n being dead. Anyways, ah was mostly jest tired. Tired o' being treated like a god, ah guess. Tired of tryin' to live up to muh image as th' king, Miss Francher.

"Ahm jest a country boy, really. Ah jest had a voice that lots of folks seemed to like, ah guess." He took a bite of a pork chop and belched loudly in E flat.

"Tell me, Elvis," continued Francher, "what do you like and dislike about being a zombie in Papa Doc's community?"

"Ah like th' part 'bout livin' forever, Miss Francher. Ain't aged a day since '77 neither, and ah like that," Elvis added as he rubbed a finger along the wet dough that was his face. "Ah guess ahm jest as scairt o' dyin' as anybody. especially considering ah'd hafta face th' Lord after havin' done some of th' fool thangs ah done.

"Course, ah get to eat alla th' po' chops ah want. Shame ah cain't taste th' damn things, though." He tried to laugh, raising nothing but a puff of dust at his parched lips.

"Scuse the language, ma'am. Ah don't get many lady visitors now, and ah forget mah manners sometimes. This bein' haf blind is a bother. But, ah figger if airline pilots can stand it. ah can, too."

"Tell me, Elvis, does it bother you that even some of your own relatives are still making a lot of money off of your name and your music?"

"Nah, not really, ma'am. Rather mah relatives have it than most anybody else. Ah got no use for money now, yew know. But the music thang hurts a little. Ah really loved to sang, Miss Francher. An 'ah miss th' audience and performin' some. An' th' stamp thang, me havin' a postage stamp. Ah got people lickin' me now I could o' whooped wit' one hand."

Another puff of dust at his lips passed for laughter.

"Would yew mind if ah played a little somethin' for yew, ma'am?"

"I'd be honored, Elvis," said Francher.

Elvis sat, a pork chop still poised at his mouth in one hand. A sudden wave of sadness swept over Francher as she realized that she and Elvis were in many ways in similar situations. The idea of losing the reasons that motivated her work only to have them replaced by materialism and hedonism left her feeling empty and alone.

And, of course, neither one of them could sing.

"Oh," she said, "I'm sorry. I forgot again, didn't I? Play a song for me, Elvis."

"Thank yew, mam," he grinned and, leaning over the arm of the sofa, picked up a battered guitar. "'Course ah don't move 'round much any more like ah used to when ah'd sang. It's really easy to throw out a hip, now, Usually takes a couple of days to find it, too."

He crossed his legs, revealing his blue suede house shoes.

He strummed a chord with the pork chop, forgotten in his hand. "Oops," he grinned, and dropped it on the sofa. "Ah'd forget mab haid if it weren't screwed on sometimes.

"Now, how 'bout this:

> "Though it's sad, it's still true
> That ah cain't be lovin' yew
> 'Cause ah don't have a beatin' heart
> Please don't cry, ahm so blue
> There won't be children, too
> 'Cause ah don't have a beating..."

The third finger of his hand tore off, hanging by a spittle of flesh to its knuckle.

"Oh, hell," he said mournfully, "ah hate it when that happens. 'Course, it's not as bad as what fell off last week."

"That was... nice, Elvis. Tell me, do you ever leave Cleveland and return to our world, the world of the living? It has been reported by my own paper that you slung hash at a Burger Barn in Skokie."

"Ah tried it a couple of times; th' last thang was as a sodajerk in Brooklyn. But, when ah burned mah Whopper..."

"Yes. yes." said Beth, shaking her head in disbelief. "So Ace did scoop me on that."

"...but ah haven't gone out since ah was in Italy to see th' Pope."

"What happened with your audience? Tell me."

"They left me fer th' Beatles, mam. "

"No, dear; what happened with your meeting with the Pope? Tell me."

"Ah was never so shocked in mah life, Miss Francher. He went and slandered the Madonna. So ah took a poke at the Pope."

"Dear Elvis. My guess is that be doesn't like the singer, Madonna. But, did you at least learn something from your trip? Answer me."

"Yes'm. Ah cain't go Rome, again."

"May I ask you one last question? Tell me, even though you've given up money and fame and you're liv...you have the simple li... simple pleasures now that you missed..." Beth sighed. "Elvis... are you lonesome tonight?"

As Elvis opened his mouth to respond, his image froze in midword on the screen. In the darkness of he viewing room, Francher said, "Okay, what's the problem? Did I miss something, Dianne? Charles?"

"Wasn't me, Fanny," answered Dianne.

"I don't even have the remote," groused Charlie.

The first four, powerful chords of Beethoven's Fifth Symphony bellowed from the shadows behind Francher.

"It was I," piped a disconnected voice, "Melanie Shelf."

The opening chords of Lady of Spain were struck as the news trio turned in their chairs. A silhouette of a woman with a rectangular stomach stood in the doorway, backlit by the hall light.

"Good heavens!" bellowed Charlie, "whatever it is, it's pregnant with Lawrence Welk's love child!"

"I've, like, come on a matter of life and death," Shelf added as her fingers continued to race across the squeeze-box strapped to her torso. "Yours."

"Oh, God," said Dianne in a monotone. "She's playin" Lady of Pain."

"Spain," corrected Francher. "That's Spain."

"Not the way shes playin' it."

The remote control perched on the top edge of the accordion slipped and fell to the floor. The video recorder released itself from the pause mode, and turned itself off. The cacophony of Shelf's accordion was underscored by the hiss of gray static on the television.

"What do they call music that's so bad it hurts?" whined Dianne, covering her ears.

"Shelf abuse," said Charlie.

Francher plopped into the plush chair behind her office desk. Behind her on the pale, green walls hung framed awards from past news stories. These included The Inkpot for her expose of the Speilberg Conspiracy. Her beige, American-modern desk was as meticulously organized as was Francher's life. The only discordant note in that life was the petite, sandy-haired woman who sat across from her playing a mournful Tip Toe Through The Tulips on a battered accordion.

Francher watched the woman remove her black beret with a nervous hand after she stopped playing. The musician wiggled deeper into her chair. Every instinct that made the newshound the best in the business was screaming that this was a major story waiting to be told. And every experience that had honed those instincts into a hard cynicism cautioned that something in Francher's office stunk besides Shelf's performance.

"Are you sure this session is, like, cool?" asked Shelf, twisting a blond forelock with a finger. "I mean, are there any... Motelites, like, makin' the scene—er, workin'—for Global Star Tonight, Ms. Francher?"

"Motelites?" Beth chuckled involuntarily at the mental picture of Ace Montana worshiping at an altar to Spike Jones singing Amazing Gracie. "Ms. Shelf, people in my line of work usually worship bylines and booze. Believe me, we're safe. Now, do you mind telling me from whom we're safe?"

"But, you're, like, hip to that, aren't you, Ms. Francher? I caught your jam sesh with Michael, the Archangel cat when you were in Italy, and you seemed, like, hep to the Big Bopper, you know, the Great Round Square in the Sky?"

"Well," said Francher, tapping a pencil in mild irritation against the edge of her desk, "if by 'Great Round' you mean... God, let's just say I'm no longer an atheist after that little interview. But why would Michael mention Motelites? He likes music."

"Now, Ms. Shelf, what's this about the matter of my death?"

"Oh, it's not only yours, Ms. Francher. Come two weeks tomorrow morning, and every righteous cat on earth may be pushin' up daises in the boneyard if the Motelites are cookin' with high octane. Or maybe I should say 'unrighteous cats'. That's why I'm here."

"I wasn't aware that the Motelites had that much... clout. Why not just start at the beginning and tell me what I don't know."

"I know the Motelites were founded by a traveling Jew's Harp salesman named John Smith. He lived hand-to-mouth back then. That he probably signed in at almost every motel, hotel and YMCA in America during his career before he received his 'revelation' into the nature of God and the universe. I think he was watching an old Laurel and Hardy movie, wasn't it, when 'God' spoke to him?"

"He was like, watchin' the boob tube, Ms. Francher, when he received the first revelation for the true form of worship Motelites call 'Lip Service'. Until that night in that Howard Johnson's, he'd been a solid square, out for nothing but gettas," said Melanie as she pumped new air into the accordion. "He even flipped his lid over X-Xavier C-c-cugat," she shuddered involuntarily, "...until that Great Jive Cat said 'Open the door, Richard' and John walked in!"

"Great Jive ... do you mean Maynard Krebbs?" asked Francher, catching herself tapping her pencil to the rhythm of Shelf's accordion.

Shelf stopped in mid-phrase in her song, her fingers frozen over the keyboard of the squeeze box. "I don't mean to be disrespectful, Ms. Francher, but we're talking cool bebop, here, not stale '50's television. How, I mean, like cornball can one get!?"

"You tell me, Ms. Shelf. And while we're on the subject of 'talking cool bebop', Melanie, I must be frank with you. Drop the beatnik talk. It's difficult to follow and as irritating as Ace Montana's overinflated ego."

"But, like... but, it's the High Litany of Lip Service! It's almost as important as, like John Smith's second most important ritual... Hand Jive."

Unconsciously, Shelf launched into a faltering version of Feelings on the accordion as she looked at Francher with sheepdog eyes.

Francher rose from the chair behind her desk, and leaned across its organized surface, her knuckles on her desk calendar. With an eyebrow arched over her left eye, and fire burning in her pupils, Francher barked.

"That's it! Even my impending death isn't enough to put up with your double talk and that damn torture rack from Hell on your chest, Ms. Shelf. Either drop the accordion with the dialect or find yourself another newshound. I recommend Ace Montana or Kirsten Lane, neither of whom knows diddly-squat about music or English."

Shelf let the air sigh in a mournful gasp from the accordion, and began to unstrap the instrument as she looked at Francher. "I... a'll be doin' me very... best," she whispered.

"He... dat be John Smith... gits de idea from one av them, well them vibratin' beds, ya know. Ya put in a quawter...

"Well, it be revealed ter John dat de Great Rou... dat, eh, God an' all dat he created be vibration. Movement. An John figgered oot dat de closest dat man gits ter God be threw de sounds we be makin'—music, werds, and de like. An' dat de highest expression av man's intellect be music, an' de highest expression of dat music be Liberace, oi'm thinkin'... and maybe, Barry Manilow, and, of course, Cab Calloway."

Francher looked at the musician in her black pull-over, black Capri slacks and sandals. The little, black scrap of cloth that was Shelf's beret lay on the arm of her chair. Moments of silence fell like drops of water into cotton. Then Francher sighed.

"You're a bait worse than death, Melanie Shelf. Do you know the difference between a great reporter and an overcast day?"

"Both have gloom for improvement?"

Francher sighed again.

"Ms. Shelf. Can you play Stairway to Heaven on that thing and then take them?"

Francher watched the young woman restrap her accordion with some enthusiasm. John Lennon's quote that he'd rather have been a carpenter than a musician flashed through the newshound's mind, and she made a mental note to ask Lennon just what he meant by that the next time she was in Cleveland, Switzerland.

"The difference is great reporters don't hide 'the light'. The truth, Melanie. I'll tell you what I know. You need to tell me what I don't know. Remember?"

"So, John Smith believed he'd received a 'revelation' that God wants everyone saved, and that dead and living atheists can be prayed into heaven despite their sins and over their objections. That's why the Motelites gather names for their giant, genealogical library. Microfiche are too small, so they keep them on Microwhales."

"Frankly, Melanie, this all seems fairly harmless. Could we cut through the theology and get to the chase? I've got a seven o'clock interview with Donald Trump over on Fifth Street. If it rains, it plays havoc on the cardboard box he lives in."

"Well, Fanny," said Melanie as she started the opening bars to Stairway to Heaven, "like, the Motelites have this groovy library in Rose Butte, over in Utah. And they've been, like, collectin' the monikers of every hepcat who ever cut a rug. They put those names onto microwhales and into these drooly computers and. turn 'em into numbers', into God jive. Dig?"

"Numerology?" asked Beth. "Go figure."

"I'm dyin' if I'm lyin'. I'm hep 'cause I was a word bird at Rose Butte until only two days ago."

"A word bird. But wouldn't a hep-eat cat a word-bird?" Francher smiled.

Melanie blushed deeply.

"A word bird is a secretary. For Maestro John Palmer himself And I thought it was sorta cornball too until he showed me..." The accordion stuttered into silence, and Melanie leaned forward in her chair. "The Sound Booth."

Francher began to clear her left ear with the eraser end of a pencil. "This's beginning to sound like a game show. 'The Name Game'? John, John, Bo-bon; banana fanna fo-fon... Jooohn."

"You don't believe me, do you, Ms. Francher?"

"Ummmm," she said aloud to Shelf. "And who is John Palmer and what is in this Sound Booth."

"He's, like, the head Fred of the 'Registry'. That's the family tree library. John's a computer genius, and he... he likes my... software." Melanie blushed, lowered her head, and struck the opening chords of Love Story on her squeeze box.

"Excuse me?" grinned Francher. "Did he have a chip on his shoulder?"

"No. No. I sorta flipped my lid over his floppy disk. We... we... networked, Ms. Francher. Please. This is serious.

"Oh, I know what you're thinkin' How could a cool chick like me fall for love bytes with John." Melanie threw her head back, giggled and pressed her palms together in front of the accordion in ecstasy. "If you ever laid your peepers on him just once... ! He's got a cleft palate, a sharp wit and a basso profundo voice that twangs my strings! I fell on him like vibratto on a whole note.

"I meant for him." Melanie blushed again. "Not on.

"We were, like, watchin' the Wheel of Fortune one night, eatin' Wake Watchers frozen dinners, and this cluck named White was movin' her vowels. That's when John let slip the real lowdown. That The Great Round Square is only one of 200 billion names of God. That each cat, created in the Big Bopper's image, owns one of God's names. And that if every moniker of God were, like, crooned at once, sorta like Gabriel's righteous horn, it would be the downbeat for the 'Final Jam Sesh', 'The Last Shindig', 'The Big Bail-Out', 'The Ultimate Cop-Out', 'The–"

"The end of the world, for God's sake! I get the idea. We all get knocked off of the hit parade of life!"

"Well, not all, Ms. Francher."

"Oh, yes. Let me guess, now. All but the chosen few, and you and John and the Motelites are the chosen few."

"'All who aren't checked in will be checked out'. It's not, like, the end of the world either, Ms. Francher. It's sorta like the beginning of eternal bebop. The climax of the song. The second of coming of..."

"Yes?" coaxed Beth. "Jesus Christ? Mohammed? Buddha? Jimmie Carter?"

"The coolest hepcat of all time, Ms. Francher. The dreamboat that every bobby-soxer blasts her wig over."

"Chocolate? Henry Kissinger? Bon Jovi?"

"Little Jimmy Dickens," gushed Shelf with reverence.

"Al..." the name died in disbelief on Francher's lips. "But, that's just crazy?!?" Francher rubbed a hand across her forehead as she rested its elbow and her other arm on the desk. "Little Jimmy Dickens, The King of Bebop..."

Melanie leaned across the accordion and looked with dead seriousness at Francher. "True. No one can hear Al on the accordian singing May the Bird of Paradise Fly Up Your Nose without having tears come to their eyes."

"I dont doubt that." Francher sat back slowly in her chair and began cleaning air from her right ear with her pencil. "Ruptured eardrums hurt. And the 'Sound Booth', Ms, Shelf? Could you tell me what that is all about?"

"I ... I only saw the door. John said he'd like, open-that-door-Richard the next night. But that never went down 'cause after John bailed-out that night. I... was caught. Terminated. Fired as his word bird."

"Caught? Caught doing what?"

"C-caught," stuttered Melanie, her face a deep scarlet, "in a moment of weakness. I knew it was wrong, but it was an old habit from another life, before I met John or knew anything about bebop! I swear, I didn't do it to hurt anyone!!"

"Melanie, I am surprised. Was it cocaine?"

"No, Ms. Francher. C & W."

"Curds and Whey?!"

"Oh, no," said the accordionist, "that would be cheesy. It was Merle Haggard. On the radio. I was country before I was cool although it destroyed by shelf-respect."

Francher rose from behind her massive desk and extended her hand to her guest. "Ms. Shelf, I'm afraid I don't have an achy-breaky heart either. You might try the religion editor, Ms. Madeline O'Hara, at the Star downstairs or a...'lesser' paper, like the New York Times. But I'm sure my audience is uninterested in an internal dispute among the Motelites, and I just don't buy this end-of-the-world stuff from one more cult among many. For starters, if this giant blast of sound is going to kill off the unbelievers among us, I don't for the life of me see how the Motelites could escape their own doomsday device."

Melanie's fingers left the keyboard of the accordion, and, lowering her hand into a pocket in her slacks, she pulled out a pair of flesh colored, plastic ear plugs.

With an edge of disbelief in Francher's question, she punched her intercom. "Miss Molly? Beth. Listen, honey, I want you to buy me a pair of ear plugs. No. Ace is in Singapore. No. Listen, I know it's not in your job description, but I'm playing a hunch, and I need your help. Okay. Okay. Yeah. When you're finished reporting me to the union, do it. Now!"

Melanie looked across the great, beige desk at Francher and sighed. "They, like, are recording those names. They say that all may be saved, even the tone deaf. But I was afraid even a slick chick like you might not dig my righteous jive, so I brought this." She threw a binder of papers across Francher's desk that toppled into a heap in Beth's lap. In the middle of the cover was a paper sticker that read: God Bop.

"I... swiped it from John, Ms. Francher. Do you dig what bebop means? It's improvised solo's in dissonant idiom's with complex rhythms, and a continuous, highly florid melodic line.

"To me, it only means I'm so lonesome I could cry."

Francher watched as tears begin to well up in the accordionists' eyes as her fingers faltered on the keys of the squeeze box. "Take five, Melanie. It's always tough to stand by your man."

"Tougher for some more than for others," Dianne added without looking at the news hound.

"It was my solid dreamboat that turned me in, Ms. Francher. John. He was a square in cat's skins. He beat me eight to the bar."

"No need to exaggerate."

"No really. There were seven other Motelites; I was ninth and he was eighth to the bar. I had a Spitzer and he had a Wallbanger. That's when he turned me in."

Francher skimmed the pages of the document on her desk as Shelf's sobs replaced the accordion as the only sound in the news anchor's office. She looked up after a few moments, and said quietly, "How many Motelites does it take to end the world, Melanie? Five thousand? Twenty thousand?"

"Eight," responded Shelf, wiping tears from her eyes. "One to activate the sound booth and seven to turn the ladder."

Francher passed a facial tissue to Shelf. Her intercom squawked into life. Miss Molly said, "You owe me big. This was a real double waste of my time, Francher. Every store I've called, and I've called plenty, is sold out of car plugs. Do I have to keep this up?"

"That's enough, Miss Molly; go back to doing your nails," said Beth, almost in a whisper. She looked at Melanie Shelf. Shelf looked at her. Dianne looked at Beth. Beth looked at Dianne.

"Honey, a good news hound can smell a story a mile away, and your story smells to high heaven." Francher turned to Menace. "Menace. Listen, book our two best agents on the first available flight to Rose Butte, Utah. They're going to the biggest jazz festival in history."

"Rose Butte?" said Menace. "Rose Butte? I could get some shots at Mount Everest this time of year, Fanny."

"A butte by any other name still smells as sweet," said Beth as she looked up at the agonized expression on Shelf's face. "And you and I have that expose on geriatric escort services to wrap up ... you know. Call Girls On Hold: We hook more than rugs!"

"I know what you're thinking," said Francher, holding up her palm to motion Shelf back into her chair, "But you've got to understand that I can't cover every story that crosses my desk. I do have the best staff in the industry, Hortense Smedley and Buck Upp Katsulas were pros before Ted Kopple bought his first rug. You'll meet them in just a moment. But, my best advice to you is to get rid of the accordion before they arrive and keep upbeat about everything. They don't have my, er, love of music, Melanie."

Shelf shimmied out of her squeeze box and sat it at her feet on the floor, Francher glanced at Shelf's boyish figure and shook her head.

"Now, I know why you wear that thing, honey. You're really flat."

"Ooh, dear!" blushed Melanie as she leaned forward and patted the top of the accordion. "I had no idea. I'll get it tuned real quick."

The sweeping checkerboard of white and beige tile stretched forever in all directions. And like a lost schools of fish, hundreds of passengers and visitors washed through the terminal, eddying and pooling with each announced departure or arrival. Their low but pervasive roar filled every nook and cranny of the massive, teaming building.

A giant clock on the wall of the airport read six-fifteen. An old tattered derelict licked insanely at the clock's face. And before that clock stood two old, grey-haired women, one tapping a finger on the watch on her left wrist.

"Dirty clock licker," said one old matron.

"Dang it, Smedley, my watch says eight thirty-two. We've missed our plane again," said Muck Upp Katsulas, the other old woman. An Asian, she was wearing the distinctive white garb of a private nurse.

"No, no, no," said Hortense, tapping the tip of her umbrella on the tile floor. "I bought that watch for you for Christmas and the man said a Rollex is guaranteed for life."

"Sure, but this is a Timex,"

"Excuse me ladies," interrupted a male voice. "Both Hortense Smedley and Muck Upp followed the sound of the voice to its source, a seedy, unshaven man in his early forties wearing a trench coat. He opened the coat like a cape at the movement of their heads.

He was naked underneath the coat except for his shoes. Both sides of the coat's lining were covered with wrist watches of every description.

"I've got one for every fashion statement and budget. Couldn't help but overhear, and I've got what you need", he added, and without releasing his grasp on his lapels, he pointed.

"Look where your short hand is pointing," said Hortense with some distaste. When he looked, Hortense struck him hard on the side of his head with her umbrella, and he fell to the floor with a thud.

"Cold-clocked by an old woman," said Muck Upp to the body at her feet. "You should be alarmed."

"He should learn some manners," Hortense groused. "It's impolite to point."

"It was a small offense," said Muck Upp. "Now, why did you go and do that, Hortense, sweety?"

"Kismet," answered Hortense. "It was his time."

Arm locked in arm, both of the women stepped over the naked exhibitionist to the sound of scattered applause. Hortense and her nurse moved through the crowds draggin' their baggage behind them by cords. Both the old Caucasian woman and her Japanese nurse looked every day of sixty-five. Both were dressed in grey tweed suits, and were confused by the vastness of the terminal. They were lost. Their eventual arrival at an airline ticket desk was more a matter of accident than intelligence.

"Miss," said Hortense to an attendant working at a compute keyboard, "Im looking for departure gate 47."

There was no response to Smedley's question from the attendant, and the old woman's nurse leaned over, cupped a hand around her mouth, and shouted, "I don't think she heard you, ma'am!"

"I know that! Miss," the old woman began again, louder, "I'm Hortense Smedley, and this is my nurse, Muck Upp Katsulas. We're looking for departure gate 47. I've got tickets to your Butte."

"That one in Utah," added Muck Upp.

The airline attendant smiled slightly to herself and continued to enter data into the computer. Rage began to animate the wrinkled and heavily powdered face of Hortense. Instinctively she reached for the .45 bluenose strapped in its holster beneath her tweed jacket.

"Here, let me try," intruded Muck Upp, restraining Hortense's hand.

"I... can... handle... this," said Hortense through clenched dentures, And raising her blue umbrella from its place by her baggage on the floor, she began rapping the countertop sharply. An audience began to gather around the drama behind her, punctuating her umbrella raps vith "Punch her lights out, grandma!", "Let her have it, lady!", "Give her what for!", and "Tweak 'er nose smartly,

Mary Poppins!"

"Are you deef!" shouted Hortense, waving the umbrella in the air and pounding the countertop with an ineffective fist now. As she shouted, Muck Upp moved around the corner of the counter, found the electrical plug to the computer, and pulled it out of the wall socket.

"So much for the infinite power of the computer," said Muck Upp to no one in particular, and waved the end of the electrical cord about for effect.

"Damn it!" howled the attendant, looking up into the blazing fury of Hortense Smedley, a punk rocker with a butterfly wing haircut, an angel with a broken wing, a family of four from Idaho, and a terrorist with two straps of dynamite criss-crossing his chest.

"Oh! Oh, excuse me; I didn't..." she stuttered, and took a flesh colored, plastic ear plug out of her left ear. "I'm so sorry, ma'am. I wear these because," she gestured at the air filling the massive terminal, "because of the noise, you know. It's Barry Manilow, you know."

"What?" asked Hortense. "You're listening to the radio?"

"The noise in here. It's barely manageable."

Hortense looked at her nurse, and Muck Upp looked at Hortense. And like a precision drill team, they both turned and looked at the attendant and the ear plug in her hand.

"What's your name, girl? I think I'll report you to your boss," said the old woman, shaking her gloved finger at the girl. "I've got arthritis something awful, and I don't have time to be mishandled."

"It's a lucky thing. thing you aren't luggage, then. But, please, Miss...! I'm really not in good with him anyway. I'm really, really sorry. Won't you let me help you now?"

"Do you like Barry Manilow by any chance?" asked Muck Upp as she leaned across the countertop. "Is your name Mandy?"

"Why, yes! How did you know? It's Mandy Copacabana, originally from Havana"

"I said I'm looking for departure gate 47," interrupted Hortense.

"Oh, you're right here," said Mandy. "If you'll just give me your flight..."

"Maybe I'll just take a train instead."

"Oh, surely you'd rather flight than switch?" asked Mandy with some animation.

Hortense took her packet of tickets from inside the jacket of her tweed suit and passed it over the counter. As the attendant began to read Hortense's papers, the old woman asked, "Where's one of those insurance machines: I always buy flight insurance."

"It's under the ladder where that man is painting the word Love on that billboard," said Mandy pointing behind. Hortense. The old woman turned and scowled at the painter.

"Well, I'm in a big rush. When will he be finished?"

"Oh, he'll make a little Love and get down tonight."

"There is greater wisdom," said a disembodied voice, "in placing one's trust in the Great Pilot In the Sky,"

Hortense turned to scowl into the face of the angel who was gently placing a hand on her shoulder. "Touch it again, birdbrain, and you'll be chirping Glory to God in the Highest about three octaves higher. And as for your words of wisdom, tell it to Amelia Earheart, Angel Cake!"

"Bitch," said the angel.

"Your flight will leave in ten minutes, Mrs. Smedley," continued the attendant, "and there's another insurance vending machine just over there by that guard." She turned to Smedley's nurse and asked, "May I have your name and tickets as well, Miss...?"

"Muck Upp Katsulas," answered the Japanese nurse as she handed her packet of tickets to the young girl. As Muck Upp and the young girl exchanged perturbed looks, Hortense began to move away from the ticket counter. Across the crowded room, a man in front of a magazine stand looked up from the Holiday Out comic book he was reading. He watched the old woman through the two slits in the black hood that covered his head. Hortense didn't see the Scottish Ninja in a plaid kilt place the comic book back in its rack and begin to follow them.

Hortense reached the vending machine only seconds before Buck Upp, who was dragging Hortense's forgotten bags behind her. Eyeing the stoic guard standing next to the machine with mild suspicion, Smedley dropped her money into the appropriate slot. The guard was reading the current issue of Global Star. Its headline read: CoyBoys Udder Discouraging Word, Linguists Milk Discovery Dry

"Waste-of-time, waste-of-time, waste-of-time," said Muck Upp. "'What good will it do you if you do die and Kirsten collects? What good are brownie points to a dead lesbian?"

"When I want your opinion, I'll pull your soap-on-a-rope," said Hortense with some bitterness, and wrote the name Kirsten Lane in a tight, small scrawl under the designation for beneficiary on the policy. The security guard yawned and shifted his weight from his left to his right foot.

The Ninja struck like lightning. Hortense's shoulder purse was snatched from her arm even as the assassin bolted into the crowd. "Oh, my God!" yelled Hortense. "My bag!"

The guard, leaning against a wall, began to clean the dirt from under the fingernails of his left hand with the fingernails of his right hand, his paper discarded. Hortense waved her umbrella wildly in the air after the disappearing Ninja.

"Thief! Thief! Purse!! Help!! " the old woman yelled into the face of the security guard, who heard nothing.

"He stole my purse!"

"Huh?" repeated the guard, talking a tiny, flesh colored plastic plug from his left ear. A thin cord ran down to his shirt pocket and Hortense noticed a small cassette player there. Tiny and almost lost in the uproar, '...at the Copa, Copacabana,' played from the plug.

"Listen, if yer one a them Hairy Krishnas...," said the guard.

Hortense and her nurse exchanged questioning glances. Smedley hiked up her dress to mid-thigh, turned from Muck Upp, and shot into the crowd with unexpected speed. As the guard scratched his head under his cap with one finger, Muck Upp offered him an upturned palm and a half-smile.

"Adrenaline," she offered to the guard as explanation of Hortense's energy.

"Stop that Scot!" screamed Hortense at the crowd as she ran at full tilt through the terminal. A spattering of people stopped or cupped hands to an ear. A mohawked punk rocker removed his ear plugs and said, "Dauumn! " as Hortense clipped his shoulder and spun him around, almost off of his feet.

But, despite her initial burst of speed, Hortense began to slow as the flow of the crowd proved too much for her, blocking her progress. She watched the thief bobbing away as the guard and Muck Upp appeared by the old woman's side.

"Srand clear!" screamed the pasty guard, spreading his legs for balance and whipping his Global Star from his holster. "Stop or I'll shoot!"

Looking down at his hand, he threw the tabloid down and snatched his revolver from his back pocket. His first shot dropped a nun three feet to the thief's left. His second round wounded a second security guard who had just entered the chase. That guard fell like an ox, dropping a big box of doughnuts that spilled into the crowd like hockey pucks. His third shot hit resurrected Charlston Heston in the left shoulder. Heston gave him a thumbs up.

Hortense struck her guard hard against the side of his head with her umbrella. He fell to the terminal floor at the old woman's feet, unmoving. "Idiot," hissed Smedley between clenched dentures. "Those were fresh doughnuts!"

"Stand back," shouted Muck Upp, pushing her elderly employer to one side. In the crowd close to the pair stood another senior dressed in a pale, green dress and carrying a large, rectangular bag. Muck Upp snatched the bag from its surprised owner and gauged its weight like an Olympic discus thrower with the muscles in her forearms and hands. Then, spinning around faster and faster to build centrifugal force, Muck released the bag with a huge grunt.

The bag shot from Muck's grip and skipped once against the tile floor. Then sliding across that floor, it wacked against the back of the Ninja's ankles. The black garbed thief did one complete backwards somersault before he struck the floor with his head, all sprawling limbs and Scottish curses, and slid hard into a wall. He lay still.

Smedly and Muck Upp trotted up to the twisted body of the Ninja as a crowd began to form a circle around the thief.

"So, that's what a Scotsman has under his kilt," said one onlooker.

"Somehow, I expected more than Spiderman underwear," said another.

"Do you suppose that was just a random purse snatching, Mrs. Smedley?" asked the Japanese nurse.

"There's... one-way to find out," answered Hortense as she bent over the prostrate form of the Ninja. She pulled her purse from the thief's knotted fist and handed it up to Muck. "Check for papers, Ms. Katsulas," she said, turning back to the moaning figure at her feet.

"Sure," said Muck. "By the way, why didn't you just shoot the slime with your .45 snubnosed blue steel whatchamacallit?"

"It's plastic. You know I hate real guns."

"Excuse me," said Heston, holding his shoulder. "Don't you know that guns don't kill people, people kill people?"

"I hate people too."

"Excuuuuuse me, sister," said Heston, and vanished into the crowd which parted before him.

Hortense pulled the black hood from the Ninja's head. On the right side of the Ninja's skull, beginning at the edge of his close-cropped black hair, a thin cut ran the length of his forehead and wept blood. On the left side of his skull, a long mass of blond hair fell damply to the thief's shoulder. Full red lips parted, and one eye, heavily outlined with cosmetics, blinked up at Smedley.

"I've half-a-mind to slap y-you silly," stuttered the blond half of the Ninja, and, reaching up with his left hand, he slapped his own right cheek sharply.

"Double-crossing half-wit," croaked the burly, crew-cut half of the thief, and, reaching back with his left hand, he struck the blond in the nose, knocking them both unconscious.

"Oh, my God," said Hortense, "It's Hermione, the hermaphrodite!"

"The Bi-Sexual Bombshell from Bilouxi, Mississippi!" added Buck. "Known in every burlesque house from here to San Francisco. A real double-header on the strip circuit, and the star of that classic cult B picture, The Spy Who Shemed Me! What's a nice shem doing in a place like this?"

"At first thought," answered Hortense," I'd guess just another try at indirect revenge against Ace Montana for having sex with his better half. But, I'm not sure now." She held up a clenched fist and opened her fingers for Muck Upp

Katsulas.

"Is... it... dead?" interrupted the old woman whose bag had tripped the Ninja. She had rejoined the two old, breathless victims.

"Nothing a few stitches won't cure," answered Hortense.

"Ah.... sew," added Muck.

"Oh, like, dear," said the 'old woman' who was actually Melanie Shelf in disguise. "The gig is up."

In the palm of Hortense's band was a pair of flesh colored, plastic ear plugs. "It's 'jig', dear," said Beth Francher, discarding the croaking voice she had used while likewise disguised as Hortense. "And I think we just kilt ourselves a Motelite."

"I don't feel sorry for 'poor' Hermione," groused Muck, a.k.a. Dianne Menace, to Fanny Francher. "Between the three of us, shem was the only one who always had a date on Saturday nights. I just want to know for sure why he... er.. she, well, whatever, snatched your purse, 'Hortense'."

Both women, who were continuing to impersonate old ladies in an effort to throw off their enemies, situated their bags in overhead storage and under their airplane seats before collapsing into them.

"My guess," answered Fanny, "is that the Motelites think I'm carrying the God Bop papers. That's why I asked you to check my purse for the duplicates we had made back at the GS offices. They were still there, as you know. It is standard for the course in these situations for the, eh, offending parties to keep an eye out on possible leaks, i.e. Melanie Shelf. It is also possible that Shelf is setting us up for a fall and is still a Motelite through and through."

Fanny offered Dianne a complimentary airline packet of honeyroasted Caviar.

"It is possible, of course, that half of the passengers on this flight are also Motelites. Or that we're just being paranoid. Choose the one you like best at this point."

"And that brilliant deduction is why you're a highly paid news anchor and I carry a camera, right?" whispered Dianne.

"No. Because I have better legs."

"Where do you keep them? Anywhy, the stupidest move I ever made was following you to Global Star Tonight after we broke the Speilberg story. I made a fortune on my serial killers portraits. My shot of the guy who offed the Lucky Charms leprechaun is still pulling royalties."

"Keep your voice down," hissed Fanny.

"Why? We're most likely the only one's in the whole plane not wearing ear plugs!"

"We don't know that for sure." A long silence between the two followed.

"And just why did you focus attention on us back at the terminal by throwing the purse at Hermione? You know the God Bop papers we are carrying are duplicates and it did not matter if Hermione stole them."

"This girdle cuts off the circulation to my brain."

"It can't help sitting on it either."

A disembodied voice interrupted. "Excuse me, ladies. I'm Paula Pom, your stewardess for this flight. Are you both comfortable? Is there anything I can get either of you? Coffee, tea... or me?" The stewardess lost control of a giggle.

"Well..." started Fanny, inspecting every inch of the towering blonde hostess. Dianne elbowed her.

"I'm sorry, but I just can't resist that line. It's so inane, so stereotypical, that it just cracks me up every time I say it!" said Paula. "Coffee, tea... or me?" The stewardess lost control of a giggle

"You certainly are a big girl for a hostess," said Fanny.

"Oh, it's my Swiss heritage, I guess. It's a little embarrassing sometimes, and it's hell getting dates—men are so easily intimidated—but all for the best, miss. 'Course, I inherited a knack for Swiss movements. Clean your clock, ma'am?"

"Excuse me?" asked Fanny.

"Just another joke," giggled Paula. "We don't have a movie on this flight, so management asked for us to entertain the passengers. But my size did get me a college scholarship to Notre Dame."

"Basketball?" asked Dianne.

"Okay," answered Paula. She pulled a remote control from a pocket and pointed it at the far end of the plane. A hoop descended.

"No," said Dianne, "I don't want to play basketball. I thought you might have gotten your scholarship to play the game."

"Why, yes, how did you ever guess!? I played quarterback. Now, may I get you ladies something to nibble on?"

"Well..." said Fanny. Dianne punched her in the ribs.

As the stewardess moved to a nun and priest seated behind Fanny and her 'nurse', Fanny pulled out a copy of Nude Photography: Art in Arrears, and spoke under her breath.

"I hope she's a teetotaler," said Fanny

"Why?" responded Dianne without emotion.

"Because that would make her non-alcoholic, and lips that touch liquor never touches my–"

"That," interrupted Dianne, "is a Motelite in drag if I ever saw one."

"And that brilliant deduction is why you followed me from Houston," grinned Fanny as she pulled the privacy earphones from their compartment and placed them over her ears. She jerked them off instantly, holding the set in front of herself like a poison snake. Her face was drained of color.

"Now what's wrong?" asked Dianne. "Did you stumble on a centerfold of Kirsten... again?"

"B-barry Manilow," said Fanny, pointing to the earphones. And both of the old women fell into a nervous silence as Fanny replaced the earphones in their compartment,

That silence was broken by the stewardess carrying a tray with two drinks and several packages of honey-roasted Caviar.

"Your drinks, ladies," smiled Paula as she leaned down and forward, offering the tray to Fanny and Dianne. "I hope you won't think me nosey, but you look oddly familiar to me, Ms. Smedley. Have you ever flown me before?"

"This is her first flight," interrupted Dianne as she took her bourbon and gave Fanny a 'beware' look. "Fear of flying."

"But, I'm almost sure I've seen you somewhere before. Have you ever been to Switzerland, Ms. Smedley? Have you seen my Alps?"

Fanny took her drink from the offered tray, and smiled at Paula. "Much as I'd love to, I swore off mountain climbing months ago. Arthritis. Caught it in Montana. It's a real pain in the butte."

"Punny you should say that," said Paula. "You look well traveled. Have you ever been to Rome? Paris? Salt Lake City? Ada, Oklahoma!?"

Fanny sipped her drink and shuddered involuntarily. She squinted up at Paula Pom, leaning slightly forward in her seat. "Why, I most certainly have been to Ada! That's where I married my dear, departed husband, Ace Montana! You remember that, don't you, Buck Nekked, dear?"

Paula Pom dropped her metal tray, scattering cups and saucers everywhere. Paula reached up to the buttons of her uniform blouse and yelled, "Do you remember Homecomig '82, Francher!"

She ripped her blouse open exposing a football jersey, orange and black, emblazoned with the number sixty-nine. Stuck in the waistband of her skirt was a plastic squirt bottle. From behind them, leather straps whipped around Fanny and Dianne, pinning both to their seats and spilling their drinks. The nun and priest behind the elderly couple genuflected and tightened the straps with a jerk. The jerk then rose in disgust, and moved to another group of seats.

Paula Porn pulled the squeeze bottle from her waistband and waved it like a gun in front of the women. From somewhere in the plane, a woman screamed, "My God, it's a hi-jacking!!" and the airplane erupted in screams, chaos and facial blemishes.

"Oh, God," said Dianne emotionlessly, "She's gonna squirt us to death."

Paula laughed demonically as she pulled a blonde wig away from her head. Her voice fell an octave. "Not Paula Pom, you naive old fools; Herve Kurtzman!!

Tight end. Ada Cougars. Almost state football champions, but you know that, don't you, 'Ms. Smedley'? Or should I call you...

"Fanny Francher!"

"Oh, God," added Dianne emotionlessly, "she's gonna cliche us to death."

As some semblance of order returned in response to Herve's commands, and the noise dwindled away, Kurtzman leaned in close to 'Hortense' and pulled the gray wig from 'her' nearly bald head.

"My," sneered Herve, "things are getting hairy."

Using the big palm of his hand, Herve slowly smeared the make-up that had served to disguise Francher as an old woman.

"My, don't we look stupid," he sneered into Francher's face.

"Yes, Herve, but mine comes off."

"Fanny, Fanny, Fanny," he rubbed the nickname into her face, verbally, "I'd expect something more clever than that from you."

"Wish I could return the compliment. Wait! I've got it! Buttface, buttface, buttface!" Francher mocked.

Muck Upp, a.k.a. Dianne Menace, her own wig knocked askance when strapped to her seat by the priest, hissed at Francher and punched her in the ribs with an elbow. "Why don't you antagonize him so he'll torture us before he kills us, Fanny?!"

Herve laughed deeply. "Everythin' okay back there, Anthony? Augustine? The straps good and tight?!"

"I don't know about good," said Anthony, the 'priest'. "But day ain't goin' nowhere."

"Ditto," added the nun. "Dey's tighter dan a jockstrap on prom night. Speakin' of which, you look especially hot in dat collar tonight, Father Anthony."

"Ach de liber, Augustine," barked Herve. "Shut up yer face."

"Sorry Herve. Bad habit," blushed Augustine, pulling at his nun's robe.

"The Motelites put you up to this, didn't they, Herve?" asked Francher calmly.

"Motelites? What th' hell's a Motelite?"

"It's onea dem lil' lights what plugs ina outlet at the motel, Herve," grinned Augustine.

"I'll have none o' that," growled Herve. "Shut up yer face again. It don't matter nohow. We don't need no help in takin' our revenge on the media whore what cost us the state football championship! We were," Herve spread his thumb and forefinger an inch apart, "this close!"

"Amazing," said Francher. "That's also how close you've ever been to a woman." Menace punched her hard with an elbow.

"Herve," Francher began again, "I didn't cost you anything. If memory serves, the Cougars had sealed a deal with Satan... one sacrificed virgin for each football game won."

"We were young and he fooled us, Fanny," pouted Herve, waving his plastic squirt bottle absentmindedly. "Satan appeared to us at a Pep Rally as one of the Three Stooges. But he was a wolf in Shep's clothing."

"Uh-huh. You used the skin of those women to make the footballs used in the games. Now, clue me in. Was I on the team when the deal was sealed? Did I participate in any of your black masses? Then explain how I'm responsible for your lost charnpionship."

"You told, you told, you told!!!" Herve whined while he stamped his feet in petulance. "Two hours after yer story broke, there was a cloud o' cigarette smoke hangin' over Ada, and not a single virgin left in town!"

"You were down to the chess club and the Star Wars crowd anyway. And now you're going to kill me and my photographer. How will that change the past, Herve? How will that get you your beloved championship? What's done is done."

"Oh, no, no, no!" grinned the jock. "I'm not goin' to kill you! That's much too simple, too humane. I don't want yer soul. Satan already owns you journalist types. I wantcha to suffer like us."

"Good God," said Menace. "Fanny, I think he's gonna turn us into impotent, drooling Neanderthals! He's gonna force us to read Sports Illustrated."

"I wantcha to lose everything you got, Francher. Your money, your fame. This plastic bottle is filled with acid! I want yer face, ya..."

Francher jerked forward snapping the leather strap from the priest's grip. In one motion, she reached under Menace's seat, grabbed a bag and swung it against the window next to the photographer. The window shattered.

The giant 747 lurched, throwing Herve off his feet. Chaos broke out among the passengers and the airplane began a slow fall into eternity as a tremendous suction gripped and sucked loose items out of the broken window.

A giant robot lurched down the aisle. "Warning, warning, Will Robinson!" it droned. "Danger, danger!"

Will Robinson fastened his seat belt. Tiny, red lights blinked on and off, an alarm blared, and dozens of plastic oxygen masks dropped from their receptacles over the passenger's seats.

As the 747 began to decompress, Francher yanked the strap from Menace, and turned to Herve, staggering in the aisle. As the newshound grabbed the quarterback by his jersey, Dianne crawled out of her seat behind Francher.

Beth fell back on the empty seats, a knee planted in Herve's stomach and jerked Kurtzman's writhing body forward.

"NOOOO!" screamed the jock as be struck the gaping window and was sucked through the opening up to his hips.

Francher watched Herve's legs flail. "Your first mistake was I'm not just a face," she hissed under her breath. "I'm also one hell of a right hook."

On the floor behind Francher, Menace was beating the priest's head against the carpeting to the sound of dull thuds. And an old woman in pale green was bludgeoning the already unconscious nun with her purse.

"Hail Mary, full of Grace," said Menace, and pounded the priest's head against the floor. "Hail Mary, full of... "

"Y-you're... forgiven... a-already," the priest gasped.

The photographer glanced up, gave Beth a wink, and let the priest's head fall with a final thud to the floor. Glancing to her left, Menace saw Will Robinson sitting small and very frightened in his seat.

Will seemed lost in the space.

The plane leveled and began to return to normal compression. A frantic pilot was trying to gain some control of the passengers. The old woman in pale green joined Francher, grinning and wiping the sweat from her brow.

"Did we do, like, swell, or what, Fanny?" she asked, pulling off her own gray wig and tugging at the wrinkled latex that concealed the youthful face of Melanie Shelf.

"Just crazy, Melanie; the ultimate cool," said Francher. "Outside of blowing our cover to a plane full of possible Motelites, I'd say saving our skins and sacking three murdering Satanists from Oklahoma isn't a bad days work. Let's hope the pilot agrees."

"Did you have to throw that one bag out of every bag I brought?" groused Dianne as she fell back into her seat beneath the now still legs of Herve Kurtzman. "My favorite Nikon was in that bag, Beth."

"Was this your medical camera, Dianne? The one that doctors your photos?" Menace did not smile.

"I set your Nikon on automatic timer when I threw it through the window, honey," grinned Francher. "If it's any consolation, you captured some great Kodak moments on the way down."

"What the hell happened here?" bellowed the flustered pilot of the airplane as he moved down the aisle towards Beth and Melanie. "I'm Captain Cirk. Can you enlighten me?"

Do I look like Richard Simmons," answered Francher looking at Cirk's substantial girth. She began to rub off what was left of her Smedley make-up with a handkerchief. "Can we talk in private? I'm Beth Francher and this is Dianne Menace, both of Global Star Tonight. And this is..."

"Oh, geeze," blustered Cirk, running a hand through his hair which slid awkwardly over his left ear. "Are we on American Idol right now?"

"I'd start by restraining these three murdering hi-jackers, Captain," added Menace.

"Murderers...?!? Hi-jackers?!? My, you ladies are enterprising..."

"The 'nun' and 'priest! need your attention as well," added Francher. "This one," she jabbed a finger at Herve's buttocks, "is busy learning to suck up to his superiors. I'd say he's got about five minutes before showtime."

"You've certainly raised a stink!" said Cirk, pulling out a walkie-talkie. "I've got to call my valet." He spoke into the device.

"This is Captain Cirk. Clean me up, Scotty."

As the backside of the plane's pilot disappeared down the aisle, Melanie leaned close to Francher and whispered, "The Motelites. They're, like, hip to our session, aren't they?"

"No, honey. These aren't Motelites. These jocks try this about once every year. It comes with my job. I must admit that your coming with us over my objections certainly proved prudent, however. Thanks for back there."

"How'd ya know that fly pie wasn't for real, Ms. Francher?"

"For starters, they don't serve Gatorade on 747's, which is what Paula Pam served to me. So, I gave Menace our standard 'Ace' signal, tensed up and leaned slightly forward. That move was almost involuntary, just preparing for whatever happened. But it was just what I needed when we were strapped to our seats. It gave me the slack I needed to jerk free. Lucky move on my part."

"Well," said Menace as she patted Herve's butt, "at least this year the Ada Cougars sent a tight end."

Beth walked around the side of the blue Ford Escort and kicked the left front tire, hard. A sign stuck on the inside back window read: Info Babe On Board. Beth made a mental note to not laugh at Menace's joke.

"Why the hell does Wood do this to us?" said Beth. "A Ford Escort? For God's sake, Kirsten Lane gets a Jaguar on assignment to cover a kitten caught in a tree. Ace gets a flakin' privatejet to go to the bathroom, and I get a Ford Escort. Next, it'll be reservations at the Bates Motel. And you know what motto they use."

"Swish or cut Bates?" asked Melanie. "Maybe if slept with Gephard like Lane and Montana, you'd get a Cadillac." Dianne shoved another suitcase into the trunk of the Escort and Shelf picked another bag from a pile.

"That's not real funny, and I don't appreciate the slur against Kirsten, Dianne. And you don't really think Gephard would, you know, with Ace?!"

"Gephard would boink a goat on a fool's bet. Double or mutton—Ace, on the other hand, is the straightest man in the world. He once punched out a Christmas caroler for singing about 'gay apparel'. But that'sjust a rhetorical question so you can grouse and stomp around while I load the equipment. You prima donna's really get my goat."

"The chicks, like, got a point on the bags," said the former Motelite. "The sooner it's loaded, we romp on the juicer and split this dump, the sooner we dump the rest of these cornball disguises, reet?"

"Groovey, " said Menace with a splash of vinegar in her voice.

"No, I mean, really," said Beth as she moved to the truck and began to heave a bag to its rim. "It's around eight-thirty. I'd guess a three hour drive to Rose Butte. When do they close the Motelite Registry?"

"Never. They, like, bebop around the clock, feedin' monikers into the computers."

"Well, I'm tired and hungry, and they arent going to kill everyone on Earth for eleven more days, so I vote we find a motel, said Francher, slamming the trunk lid.

"NO!! We can't crash at a motel, Beth! They've probably got every flop house in Utah bugged!" protested Menace.

Francher opened the driver's door to the Escort as Menace and Shelf moved to the passenger's door. "I don't think they'd buy a film crew from Global Star Tonight arriving unannounced at eleven thirty to cover a genealogy story."

"That's solid, like she said," added Shelf. "It's, like, dust city between here and Rose Butte, and, like, no one will be on the road. It'd be hip to, like, catch some zzz's in the heap, outta sight, man."

"I think she said we'll be driving through a desert to Rose Butte," interjected Menace as she climbed into the back of the Escort. "And no one would see us sleeping in the car."

"I dig, Dianne," answered Beth as she crawled behind the steering wheel. The newshound turned the key that had been left for them in the rented car, and the motor roared into life. Francher pulled out of the parking lot, crushing Melanie's accordion under the Escort's left rear tire where Beth had left it.

"What was that?" asked Shelf. "It sounded like a choking owl?"

"Speed bump," answered Francher.

"It might be a good idea, Melanie, if you use the travel time to fill Dianne and I in on some background on this John Palmer. In English, please. How did you meet him?"

Well, a drip chick friend of Your's Truly, like, asked me to a hot jam sess to meet some new hepcats. The place was a real boneyard, really squaresville, and no one would make with the swing until some coot cat said 'open the door,

Richard', and he hoped in. It was, like, instant chemistry, and I could see by the mellow drape of his sack that he was one B.T.O. I decided on the spot that he'd be my pash-pie or I'd just die!"

The silence in the car accentuated the purr of the Escort.

"I think her mother was scared by Dobie Gillis when she was pregnant with Melanie," said Menace from the back seat.

"Wouldn't that be Shelf abuse?" quipped Beth. No one laughed.

Francher sighed, her patience thinner than usual. "Obviously, you didn't die," she said. "What happened then?" The Escort passed a billboard advertising Preparation H ointment. Not inappropriate, thought the reporter, for the pain in the butte that lay somewhere ahead in their futures.

"We, like, bailed out of that square shindig, and he took me to his pad. That's where I found out he was a sound scientist, a righteous cat with mega gettas who knew how to spend it. He set me hep about the Motelites and the Universal Vibrator. And he blasted my wig ... all night long, baby."

"Sex?" asked Menace, yawning in the back seat.

"No, thank you, I'm like straight. And, I, like, flipped my lid when he said he'd get me a secretary gig at the Registry. Jeepers, I was a real bobby-soxer, wasn't I, Dianne? Stupid. I was so stupid."

"Love is blind," said Francher. "And has no seeing-eye dog."

"Love is a fool's path with no warning signs or Texaco rest stops," added Menace.

"Love is a disease without cure or Medicare reimbursement," sighed Francher, shaking her head.

"The heart is a poor philosopher with a mail-order degree from Jamacia," said Menace, chewing on a fingernail.

"The heart, when broken, lies like a bloody mass of rancid catgut," added Francher.

"Oh, is that from Socrates?" asked Shelf, looking up from her fingernail.

"Hallmark."

"Oh, you fracture me, Miss Francher. I know a super-cool chick like you could never be that cornball. Hallmark?"

"I wish it were true," said Beth, softly, "but love makes a fool of every man, every woman, everyone sooner or later."

"I know this is, well, kinda personal, but is there a solid Jackson in your life, Miss Francher?"

The silence was like a weight in the Escort as Francher glanced away from Shelf and out of the driver's window into the deep blue of the desert night. The bobbing head of the fuzzy toy dog on its dash didn't help her mood. Neither did the billboard advertising Count Dracula's newest paperback, Love Sucks. The sky was so clear and blue, undiminished by city lights, that it was mesmerizing. Rose Butte was only an unseen but felt presence. A car passed and, eventually, a second before Francher turned to Shelf. The shadows in the car and the dashboard lights seemed to soften the chiseled, Grecian beauty of the newshound.

Suddenly, a deer was frozen on the highway by the car's headlights. The Ford struck it with a violent thud, tearing the animal into a bloody rain of body parts and entrails that washed over the windshield.

Francher turned on the wipers.

"Yes," she said softly. "There... is some one.. dear to me." Menace began to snore brokenly in the back seat, slumped against a door. "Oddly enough, another reporter named Lane. We fight like cats and dogs when we're together, and Lane is an unethical, back-stabbing jackal when it comes to breaking a story. But I've never met anyone more painfully honest, and honesty is a very rare commodity in this crazy world."

"How do you know she's honest?" asked Shelf.

"She told you I don't have a chance in Hell."

"How did you meet this Lane character, Miss Francher?"

"Call me Beth, honey. This business makes strange bedfellows, Melanie. I was down in New Orleans about a year and a half ago during Mardi Gras. I'd been assigned to cover a story about a satyr who seduced women in laundromats. The newspapers were calling him the 'Satyr of Suds' for lack of professionalism. Unknown to me, Lane had been given the same assignment by her editor, Frank Gephard. Lane pulled every trick in the book to beat me to the story. And I wrote the book on tricks."

"Were you, like, furious with this Lane cat?"

"I must admit, she almost got my goat on that one."

"You're kiddin? You're an infobabe and a shepherdess, Miss Francher?"

Francher searched for any hint of humor in Shelf's face and found nothing.

"I posed as a housewife," she continued, ignoring the musician, "with enough dirty laundry to be a senator, and just about lived at the Clean Yer Whistle laundromat. It was a cheerless job, but I knew the tide would turn.

"It happened during the rinse cycle. I glanced up from reading an article by Ace Montana in the Global Star. I believe the headline was: Queen Charles the First, Pregnant. Across the double bank of washers stood a ravishingly beautiful woman with clear, perfect skin, large, deep-brown eyes, horns on her forehead and thick, curly brown tresses cascading to her shoulders. She wore a button reading: Men wear attire... I wear satire."

"Jeepers! " exclaimed Melanie, "the satyr was, like, a chick? Why would a chick be seducing.... euuuh! That's disgusting!"

"Women get horny too," said the newshound, icily.

Francher gave Melanie a long, silent look before turning her attention back to the dark road. A length of the deer's intestines that had caught under the windshield's wiper was sucked away by the wind.

"I wish I knew how you can mend a broken hart," said the infobabe.

"Don't bail out now, Ms. Francher," said Shelf. "Why'dcha stop? What happened next? Weren't you, like, wigged out?"

"If you mean was I afraid," resumed Francher, gazing straight ahead through the windshield, "I had nothing to fear. Menace was in a dryer with a camera hidden in her chest."

"Wow! She has a photographic mammary?"

"She's quite dependable in a crisis, and static-resistant, too," continued the newshound. "The satyr winked and asked if I'd be a lamb and loan her some Woolite. I filled a cup, leaned over my washer and threw the detergent in her face. I jumped up on the washer, and then over the entire bank of machines and tackled the satyr."

"Swell!" exclaimed Melanie with some excitement. "You put her in places with bright, shiny faces, Miss Francher?"

"Would you stop with the Miss and Ms. Stuff. It's very annoying. Well, we fell in a jumble on the floor, and I tore away the brown wig and the horns; I'd known they were fakes. I've worn enough disguises on my own to spot a phoney a mile away. And that's when a photog in the clothes hamper next to the satyr jumped out and snapped the picture that still sits on my desk at the Global Star Tonight offices."

"Drooly! So, you and Menace stopped the satyr con? But... what's that got to do with Mr. Lane?"

"The photographer wasn't Menace, that's for sure. She couldn't get the door of the dryer open. That photograph isn't of me and the satyr of New Orleans. It's of me wrestling with Kirsten Lane."

"Kirsten ... Lane? The satyr was Mr. Lanes sister?"

"No. Kirsten had been assigned to cover the same story, remember? She'd disguised herself as a female satyr to lure the real goat into the Clean Yer Whistle, and the photographer was one of the Star's best, named Alucard, also on assignment with Kirsten. The police got the real goat at the We're Never Clothed all-night laundry on Saturday night."

"So Kirsten is Mr. Lane's niece on his mother's side once removed?"

"Kirsten Lane is the 'satyr' that won my heart."

"Oh... dear," stammered Melanie in a tiny voice full of embarrassment. "I didn't know you were a one-note samba."

"Don't worry about it, honey. Now, why don't you turn on the radio and catch some tunes for us, Melanie. The drone of this engine is making me drowsy, and it's a little warm in here. Could you crack your window a bit?"

Melanie flipped on the car radio. The car filled with Barry Manilow singing I Mangle The Songs. Her face etched with trepidation and cast in odd shadows by the light from the radio, Shelf turned to Francher.

"Tha-that's, like, jest a coincidence?!?"

"Of course, Melanie. Just turn the dial to another station, answered Francher. "No need for trepidation. See if you can find the All Usher All The Time station."

Shelf twisted the dial to another station. The radio sang '...that make the whole world sing. I write the songs that...'

"Oh, God," whispered Shelf, and twisted the dial again. 'I write the songs that make the young girls cry...' wailed the radio speakers. "It's happening! They've found us!"

"Now, don't panic," said Francher. "Maybe it's Manilow's birthday today, or, God forbid, he's died. Try an AM station."

Melanie flipped a switch on the radio to AM. She twisted the dial again, her hand shaking and a line of sweat leaving a wet trail down the side of her forehead.

"It's five after midnight on a beautifully clear night in Utah, with no chance of rain and a high tomorrow of ninety-five degrees," chatted a voice on the radio. Melanie sighed and shuddered involuntarily.

"See," noted Francher, "I told you it wasn't necessary to shudder involun–

"And now," interrupted the disembodied voice from the Escort's dash, "we reprise Barry Manilow's Copacabana."

Melanie's hand was frantically on the radio dial, flipping through one station after the next. Every turn of her wrist caught another fragment of another Manilow song.

"Oh God, oh no, oh God, oh no, oh God, oh no," she muttered as she turned to Francher with unspoken horror. "They've started God-Bop early! We're all gonna die! We're gonna die! Die! Die!"

"Did someone say pie?" asked Menace, removing an earplug from her right ear.

Francher looked into the Escort's rear-view mirror as she reached across the gear-shift to put a hand on Shelf's arm, as much to restrain her as to offer her some Shelf protection.

"Oh, hell," Beth hissed to herself "Not now. Not again."

The headlights began to flicker and play a wild dance across the dark asphalt of the deserted road, and the Ford began to shake. In the back seat, Menace put her earplug back in.

"Piece of junk! " Francher barked, slapping the Escort's dash. "If it had a cellular phone, at least I could call home." The dog on the dash began to glow eerily.

"Remember that trepidation of yours a little earlier? Well..."

The car's electrical system failed. Loose objects on the dash, seats and floor of the Escort that had been jumping like grease on a hot skillet began to dance in mid-air, defying gravity. Francher fought for control of the car as the motor shut off like someone throwing a light switch.

"It's the Motelites, It's the Motelites!" screamed Shelf.

"DON'T THINK SO," yelled Beth over the racket of the rain of flying objects inside the Escort. "MORE LIKELY, ANOTHER CLOSE ENCOUNTER OF THE ABSURD KIND! DON'T LET THEM SEE FEAR! AND, FOR GOD'S SAKE, DON'T LET THEM RUB THEIR MIDDLE FINGER IN THE PALM OF YOUR HAND!!"

"WHY?!"

"IT'S THE SAME THING AS SEX FOR A MARTIAN!"

"IS IT OKAY IF I WEAR A GLOVE?"

"SURE, IF YOU WANT TO RUIN THE SPONTANEITY!"

The Escort rolled to a stop, elevated objects fell with a clatter, and an unnatural silence fell over the car. The dash dog landed in Francher's lap. The news hound turned to Shelf, who seemed frightened beyond reason, and gripped her arm hard.

"Now, listen. This has nothing to do with the Motelites. These are probably Martians sent by Speilberg. He's been after me ever since he made that movie about zombie salmon."

"Oh, I saw that," said Melanie. "Spawn of the Living Dead."

"You'd think they'd at least be original," said Beth as she looked out her rear-view mirror again. Distant, red points of light hung behind the Escort. Instantly, the car was flooded with blinding, multi-colored light, the air inside became oppressively heavy with the smell of ozone, and a muted roar filled the desert night.

"Dianne, pretend sleep!!" commanded Beth of her sidekick. Menace snorted like a warthog deep in sleep.

"What is that, like, about?" asked Melanie.

"Martians take things very literally. Since reporters are called news hounds, I'm hoping they'll mistake us for an unusual breed and 'let sleeping dogs lie'."

Moving like a gigantic wave, the light crept up and beyond the back window of the Ford and washed over the road in front of the car. Melanie Shelf buried her face in her bands, and although Francher could't hear them for the outside chaos, she knew Shelf was sobbing into her hands. Francher put on a pair of sun glasses. Menace grunted and turned over to face the back seat.

"Stay cool," said Francher, "and do whatever they say except the Hokey

Pokey. That's a weird, sexual fetish for Martians. Open your door and step out. Maybe they won't see Dianne in the back seat."

As she began to follow her own instructions, a monstrous flying, neckless banjo ablaze in light settled to the road a dozen yards in front of the car. Francher stepped out onto the hot asphalt and slammed her door. Then moving slowly to the front of the Escort, Francher glanced over to locate Melanie.

Melanie stood a dozen feet in front of the car, her face and body thrown in relief by the powerful lights of the flying banjo. No sign of fear marked her underlit face. Her eyes were cold and hard, and strapped to her chest was a small bag.

"Mel," hissed Beth, "what in God's name are you doing?" But Shelf's fingers were already on the holes of a kazoo she had pulled from the bag, playing a riff of nine notes. The roar from the flying neckless banjo died into silence like the revving down of a dozen, massive jet engines. The silence that hung over the dessert was startling, and Francher realized she could now even hear the distant chirp of crickets.

The neckless banjo suddenly boomed out the same nine notes in answer in Shelf's kazoo. Melanie responded with another, identical set of notes. And Beth's expression of calculated caution melted into one of hard cynicism.

"What are you doing?!" yelled Francher. "I was joking when I said you should blow it out your old kazoo!"

"Music is God's language, and this is one of God's messengers!" The flying banjo answered Melanie's musical statement with an identical repetition.

"What are you saying, for God's sake?" muttered Francher.

"A mathematical formula expressed through foot and tone that equivocates the word 'welcome'," yelled back the kazooist.

"It sounds like Dueling Kazoos by George W. Bush and Chris Dodd!" shouted the news hound. "Hey, they had to do something to make a living after the economic bailout!"

"It is Dueling Kazoos!!"

"But where did you get that thing in your mouth?" yelled Francher. "I destro... eh, accidently backed over that accordion thing back at the airport."

"You don't think I'd travel without a backup, do you?" replied Shelf "After all, music is my life!"

A mouth split the metal underbelly of the spacecraft, spilling out a river of light over the highway. A metal tongue rolled out from this gaping aperture and hissed to a stop on the asphalt. And like a splatter of inkblots in the light, shadows began to float out of the mouth of the spaceship.

Those inkblots grew and mutated into disjointed things of bulbous heads, elongated necks, disproportionate and multiple limbs... TV actors and actresses.

As they tottered through the light and down the ramp towards Francher and Shelf, Melanie released the kazoo. The first figure broke free of the light.

"Oh, God," gasped Francher, "it's worst than I thought. And I thought they were congressmen."

The clumsy, awkward figures were dressed in dark-blue marching band uniforms with gold epaulets at the shoulders, and conical, plumed caps. One of these figures stepped away from the mass of swaying bodies, a baton held at its hip with a gloved hand.

"Trumpet, cornet, bugle," tallied Francher, "trombone, Wagner tuba, double-B-flat baritone, french horn... it's.... it's a brass band with George Segal on banjo and Barney Frank on mouth organ!"

"Sweet Bach!!" gasped Shelf, "it's John Palmer!"

"John Palmer is George Segal?"

"He is in this story unless you wanna get us sued," gasped Shelf.

The band began playing an arrangement of the Beatles' Sgt. Pepper's Lonely Hearts Club Band as Palmer moved away from the group and towards the stunned kazooist. Palmer raised his baton high, and said, "Sweeet. It's Fanny Francher, taken the bait. She'd danced with the devil, and now it's time to pay the piper!"

Francher stepped forward and extended her hand. "I gather that I need no introduction. Mr. Palmer, we're here tonight to do a feature for Global Star Tonight on the genealogical facilities of the Motelites, and have no bone to pick with aliens."

Palmer stared at her hand. "What! No glove!! " He leveled his baton at the news hound. "Are there others in this ensemble? Do none of you practice safe sax?"

"We're it, Mr. Palmer. My equipment is in the trunk, and according to the International Alien Convention–"

"We're not aliens," interrupted Palmer. "We're only actors playing aliens." He turned to his band. "Search the car!"

"I know we should have called the F.A.I.A. before we started this trek, but I was working on an extremely tight schedule," continued Francher. "If we've caught you at an awkward moment, we could come back tomorrow."

Palmer sneered. "Do I look like a fool, Fanny Francher?"

"Yes."

"Well, I'm not. I'm only an actor playing a fool. Furthermore, we care nothing about the Federal Agency of Invading Aliens, Ms. Francher. I know why you are here, and I know that you know that I am the leader of the Motelites."

"It's 'Illegal Aliens", and I thought you were an actor playing the leader of the Motelites." Behind her, Francher heard one of Palmer's men yell, "There's a woman asleep in the back seat!"

"You're kidding," said Francher. "Those insurance salesmen are sure tenacious. You really are in good vans with–"

"Stop!" boomed Palmer. "The time for false notes is over, news hound. You're here to expose the Motelite's Grand Finale for a world full of plebeians, and I'm here to ring down the curtain on your little comic opera. And, of course, our alien accompanists are here to watch me stop you. They just love revenge. And to watch."

"The woman asleep in the Escort had nothing to do with the Speilberg expose. You have what you came for, so leave the photographer to her dreams."

"You're articulation is perfect, Fanny," said Palmer as be smoothed a wave of hair back into place on the side of his meticulously groomed head. "But your performance is seriously flawed."

"That's a wrap. Drag her out of the car, boys!! "

Francher coolly evaluated the man standing before her as Barney Frank gave a final toot on his mouth organ and began to rouse Dianne Menace from her sleep. Despite the band uniform that hid most of his body lines, Beth guessed Palmer's five feet, eleven inches were built of hard-edged muscle. His brown hair was close-cropped, but full of subtle waves, his cheeks and chin were sharp, clean lines, and his skin was an olive brown. Palmer's eyes were brown and well spaced. Francher noted that he was not to be underestimated, and that Melanie's infatuation with the head Motelite was probably justified, even though he was a man. And even though he was not the man he claimed was John Palmer.

Still struggling, Menace was dragged to Beth's side by a tuba player and a cornetist. "A has-been actor playing at world conquest?" asked Dianne.

"I think you've put your finger on it, Dianne," said Francher with a secret wink to her camera woman.

"Yeah, yeah," answered the still sleepy photojournalist as she hung her left hand from the lapel of her blouse with its ring finger pointed directly at Palmer. "Yeah. You look vaguely familiar. Didn't I see you strumming the old banjo on America's Got Talent once?"

"Enough of this discord. You and I are going for a little ride to Rose Butte in a spacecraft. I promise you'll see much more of me than you'd hoped. In fact, I may be the coda to your life's symphony. Take 'em boys! Swearin' to God, we're gonna have a hot time in the old town tonight!"

Moving with trained syncopation, Palmer's musicians discarded their instruments and advanced on Francher and Menace. Melanie Shelf stepped out of the shadows and put her arm through John Palmer's crooked arm.

"Ali, Melanie Shelf, my little sonata."

"Did I do good, Maestro?" asked Shelf with an imploring, totally devoted look. "I got the infobabe and her flunky!"

"Better than good, sweetheart. You did well." And, opening his mouth to its limit, he kissed her deeply.

"Yuck, that's disgusting," said Francher as a musician at each of her arms began to drag her and Dianne into the light.

"Don't be coy, Fanny," said Menace as she slowly waved her ring finger in a broad arch across the mouth of the flying neckless banjo. "You've seen french-horn kissing before." And, one by one, Menace, Francher, the band, Palmer, and Melanie were each swallowed up by the light.

The gaping mouth of the spaceship sucked up its metal tongue and sealed itself, throwing the desert once again into darkness. The saucer hovered momentarily just above the highway, its muted roar racing up the scale in pitch by several octaves. Then it shot like a bullet into the night sky.

On the deserted asphalt below, Francher's rented Escort coughed into life, its headlights flickering on. Its motor caught, revved, and the car slowly crept forward and veered to the side of the road.

"I write the songs that make the whole world sing," sang the Ford's tinny radio to the empty sky.

An assortment of animals on the side of the road watched the saucer vanish. In union, they began to strip the Ford.

"**W**elcome aboard Transworld Flight 69," said the small, mechanical voice of a computer set in a wall of the saucer. "Destination, Rose Butte. Estimated time of arrival, nine minutes. I'm your host IAJ. Please feel free to ask questions; we are here to serve mankind... with relish. Tips are appreciated."

"Hello, Fanny. Dianne. Fanny... famous, gooood. Menace good!"

Beth Francher looked down into the grey, parchment face of Deep Neck, a grin splitting its jaw. The last time Beth had seen the little alien, he had been trying to sneak a peek up Kirsten Lane's skirt while he was operating the elevator in the Global Star building.

"Surprised to see me?" the alien asked. "Still want to be me?"

"Not as much as disappointed," answered Francher with no show of emotion. "I'll admit I won't be recommending former world traitors and scumbags for positions with the Global Star again."

"Ooooooh," said the alien, the tip of its finger beginning to pulsate with an orange-yellow light. "It cut deeeep!" He placed this finger on his own chest. "Heeeeeal... heeeeal... heeeeeeal! Shut mouth, Fanny, or Deep Throat mutilate news-cow!"

"I'll admit you've got the balls. 'Course, they originally belonged to Bull Durham."

"Let me cut news cow!!" screamed the alien. "Let me cut news cow!!"

"Enough, Deep Neck," interrupted John Palmer. "You got a beef, take it up with management. I've got a news cow... er, news hound to silence."

"So, this whole God-Bop thing is just another attempt at revenge," observed Francher, shaking her head in disbelief "What'll it be? Sledge hammer? Chainsaw? Ginsu knife? You playing "Swanee" on the banjo?"

"Shut up," snarled Palmer. He beckoned an alien to his side. Oddly different from Deep Neck, this extraterrestrial had three eyes on its chin, a mouth in its forehead and no nose. "We actually wanted Ace Montana, but he was overseas."

"Bind them! And don't be gentle about it, Samsonite."

Deep Neck and the three-eyed Samsonite approached Francher and Dianne, pulling what appeared to be short bands of light from their tunics. "Put your hands behind you, ladies," said Deep Neck, "and try not to enjoy the handcuffs too much."

"My, how quickly we lose the alien speech slur along with any sense of loyalty to Earth. Is this really necessary? It's not like I'm going to jump off a flying saucer moving at 700 miles an hour. I've seen what that did to Deep Neck."

"My dear," answered Palmer, waving an arm in a broad arc that took in most of the visible interior of the spacecraft, "look around you. This isnt a New York subway. It's a delicate and simply amazing piece of work, a symphony in steel. I don't want to find your finger in the interspatial warp thingamabob just in case you really get desperate and stupid."

"Why would I horn in on your character traits?" sneered Beth.

Francher took inventory of her surroundings just for the very purpose Palmer had mentioned. The walls of the ship looked like milk-colored membranes stretched over a light bulb. Semi-transparent, they seemed to pulsate from a hidden source of power, although there was no perceptible movement. Large posters of famous aliens adorned each wall: ET., Alf, Al, Superman Gore.

Almost below her range of hearing, a low hum seemed to fill every inch of the flying saucer. A maze of curving corridors ran like spikes from where Francher and Menace stood, disappearing as they curved away from the news team. On the floor, a separate colored stripe followed the curve of each corridor.

"Let's go to Palmer's office," said Melanie. "Follow the yellow hick's road."

The band of light being tied around Beth's wrists behind her belt felt cool and soft. "Even if I ran away, where would I run to, Palmer? We're not in Kansas anymore. And I wouldn't know an interspatial warp thingamabob from a thermonuclear sitz bath."

"Do as you are directed," said Palmer. "I've simply no time for this interlude, and no patience to refrain from speeding up the process if you don't shut up. I've got a world of pagans to kill in only ten hours."

"Hey, I not jump out of saucer!" interjected Deep Neck.

"Ten hours?!?" said Beth, wincing as the alien behind her pulled the light cuffs tight against her flesh. "What happened to eleven days?!?"

Palmer grinned as he stroked Melanie's blond hair. He leaned close to her head and kissed her earlobe. "I'm really impressed with you, dear. They bought your little falsetto song, hook, line and sinker.

"My stupid, little media pigs," added Palmer, "if you'll follow me, all will be revealed. Our arrival at Rose Butte is only..." he checked the tiny batons of his wristwatch, "Seven minutes away."

"Well, I'll admit I never thought it'd end like this," said Francher. "Not with a bang, but with a wimp. But its obvious this little saucer has brought us to the point of no return."

The entourage began to move down a long, white corridor of the spaceship that curved into nothingness on their left. Palmer unconsciously raised and lowered his baton to the cadence of his own steps. On occasion, the tip of the baton struck the floor of the craft, without sound.

They passed a room marked THERMONUCLEAR Sitz BATH.

"This stuff isn't really metal, is it?" Menace noted, thudding the heel of her palm against a wall as they moved silently down the hall. "Just as phoney as that baton you use as a sexual crutch, eh, Palmer?"

"Ah, Menace, Menace, Menace. I'd expect such a butch statement from Francher's... pet. But you are surprisingly observant and correct. This ship is actually organic; a living creature bred through the incredible advanced science of these marvelous little leather suitcases we call aliens."

"A living creature?" repeated Menace. "Not female, I hope, or it won't be safe from Ace Montana."

"Don't mention his name!" snarled Palmer. He softly stroked the ships's membranous wall. "She had to undergo a year of therapy after one date with that sexual deviant!

"It's the same science that supplied the Motelites with the computers and softwear needed to accomplish God-Bop, which is quite real, I assure you. The very same technology that gave the world such space-age wonders as Tang and mood rings.

"I give you that information, Menace, because you have no better chance of damaging this living skin than you would have if it were steel.

"You see, this is actually a joint venture to bring about your death, Francher, and to conquer the world. When you exposed the alien's attempt at world conquest through Speilberg, they simply looked for another avenue of conquest. What they found was John Smith. And what John Smith found was the man to supply the charisma he lacked... me."

Menace snapped the fingers on her real hand. "I knew I recognized you. Your name isn't John Palmer at all. You're Zamfir, Master of the Pan Flute. "

"Close," said Beth, "but not close enough. He's Leon San Dunes, a second-rate, Las Vegas lounge act."

Palmer stopped his parade and bowed deeply from the waist. "I am honored, but not surprised. Yes, I am the famous stand-up comedian and musician. In fact, I first met and joined John Smith to form the Motelites at a command performance."

"Yeah, you'd signed a contract, and management commanded you to perform. At the Motel Six. You were never more than a third-rate lounge lizard."

John straightened slowly, ignoring Menace, a fire burning in his eyes. His hands shook slightly. "I am the co-founder and current messianic leader of one of the world's largest and most powerful cults, Ms. Francher. I started the joke that started the whole world laughing, And John Smith–"

"Is dead," interrupted Francher. "I remember they found him with a clarinet up the old kazoo. And I bet I know who killed him."

"Ah, 'martyrdom' is so financially beneficial, and so very easy to... arrange. And, I must add, it makes it easy to move up through the ranks quickly when one can promote oneself. But we digress, Menace. Francher. We are here."

The corridor broadened out into a circular room furnished with three rows of chairs facing a blank wall. Unlike the other walls in the saucer, this one was opaque. Above the arch of the door to this room was a sign that read: The Leon San Dunes Lounge.

"A nod to my past as an international star," said Palmer. "A nice gesture from my alien brothers. Please, be seated."

Reaching out and touching a hidden stud in a wall, a section of that wall slid open, revealing a huge porthole behind Palmer. Beyond this window and much in the distance stood Rose Butte, barely a bump on the horizon. Below the porthole and moving in a blur of indistinct forms and slurred colors was the flat Utah desert.

"Ah," began Palmer, pointing to the screen and grinning at his captive audience, "soon, our molehill shall be a mountain." Deep Neck and Samsonite strapped Francher and Menace into chairs. Finished with their tasks, the two aliens joined Shelf in a row of seats.

"Inside Rose Butte are the great caverns of the Registry, and even as I speak, every name of every human who ever lived or lives today is being entered into our computers and converted into numbers."

"Just curious, mind you," interjected Menace, "but howja spell 'alien dupe' in numbers, tuba breath?"

Palmer ignored the comment, and reached once again to the smooth wall of the spaceship and touched a hidden stud. The lights dimmed, a microphone and stand began to rise from the floor before Palmer, and the spaceship's computer simulated a drum roll and cymbal crash.

"Now, for your in-flight entertainment," intoned the computer, "direct from his sell-out performance at the International Convention of Motelites in Salt Lake City, Utah, that Maestro of Mayhem, the Conductor of Clowns, the Bandmaster of Brouhahahhaha, it's Leon San Dunes!"

"Someone's gotta be Zamfir," Menace muttered.

As the room filled with canned applause, Palmer looked past his captive audience to an imaginary stage manager. "Is it time, yet?" he asked. "Heidy, heidy, heidy! I'm Leon San Dunes and you're not!"

"You know, you're a pimple on the butte of life, Palmer," said Francher.

"That was our stage manager at the Leon San Dunes Lounge," continued Palmer, pointing a thumb at his non-existent boss. "I learned to respect stage managers when I was in vaudeville, a long time ago. Gosh, those were the times. Boy, were they bad! I wasn't funny, always, ya know. When I started in vaudeville, I lost twelve stage managers before I realized that when they gave the (Palmer drew a finger across his throat) sign meaning out-of-time, they were actually cutting their throats." The computer simulated a rim shot on a drum, and cymbal crash.

"Boy, I've had some lousy times. Boy, I've had some great times. At that time, I was really flattered when the cast told me to 'break a leg'...until I caught them greasing my shoes!" Canned applause filled the room.

"It's true. And I loved it when the theater owner asked me to hang around after the show. He even gave me the rope!" Applause was followed by a rim-shot and cymbal crash from the saucer's computer.

"Time was, I'd walk into any auditorium for an audition, and dance to any time signature: 2/4 time signature; 3/4 time signature. Shakespeare's signature. They loved it." Palmer did a short tap dance. "But, my act has died on the stage a time or two as well. My fans used to beg for my autograph. Some wanted two or three signatures. The insurance companies required it."

The room filled with canned laughter. "No, please, please," said Palmer, waving the imaginary applause down in volume. The computer complied with his gesture. "There'll be time enough for that later.

"You know, there are some people who say time stands still. But, I think it keeps marching on. And I'll never forget the first time I played Vegas." Palmer looked up and behind Francher and Menace as if a great marquee hung there. "Leon... San Dunes!! Standing... room... only," he read the imaginary marquee, accenting his words by sweeping his arm in an arc and flicking his fingers at the end of each word. "I was booked in the Men's Room." Rimshot. Cymbal.

"I didn't mind even playing to the audience's backs, but it hurt when they wouldn't applaud." Hard rim-shot, cymbal-smash, extended applause from the computer.

"And I'll never forget the first time I fell in love. Comer of Times Square. She had great... timing.

"Oh, I know you wouldn't think it to look at me, now. Some say I'm out of step with the times. So, for the time being, I'm taking some time off." He removed his Timex "But I still believe my time will come. Happens every time.

"In the meantime, take some timely advice from an old-timer. Don't waste it. Because, time is of the essence, and wasted time is time wasted," quipped Palmer as he dangled his watch at his captive audience. "Got that engraved on my Timex." Palmer laughed. The computer laughed.

"I was big, once upon a time. It's true. See." John pulled a copy of Time magazine from beneath his band tunic. "That's me! In the cast of the Rocky Horror Picture Show doing the Time Warp again. I still dance anytime signature: 3/4 time signature. 2/4 time signature. Irving Berlin's signature... anytime!" Palmer threw his hand back and tossed his watch at Francher and Menace.

"My, how time flies!!"

Palmer danced as the canned applause died away, leaving only the constant hum of the banjo saucer to fill the room. The lights rose automatically. Menace yawned.

"I'm still curious," she said, ignoring Palmer's entire show, "howja say you spell 'alien dupe' in numbers?"

"Shut up, Shut up, Shut up!" shouted the Motelite, turning his back to his captives. For a moment, his shoulders hunched and his hands obviously covering his face, Palmer sobbed into his hands. Then, straightening his back and lowering his arms, the once 'great' comedian turned again to Francher and the bound camerawoman, his face red and slightly swollen.

"I... am... nobody's... dupe! You took the hook I baited! You are the dupes!! I am the meister baiter!!"

"Gotta hand it to ya," said Menace. "When you're right....handed, you're right."

"Yeah, yeah," added Beth. "Same thing Speilberg said when we caught him with his film exposed, bugle brains. But I sorta know different since it was I who took the anonymous phone call from that little leather-necked geek, Deep Neck, there."

"Is that true?" demanded Palmer of the extra-terrestrial now standing by Dianne's chair. "You little over-night case!!"

"Y-yes," stuttered Deep Neck. "The fall from the banjo saucer rattled my bra—"

"And I was the one," interrupted Menace, "that recorded everything he spilled to Francher at the McDonald's in Houston. Whining about how he should have won the Oscar and all of that. And didn't get his fair share o' th' profits. Hell, he knew the deal the aliens struck with Speilberg. They supplied the saucers and all of the aliens, reducing the director's overhead to nothing. He knew they'd get a cut of the profits in return to use to finance the invasion of Earth. And it was that little leather suitcase that suggested the film would desensitize the public to the image of bug-eyed monsters eating their brains for lunch as an added bonus to the deal. What does Speilberg get? Only the title of the undisputed World Director of Film.

"I should have known that if Deep Neck would turn on Speilberg and his own kind, he'd sell the Global Star out as well."

"Eat blabflap and die, human scum," said Deep Neck.

"Kiss my undulating buttocks, dung-face," spat Menace.

"Lather my—"

"Stop it! Stop it!" shouted Francher. "This isn't some stupid Ace Montana game!"

The bump that was Rose Butte on the horizon had now grown to a substantial mound framed by the huge porthole in the wall of the saucer. Deep Neck pulled his tunic down and taut, smoothing out its wrinkles as he evaded Francher's glare.

"While you all are debating the virtues and vices of Martians, that butte is getting bigger and bigger by the second. Aren't we going a little fast, Palmer?"

"I am in complete control," sneered Palmer. "I can stop this baby on a dime and get nine cents change."

"At 700 miles an hour, Sergeant Pepper, it looks like we're going to smash into that dime in about one minute!" said the newshound.

Palmer brushed his fingers over the surface of the wall next to the porthole. Lights played beneath his fingertips. "I'll decrease our speed until we'll float into Rose Butte like a feath... oops."

"Oops what?" asked Menace, fidgeting in her chair. "Oops as in I forgot to let the cat out, or oops as in the controls aren't responding?"

"What's that gash in th'... my God. It's a butte hole," whispered Francher, struggling against her clamps.

Rose Butte blew up in size like a balloon beyond the porthole. The butte hole had grown to a crevice, still much smaller than the saucer. Sneer gone from his face, John Palmer played his fingertips over the wall again. "I am in control," be said to himself "I just misjudged the... oops."

"Goddamnit, Palmer, this isn't fanny!!" shouted Menace.

"What's wrong... here... Deep Neck, could you just look...?"

"I'm not... pilot, Palmer. I... in espionage... 'member?"

"Well, could you just get an engin... oh, sweet mother of music. Code yellow! CODE YELLOW!! I CAN'T STOP THIS THING!!!"

"We're going to die," whispered Melanie, her body pressed deep into her seat. An alarm began to sound.

"Prepare for Emergency Landing Procedure! " shouted Palmer into an invisible intercom in the wall.

Rose Butte filled half of the great porthole as Palmer ran to a chair and began to strap himself down. "Melanie!" he yelled, "strap in!!

Deep Neck was on top of Palmer, shaking the bank leader and pounding his head against the seat like a madman. "I DON'T WANT DIE!! SPKMSPTB RMSRTY HELKJZXSTS!!!" the Martian screamed as he reverted into his own language.

"W-w-we a-are g-g-going t-tooo d-d-di-i-ieeee," stuttered Palmer under the rhythmic beating from the alien.

"I.... I love you, Palmer," whispered Melanie.

"Of course you do," replied Palmer as the flying neckless banjo plowed straight toward the butte hole. "And no buttes about it."

The saucer struck.

And passed through the mountain like light through a fog.

Francher opened her eyes in response to Palmer's deep throated laughter. The Motelite was clutching his sides and laughing on the floor, overcome with mirth.

"God... I love it... when... that happens," chortled Palmer between bursts of laughter. "Got ya! Got ya! Got ya!! Who says I wasn't... a... great comedian?"

Deep Neck was clucking like a chicken, the closest approximation of human laughter available to the alien. "I should have won... Oscar!!" he gasped. "Badaw Bakaw Badaw!!"

"Of all people," chided Palmer, "the great Beth Francher should know these aliens are masters of special effects. You really disappoint me, Fanny."

"Don't be," said Francher. "From the moment I saw you, I knew you were a fake."

"You bastard," sobbed Melanie, rising from her chair. "Why didn't you tell me!"

Palmer took a big pinch of Melanie's left cheek. "Is'urn my boogie woogie baby waybe feelum out-of-step. Is'um she throwin' up? Is'um she not got it on'um da ball?"

Melanie brought her knee up forcefully into Palmer's groin.

"With some'un to spare'um," said Shelf.

The flying banjo sank like a sigh to the floor of a landing field cut from the heart of Rose Butte. As Deep Neck began to unstrap Francher and Menace, Beth surveyed all she could see of the cavernous room through the spaceship's porthole. Its vast ceiling rose three hundred feet above the flying saucer, and a massive tunnel had been cut at a parallel to the landing field's entrance from virgin rock. It curved away to the right of Palmer's craft, and disappeared in the distance.

Francher watched as two despondent workers wearing black tuxedos were painting parking strips about two hundred feet in front of the saucer. She recognized them as the actors from TVs Mork and Mindy. And beyond these painters, built only a few feet away from the wall of the cavern, stood a mahogany desk, twenty feet long.

Below and before the saucer stood an alien waving two flashlights tipped with red cones. It was TVs Alf. Alf moved towards the saucer, the alien's abrupt torso making every step an experiment in balance.

Palmer took a ring of keys from his pants pocket and dangled them over the open palm of the alien. "One scratch, Satchel, and you'll be washing meteor craters on Saturn."

"Oh, I very careful, careful. Learned lesson," mocked the extra terrestrial in a voice that sounded like chalk on a blackboard.

"Tip?" it added, holding out a three-fingered paw.

"Sure," said Francher. "Here's one. Don't listen to Larry King on an empty stomach."

"And get yourself some industrial strength carpet cleaner," added Menace, wrinkling her nose from its smell.

"Now, back to our earlier conversation, Palmer, in which it was obvious you couldn't tell me about this Motelite plot because you don't know to tell. My guess is that you're really just a figurehead," she continued as they began to move down the ramp, "a public relations man for the Martians, used to divert attention away from the real brains of this operation."

"You guess wrong again, Francher. You guess wrong a lot for a journalist on national television. But they don't really need brains. Just a pretty face. Looks like you struck out in both categories." Palmer turned on his heels and waited as the rest of the party descended the ramp. He grinned as he watched the muscles play in Francher's jaw.

"While I don't have to tell you anything, I am certainly in a position to tell you anything I wish, Fanny. The glitch in our endeavor was that new babies with new names are being conceived and born every second. Our computers were limited and our ultimate goal was hopeless until the Martians supplied us with new equipment through their front, Bill Gates. We're now able to extrapolate—predict, if you will—the names of those just conceived and about to enter the world.

"It wasn't easy, but two things helped us out: Japanese technology... and the fact that Bill Clinton is finally impotent. The latter fact certainly proves that there is a God," Palmer concluded.

"All it really proves is that Hillary is a good shot," Beth retorted.

The ramp shrunk back into the flying saucer, and Francher watched 'Satchel', the parking attendant, waved at them through the porthole with an odd, one-fingered, alien gesture. The whine of the ship began to rise through the scale by octaves as Deep Neck joined Palmer and the news hound. The saucer jerked into the air and shot into the tunnel that ran parallel to the entrance. It tilted on its left side as the right edge of the spacecraft scraped the wall, filling the cavern with the scream of tortured metal and a light show of sparks. Palmer clenched his fists at his sides, ground his teeth, and turned a deep shade of red in the face.

"Insurance for a flying saucer must be astronomical," observed Francher.

"Only if you spring for comprehensive," Palmer hissed through clenched teeth.

An odd alien like a large ivory colored oval with a human face in bas-relief on it sat behind the registration desk.

"What in God's name is that?" asked Menace as the entourage approached the desk.

"That," said Palmer with some disdain, "is one of the greatest actresses on Mars. Regrettably, because of budget constraints, she can only make a... cameo appearance."

The cameo looked up and reacted with excitement as Palmer and his captives arrived. "Oh!" she squealed to a co-worker, an old man with antenna on his head, "it's, like, that famous boob tube cat, Martin! Ya know, on Global Star Tonight! I jest can't believe she's, like, here, for real, in the flesh and all!"

Francher looked at the old man. "Aren't you the guy who played on My Favorite Martian on TV?"

"Hey!" said the actor, "there are no small parts, only small actors! And it was Third Rock From the Sun. Please sign in!"

"No need," Palmer said as he waved to the two workers. "Pre-registered! I'll be taking care of these guests personally!"

"Maybe you can help me understand something. Why do these Martians come in so many distinct and different forms?"

"They'll shake hands with anything."

As Palmer and his captives passed the desk, all overheard the same cameo Martian say, "I jest can't believe she's, like, a thesbian!!"

"Well," said the Conductor with a greasy smile, "I see I'm not the only one with an ill-kept secret."

"Here's another, Palmer. It's understandable for someone whose personality quirks led him to be a professional liar blind to his own faults. But the easiest way to get one to divulge information is to question his authority to do so."

"At least I'm not an ornament in a queer hairdo," sneered Palmer. "A lesbow."

"Cute pun. But men like you are the reason I became one."

"Why do you, like, take that jive off of her?" demanded Melanie of Palmer. "She's been dumpin' on you ever since we split dustville."

Palmer brought the group to a halt in front of an elevator recessed in a cavern wall. He pressed the up button, turned on his heels, and faced Francher with a smile she couldn't quite decipher. He did not look at Melanie Shelf as he ran the backs of his fingers down Beth's cheek, slowly.

"Because, when I look in her eyes, I see myself."

"Could be these," said Francher, removing her sunglasses. "When I look into your eyes, all I see is the back of your skull."

"Hey, what is this, John?" complained the accordionists, scowling first at Palmer and then at Beth.

"Melanie, my dear, I believe you are needed in the Sound Booth." He waved her away without turning from Francher.

"Hey..." began Shelf, but her sentence was cut short as Palmer turned abruptly on his heels and drove a look of molten hate through her with his eyes. "Now," he commanded.

The elevator pinged, and its door opened as Melanie stood, slack-jawed and ftightened, riveted in her position. Palmer directed Menace and Francher into the elevator, followed, and punched a floor designation on the wall panel. The doors closed as Melanie still stood transfixed, sobbing.

"Do you believe in auras, Ms. Francher?" asked Palmer.

"You are a real hound dog," said Francher. "Have you no concern for your little girlfriend's shelf-esteem?"

"I think he wants aural sex," said Dianne, leaning against a wall.

"You are exactly right again, Beth. May I call you Beth? Do you believe in auras?" said Palmer, ignoring Menace.

"It's my favorite part of Le Bohme."

"And a sense of humor. Well, I see something in your aura that might even surprise you. We are very much alike in some ways. A different time and place, and we'd have made the fat lady sing."

"Hey!" barked Menace. "I'm not fat! I'm just naturally big boned, which is more than I can say for the Kareoke Kid, here," she added, pointing at Menace.

The elevator slid to a stop, and its doors opened onto a long hall, its walls heavily decorated with musical instruments. As they moved into the hall, Palmer began to point out individual pieces.

"Menace, your room is on this floor. I'm sorry, but I must separate you girls tonight. Can't take chances, you know. You'll find your accommodations uncomfortable, and there is no room service. I decorated this room myself, so I'm sure one with your education will fail to understand the motif as well."

"Alphorn, lituus yuchchyn," Menace said as she catalogued the musical instruments in the hallway. "Shakuhacki, pyiba, balalaika. Bust of Slim Whitman. Epidermis flute."

"I am impressed," said Palmer as he threw open a door to one of the rooms and stepped inside. "You do understand the motif. My estimation of you has risen, Ms. Menace. I had no idea you were a student of the classics of music. May I ask who was your favorite?"

"The Singing Nun," said Menace. "She's a hard habit to shake."

The smile vanished from Palmer's face as Menace moved into the room. "Then you may even enjoy dying in the morning," he said, stroking a small stature of The Partridge Family. He stepped into the room.

"And where will I spend my last night?" asked Francher. "A performer on the stage of a third rate musical."

"You're really stressed out, aren't you?" asked Palmer. "All that infobabe pressure. Is my hair in place? Do my nails look good? How is my eye shadow? How do you pronounce those foreign names like George W. Bush? In the great cosmic symphony, you're just not in step with the beat.

"Fanny, do you suffer from... syncopation?"

"Nothing a good bowl of prunes won't cure.. Maestro," said Francher, "or a rerun of your 'comedy' act."

Palmer moved back through the door, closed and locked it behind him.

Tchaikovsky's "Nutcracker Suite" hung like a muted whisper in the room. Francher caught herself pacing in rhythm to the music as she moved through the deep, white carpeting. In a fury at herself, she sat down heavily on the single bed. Palmer had searched her purse and left it on an end table by the bed. He had not searched her pockets, however, so she had emptied and hid her precious contents the minute he'd left the room. She made a mental note to herself that Motelites were certainly not professionals as abductors. She debated removing her micro-cassette recorder from the strap on her inner thigh and decided it wise to do so. It followed her other secret items to their hiding place.

She reviewed her situation. She knew that Rose Butte stood alone in the desert. There were no buttes about it. Her room was obviously decorated by Palmer and did not look as if it had been carved from the naked expanse of Rose Butte.

But the room was butte-ugly.

The bed she sat on was covered with satin sheets and a heavy comforter imprinted with the grinning faces of the forgotten teen musical group, the New Kids on the Block. Above the bed hung a velvet painting of Elvis in an elaborate, gold frame On the small table by the bed was a cheap, plaster bust of Pat Boone. Across from the bed, great windows had been carved from the stone, and beyond the window stretched a startlingly beautiful desert landscape highlighted by a gibbous moon.

Francher stood frozen at the window, eyes wide with surprise. Then she shook her head and turned away. It must have been the clouds, she thought, or the persistence of her mild case of syncopation.

Little boys don't ride bicycles across the face of the moon. Then she remembered that they did. Ace had broken the story years ago.

As was true in the hallways of this mock hotel, the conductor's walls were decorated with an array of unusual musical instruments, many of which Francher could not identify. Although the room was filled with the sweep of the "Nutcracker Suite", she could not find the source of the music... or a source of escape.

It was obvious to her why Menace had been locked in a lesser room many floors beneath her while she lay on Palmer's bed in his penthouse. That was why the micro-cassette recorder shared the secret hiding place of her other personal items.

She absentmindedly picked up one of Palmer's magazines from the end table by the bed. It was Penthouse And Garden. She flipped through the magazine to its centerfold. Madonna's featured apartment was naked. The garden was bare. Disgusted, she tossed the magazine aside.

It was also transparent to the news hound why Palmer had left the room, locking the door behind him. She lay back on the cool, satin sheets of the bed and closed her eyes, her mind wandering back to a laundromat in New Orleans and the clean, beautiful lines of Kirsten's face beneath a false, curly wig and horns. Her mind was better used in memory for the moment. The horrifying mental picture of millions of human beings collapsing and dying, their cars and brains scrambled by the massive sonic blast of the Motelites, made Kirsten Lane's visage a welcome escape, indeed.

That mental picture was uppermost in her mind when a rap at the door interrupted her reverie. She glanced up at the steel door that had been poorly camouflaged by imitation wood grain. "A little loining is a dangerous thing," was scrawled in lipstick on the door.

"Whomever it is, get lost," she said to the door.

"C'mon, Fanny don't be cruel. I'm a desperate sinner and you're my only salvation."

Beth was on her feet and at the door before Palmer's final word had faded. "What do you hope to gain by this," she demanded with a cheek pressed against the cool surface of the steel door. "It's obvious you're no fool, so why have you decided to spend the rest of your life in a world full of alien geeks and wide-eyed fanatics, star-man?"

"Would you like some supper?" answered Palmer's muffled voice. "I'm not a cruel man, Beth, just a pragmatic one. Even a murderer gets a good meal before his execution, and you have killed me softly with your song."

Francher moved back slightly from the door as locks were thrown in response to her silence. As it opened, she moved back to Palmer's bed and sat on its edge, her otherwise shaking hands under her thighs.

"Well, it's been a long time, Fanny; you look marvelous," said, John, framed by the doorway. He carried a flat tray full of still steaming food. He wore a flimsy, blue Teddie cut high at the hips.

A single-rose sat in a white vase on the edge of the tray. "If my memory serves, it's everything you like: an eight ounce steak, medium, double-baked potato with sour cream and butter, corn, fine coffee... and me. Where can I put this?"

"John Palmer, Jack Jermane or Leon San Dunes—whatever your real name is—I'd guess you can put it where the shoeshine boy never shines."

"You haven't changed a bit, Fanny," he said, grinning. "Well, just a bit." He kicked the door shut behind him. "The Rhoades Scholar tempered with a touch of the common ma... woman. And that Leon San Dunes thing. That was a great scam until Ace caught me. I'd put 'em to sleep with my jokes while my partner picked their pockets."

He sat the tray down on an endtable by the bed. "And I haven't changed a bit because there's nothing to change for the better."

"That's the true mark of a con-man, 'John Palmer'; if they've really got it, they believe their own con. I've got to give credit where it's due. This Motelite scam has got to be your masterpiece. And I do like you in blue."

"It is better than the mermaid switch you exposed in Oklahoma, isn't it? I'd have never forgiven that if it'd been the only thing of mine you'd exposed in the state, Fanny."

"It was juvenile. And as for the other expose, I was young."

"You are still young. We were both younger then, and stupid." Palmer moved to the edge of the bed next to Francher. "That's the usual requirement for failing in love.

"But now is now, Fanny. I am not a mad scientist bent on conquering the world, and I have no intention of disclosing my plans to you so that you may conveniently defeat me and save the Earth. This is the real world and not the fantasy printed in those sleaze-papers like the Washington Post and the New York Times.

"Join me. You'll be rich, powerful and famous, not to mention satisfied. Presidents and kings will curry your favor. I'll change the name of Rose Butte."

"Ummmmm. Francher Mountain?"

"No. Rose Fanny."

"I was never in love with you, Leon," said Francher with distaste written all over her face. "You're right; I was young and stupid, inexperienced and impressionable. It meant nothing beyond animal lust. And I'd already guessed that everything you or Shelf has told me about God-Bop is a lie, or, at best, a half-truth. Don't overestimate yourself"

"It must have meant something more than that," said Palmer, brushing her hair that lay against her shoulder with his fingertips. "You're gay now. I must have spoiled you for all other men."

"Surprise, Leon. Have you ever read how celebrities have to protect themselves from over-zealous fans? Well, women celebrities have to protect themselves from over-sexed men as well... like you. And a lie that disgusts eighty percent of them is much cheaper and more convenient than a half-dozen bodyguards."

Palmer rose from the bed and walked to a wall decorated with musical instruments. "I haven't been unaware of your obvious lack of fear at the prospect of dying by my hand. That leaves me three scenarios. You have made sure that an army of clog-dancing head hangers are even now surrounding Rose Butte and will stop GodBop, saving your beautiful neck after you have your story.

"That's out. Hermione and the Ada Sod Squad made sure you weren't running any end plays around John Palmer. Your uncovering their little ploys did nothing to subvert their real missions. Motelites: 1. Global Star: 0.

"Or you may believe that God-Bop is only another clever con on my part. I'm sure your research department must have checked 'John Palmer' out before you ever left your offices at the Global Star. And I don't underestimate you.

You never miss a trick; that's why you're the best on television. So, recognizing a great story and thinking you'd face no danger at my hand, you made your reservations and here you are...

"That's out. It's time to face the music, babe, and it's Requiem for an Info-Babe with a bullet on my Hit Parade.

"And that brings us to my third guess, and the one I believe drew you here like a magnet. We had something very special once," said Palmer huskily. "And there's no reason we can't polka... again. " He moved to Francher and, taking her shoulders in his hands, lifted her slowly from the bed as he also rose. She traced the edge of his lower lip with the tip of her finger as she rose. His face was suddenly buried in the nape of her neck, and she felt the hot breath of an old and not forgotten lover.

"Honey," Beth cooed," you're wrong as usual." She pushed him back with the palms of her hands and stepped away from the Motelite leader. "I don't sing duets with men who plan to kill me. Call me old-fashioned."

Grinning, Palmer moved once again to a bedroom wall decorated with musical instruments.

"One of the advantages of power, Fanny, is that you generally get what you want. And my little collection of musical instruments was gathered for me by my devoted followers from all over the world. And my prize piece of them all is also the rarest. It was indeed the first of its kind, and very old." He took an ancient instrument from its mounting and strapped it over his chest. Do you know how to... play... pipes?" asked Palmer.

"Just pucker your lips and blow," answered Francher, her head lowered and her eyes half closed. She leaned her back against a wall for support, her open palms pressed hard against its cool surface. John began to play.

"Don't," said Francher, almost in a whisper. "Not that song. Not Feelings. That was... our song."

Palmer moved close to Francher, the melody dying into a single note as his fingers left the bagpipe and moved to her stomach. He began to follow the curve of her ribs up. "Baby," be whispered eerily over the dying note from the bagpipe, "an alien will come for you at six in the morning. Follow it. Do whatever it says. My... chosen... people won't suffer God-Bop. There's a pair of ear plugs with your name on them."

His mouth left the bagpipe and discovered her lips, soft and wet beneath his own. The crush of their bodies collapsed the bagpipe between them, and its strange, diminishing wail left the Nutcracker Suite to refill the room again. Francher covered his hands with her own, and, throwing back her head, she began to sway to the very real but unheard music of passion.

"Leon," she whispered, "about your... earplugs. The one's with my name of them. " She leaned in close to Palmer's neck and hissed the words against his skin. "The writing must be...very small."

Palmer's kisses followed the line of her jaw until, hungry, they found her hot, wet lips again. He kissed her deeply, his powerful hands pulling her hips against his own.

"Oh, God," whispered Francher as they fell, together, in a slow tumble to the floor, her body responding to the hot, masculine weight of her lover. "Is... is that... your baton... or are you just... happy to... uh... see me."

"It's my baton," whispered Palmer. "And we're both happy to see you."

Also a whisper, Francher heard the "Dance of the Sugar Plum Fairies" replace the "Nutcracker Suite" as it ended. Deep in her mind, its beat was matched by her unspoken words repeating over and over. Oh God... forgive me; oh, God... forgive me... oh, God, forgive.

Lost in their reverie, neither beard the creak of the door to Palmer's penthouse, or saw Melanie Shelf as she watched the rhythm of their writhing bodies and sobbed.

Glitter Plenty stood in the open doorway to Palmer's penthouse. She wore black leotards and thigh-length black, leather boots and a puzzled expression. The antenna that rose above her blonde, shoulder-length hair at her forehead sparked. As Ace would say, she wasn't bad looking for a bug-eyed alien.

"Fanny ready?" chirruped the moon maiden in her high pitched, broken English. "News dog come."

"Is it six already?" asked Francher as she rose from Palmer's bed and slung her purse over her shoulder. She glanced at her wristwatch. "Time flies when you're being done."

The humanoid Moonite shrugged her shoulders and raised her hands, palm up, to mid-waist. "News puppy come..."

"Yes. But what business is..." started Beth, but the alien had already moved beyond the open door. Francher quickly checked her purse and, reaching down to her right thigh, punched the play and record buttons on the micro-cassette recorder hidden under her clothing. She moved to the door and glanced out. Just around the edge of the opening stood Glitter Plenty and a second alien.

"Who's this?" asked the journalist." What's it doing here?"

"This is Duffle," muttered Glitter's assistant, pointing a finger to itself.

"Duffle is bellboy, " said Glitter Plenty, pointing to the little creature. It stood bent almost double, a great hump disfiguring its back. One eye was misplaced and larger than the other, and its right arm hung limp by the right cheek of its enormous butt. "He from BabyGotBack planet."

"Poor thing," observed Francher. "At least he has a job that matches his capabilities."

"Not really. He has a degree in theater from Notre Dame."

"Nice bell bottoms," said Francher. "But I have no… bags… to be carried."

"Oh, no. Bellboy not carry bag," explained the Moonite. "Genetically engineered to maintain Motelite bell. Duffle work in perfect harmony with others in Sound Booth."

"Hmmm. Sorta quasi-modal," said Beth.

The disfigured alien scampered down the hall as Glitter motioned frantically for Francher to follow it.

"Get Fanny in gear," urged the tiny Motelite. "News basset slooow!?"

"Where is Dianne Menace? Menace is supposed to be here. That was my agreement with Palmer."

"Menace at car. Waiting. Fanny, hurry!"

Francher started to object to being called "Fanny" by anything looking like a cartoon alien, but decided it was a waste of time and energy. The hunchbacked monster had already opened the elevator door at the end of the hall and stood waiting, giggling as the elevator tried to repeatedly close itself only to be stopped by the genetically engineered bellboy's butt.

Francher joined the Motelite as they moved down the hall. "Rear Sergeant Duffle," snapped Glitter, "what are you doing!?"

"Trying get... rise... outta Glitter," grinned the alien.

"He is sorta cheeky," said Francher. They entered the elevator just as a second door on its opposite side opened.

"We ... here," said Glitter, stopping so suddenly that Beth almost fell over the tiny alien. A plaque over this second door read: Sound Booth.

"There must be some mistake," said Francher. "I'm not supposed to go in there." She looked down at Glitter Plenty and into the barrel of a ray gun. For a second, she weighed her chances of wrestling the gun from an alien half her height before it could discharge the gun, and abandoned the thought.

"Surprise, news poodle," Glitter sneered. "You screwed... again!"

"Surprise? Not really," muttered the news hound. "Nothing Phazers me much.

Francher moved through the doors with Glitter and her hunchbacked bellboy onto a platform that overlooked a gigantic cavern a hundred feet below. A handful of aliens as tiny as ants moved about the floor of the Sound Booth. Tiers of computers rose about twenty feet in height, humming as thousands upon thousands of names flooded into them even as Francher watched. She guessed that hundreds of Motelites and aliens fed these computers from obscure rooms honeycombing Rose Butte, and a shudder ran through her as she realized that her name was stored somewhere in those banks of machinery.

In the middle of the cavern was a gigantic marble statue of Slim Whitman.

On the most distant wall from the news hound, a huge bell like the ear of an old phonograph stood pointing at a forty five degree angle to the ceding. A spiral walkway twisted up and around the bell to end in a small, metal platform at its lower lip. And on the platform stood Dianne Menace, sleepy, grouch, seared and still bound with light cuffs, Melanie by her side. A white mutt with black spots sat on its haunches at the bell's base, one ear cocked towards it.

"Go," ordered the Moonite, "go." Glitter Plenty nudged Francher forward with the tip of her ray gun.

As Francher and her two guards began to descend to the cavern floor, Glitter Plenty spoke into a device on her wrist. "Code green—God Bop; repeat, code green—God Bop." The metallic click of their heels on the ramp became a rhythmic accent to the swelling hum of the huge computers. Francher watched as aliens of almost every conceivable description began to scurry to stations at the banks of computers. And, as each reached its designated post, protective earphones were secured over what passed as ears for the extraterrestrials.

When Beth, Glitter Plenty and Duffle reached the cavern floor, the bellboy scurried ahead with an awkward lope, filled with obvious excitement.

"I forgot to tip him," said Francher. "Blast it."

Glitter fired her ray gun, barely missing the journalist and blasting Duffle in the back. The alien went down; a mass of writhing arms and legs. Beth made a mental note not to use certain figures of speech around Glitter Plenty.

"This huge up-ended bell," said Glitter with an indistinctive wave of her arm, "took us over five years and four hundred Japanese scientists to engineer. It can withstand vibration not even imagined by humans. Even Two Live Crew."

"She don't know me very well, do she," said Francher, still staring at Duffle's charred and lifeless body.

"Soon, you will see raised handles on the interior curve of the up-turned bell. Count them, and you will find four."

"If I don't count them will I find three?"

"Just the proper number," continued Glitter, ignoring Beth. "For two human arms and two human legs. You see, Fanny Francher, we have planned long and well for our revenge."

As they approached the base of the spiral walkway, Francher saw Melanie Shelf leaning against its railings. She wore a uniform like the ones used by the brass band that had greeted them in the desert.

"Ah, Melanie! The girl voted most likely to serve mankind... on a silver platter."

"Ah," sneered Shelf, "good morning, Ms. Francher. Hope you had a nice... peaceful... evening. Sweet dreams of Kirsten?"

"You know me," answered Francher, yawning. "Trapped in a bed I never made."

A deep, red blush of color began at Shelf's neck and crawled up her face. "Welcome to the Sound Booth," she said through gritted teeth. "I thought sure you'd enjoy seeing the Motelites control center before you... split."

"Then, need I ask where is John Palmer?" asked Francher.

"Your question surprises me, Ms. Francher. Didn't he tell you he was... coming?"

"What do you hope to accomplish with all of this double talk, Melanie? And, for God's sake, why are you selling out your own kind to these rejects from a gene pool?"

My... own kind?" said the Motelite as she paused on the bottom steps of the walkway. She reached up and snatched the black beret from her head. As she shook her short mane of dishwater blond hair loose, Francher saw the pair of antenna the beret had so successfully hidden. "And as for one... selling out... you and, and... " her voice broke as tears welled up in her big, grey eyes. "You and John are the experts at that!"

"I think I understand now," said Francher. "You'll make quite sure that John's side of the deal with your... people... is carried out to the letter. A double spy. And I will be forced to watch the destruction of almost every normal human being on Earth because hell hath no fury like a woman spermed."

Melanie sneered as she continued to climb the walkway. It was a sneer Francher could not see as she followed the alien up the stairs, but could hear in the inflection of each word.

"Why, Fanny, I wouldn't hear of it," said Melanie. "And neither will you."

As they reached the platform that ran parallel to the giant mouth of the resonance bell, Francher gave Dianne a wink and smile. "What did that mean," demanded Shelf, turning on the news hound to catch the gesture.

"I always carry an Ace in the hole," said Francher.

"Don't he wish," added Menace.

"Your optimism is ill spent today, Francher. Although I would savor your seeing Kirsten shaken into atoms, you lying slut, you won't watch that particular dance of death. Because you'll be doing the Watusi with the Grim Rapper."

"That's reaper, but I can understand how you couldn't tell them apart. Since you also can't tell a real man from a cheap imitation," said Menace.

Dianne was shoved roughly against the cavern wall by Glitter Plenty as Shelf moved to a control panel inset in the stone next to the monstrous bell.

"You'll be staying, Menace," said Melanie. "Nor will your ears be covered as the pitch of this magnificent bell begins to rise and split your ear drums. No pictures today, either. Your head will have exploded long before the pitch will have raised even enough to reconstitute the Motelite's savior. And this," said Shelf, holding an audio cassette in her hand, "this little surprise will repay my faithless lover. I will kill three turds with one tone."

Shelf pushed two buttons on the control panel that sparked a dozen lights into life. She inserted the cassette with a shaking hand.

"You will fail, you know," said Francher. "I was onto this from the moment you botched Lady of Spain on your squeeze-box at the Global Star Tonight offices. Even as we speak, this whole library is surrounded by hundreds of very angry music critics."

Shelf threw back her head and laughed. "And this entire facility will resurrect Bert Parks! You know nothing!"

Shelf pressed another stud on the control panel, and a metallic cylinder rose to a foot in height from the board.

"This is so clichéd," Francher snarled.

A pulsating alarm filled the cavern as Melanie twisted an outer sleeve on the metal cylinder and watched it sink back into the control panel.

"Even if it were true, nothing can stop God-bop after the final sleeve of this fail-safe system sinks back into its receptacle."

Shelf twisted a second outer sleeve that sank out of the grip of her hand. A mechanical voice joined the alarm in the cavern.

"Step Two, God-Bop, instituted. Identify to proceed. FIVE MINUTES TO DISCONNECT," intoned. A digital screen came to life on the control panel and began a silent count down of the remaining seconds.

"Pull her up, boys!" commanded Shelf

Francher felt multiple hands on her body, and realized that several of the genetically engineered dwarves had joined her on the platform. She did not resist. Could be worse, she thought. At least none of the hands belonged to Ace Montana.

Glitter Plenty moved to the news hound's side and grabbed her left arm. The fail-safe alarm rose a step up in pitch as Melanie punched in an identification code. A mechanical voice intoned: "STEP THREE, GOD-BOP, INSTITUTED. All unnecessary pets forgotten in distant rooms requiring close to four minutes, thirty seconds to retrieve should now be retrieved to heighten suspense."

"Now," said Melanie, absorbed in manipulating the controls of the doomsday machine. "Strap her to the bell now!"

Francher slipped her purse from her shoulder. "This has gone far enough..." she began.

The sound of an electrical discharge broke Francher's sentence and she turned to watch Glitter Plenty crumple to the floor of the ramp. There, the alien spasmed and lay still as her antennae sparked.

"Have you no Shelf control? No Shelf respect? The auditorium is packed and you still ring my chimes?"

"JOHN!" gasped the Moonite at sight of the Motelite leader.

Palmer stood at the mouth of the platform, his ray gun striking a second dwarf even as Melanie turned. In a strange mixture of anger and fear, a third bellboy pointed his own gun at the Motelite. "Die quick and endure poverty!" hissed the alien as he fired. But the shot was wild, and Palmer added a third jerking body to the metallic floor of the platform.

"John, I can explain," said Shelf, backing away from the advancing conductor.

"Shut up and face the music," said Palmer as he joined her at the control board. He slapped the remaining portion of the metal rod into the control panel.

"Allow me," he added with a greasy smile," and Palmer pushed another series of buttons on the board. The fail-safe alarm climbed in pitch and volume by several decibels as the computer rasped: "Oh, boy, you've done it now!! God-Bop!! God-Bop!! GOD-BOP!!!"

Huge camouflaged doors in the ceding of the cavern began to slowly yawn open as Melanie grabbed Palmer's arm and yelled over the growing hum on the bell."JOHN! I CAN EXPLAIN! I LOVE YOU! I LOVE..."

Palmer shoved Shelf backwards, hard. "I love you, too, bitch," he said as the Moonite tripped at the lip of the bell, tottered as she tried to catch her balance by waving her arms wildly, and fell. Her scream was absorbed instantly by the rising volume of the hard driven banks of computers and the scream of the upturned bell.

"I must be better than I thought," said Francher. The doors in the cavern ceiling were completely open now, and a round panel in the floor of the cavern slid open. Rising on a stage that rotated slowly, Francher and Menace watched as a grand piano appeared, decked with a lit candelabra.

"It's worse than I thought," said Francher. "He's bringing back Liberace."

"You fools!" shouted Palmer. "You musical morons! Bert Parks? Liberace? Manilow? Frankie Valli? All smoke and mirrors! Today, the greatest composer and musician of all time shall rise and clean the earth of its idiots. Today, I resurrect Al Yankovic! He placed earphones on his head.

"Move to the bell," demanded Palmer, his face wild with passion as he waved his ray gun at Francher.

"I don't think so," yelled Francher.

"MOVE IT!!" screamed Palmer.

"I'M PREGNANT," Francher screamed back at him.

Palmer stepped over the body of Glitter Plenty as he moved to the news hound, his eyes hard and cold. "I don't buy it!" he shouted over the noise. "And even if I did, so what. You think I wouldn't sacrifice an unborn child with the rest just because it's yours?"

"AND YOURS!" Francher pulled a case plastic tube from her purse, a home pregnancy test. A + marked the spot. "You underestimate my willingness to... sacrifice for humanity. You see... I AM GAY. Last night, my body was with you, but my mind was with Sharon Stone."

"Yours, too?" yelled Palmer.

Menace had fallen to her knees and was desperately trying to remove the earphones from a fallen dwarf. The entire cavern seemed to vibrate with the power of the sounding bell, and a thin wisp of dirty smoke began to curl from its metal throat up into the air, whirling from the agitation of the powerful vibrations.

"NO! It's a lie!" shouted Palmer, red faced, his hands shaking. Francher saw his finger tighten on the trigger of the alien weapon.

"Does your computer extrapolate the names of unborn children with gay mothers?" yelled the news hound, waving the tube in Palmer's face.

"The computers... extrapolate... any sexual combin..." Palmer's hand and its forgotten ray gun fell to his side as the blood drained from his face. He screamed into the wrist-radio on his other arm, "ABORT! ABORT GOD-BOP!!! ABORT!! ABORT! ABOR..."

The wrist-radio shattered.

"Oh, God, "mouthed Francher in horror. "It must be Memorix."

Francher's face was twisted with pain, and the tube felt from her fingers as the wisp of smoke grew into a swirling, dirty tornado, screaming in the cavern. Below the news hound on the cavern floor, the aliens manning the banks of computers fell, one by one, writhing on the tile and clutching at orifices that approximated ears.

Menace managed to force Glitter Plenty's earphones off of the alien's head by using her opposing shoulder and the platform as wedges, and was struggling to force them over her own ears. As Francher struggled over the bodies of the fallen dwarves clutching at her own ears, she saw Palmer stumble to the master control panel.

Palmer was muttering feverishly as his fingers flew over the master board, even though his words were lost in the screech of his own doomsday machine.

"Gay. Pregnant. Gay. Pregnant."

Even this whispered chant died on his lips as his eyes fell on the tiny window of the CD player in the control panel. In Melanie's small, cramped handwriting, the label read: The Best Al Yankovic.

He jerked back from the panel and turned, his face twisted with fear. He screamed into the roar, "STOP IT!!! STOOOOOOOOP-PPPPPPP!!!!!!!!!!!"

Shaking his fist at Francher, who now knelt by Menace's side of the platform, he yelled with maniacal power, "YOU... BITCH! AT LEAST YOU DIE!!!"

His eardrums burst. Blood trickled from both of his ruptured ears down the nape of his neck as he stared up into the funnel of the tornado cloud erupting from the up-ended mouth of the bell and twisting up and through the gaping aperture in the cavern roof. He snatched the useless earphone from his ears, raised the forgotten ray gun in his hand, and moved towards Francher and Menace.

A monstrous figure began to form in the dingy, swirling cloud of sound and dirt. A hideous, deep choke became a titter of laughter that rose and rose higher and higher in pitch. Palmer stopped and faced the perverted monster of ozone, fire and dust bunnies with a look of hope that instantly dissolved into horror as vague lines took on sharp edges.

Francher collapsed at Menace's side, the confiscated earphones askance but in place over the camerawoman's head. Menace tried painfully to crawl to the master panel, but failed and collapsed, laying still, her hands still bound behind her. Francher fought her way back to consciousness, and opened her eyes. She saw Palmer shaking his fists at the thing in the tornado of winds, and she saw the blasphemous thing in the dirty cloud holding a ukulele.

"Oh... sweet... God... " she muttered, and began to pull herself desperately towards the panel on her elbows and knees. Only half consciously, she recognized the worlds of naked flesh and the grass skirt and the tiny mustache and the voice, hideous beyond human understanding. She had heard it once at a revival theater when she was a child, and had cried for hours.

It was Yankovic singing Aba Daba Honeymoon.

Palmer stood rigid, paralyzed by the thing that sang above him in the whirlwind. And as the pitch of the sound bell straddled the edge of human hearing, an enormous, fat hand plucked Palmer from the ramp, his head pinched between Al's monstrous thumb and forefinger. Yankovic's head bobbed like a toy hula babe on the dash of a car as he sang Abba daba daba sang the monkey to the moon.

Then Al popped Palmer's head.

Francher reached the control panel just as she felt a heavy thud on the platform behind her. Turning, she almost tripped over the bloody, headless corpse of John Palmer crumpled at her feet. Ignoring the behemoth sucking the blood from its fingers, Francher began to break everything possible on the panel, bloodying her hands as she screamed, "DIANNE!! HOLD ON!!"

Beth's eyes fell on the CD player recessed in the panel and the cassette whirling inside. She clawed at the tiny window protecting the cassette franticly as, behind her, she sensed the monstrous hand of the dead comedian descending again.

Francher curled her fingers tight into her palms. raised her hand high above her shoulder, and screamed, "HEEEEEEEYAAAHHHHH!!!" With all of her strength, she rammed her knuckles into the CD player. A ribbon of tape instantly wrapped around her cut and bleeding knuckles, the player jammed.

The monstrosity in the dirty cocoon of smoke and grass and wind gagged in mid daaaaabaaaaaaa. Like a jet engine revving down, the roar in the cavern began to implode and drop in decibels. The cloud inverted, swallowing itself back into the throat of the bell.

"NOOOOOOOooooooo!" screamed the wraith of Yankovic.

"DIE YOU LOUSY BELL-WHETTEW!" screamed Francher.

And the sound was gone.

Francher was shocked to hear the echo of her own scream in the silence of the cavern. Menace was crying on the ramp. The sound of her crying was frightening. And, calling the last ounce of her physical strength into play, Francher stumbled away from the control panel to the camerawoman's side.

"Ya... ya got a... key to this thing?" gasped Menace, raising her bound wrists in a feeble gesture.

"What?" asked Francher, kneeling.

"Oh, God, she's... deaf."

"What," asked the news hound, fumbling with the light-cuffs.

"FANNY! FANNY YOU'RE DEAF!!"

Francher dug out a slag of wax from her left ear with the small finger of her left hand. Still dazed, dirty and physically shaken, she grinned weakly, and said, "Don't... call me... Fanny. I can read lips... remember?"

Menace's light-cuffs separated. "I feel like... I've been goosed by... Ray Stevens."

"You almost ended on a sour note, sugar," said Beth. "Grab hold of my shoulder. Up.. we... come."

"What happened?" asked Menace.

"Later, Dianne. Let's go home."

Her arm around Francher's shoulder, Menace smiled weakly into the newshound's dirty face and whispered, "That's... sound... advice."

Like a gun shot in the cavern, the entrance to the Sound Booth exploded inward. A swarm of music critics burst into the cave. They carried Uzis on their hips. They began spraying the banks of computers with popcorn bursts of shells as a unit leader lifted a bull horn to his mouth.

"EVERYONE FREEZE!!" roared the bullhorn. "THIS IS THE EPA... AND A COUPLE MUSIC CRITICS. YOU'RE UNDER ARREST FOR VIOLATION OF THE CLEAN AIR ACT!"

"...clean air act," echoed and died away with the gun bursts in the cavern. Menace grinned weakly.

"So you... did notify the EPA, Fanny."

"Hey," groused Francher. "I always cover my butte."

Francher looked at Menace. "It's over. The horror is over."

"Not quite," answered the weary camerawoman. "What about Palmer's child?"

"Are you kidding? I always carry a fake home pregnancy test with me. It's a sure fire cure for horny men. Well, except for Ace, of course. He still thinks he can 'cure' me.

"We still have to drive back to New York City in the Escort."I almost hate to leave. After all, you have to adroit... "This is a butte of a mountain."

EPILOGUE

It was a Yellow cab. Inside and out.

The tires of the taxi screeched loudly as the car whipped around a corner. In the back seat, Ace Montana was thrown against the door as were some small, creeping things.

"Hey!" he yelled at the driver. "What's the fu***** hurry?"

"Sorry, Mac," the cabbie replied. "I got a hot date tonight."

"Yeah? Well, trust me... as ugly as you are, it can't be that hot a date. Not unless you are really into camels."

"Better than having one in my mouth all the time," the cabbie snapped.

"Let me guess," Ace said. "You majored in customer relations, right?"

The next instant Ace was thrown violently forward, nearly hurtling over the seatback as the cab came to a squealing halt. The driver nonchalantly turned off his meter.

"Here we are," he said curtly. "The Menaheim Building. Now, get yer butt out."

"With pleasure, just as soon as I push my spine back into place."

Ace crawled out of the back and stood next to the cabbie's open window, counting out the fare. As he handed the money to the driver, be grinned wolfishly.

"I suppose you'd like a tip, too?"

"Piss off, buddy."

"No. No. I insist, my good man. You've been such a delightful traveling companion. Here's your tip." Ace leaned down so he was looking right into the cabbie's eyes.

"I'd get to a fire station just as quick as possible."

"That's your tip?" the cabbie growled, "Get to a fire station? Why the hell should I?'

"Because some careless individual left a lit cigarette—a Camel, I believe—in your beautiful cab... and now the back seat is on fire."

"Huh?" The cabbie turned to see smoke beginning to billow up from the rear upholstery.

"Holy Cow!" he yelped. Slamming his foot on the accelerator, he roared away from the curb.

"Now you'll really have a hot date!" Ace called after him. He only regretted he'd miss the cabbie's expression when the driver began counting the fare. It was Monopoly money.

The Global Star offices were nearly empty, as Ace had known they would be at this hour of the night. Ordinarily, he would have gone straight home after returning from Singapore, but Gephard had wanted to speak with him about something.

He spotted Uge Nochers walking toward him.

She seemed not to have noticed him, her eyes staring blankly ahead of her. She was walking stiffly, as though in a trance, her arms were crossed, holding up the torn front of her dress. She ignored the framed poster on a wall, an old one of Gephard as poster child for Planned. Parenthood. Its caption read: Would You Want One of These?

"Hey there, sweetheart," he called by way of greeting.

Uge continued to walk toward him, but she said not a word. Nor did she acknowledge his presence in any other way. As she drew closer, Ace could finally see clearly that the fabric of her dress was indeed torn.

"What happened, babe?" he asked cheerfully. "Did the titmice finally get to you?"

"Oooooh!" Tears welled in Uge's eyes, and she raised her hands to cover them, This in turn caused her to release the front of her dress, which fell down to reveal her bra.

Realizing that she bad inadvertently exposed herself to Ace, she grew even more distraught. Sobbing loudly, she pushed past him and ran into the women's restroom. Ace stared after her, smiling in appreciation.

''Whoa! Nice fashion statement there, Uge." The image was indelibly etched in his mind. "Let's see some queer designer top that," he chuckled.

As usual, Ace didn't bother to knock on the door of Frank Gephard's office, preferring to just walk in unannounced. He was somewhat surprised to see the editor hunched over an ancient manual typewriter slowly and painfully tapping at the keys with two fingers.

In the middle of the room, in front of Gephard's desk, Lon Alucard was lying on the floor. A number two pencil was protruding from his heart, and he was obviously dead. Thin wisps of smoke were beginning to rise from his body.

Ignoring the corpse, Ace stepped over it and flopped down into a chair. He pulled out a cigarette and lit up, watching Gephard's attempts at typing with undisguised amusement.

"What killed him, Frank?" he said at last. "Lead poisoning?"

"Don't bother me right now, Ace. I've got a big story here, and I'm going to write it myself."

"Give me a ****in' break, Frank. I mean... if you could write, you wouldn't be an editor, right?"

Gephard stopped his pecking and spun around in his chair. "Listen up, Montana. I'll have you know I'm a damn good writer." Ace noticed he was sitting on the New York City phone directory just to reach the typewriter

"Yeah, right. You and Joan Collins. So, tell me, Frank," Ace finally took another look at the corpse lying on the floor. The body was rapidly deteriorating into a pile of ooze. "What's the story with Alucard there?"

"I killed him, Ace," Gephard replied, pausing between each word for dramatic effect.

"Oh. Any particular reason... or just exercising your short temper?"

"I had to do it, Ace. He was about to bite Uge."

"GGGG's, Frank, what's wrong with that? I mean, if nibbling on some babe was a capital offense—they'd have fried my taters when I was four."

"No, you don't understand. Neither did I, at first, though I should have." Gephard slumped in his chair, dragging one hand through his white hair.

"All the signs were right there in front of me, you know?" the editor continued. "Alucard could only come out at night. He was anemic. He hated garlic and mirrors. He had fangs like a pit bull. And he was from New Hampshire, for Gods sake."

"Are you sayin' what I think you're sayin' Frank?"

"You got it. All you have to do is spell his name backwards. The guy was the best photographer we ever had, but in the end he turned out to be nothing more than a lousy, slimy, filthy, stinking, disgusting, blood-sucking homosexual.

Ace looked at Gephard.

Ace looked again at the smoldering pile of vampiric ashes that had been Lon Alucard and shook his head sadly.

"God... I hate when that happens."

ABOUT THE AUTHORS

MEL ODOM

Mel Odom has written more than thirty books in the popular Executioner series, the 129th book in The Hardy Boys Casefiles series, and participated in six anthologies: October Dreams, 100 Wicked Little Witch Tales, Zodiac YA, Don't Look Back, Sixth Sense and Dark Shadows. Recently inducted into the Oklahoma Hall of Fame for his work, Mel has also written the first book in a Forgotten Realms series, Forgotten Realms: Lost Library of Cormanthy. In the TSR highly successful world of adventures, his work also includes ER.E.E.LANCERS and F.R.E.E.FALL.

Odom has penned two FASA ShadowRun gaming novels, Preying for Keeps and Headhunters. Lethal Interface has been released in Russian and German editions. Stalker Analog also bears the mark of his pen.

Ever restless and typing with both feet as well as with both hands, the prolific writer has also written Bitter Fruit and Neon Chill in the Deathlands series, several players guidebooks including for Harlan Ellison's I Have No Mouth And I Must Scream, Angel Devoid: Face of the Enemy, and Cybermage. Omega Blue and Omega Score, two futuristic thrillers, are about a special ops FBI team who go after only the biggest of the Most Wanted.

Hart of Darkness is Mel's only excursion into the world of comic books. This four-issue miniseries was published in 1991 -92.

―――⦻―――

R.A. JONES

The concept for Global Star sprang naked and ready to be clothed from the head of R. A. Jones. (He often springs that way himself while not penning one of his successful comic book series). Yes, Global Star sprang from

Jones as he sat on the couch at Mel Odom's house after a convention in Oklahoma City in 1994. Yes, it sprang and then was fully clothed in cheap hand me-downs by Odom and Vance and Jones, totally sober. Hard to believe, eh?

Who can forget Jones' comic book series including Dark Wolf, Scimidar, Fist of God, The Ferret, The Protectors, White Devil, Pistolero, Merlin, Sinbad", Showcase '95, Harlan Ellison's Dream Corridor, Star Trek: Deep Space Nine and CyberTrash. Who can forget Bulletproof Monk and Automaton for Image, Wolverine/Captain America for Marvel, and King of Hell for Tokyopop. Who can forget the comic book series done with Michael Vance like Straw Men and Bloodtide, or the first three or four years of R. A. work with Michael Vance on the syndicated Suspended Animation comic book reviews column? Who cannot remember his uncredited work on Vance's book, Forbidden Adventures, or his co-ghosting with Vance of the novel The Equation?

Who (is it you?) read his short story, Good Night, My Johnny Boy, in Chic (where he first learned to spring naked), or his famous Around Tulsa weekly newspaper series in Applause magazine inside the Oklahoma Eagle newspaper?

Did you know that he wrote Comics in Review for Amazing Heroes magazine from 1983 to 1986, that he was the story editor for Elite Comics, or wrote movie reviews for the Broken Arrow Ledger newspaper? Who knew that he could even write and star in a television commercial?

Who? I don't know. I forgot.

MICHAEL VANCE

Michael Vance was born on July 18, 1950 in Oklahoma City, Oklahoma. Vance was first published in The Professor's Story Book chapbook at the age of eleven and became a professional freelance writer in 1977. He has been published in dozens of magazines and as a syndicated columnist and cartoonist in over 500 newspapers. His history book, Forbidden Adventure: The History of the American Comics Group, has been called a "benchmark in comics history". It was reprinted in Alter Ego magazine #s 61 & 62.

His magazine work has been published in seven countries, and includes articles for Starlog, Jack & Jill and Star Trek: The Next Generation.

He briefly ghosted an internationally syndicated comic strip, and his own strip for five years called Holiday Out that was reprinted as a comic book. Vance also wrote comic book titles including Straw Men, Angel of Death, The Adventures of Captain Nemo, Holiday Out and Bloodtide. Artists with whom he has worked include: Wayne Truman, Richard "Grass" Green, and Dave (Alley Oop) Graue.

His work has appeared in several comic book anthologies, and he is listed in two reference works, the Who's Who of American Comic Books and Comic Book Superstars.

His twenty seven short stories about a fictional town called "Light's End" have been published in Media Scene, Holiday Out Comics, Dreams and Visions, Maelstrom Speculative Fiction, Whispers From the Shattered Forum, On Spec, Whispers from the Shattered Forum, Lovecraft's Mystery Magazine and many others. Most have been recorded by legendary actor William (Murder She Wrote) Windom and some were released on cassettes and CDs. One of these stories, The Lighter Side was nominated for the international 2004 SLF Fountain Award for Best Short Story.

Vance's weekly comics review column, Suspended Animation, has been continuously published for more than nineteen years, currently reaching more than 700,000 readers in fanzines, newspapers, and on over eighty websites. At its peak, it was read by approximately 4,000,000 readers a year. It is the longest, continuously published, comics review column in the world.

In his career, he worked in newspapers for twenty-two years as an editor, writer and advertising manager, creating three successful newspaper magazines. He also worked as an advertising copy writer, journalist, novelist, historian, graphic designer, in public relations, as a grant writer, cartoonist and columnist.

Vance also created the new Oklahoma Cartoonists Collection housed in the Toy and Action Figure Museum in Pauls Valley, Oklahoma.

He is currently communications director of a nonprofit agency, the Tulsa Boys' Home, in Tulsa, Oklahoma. He is a Christian.

82669203R00128

Made in the USA
Columbia, SC
19 December 2017